54

54

WU MING

Translated from the Italian by Shaun Whiteside

WILLIAM HEINEMANN : LONDON

First published in the United Kingdom in 2005 by William Heinemann

1 3 5 7 9 10 8 6 4 2

Copyright © 2002 Giulio Einaudi editore s.p.a., Torino

Translated from the Italian, 54

Translation copyright © Shaun Whiteside 2005

William Heinemann
The Random House Group Limited
20 Vauxhall Bridge Road, London, SW1V 2SA

Random House Australia (Pty) Limited
20 Alfred Street, Milsons Point, Sydney
New South Wales 2061, Australia

Random House New Zealand Limited
18 Poland Road, Glenfield
Auckland 10, New Zealand

Random House (Pty) Limited
Endulini, 5a Jubilee Road, Parktown 2193, South Africa

The Random House Group Limited Reg. No. 954009

www.randomhouse.co.uk

A CIP catalogue record for this book
is available from the British Library

Papers used by Random House
are natural, recyclable products made from wood grown in
sustainable forests. The manufacturing processes conform to
the environmental regulations of the country of origin

ISBN 0 434 01293 9 (Hardback)
ISBN 0 434 01294 7 (Trade Paperback)

Typeset by Palimpsest Book Production Limited, Polmont, Stirlingshire
Printed and bound in Great Britain by William Clowes Ltd, Beccles, Suffolk.

For Gilberto Centi

Contents

'Postwar' means nothing.

What fools called 'peace' simply meant moving away from the front.

Fools defended peace by supporting the armed wing of money.

Beyond the next dune the clashes continued. The fangs of chimerical beasts sinking into flesh, the heavens full of steel and smoke, whole cultures uprooted from the earth.

Fools fought the enemies of today by bankrolling those of tomorrow.

Fools swelled their chests, talked of 'freedom', 'democracy', 'in our country', as they devoured the fruits of riots and looting.

They were defending civilisation against Chinese shadows of dinosaurs.

They were defending the planet against fake images of asteroids.

They were defending the Chinese shadow of a civilisation.

They were defending the faked image of a planet.

The Background

I

ITALIAN SOLDIERS!

The Slovenian people have launched an inexorable struggle against the occupying forces. Many of your comrades have already fallen in that struggle. And you will go on falling day after day, night after night, for as long as you remain tools in the hands of our oppressors, and until Slovenia is liberated.

Your leaders will lead you to believe that the Slovenian people love you, that you are being attacked only by 'tiny numbers of communists'. This is an insolent lie. All Slovenes are in accord with the struggle against the occupying forces. Under the leadership of the Slovenian National Liberation Committee, our entire people has organised itself into a single invincible liberation front.

ITALIAN SOLDIERS!

Your superiors are concealing from you the desperate situation into which Mussolini has hurled the 'Italian Empire' by selling it to Hitler. They are hiding from you the fact that Abyssinia, for which Mussolini spilled so much Italian blood, is no longer in Italian hands. They are hiding from you the impasse that Italian troops face in all of their African colonies. They are hiding from you the losses that Italian troops have suffered in the Balkans, and the fact that western Serbia, Montenegro, most of Bosnia and Hercegovina, Lika, and parts of Dalmatia have already been liberated. They are hiding from you the terrible losses and torments inflicted upon Italian troops by the crushing weight of Russian weapons on the Russian front, and by the unbearable Russian winter. They are hiding from you the chaos that is breaking out in Italian cities as a result of the growing food shortages, the result of continuous bombing by the British Air Force, and the growing discontent of the Italian people with the policies of the warmonger Mussolini, who is plunging Italy into the abyss.

ITALIAN SOLDIERS!

Understand what the Italian populace at home is coming to understand more and more, that Hitler is pushing you on all fronts: in Africa, in the Balkans, in France and in the USSR, so that you will be unable to form a resistance in your own country when he attacks 'Allied' Italy, just as he has attacked 'Allied Yugoslavia'. Understand what any blind man must understand today, that Italy, as long as it gives allegiance to Germany, will suffer a terrible defeat at sea, on land and in the skies, at the hands of the united forces of Russia, Great Britain and all the freedom-loving peoples of the world.

Understand, Italian soldiers, that the only way out for you and for the whole of the Italian people is to turn your weapons against those who have brought both you and us nothing but misfortune, to turn them against Mussolini's fascist gang! It is vain to claim that you too condemn the bestiality of Hitler and Mussolini, that you too wish to see the end of fascism and the end of the war. You must use your actions to demonstrate your love of freedom and peace, your hatred of the oppressors, both yours and ours. Otherwise what awaits you is ruin, both yours and theirs.

ITALIAN SOLDIERS!

The Communist Party of Slovenia appeals to you:

Do not carry out your superiors' orders, do not fire on the Slovenians, do not persecute the partisans, but surrender to them, do not stand in the way of our liberation struggle!

Attack and disarm the fascist militia, the agents of OVRA and all those who are forcing you to fight against the Slovenian people.

Destroy the Italian armed forces, destroy the stores of weapons and food unless you can give them to the partisans, destroy the means of transport of the Italian army, lorries, motorcycles, horses, roads, railways, etc.!

Do not let the Italian armies be posted to the Russian front, to die for the lunatic Hitler and his satellites! Demand to return to your homeland!

Desert the Italian army, our people will be glad to help you! Give your weapons and ammunition to the partisans and the Popular Defence.

Join the Slovenian partisan units and help them, guns in hand, to bring to an early conclusion the absurd butchery of war, so that you can very soon return to your homes, to your poor abandoned mothers, wives and children, and establish a true sovereignty of the people in your own homeland.

LONG LIVE THE COMMON STRUGGLE OF ALL PEOPLES AGAINST FASCIST BARBARISM!

LONG LIVE THE USSR AND ITS INVINCIBLE RED ARMY, THE MOST POWERFUL DEFENDER OF FREEDOM AND PROGRESS!

LONG LIVE STALIN, THE LEADER OF THE PEOPLE AND WORKERS IN ALL COUNTRIES!

LONG LIVE THE COMMUNIST PARTY OF YUGOSLAVIA!

DEATH TO FASCISM — FREEDOM TO THE PEOPLE!

Central Committee of the
Communist Party of Slovenia

Someone had written 'SMRT FAŠISMU' in red paint on the peeling wall.

The men had been lined up in front of it.

Their faces were blank. Closed, absent. Like the windows of the village.

The captain yelled orders at the unit. The Italian soldiers assumed their positions, rifles shouldered. Almost all of them reservists. The officer was the youngest, with a well-trimmed moustache and a grey garrison cap tilted on his forehead.

The condemned men raised their eyes to look their butchers in the face. To be certain that they were men like themselves. They were used to death, even their own, they had grown accustomed to it over thousands of generations.

On the other side eyes lowered, reflected sensations.

The two rows of men faced one another, motionless, like statues abandoned in a field.

One of the condemned men rubbed a foot against his leg, a movement at once automatic and grotesque.

The captain turned to face the houses and called the interpreter over.

'The inhabitants of this village have given refuge to communist rebels. The same ones who cold-bloodedly murdered two Italian soldiers last night.'

The interpreter translated.

'You have been warned! Anyone who offers refuge to bandits, anyone who offers them protection and lodging, is guilty of collaboration and will pay with his life!'

The officer let the interpreter translate once more.

'Today, ten inhabitants of this village will face a firing squad. Let this serve as an example to anyone who seeks to help the bandits infesting these mountains!'

When the interpreter had finished, the captain stood where he was, his leather boots planted firmly in the mud, as though he expected a reply from the cluster of silent houses.

Not a sign of life. Even the air was still.

He yelled, 'Company! Ready!'

An awkward movement ran through the row of soldiers, as though only some of them had received the order and the others had joined in afterwards. A rifle slipped out of someone's hand.

'That's an order, for Christ's sake! An order!'

At that moment three soldiers exchanged a nod of intent and swung the barrels of their guns around. One towards the captain's head, the other two at his fellow officers.

'Stop it, all of you! No one's going to be shot here.'

The captain blanched. 'Capponi, what the bloody hell do you think you're doing? Farina! Piras! I'll have you court-martialled!'

The other soldiers looked on in astonishment. Shrugs, unease.

'Captain, drop your gun.'

'This is desertion, you're crazy!'

'Drop the gun or Farina will shoot you.'

The officer didn't move, the weapon was pointed at his temple, his teeth were clenched with rage. His thoughts raced, paralysing his brain.

'Captain, if you drop the gun we'll let you go.'

He hissed, 'Capponi, I always knew you were a fucking communist. And what do you think you're doing? Eh? And the rest of you, what the fuck are you doing standing there like idiots? Do you want to get shot too?'

No one replied. Eyes met, but just for a second. No clues about what to do. They knew only that if they disarmed their comrades they would have to shoot them along with the others.

The line broke up; they went and stood, unsure what was going to happen.

The men against the wall stared wide-eyed at the scene.

'Chuck the gun away.'

The officer's jaw was locked so firmly that he couldn't say a word. He took the weapon from its holster and let it fall to the ground.

Capponi picked it up and slipped it into his belt.

'You can go,' he said, turning back to the condemned men. 'And so can you.'

He waved a hand and, incredulously, one after the other, they ran for the mountains.

'Listen carefully, all of you. Anyone who wants to come with us, Farina, Piras and I are heading off to find the rebels. You do what you want, but as the captain said, if our men catch you, they might well shoot you, because you stood and watched. And you did the right thing, because killing people like these is a job for pigs.'

The three men picked up their rucksacks and put them over their shoulders.

'Oh, one moment, Romagna, you got us into this situation, you've got to get us out of it.'

'No, *romano*. It was Cavaliere Benito Mussolini who got us into this situation. Now it's up to each of us to make our own decisions.'

'And what about us, where are we supposed to go?'

Farina passed them with a box of ammunition he had removed from the truck they had arrived in. 'You come into the hills with us.'

'Where the bandits are? But they'll shoot us!'

Capponi shook his head. 'Don't you worry, they won't shoot us. You follow me.'

'Yeah, don't worry,' he said. He headed towards the truck, cursing.

'What are you doing? Are you going with them?' asked one of the others.

The Roman shrugged. 'What am I going to do here?' He pointed to the captain. 'I don't trust him one bit. Whatever happens he'll bang us in the slammer. And he's just as capable of having us lined up and shot. Never liked him anyway.'

He picked up his rucksack again. 'If my wife could see me now . . . Fuck the lot of you, your father and your –' As he turned around he caught a sudden movement, the captain taking something out of the interpreter's belt.

'Oi!!!'

Vittorio Capponi fired first, and the captain fell flat, his skull shattered. A dark object rolled at his side.

'It's a hand grenade!'

They all threw themselves on the ground, hands over their heads, holding their breath.

Nothing happened.

After a while someone opened his eyes again.

Then he stretched his neck.

Finally he risked going over to it.

They were all frozen, looking at the spot where the officer's body lay, and which could have sucked their lives away.

Someone thanked the Madonna del Carmine for making the Duce's weapons so crap.

Someone else spat.

The interpreter sat where he was with his hands in the air. 'Don't shoot, 'Talians! Don't shoot, me innocent!' But no one paid him any attention.

Farina nodded to Capponi to move. 'Come on, Romagna, let's get going.'

The three of them set off up the path at a fair old pace, with the Sardinian in front as a scout.

The Roman, unconvinced, followed them, stumbling and turning around several times to look at the corpse, almost as though he expected to see it getting back up. The others said nothing. Dejected gestures. Finally, one at a time, they picked up their rucksacks and set off in Indian file behind the others.

II

The architect and poet Carlo Alberto Rizzi left home at ten o'clock in the morning. His beard perfectly trimmed, tall, slim and as proud as though he were posing for an equestrian statue, he looked around for a moment, adjusted the tricolour flag bundled up under his duffel-coat and finally set off towards Sant'Antonio Nuovo, where the students would shortly be assembling.

The sound of distant voices, shouting and singing, carried on the wind. The city was demonstrating against General Winterton's abuse of power, and for the restoration of Trieste and all the occupied territories. The processions had been organised the previous evening, and couriers had run from house to house in defiance of the checks by the Anglo-Americans who had occupied the city for nine years.

Nine years, during which Rizzi had sent letters to the papers, dispatched petitions to the authorities and declaimed fiery patriotic poems in theatres and cafés.

At the age of forty-six, Rizzi thought of himself as 'a liberal of the old stamp', and he grieved for his city, occupied by the Germans in '43, by Tito in '45 and by the Anglo-Americans shortly after that.

The great powers didn't want the people of Venezia Giulia, Istria and Dalmatia to be able to choose their own fate, as Italians among Italians. Trieste had become a limbo, scornfully known as the 'Free Territory'. Neither here nor there, neither fish nor fowl: the city and the northern territories assigned to the Allied military government and identified as 'zone A'; to the south of the city boundaries, 'zone B' administered by Yugoslavia. The humiliating imposition was sanctioned by the so-called 'Peace Treaty' of '47. But whose peace?

The streets of Trieste were patrolled by the police force of the

AMG, whose riot squad had been nicknamed 'Tito's Fifth Column' because of the violence with which it suppressed the demonstrations by the Italians. As to Zone B, Tito used an iron fist to eradicate every last trace of Italian identity.

It was time for them to regain their lost dignity. Perhaps that very day, 5 November, would be the day of truth.

Sleepless, incapable of interrupting his own ruminations, he had watched dawn rise from the window of his bedroom.

On 8 October hope had almost been rekindled, with the promised restoration of Zone A to Italy. But on 3 November, the thirty-sixth anniversary of the liberation of Trieste, General John Winterton had forbidden any patriotic commemorative demonstration. Despite the prohibition, Mayor Bartoli had hoisted the tricolour on the roof of the city hall. Winterton had ordered it to be furled and confiscated, subsequently refusing to return it to the council.

On 4 November, the anniversary of the victory of the Great War, Rizzi had gone to the demonstration in Redipuglia, the first village beyond the 'border'. In the military cemetery, a large crowd was commemorating the liberation from the Austrian yoke by demanding liberation from the Slavic one. Rizzi's eyes had misted over at the sight of the delegations of the occupied cities: Zara, Cherso, Lussino, Isola . . . Unforgettable. That evening, returning to Trieste by train, the men and women had not gone home in dribs and drabs, but had filed through the streets in little processions, and then merged together in a large spontaneous demonstration. In the Piazza dell'Unità, by now more than a thousand people had stopped in front of the city hall and the Caffè degli Specchi. An English police officer had come out of the main entrance of the Prefecture, attacked and beaten the procession's standard-bearer and torn the tricolour from his hands. At that very moment the riot squad had arrived, all black raincoats and rifles, and taken on the demonstrators. They, Rizzi included, had defended themselves by smashing up the chairs and tables of the café, using the legs as maces. During the chaos, Rizzi had, by some miracle, succeeded in recovering the standard-bearer's tricolour, which he now had about his person, folded up between his jacket and his coat.

The commotion had continued in front of the Verdi monument in the Piazza San Giovanni, in Piazza Goldone and in the Viale XX

Settembre, where the crowd had attacked a cinema reserved for the English officers. In the midst of all this confusion, a police van had crashed into a trolley bus: ten policemen injured.

In Via delle Torri, where the street was being repaired, the demonstrators had tried to erect a barricade using crash barriers and a steamroller. The police had replied to flying stones by firing into the air, then ten jeeps had broken through the roadblock and trucks full of police had come by way of reinforcement.

The clashes had reached as far as the Chiozza arcades.

All in all, twenty people had been injured. Sixteen arrests.

The students, and others besides, had decided to go to the piazza the following morning. All the processions were to converge under police orders.

Because of roadworks, the street in front of the church had been torn up. On the demonstrators' side there were carts, bags of gravel, some pickaxes and a heap of broken paving stones. Two roads led into the little square, Via XXX Ottobre and Via Dante. On the corner of Via XXX Ottobre was police headquarters, dangerously close.

Among the 200 fearless fighters surrounded by the riot squad there were schoolboys, university students, some old irredentists and various citizens of no particular politics. There were also some ex-fascists, but, heavens above, were they not Italians too?

The riot squad was reinforced by jeeps covered by metal netting, armoured cars, at least 300 police officers wearing steel helmets, and carrying truncheons, carbines and rucksacks containing tins of tear gas. They looked pretty threatening, but . . . was it the moment of truth, or was it not? Rizzi unfolded the tricolour and started yelling at the top of his voice.

Eventually one of the commanders left the ranks, walked towards the crowd and stopped right in front of Rizzi, staring him straight in the eyes and clutching a riding crop. There could be no doubt about it, he was the same provocateur he had seen the previous evening. Pale as a sheet, with a face colder than the *bora* in December. Silence fell. Without lowering his eyes, Rizzi threw the flag over his shoulders. With a horrible English accent, the man said:

'This is to be the only warning, there will be no others: hurry up, all of you, go home!'

Rizzi thumped him in the sternum, knocking him backwards. The police officers were unable to retaliate immediately, because the demonstrators blocked them with a hail of stones and handfuls of gravel. A pick was also seen flying through the air, missing the bonnet of a jeep by only a few centimetres. Then the charge began, and the impact was terrible.

Rizzi found himself running a gauntlet of kicks, punches, and blows from batons and rifle stocks, 'Son of a bitch!' in English, although he didn't know what it meant, 'Son of a whore' in Italian, which was one he did know, insults in Slovenian, and splatters of red. He and some others managed to get inside a church and close the door. There were more than thirty of them, all breathless.

One of them was Enrico Pinamonti, thin and bespectacled, a secondary school teacher with anarchist ideas. What was he doing there? Rizzi barely knew him, they had never gone beyond hello and good evening, and now they were besieged together.

'Good day to you, Pinamonti.'

'Hi, Rizzi. We'll see whether it's a good day or not. It could be.'

Outside there was a terrible commotion, shouts, sirens, people hammering on the door. The parish priest arrived, completely out of breath.

'What on earth's going on?'

A middle-aged man with a tricolour kerchief around his neck replied, 'Is this not the house of the Lord, father? You must give us asylum – those people outside are worse than the Germans and Tito's men put together!'

The priest walked over to the door and shouted, 'Listen to me, I'm the parish priest. This is the territory of the Holy See, conse-crated to St Anthony of Padua. It is the house of God. If you break down this door, you will have profaned a sacred place. Cease your hostilities, I will speak to the people in here and persuade them to leave, as long as there is no further violence!'

'Fucked if I'm leaving this place when that lot are still out there!' said a mop-headed young man.

'If we're going to take 'em, I'm going to dish 'em out as well!' said a man clutching a long bronze candelabra as though it was a pike.

'What are you doing? Put that down this minute! Why didn't you stay out there, if you're so bold?' shrieked the priest. Meanwhile there was not a sound from outside . . .

. . . At that very moment the door was burst open by the jet of water from a big fire truck, which immediately drenched everyone inside the church, opening the way for an even more violent charge. At the sight of the flooded church, the priest turned purple, and if had he not been a man of the cloth he would no doubt have cursed. He started shouting, 'Where is your leader? I wish to speak to your superior officer! Immediately!'

His words went unheeded; the slaughter had already begun. A few students had their skulls broken with rifle blows. Blood mingled with water. The man who wasn't going to take them without dishing them out swung the candelabra around his head, then brought it sharply down on the shoulder of a policeman, hit another in the stomach, and was finally overcome by at least seven police officers, hurled to the ground, and kicked until he had stopped moving.

Everyone who had been besieged in the church was arrested and dragged away. All but Rizzi and Pinamonti.

A moment before the police burst in, the architect and the teacher had hidden themselves in a confessional. Just by a hair, they had escaped being beaten up and arrested. They stayed in the sacristy talking about what had happened, while the priest went to deliver his protest at police headquarters, saying that the church had been profaned and that even if the sky should fall he would reconsecrate it that very afternoon, in front of the faithful and all the people of the city.

'Pretty spirited for a priest!' remarked Pinamonti, then looked at Rizzi and added, 'That was a good slap you gave the commander.'

'That wasn't a slap, it was a push,' said Rizzi pedantically, his mood darkening.

After almost a minute's silence, Rizzi sighed and declaimed in a low voice:

> 'Poor homeland, racked by the abuse of power
> Of the wicked and the vile.'

'Ah yes you're a poet. Pretty words, but I didn't go to the square

for my "homeland", strange though it may seem. I'm an internationalist, I don't believe in homelands.'

'As a matter of fact I was wondering why you –'

'If there's a challenge to police violence, I have to get involved.
And besides, I'm neither an irredentist nor a slavophile, nor am I a
supporter of Togliatti, who changes his mind about Tito every day,
following directives from Moscow.'

'I don't understand, I'm afraid. Whose side *are* you on?' asked Rizzi,
narrowing his eyes slightly and stroking his beard.

'What I'm trying to say is, whatever happens in the end, we still
have to fight our own bosses, Slovenian and Italian, all together.'

'So what are your hopes for Trieste?' asked Rizzi, curious about
this unfamiliar point of view.

'First of all I want Winterton and his gang to leave. After that, we
should maintain the internationalist fraternity between Italian- and
Slavonic-speaking workers, and reject all racial and patriotic claims.
We've had enough of that kind of nonsense, dangerous rubbish about
blood and soil, before and during the war. I know you don't agree.'

'How could I? You're comparing the Führer's ravings about Aryan
purity with the legitimate desire to reunify the peoples of Italy in a
single country! I'm an old liberal, I've always been anti-fascist. It's
hardly my fault if words like "homeland" have been sullied in the
mouths of rabble-rousers. Ask the citizens of Pola and Zara whether
they don't want to be freed from Tito's yoke! Families have been
broken up, there's a diaspora –' His voice choked in his throat, and
Pinamonti took advantage of the fact.

'Let's drop the biblical stuff! Words like "diaspora" merely exacer-
bate an artificial quarrel. Grudges divide people who should really be
fighting shoulder to shoulder against their exploiters. My dear Rizzi,
I don't doubt your honesty for a moment, but the homeland you want
to reunify is the homeland of the bourgeoisie, the Christian Democrats,
the bosses, who were all fascists the day before yesterday, and who then
put on democratic clothes, and it's not as though the Italian police
behave any better than the Allied Military Government, either. Do
you think we in Trieste would be any better off if they were wielding
their clubs on the orders of Rome rather than the AMG? Utter
nonsense. And I'd go so far as to say that nonsense of that kind enables
the AMG to marshal its forces of repression all the more effectively.'

'Meaning?' Rizzi interrupted him. He wanted to know where Pinamonti's acrobatic reasoning was taking him.

'Trieste is divided between an irredentist Italian majority, a Slovenian minority and an "independentist" Italian minority: a good reason for bringing Italians from other provinces, Slovenians and independentist Triestines into the Italian police. In that way, Italian police repress pro-Slav demonstrations, while Slavs and independentists, as happened just now, beat up the Italians. It's that race hatred, which you call "patriotism", that fuels the machinery of the AMG, and perhaps other state machinery as well.'

'So are you some kind of anarchist? What sort of formation do you serve in?'

Pinamonti put his hand under his coat, took out a folded newspaper and passed it to Rizzi. It was a fortnightly paper called *The Communist Programme*. Rizzi unfolded it and skimmed it for a few minutes, lingering over the account of a meeting of the Internationalist Communist Party, which Rizzi had never heard of before, and which had been held in Trieste, of all places, during the summer.

'What on earth is this Internationalist Communist Party? Are you a member?'

'Actually no, but they have ideas very similar to mine. They don't side either with Moscow or with Belgrade, they hate Stalin and they maintain that Russia is a capitalist country.'

'Weird. Who's in charge?'

'No one, but the most highly regarded exponent is this fellow Amadeo Bordiga, who founded the ICP in 1921 and was expelled a few years later.'

'I think I've heard the name. Anyway, my dear Pinamonti, I was there when Tito's Fourth Army fired into the Italian crowd on 5 May 1945. You can analyse all you want, but when it's a matter of life and death you've got to unite your forces, and I'm convinced that Istria, Fiume and Dalmatia would rather stay with us, with people who speak their language, rather than with brigands who express themselves in grunts and throw people in sink-holes in the Carso. You go on thinking whatever you want, and I'll go on using the words I prefer, "homeland" included.'

Pinamonti said nothing for a few seconds, then shrugged and said,

'My dear Rizzi, you do what you want, too, but because you're a decent guy I want to warn you that, as a patriot in this time and place, you're going to get fucked one way or another.'

And on that serious note their debate concluded.

At four o'clock in the afternoon, the bells of Sant'Antonio summoned the faithful. The parish priest was reconsecrating the bloodied church. The steps and the surrounding streets were crammed with people, the atmosphere was tense, and police jeeps were already assembling. Half an hour later, the priest came out in procession and, holding the cross aloft, began to bless the external walls. Silence. Men took their hats off. Everyone present crossed themselves.

Rizzi and Pinamonti, mingling with the crowd, studied the British police, their fingers drumming on their weapons. The same officer as before – identified by some as a certain 'Major Williams' – ordered the 'assembly' to be broken up. Once again some people launched a hail of stones while the congregation tried to stop them and the priest tried to perform his function. From a side road came the rattle of rifle fire, first in the air . . . then at head height.

Panic: in the general scramble the wounded were carried over people's shoulders, but the police obstructed and beat those who were trying to help. On the church steps, everyone could see big patches of blood. The priest and his congregation fled inside, but the pursuit continued right up to the altar, the hoses drenched the nave, and voices were heard crying, 'There are people dead! There are people dead!' and 'Christ almighty, they're trying to kill us, fight back!'

Rizzi lost sight of Pinamonti, then he lost his tricolour, and finally he took a bullet in his backside, which passed through his right buttock and emerged on the other side, just grazing the joint of the femur. Pinamonti got away with a truncheon blow to the temple and a few kicks in the kidneys.

A sixteen-year-old boy died from a bullet to the heart. His name was Pierino Addobbati, said to be the son of an exiled doctor from Zara. Everyone remembered the little tricolour ribbon in his blood-drenched buttonhole. Another casualty was Antonio Zavadil, a sixty-year-old maritime waiter of Czech origin who had become a naturalised Triestine. There were twelve serious casualties and about forty arrests. The police smashed up the headquarters of the Movimento Sociale

Italiano and the 'Flame' athletics club, to create the impression that they had been putting down a neo-fascist demonstration.

The Italian correspondents of the British newspapers spoke of the 'thuggish actions' of 'neo-fascist gangsters'.

From Rome, Prime Minister Pella exhorted the people of Trieste to 'maintain the calm of the strong'.

The following day a general strike was declared. The tension mounted until, at around ten o'clock in the morning, clashes and gunfire resumed. On the corner of Via Mazzini and Via Milano, demonstrators overturned a police jeep and set it alight. The offices of various Slovenian and independentist associations were invaded and smashed to pieces. Someone threw a hand grenade at the Prefecture. In Via del Teatro, the police opened fire on some people who appeared at the window. That day, 6 November, the police killed another four people, injuring thirty.

When Rizzi heard of this, he was lying belly-down on a hospital bed, humiliated and exhausted, and more concerned with his own backside than he was with his homeland.

That man Pinamonti was either a prophet or a jinx.

III

A substance that relaxes the heart and the sphincter, a nectar that eases rebellion in the muscles, fairy tales told to bones and joints. The bitter fruit of *papaver somniferum*. The hand of a Turk, a Laotian, a Burmese. Firm thumb, sharp blade, latex that touches the air and clots. Brown mush that sticks to the fingers. Filaments and finger-tips, children playing with pine resin.

Chandu, prepared opium. Loaves that fill boxes that fill trucks that meet waiting planes or ships. Compliant customs men, blind eyes turned by states and armies, investments passing from bank to bank. A kilo of opium becomes 100 grams of morphine, which become 25 of pure heroin, which is mixed with talcum powder, plaster of Paris and who knows what else.

For every dollar spent on opium, 5,000 are earned.

Goods that every trader dreams of, the additive that every circulatory system yearns for.

Intersecting routes. From Turkey to Sicily via Bulgaria and Yugoslavia. From Sicily to Marseilles. From Indo-China to Marseilles on the ships of the Foreign Legion. From Marseilles to Sicily.

From the Mediterranean to America.

The French Connection
The tie tight around the arm. Needle jabbed in the hollow of the elbow pierces the vein, clearly visible beneath the dark skin. Squirt of plasma, red blood cells, white blood cells, useless platelets flung into the outside world. The curse involves the Creator. No one hears it.

Apart from the Creator.

And the cockroaches, from behind the skirting board.

But who knows whether the Creator really exists. And cockroaches have no ears.

Body: a shell of trembling jerks, not a muscle that does its duty without protest. Blood of the walking dead, the smell of acute gingivitis, cold sweat.

The musician presses a handkerchief to his mouth. Sighs. Ties the tie around the other arm. Hard to press the plunger of the syringe. The hand less used seems to belong to someone else. The brain cannot direct it. *Calm, calm, breathe and try again.*

There we are, no problem. Hot serum begins to flow.

Euphoria and well-being, one thumb after the other.

He unties his Brooks Brothers tie.

Silent fart of bliss. Smile. *Happy Christmas.*

PART ONE
Šipan

Chapter 1

Magione was first to the enclosure, accompanied by the jockey wearing the blue and gold colours of the stable. He started walking round, shaking his neck, as though to ease the tension. A four-year-old tawny thoroughbred, thin, sharp muzzle, good season in '53, placed plenty of times, two wins. Behind him, the jockeys introduced the other animals, superb, just shy of eighteen hands at the withers, their breath vanishing in the sharp afternoon air. Giuseppe Marano stroked the neck of his Ninfa, his absolute favourite, although he knew he was the more nervous of the two of them. He glanced quizzically at the spectators, then finished his tour of the enclosure, checking all the details. The filly snorted a few paces away from Lario: the colts weren't doing too brilliantly. Then Verdi, Augusta and Redipuglia, very handsome too, but they'd be placed at best although Augusta might do well if the going was heavy. Until the previous day, before the clear sky of that winter Sunday, it had rained on Naples and the going was still soft. Monte Allegro, the most nervous of the group, turned up snorting and pulling at the bridle, ignoring the voice of his trainer, who seemed to be whispering something to calm him down. Nothing new there: Monte Allegro was one of those animals that are hard to control, that gulp down the first thousand metres before collapsing at the finish.

In the stands, Salvatore Lucania lit a cigarette and watched the wind carry off the first breath of smoke. He had had to take off his gloves, and now he was almost regretting the fact: it was bitterly cold. He turned towards Cavalier De Dominicis and said, 'Wasn't this supposed to be the *città d'o sole*, the city of the sun? Fuck, it's so cold you'd think we were in New York!'

The *cavaliere* laughed, immediately followed by the cluster of people surrounding him. Lucania wrapped himself up in his camel-hair coat and went on smoking.

The two journalists came over to him, notebook in hand.

'Signor Lucania, they say that Eduardo is interested in a film about your life. Have you met him?'

'De Filippo? No. Great person, great artist, but they won't let him make that movie, I can assure you of that.'

'So, tell us, who would you choose to act you on the screen?'

Lucania adjusted his glasses. 'Cary Grant, of course. Of the Italians I like Amedeo Nazzari.'

A grim and unambiguous look was fired at the press, warning them not to go too far. The man responsible was Stefano Zollo, bull neck crammed into his thin tie, with Victor Trimane at his side. His job to make sure that the boss wasn't disturbed by people coming and going.

'The horses are coming on to the track,' announced the loud-speakers.

The jockeys, already in the saddle for the warm-up, were making the horses stride to test the going. Ninfa looked like a white princess in the midst of the black horses. Marano fastened the crop to his wrist and pressed his cap low on his forehead. Lario caught the smell of a female and shook his head. Then Verdi and Magione passed, followed by Augusta and Redipuglia. Bringing up the rear was Monte Allegro; the black horse held his head high, his teeth bared, and Cabras, the Sardinian jockey, had trouble keeping him under control, and kept on talking to him and stroking him without any great success.

Saverio Spagnuolo waited for the boy to come back with the odds from the bookies. He saw him speeding towards him, coming over to whisper, 'Savé, Ninfa's at 21.'

Spagnuolo nodded and turned back towards the guy who had called him over: 'Listen, pal, Ninfa is the absolute favourite, I can give you 10–7, no more than that. But there are the other horses as well if you want them, and their odds are higher.'

The other man gripped his hand, passing him the rolled-up banknotes. 'You're trying to get me to make a dick of myself. 10–7 is fine. Ninfa to win.'

'As you wish. Take care of yourself.'

The clandestine bookmaker eyed the horses striding along the track and remembered his instructions: keep the odds as low as possible.

He scribbled a few conventional hieroglyphics into his notebook before slipping it into his pocket. Then he sent the little boy back to the official bookies.

'Give me 20,000 on Ninfa at 5–4.'

'13–8.'

'Even with the going so heavy?' objected the punter, trying to persuade him to raise the odds.

'13–8, a bargain. If you're not happy, the bookie will give you 2–1.'

Spagnuolo gripped the wad, counted quickly, scribbled something else and pulled off a strip.

'Five thousand on Ninfa.'

The track judge gave the signal for the horses to go to the starting gates. Magione was in first, followed by Augusta. Marano held Ninfa back until Lario was in there too. Monte Allegro was still running at large, giving his jockey a few problems. His nerves also infected Verdi and Redipuglia, who started snorting and pulling on their bridles.

Gennaro Iovene closed the case of veterinary instruments, and headed for the stable door. The intense light dazzled him as soon as he was outside. He hesitated for a moment, then took the path to the right, towards the tracks, seeing the horses entering the gates in the distance. The man in the black coat, hands in his pockets, turned his back on the track. Iovene merely nodded at him, and when the man lit a cigarette he knew that his signal had reached its target.

He walked on without turning around, hearing the mounting excitement of the public

'The horses are in the starting gates. One minute to the close of betting on the totaliser,' echoed the loudspeakers.

Marano was keeping Ninfa on a tight rein. The filly stuck her muzzle through the barrier. The others were all in already, apart from Monte Allegro, who was still putting up resistance. With a series of powerful blows to his flanks, and the help of a couple of attendants, Cabras managed to get him in.

Cassazione was almost as nervous as the black horse that had been last in. He was constantly giving nervous snorts. Standing beside him, Kociss didn't feel comfortable with all that money in his pockets. It was more than he had counted in all his twenty years. He nodded to the men waiting for him over by the bookies, and slipped them the money in a single quick movement. They all set off at once, slipping their way through the punters who were besieging the bookies' counters. Kociss held out the wad of banknotes: 'A hundred thousand on Monte Allegro!'

The bookmaker craned his neck. 'What?'

Louder. 'A hundred thousand on Monte Allegro!'

The same scene was played out at the other three counters. The bookies turned round in a single motion to rewrite the odds on their blackboards. Down from 7–1 to 5–2. It had worked.

Kociss dashed like lightning to the totaliser, inside the covered building, pushed aside a few punters, and reached the betting office at the last available moment. 'A hundred thousand on number six, Monte Allegro.'

The cashier didn't bat an eyelid and handed him his receipt. At the totaliser, the odds for Monte Allegro went down from 18–1 to just over 9–1. Kociss smiled to Cassazione. 'Let's get going.'

The gates opened with a single metallic clang, spilling the horses out on to the track.

'They're off!' thundered the commentator.

Saverio Spagnuolo saw them dashing past him. He clutched the crumpled banknotes in his pockets and prayed to his mother in heaven that everything would go smoothly.

All of a sudden Magione took a lead of a couple of lengths as they approached the bend. Marano let him go, holding Ninfa a little to the side in his wake. Immediately behind them was Verdi, flanked by Redipuglia ahead of Lario and Augusta, with Monte Allegro coming along the fence.

Iovene stopped a few metres before the gate. He told himself it was because he was curious to see the race, but he knew very well that it was fear. Fear that something might go wrong. He had a permanent sense that the case was slipping from his sweaty hand, or that someone might grab it from him. The syringe inside was worth 250,000 lire. He gulped.

After 1,000 metres Ninfa began to move up, overtaking Magione,

who was running at the head along the fence, until she was head to
head. Augusta and Lario started falling behind, on the unsuitable
surface. Cabras held Monte Allegro on a tight rein, shortening their
distance from the front runners and overtaking Verdi on the inside.
Marano turned around to check the situation, and saw the black
horse gaining ground until he was right behind Magione. All he
could think, 400 metres from the end of the race, was, 'Not yet.'

Kociss and Cassazione stood by the finishing line, holding their
breath.

Two hundred metres from the line, Ninfa, thundering forwards,
swerved slightly to the side, already more than a length ahead of
Magione. In a flash Cabras slipped Monte Allegro's muzzle into the
open gap. Marano understood that the moment had come and
worked his elbows up and down as though to get the maximum out
of the horse, while actually holding back the forward surge. He saw
Monte Allegro pushing at his flanks, and stretching his muzzle
forwards before winning by a neck.

Salvatore Lucania watched the final dash with a contented smile,
while everyone around him, and down below in the stands, exploded
with rage and disbelief. Monte Allegro first, followed by Ninfa,
Magione and Redipuglia.

Cavalier De Dominicis applauded. 'Congratulations, Don
Salvatore, you've won again.'

Lucania gave a seraphic smile. 'Of course, everyone likes me. Even
lady luck.'

The cluster of people thronging around them applauded and
laughed in unison.

Stefano Zollo stayed impassive, moving only when Lucania decided
that the moment had come to go down.

Having withdrawn the pile of money, Kociss and Cassazione felt
their nerves settling, and relaxed into a laugh that stopped them from
speaking for a few seconds. When they reached the group they grew
serious again. Zollo took the piles of banknotes and made as if to
go, but the boss intervened: 'No, these are good lads, that's the phrase,
isn't it? Good lads! *Bravi guaglioni!* Let's give 'em a nice present,
Steve, they've deserved it!'

His bodyguard held out some of the money to the two boys,
keeping his eye on his boss until he had stopped nodding.

The two errand boys looked at the banknotes but didn't have the courage to take them. Five thousand lire. Each. Zollo said, 'Now clear off.'

They fled, wildly excited about the money and the fact that the big boss had deemed them worthy of his attention.

While the *cavaliere* was saying goodbye, bowing repeatedly, Zollo held out the envelope to the man in the black coat, muttering, 'Everyone will get his share.'

It was at that moment that the slap rang out. Zollo saw it out of the corner of his eye. White scarf and hat. A young man, less than thirty, well dressed, had slapped the boss's face. Not a hard slap, but a challenge, an insult. He turned around to grab him, to pulverise the lunatic, but Don Salvatore Lucania, known to the world as Charles 'Lucky' Luciano, flashed a look at him: don't react.

He stayed motionless, his eyes fixed on the moron who was playing with fire. He imprinted those faces in his mind. There were two of them, and they both had the guts to stare Luciano straight in the eyes before the swarm of associates pushed them out of reach.

Lucky Luciano smiled. The smile that Zollo knew very well, the one with which he could invite you to your own funeral. 'Don't worry, just a bit of fun, nothing of any consequence! The ability to lose is something that comes with age, my friends. Clearly fortune smiles most kindly on old men like me!'

Words that did little to ease the tension.

Zollo gritted his teeth as they made for the exit.

Chapter 2

Cold whose like only the oldest residents can remember, a long time before the war when so many of us had just been born. In all the bars in Bologna, the thermometer is the focus of everyone's conversation. Long discussions, not to say arguments, about the coldest winter of the century, as though talking about it around the stove would keep shivers and flu away.

In the Bar Aurora, until just a few days ago, most of us maintained that in spite of everything the first few days of February '32 had been the coldest in living memory. Then yesterday it said in *Il Resto del Carlino* that the temperature hadn't dropped to thirteen degrees below zero for sixty years. Someone immediately tried to contradict this, saying that, as everyone knew, the *Carlino* made up stories if it hadn't got any, and anyway *L'Unità*, the communist paper, hadn't said anything of the kind, and someone shouted from the little billiard room not to go talking rubbish, that in '32 his sow had died of cold, and that meant that it must have been at least fifteen below zero.

In the end, the question was resolved by Garibaldi, who is one of the oldest of the regulars and still hasn't gone soft in the head, even at the age of seventy-five.

'Thirteen degrees, I remember it well, I was about seven years of age. It was called "the cold of the Dead" because of Death in the *taroccho* pack, number thirteen. And if Bortolotti's sow died in '32 it's because he lived in Vergato before the war, and everyone knows it's colder there than it is in the city.'

So a verdict was reached on the cold. So after that for a few days everyone's been talking about the snow, because talking about it means judging the work of the snow shovellers, and hence of the communist city administration. And it doesn't matter if we're communists, everyone can see that the streets are in a terrible state, so everyone tries to have his say without blaming Mayor Dozza. Because basically no one wants to hand the victory to the reactionaries on the *Carlino*, which comes out every day with pictures of some snow-blocked street or other under a scandalised headline.

'I'll tell you this, I've still got a good memory,' says La Gaggia, laying out the fifteen cards. 'The winter of '27 was worse. I remember the arcades, they looked like tunnels with all the snow piled up on one side reaching up to the arches.'

Garibaldi shakes his head, folds up his cards and downs the last drop of grappa. Then he raises his eyes and his empty glass to Capponi, on the other side of the bar, too busy arguing with his brother to pay him any attention.

'Never mind remembering,' says Bottone excitedly. 'In '27 there were still people to sweep away the snow. Just try sweeping it up on Via Saragozza! You could build a whole San Luca arcade on the other side of the street!'

He strikes the table in front of Walterún, who can't make his mind up whether or not to discard. 'Come on, pal, this time we'll thrash them.'

And sure enough, barely has the Pugliese laid his two cards on the table than Gaggia, Bottone's partner, reveals four queens and gets off to a great start with twenty-eight points.

'It'll take a bit of nerve!' says Bottone, throwing down a card in the suit of coins. 'Tell me what the mayor has to do with snow in the street. No, really, spell it out for me. Does he choose the people who are supposed to do the shovelling?'

La Gaggia is about to speak, but Bottone is off. 'No, because you'd think that everyone here's a Party member. But in fact everyone knows that the snow shovellers are completely useless, they don't want to lift a finger.' He concentrates on the game for a moment, then he starts up again. 'Where's the surprise in that? Is there anyone left in the world who can do his job properly? No, all the decent people have retired, 5,000 lire a month and thanks very much, and then you've got these other blokes who are taking half a million to sit and warm their arses.' His tone rises, his voice trembles, his clear eyes widen. 'By God, they're lucky we're old,' and here, as ever, his finger starts knocking on the table, 'because if I had a button to launch an atom bomb and wipe out the lot of them, maybe a few innocent people would get killed as well, but I'd press it anyway, I can guarantee you that,' he almost shouts, throws the king of cups on the table and finds himself trumped by Garibaldi with a Moor.

Bottone is one of the best *tarocchino* players in the bar. We all know that it's almost impossible for him to make a mistake; the only thing is to hope that he gets nerves, because if he starts off on his talk about the atom bomb and the button, he can easily throw away his hand. And he delivers this speech at least once a day, on the most diverse themes, his finger knocking on the table and the atomic mushroom that will wipe out all injustice. That's why Rino Gualandi is known to everyone as Bottone, or Button.

The only one who doesn't pipe up about the snow is Walterún. Partly because he needs to concentrate on the cards, because he isn't exactly a champion player, but more importantly because he spent seventeen years in Manfredonia, near Bari, and then thirty in Milan, where he was a labourer, and he only came here twelve years ago. So his opinion does count, but it just fills up the conversation, because it's only as a matter of curiosity that he wants to know how much snow there was in the Piazza del Duomo in '28.

Anyway, the weather – the past and the temperature – is a subject for old men, the ones who treat the Bar Aurora as a second home: *tarocchino* and chatter. The ones who are still working, meanwhile, are in the billiard room, talking about sport and women. But what's important isn't so much what they're talking about, or who's doing it, you must always respect the Rule: don't speak under your breath, if you have to whisper in a corner go and confess to the priest, don't come here, no one's interested. Here we talk in threes, in fours, sometimes the whole bar all at once, because there are topics like cycling or politics that inflame people's emotions and make them raise their voices. Then there are the rare times when someone takes offence and fails to show up for a while, we all remember those, and also the ones, even rarer, when someone gets a bit plastered and the fists fly, there's a bit of pushing, a few slaps, and the more sober among us have to intervene. Like that time in '48, when Stalin threw Tito out of the Cominform, and we were all here talking till daybreak, with the shutter half down.

The younger men, on the other hand, never talk about anything at all. They pretend they've just dropped by in passing, so they never take their coats off, even if they never go anywhere. But some of them do, like the *filuzzi* dancers, for example, show up looking like they've stepped out of an American movie, with their mackintoshes on and smoking their cigarettes without their hands, and you'd think they were about to order a whisky, and instead it's always a Fernet or a Sambuca. Afterwards off they go to the dance hall, and some of them have routines that would put Fred Astaire to shame. We like it when they drop in to have a drop before going dancing, because we all feel a bit like those men with their towels over their shoulders who massage boxers before they go into the ring. Because Robespierre Capponi, known to everyone as Pierre, is the best dancer in the Party cell, in the quarter, perhaps in the whole of Bologna. And Nicola nags him the whole time, when he can't get up in the morning because he got home late, but he also knows that we're proud to have the Filuzzi King pouring our drinks, we're proud to have him in our bar.

Nicola Capponi, known to us all just as Capponi, with that deep voice of his, it's better not to wind him up. At closing time, he croaks something, gets out the sawdust and starts stacking the chairs. Then even the ones who have stayed until late get up and head for home, but almost regretfully, and you'd almost think that if they didn't have to close the place we'd just stay there all the time.

Chapter 3

They'd brought him there shortly before Christmas. A present for the troops, the showpiece for the new recreation area. Then Merry Christmas, Happy New Year, back to the family, holidays; work had been suspended and he had been left there with only two armchairs, a table, the old jukebox and the picture of the president for company.

What a situation! The inactivity was really exhausting. Doubts and hypochondria racked his self-belief. Will I still be able to do my work properly? Will they be able to get me to work so far away from home? Will I still make people laugh, keep them interested with the news, move them? McGuffin had no answers. He consoled himself by thinking about past glories, and every now and again, to keep hope alive, he peeped out of the door, hoping that someone might pay him a little attention.

Fully assembled on 16 February 1953 in the factories of McGuffin Electric, near Pittsburgh, Pennsylvania, he had been one of the first deluxe models turned out by the company. At the end of the month the Bainton family had bought him in an electrical goods shop in Baltimore. From his very first beginnings, McGuffin had proved to be a truly extraordinary television set. On 5 March, after less than a month of life, he had delighted the master of the house with the sensational news of the death of Josef Vissarionovich Dzhugashvili, better known as Stalin. Thanks to the internally illuminated tube, none of the members of the family had worn their eyes out following the interminable live broadcast of the sentence passed on Ethel and Julius Rosenberg, accused of spying for the Soviet Union and sub-sequently condemned to death. On the seventeen-inch rectangular screen, even grandmother Margaret, a half-blind octogenarian, had managed to make out the few images of the signing of the armistice in Pam Mun Jon, in Korea. It was 27 July. Less than a month afterwards, McGuffin had announced that Moscow possessed thermonuclear bombs like the ones dropped on Hiroshima and Nagasaki. That had been his final scoop. Since then, nothing. He had been switched off one evening in mid-August, and never switched back on again.

Resold for the simple fact that he didn't match the Swedish furniture in the new sitting room, and passed from hand to hand, he had ended up on a ship along with some Italian immigrants on their way home for the holidays. Bartered within only a few days for a Paperino motorcycle, he had arrived at the military base on Christmas Eve. He had not moved again since then. No one had even bothered to plug him in.

The faint light of a bicycle flashed across McGuffin's empty screen. A young boy, certainly not a soldier, was cycling along slowly beneath the streetlamps, looking furtively around. This was not a normal bike: above its front wheel, on the carrier, there was a big, wide, wooden platform.

The light grew fainter and then went out. Through the spyglass in the door, McGuffin could just make out a pair of arms and a handlebar. He picked up a strange electricity in the air. He felt something stirring inside, even though he was not plugged in. The boy. The bike. The platform. A life of flight from that dark place where everyone seemed to have forgotten him. But how could he attract the boy's attention? Deluxe model he might have been, but he hadn't been designed to switch on all by himself. And anyway his plug was lying on the floor, he could not be dragged from his lethargy.

The spyglass in the door widened with a squeak, and the boy's face peeped in.

'Take me with you! Carry me off!' McGuffin longed to yell.

But the boy appeared to need no incentive.

Chapter 4

The mirror was too small for Pierre to see all of himself in it at once. But his movements were automatic by now: he could tie the knot in his tie with his eyes closed, get his trouser turn-ups right to the centimetre, check that the back vent of his jacket was properly creased and his buttons polished.

He pulled tight on the laces of his good shoes, because he didn't like having to stop in the middle of dancing to tie them again. When that happened he felt ludicrous and vulnerable.

That Wednesday, as usual, Sticleina was the first to turn up. He stopped in the doorway for a moment, studied the bar intensely, took a long and thoughtful breath of smoke, and then threw the cigarette end away, shutting the door behind him, a moment before Garibaldi exploded, 'Shut that door behind you, it's letting the cold in!'

Capponi looked darkly at his brother's friend, as he set up the espresso machine to make him his usual *caffè corretto*.

'Where are you off to this evening?' asked La Gaggia from the table next to the stove.

'The Pratello, I'd say.'

'I see, and is there grazing to be had on that dancefloor?'

Sticleina replied with mock regret. 'Yes, but the guys from the Pratello won't let you near their women. It would be more accurate to say that we go there to hear the Bonora Trio.'

'Bring one of those girls back here for me some time, will you? I'm sure I could still cut a fine figure.'

'A fine figure of shit,' observed Walterún, trumping his trick.

Pierre contemplated himself for a long time: he studied his dark eyes, his mother's eyes, like the ones in the photograph in which she was dressed as a bride, the one that stood on the chest of drawers; the arch of his eyebrows, the straight nose, the thin cheeks. He slipped the photograph of Cary Grant from the top of the dressing table and wedged it between the wall and the mirror. He took a step back and tried to assume the same indescribable expression.

A gust of chilly air ran through the bar, and the crash of the door signalled the arrival of Gigi, the *umarein ed gamma*, the 'rubber man' in Bolognese dialect, who pirouetted his way to the bar, where he lay horizontally on top of Sticleina, arms held above his head.

'Oi, Capponi, bring me a bitters,' he said, as the applause faded away.

'So,' said Sticleina, showing himself off to the new arrival, 'don't you notice anything special?'

Gigi frowned and studied his friend more closely. 'Bloody hell!' he said, stretching out his finger to touch the coat. 'Did you get it as an Epiphany present?'

'It's camel, bought in Milan. In instalments, of course.'

'Yeah, yeah, lucky you, still living with your folks, means you're never short of a few things.'

Sticleina brought a cigarette to his lips and held out the pack to Gigi. He thoughtfully took a drag and blew the smoke out fast, with some difficulty.

'I'm not sure I'm going to be living at home for long.'

'What do you mean?'

'My dad wants me to get married. He says you can't drag a girl along behind you for ever.'

'Hm, and what does your mother have to say on the matter?'

'She says I should finish my training as a nurse. That I'll have no prospects otherwise, and a woman needs security more than anything.'

Gigi took advantage of the mirror behind the bar, the one inscribed with the word 'Martini', to check that his brilliantined hair was nice and smooth along the temples, slick and gleaming all the way to the little curls at the back of his neck.

'The older generation are always saying things are easier for us, but I think things are pretty complicated all the same. If you're with a girl, eventually you've got to marry her. If you want to marry her, you've got to have a decent wage, and then you have to wait to get married. What are you supposed to do?'

Cary Grant's faint smile was formal and elegant, and natural at the same time. His smile was a contradiction. Pierre tried to imitate it, but for that very reason he couldn't. He was better at Cary's walk, and had almost perfected his way of keeping his hands in his pockets.

Brando arrived as the church clock chimes were coming to an end.

'So, aren't you ready yet?'

'Pierre's the one who's dawdling.'

'Get a move on, Pierre, you're handsome enough already.'

He pulled down his jacket so that it fell perfectly on his shoulders, and made sure that the white cuffs of his shirt protruded a centimetre and no more, otherwise he'd look like a peasant.

Already striking a pose, he came out from behind the bar and found them standing in front of him, side by side like the three musketeers. Because that was how he saw them, just like in Dumas's novel: Athos, Porthos and Aramis. And he was D'Artagnan, the boaster, the best one.

'Shall we go?'

'What cheek! You're the only one we're waiting for!' exploded Brando.

Gigi blew a raspberry at him. 'Yeah, come on, it's getting late.'

Pierre's eyes met those of his brother Nicola, hard as nails as ever, and as always when he went dancing. He saw him turn red and holding in his rage. That look granted him no more than a few minutes of independence, just long enough to say goodbye to everyone, and he had every intention of squeezing every last second out of it. He came out from behind the bar and walked slowly across the floor, elegant and loose-limbed. He stopped at the cardsharps' table. 'See you, Bottone, I'm off. Don't win too much.'

'See you, you old rogue.'

He said goodbye to La Gaggia and Walterún, and waited for a glance from Garibaldi, like a blessing before he set off for the arena.

To Bortolotti, Melega and the rest playing *boccette* on the billiard table he gave only a nod that was meant for everyone.

Nicola's face was purple by now, he was about to explode: it was time to clear off. Pierre watched him rubbing the bar more and more quickly, and decided he had provoked him enough.

'Let's go!'

The four of them left in single file, dressed up to the nines for a party, ready for anything, like heroes entering the lists to outshine everyone else.

A moment later they were back in command, in the street, with their coats rolled up under the seats so that they wouldn't get stuck in the wheels. Each one had an elegant accessory that was all his own: Brando his hat, Gigi his leather gloves, Sticleina his father's watch and chain, and Pierre a white mohair scarf.

At their head, Gigi Mazzoni pedalled straight-backed and chest out, parting on the right, square chin. By day he was a mechanic in a factory, always covered with black oil and with a smell of engines that hit you from a long way off. But in the evening he was someone else entirely: his dancing skill, his smooth, lightning moves, had won him the nom de guerre of 'the rubber man'.

Behind him came Giuseppe Branca, a barber who, after *The Wild One* was shown in the cinema, was known to everyone as 'Brando', because of his barely detectable resemblance to the actor. He was obviously very proud of it, and from that day the familiar 'Pippo' had passed on, to make way for the high-flown 'Brando', the lady-killer; and woe betide anyone who called him anything else.

Pedalling away in front of Pierre was Aristide Bianchi, the shyest one, the one Pierre saw as Aramis. He told everyone he was a nurse, but really he was still a trainee at Sant'Orsola Hospital. Skinny as a rake, he seldom took his hands out of his pockets, but he had an elegance of his own and when he walked through the streets of the district he stuck out a mile. For that reason they called him 'Sticleina', the toothpick.

Last of all came Piero Capponi, known as 'Robespierre'. His father Vittorio had been obliged to call him Piero because foreign names were not allowed during the fascist era. But even when he was little, everyone had known him as Robespierre, and that was his real name, because real names are the ones you choose and prefer, not the ones you read in official documents. In the end he had become 'Pierre', simpler, and with a touch of the exotic that pleased him. He was twenty-two, eight years younger than his brother, but they were so different that they could have been twice as far apart.

What he had with Brando, Gigi and Sticleina, on the other hand, was more than friendship. It was an alliance of intent, reinforced by habit. The four of them were a unit, the best dancers in the district, and leaving everyone far behind was almost a mission, like fighting Richelieu's soldiers and making them see that no one was a match for the *filuzzi* dancers of the Bar Aurora.

At that moment, as they headed towards the Pratello, they felt invulnerable and united. Just like the musketeers.

Communist musketeers, that is.

Tickets into the Pratello dancehall cost 300 lire, but Pierre and his friends got in for free, because there were people who came just to see them when word got around about where they were going to dance.

They were in perfect accord with the Bonora Trio. The musicians knew the dancers' favourite pieces of music, and were happy to play them. The first one was always a mazurka, not too fast, just to warm up. Pierre paired up with Brando, and it was Sticleina's turn to twirl with Gigi.

Everyone took to the floor for the mazurka, even the women, who couldn't usually keep up with the giddy rhythms of those dances. Two or three pieces in, the rhythm started to speed up. Nino Bonora's concertina, supported by bass and guitar, sounded as though it was never going to stop. By the sixth item on the programme only the musketeers of the Bar Aurora were left on the floor. Shouts of encouragement rose up from the tables, along with applause for the more complex movements. Sticleina, emphasising his womanly way of dancing, started to sway his hips.

Once the piece was over, the guitarist Aroldo Trigari approached the microphone to announce, 'Hold on tight now, everybody, this polka is a real earthquake!'

Bonora launched in at a breakneck rhythm, and the four *filuzzi* followed the music each on his own, the couples parting and reforming each time the tune came round again. They ran through four different figurations one after the other, and by the fifth the whole hall was breathing in unison, the girls were clutching their tables for fear of being sent flying, so great was the energy with which Robespierre Capponi executed his famous 'bend-down-and-turn-around', a *pièce de résistance* in which his only rival was Neri Raffaele, known as Felino, from Borgo San Carlo.

The 'earthquake polka' was the last piece in the first session. After it, the band played a very calm waltz. The central part of the evening, for devotees, was closer to the *liscio*, or smooth, style of the Romagna than to real *filuzzi*. Anyway, no one complained, because this was the opportunity to ask some beautiful girl to dance, and that was what most people were there for.

'Shall we go on the attack?' asked Gigi, straightening his tie after all that dancing.

Pierre mopped his forehead with his handkerchief. 'At least let me get my breath back. Let's have a drink, then we'll see.'

'You just stay there, then. We'll go on ahead and test the ground.'

Gigi and the others were very well aware that more than one girl had fallen for Capponi's dark eyes, so they preferred to go on ahead in choosing their dancing partners.

'Are you dancing, *signorina*?' said Sticleina, bowing like an experienced ladykiller in front of a curvaceous brunette.

'Can you dance like a man as well?'

'Sure I can, and not just that.'

Pierre stayed at the bar for at least three or four numbers, sipping a vermouth. He knew very well that there was a girl waiting just for him. Even now, when she was dancing with a guy, she made eyes at him each time she span. Apart from anything else, she moved better than all the rest. Pierre figured she would be a fantastic *filuzzi* dancer as well, chucked away his cigarette and crushed it beneath his shoe. He crossed the floor as though it were Piazza Maggiore on a Sunday morning, keeping his hand in his trouser pocket, under his jacket, more Cary Grant than ever. Arriving in front of the girl, he offered her his arm and invited her to dance with a glance and the faintest of smiles.

After the first pirouette he asked, 'What's your name?'

'Agnese Bernardi.'

'Do you live here in the Pratello?'

'Yes, not far away.'

Pierre reflected on the rule. If you invited a girl from a different district to dance, after the first number you had to drop her and leave her alone for the rest of the evening. A second dance and it meant you were making your move.

So, when the music stopped, Pierre tried to take his leave. Just at that moment, whether on purpose or by chance, the girl lost a shoe. As he bent down down to help his partner put it back on, Agnese Bernardi clearly gave the impression of taking longer than strictly necessary. They were still clinging to one another as the band struck up once more, a quick piece that heralded the big *filuzzi* finale. The girl from the Pratello starting moving in time with the music, and Pierre, after a moment's hesitation, forgot the rule and started moving along with her. They jumped, swung, swayed and pirouetted: the couple left everyone else standing in terms of rhythm and agility. The whole place was abuzz. She smiled, she was pretty, and she really could cope even at the fastest tempo. Pierre put her to the test, and she responded in perfect harmony. They were still together by the third dance, without noticing, out of the pure pleasure of dancing. For him it was an opportunity to try out the fastest rhythms with a girl rather than Brando, his usual partner. With all the friendship in the world, it was a different thing.

Then, above the music, a male voice stood out from the others, breaking the spell of the dance. 'Right, that's enough, I'm going to smash his face in!'

While still concentrating entirely on the rhythm, Pierre became aware that something was wrong, that the rising murmur was not only one of admiration, and that the phrase that had just rung out didn't herald anything good. He took advantage of a pirouette to turn and look. At that very moment a thick-set man broke away from the grip of two people who had been holding him back, and marched threateningly towards him. The Filuzzi King extended his twirl by a turn and a half, and ended up right on top of the man, exploiting the effect of surprise and the run-up to knock him over. Things heated up. Brando took a punch to the eye without seeing who was hitting him, Gigi threw his tie around the neck of a short-arse from behind, while Sticleina was already on the ground wrestling with someone much bigger than him. Inevitably, some peacemakers tried to restrain the beasts, get between them, to hold back the hotheads.

'Come on, guys, there's no need for this!'

'Hey, we're all here to enjoy ourselves.'

'Bòna, Pirein, Pompetti's calling the cops!'

The shoving and kicking lasted no more than ten minutes, enough time for the most frenzied to give and receive at least one punch, but also enough for cooler heads to persuade the musketeers from Bar Aurora to make their way home and the Pratello guys to calm down.

'They didn't hit you nearly hard enough.'

Nicola had always been a light sleeper. Perhaps whatever it was that gnawed away inside him kept him awake. Perhaps it was the war. From the doorway to the room he looked at Pierre with a mixture of scorn and commiseration.

Pierre sank even deeper into the armchair, loosening his tie. 'And yet they know me well enough not to try it on with me again. Sons of bitches.'

He dabbed at his injured mouth with his handkerchief.

'If our mother was here she'd give you what for, I can tell you that. And you're asking for a kicking, chasing skirt all the time.'

Pierre was too tired to talk, but whenever he tried to shut up, his anger got the better of him. 'You leave our mother out of this, understand?'

'You come in at this time of night with your mouth smashed in, and tomorrow you'll be half dead behind the bar. If aunt Iolanda didn't keep on at me to keep on at you, I'd give you a good kick up the arse and there's an end to it.'

'And leave aunt Iolanda out of it too!'

Nicola's hoarse voice was filled with disgust. 'They've broken their backs bringing you up, and I hope you're satisfied. It's almost a blessing that our mother's dead!'

Pierre exploded. 'Shut up! What do you know about it? What the fuck are you always on about? Always judging, always banging on. So I like pussy, so what? I like dancing and I'm good at it and everyone admires me, you know? They look at me. And isn't there some satisfaction in that as well? But take a look at yourself, always behind the bar, always pissed off. Anyone would think you were ninety years old!'

'The bar is our bread and butter, fine, and if you don't feel like working, then you can bugger off. Clear off, away with you, on your bike, go to dad in Yugoslavia and he'll give you a decent job, breaking rocks! Go on, a bit of military service would do you the world of good if it wasn't for your heart murmur. Head murmur, more like.'

'Oh, go fuck yourself. What do you expect dad to do? We haven't heard a word from him since March, we don't even know if he's still alive! But you don't give a toss, do you? You've got to work, you're serious, you . . .'

Nicola disappeared into the darkness of the bedroom, and Pierre stayed where he was, almost lying on the armchair. He was stiff and tired and he couldn't feel the right-hand side of his mouth. He was gripped by great sadness, as he was every time he had an argument with his brother. He didn't hate him, he knew he wasn't really a bad person. According to aunt Iolanda he was afraid of loving people, afraid that they would leave. However, when he was a little boy, Nicola had seemed like a hero to him, one of the people you boast to other people about: 'My brother was in the 36th partisan brigade.' He still remembered that when the Germans had shot his brother he had wept with rage and pride. He had had to have an operation, and since then the pins in his leg had become the indelible mark of the war. As Pierre had grown up, the contrasts between them had come into being. Pierre felt that until he left home that conflict would never be resolved.

So he sat there on the armchair, pressing the handkerchief to his mouth and thinking about where he could go, without a lira, without a passport, and with a knowledge of the world that extended from Modena to Marina di Ravenna.

Chapter 5

Statement made on 8.1.1954 to Police Commissioner Cinquegrana concerning the disappearance of an expensive television set of American manufacture from the military base of the Allied forces in Agnano, Naples

My name is Salvatore Pagano, born in Naples on 21 July 1934. My mother's name was Carmela, but everyone knew her as Nennella, particularly in the Vergini. The district, I mean. The Vergini district.

I don't know who my father was, and that's all I'm saying.

But my friends, the horsemen of Agnano and other friends as well, call me Kociss. Ok, Totore 'a Maronna as well, but mostly Kociss. Don't you get it? Kociss, with a 'k', fine, it's not a letter we have in our alphabet, but the Americans and the foreigners do. K, I mean. What, don't you know the great Hungarian footballer Kociss?!

Am I a footballer? No, but it doesn't matter a damn, number one because I really do know how to play the ball, even though I'm almost twenty, because the way I got the name has nothing to do with the ball, or rather, well, it does, but it's different. Ok: you know that great team they've got in Hungary, who are going to slaughter everyone in the World Cup in Switzerland this year? Ok: they've got these players in Hungary and there's one who scores goals with his head, how can I put it? He's proverbial. He and Puskas score goals by the cartload, it's crazy. And this one does almost everything with his head, I've never seen anything like it. Kociss.

So, you've got to know that, ok, some friends and other friends too, you know how friends are, they muck about, and at the end of the day they call me that because they say that when I'm arguing with some clueless nutter, which hardly ever happens, let's be clear about that, at the end of the day, the rare occasion when it does happen and we're just ordinary people if you catch my drift, then the curses are flying and one thing leads to another, if you get my meaning, and anyway when all's said and done they say I hit them with my head, but it's only ever happened once, twice at the most, you know what friends are like, and they say that I knock them out, so that's how I got that name. But that wasn't what was important, because apart from anything else I'm here to tell you that I had absolutely nothing whatsoever to do with that wretched nuisance of a television set.

Chapter 6

Sharpen the blade on the strop fixed to the wall, moisten the soap
in the bowl with hot water, remove any loose bristles from the badger-
hair brush, soap your face, pass the razor across your face, slow down
as you get to the cleft in your chin, remove any remaining soap with
the hot flannel, inspect your face for remaining hairs. Cary shaved
with his right hand, enjoying every moment of that morning liturgy,
followed by the holy vestition: suit and shirt commissioned from
Quintino of Beverly Hills, matching tie and socks, no suspenders
because Cary's socks *wouldn't dare* slip down his calves. Derbies or
full brogues on his feet.

Archie, who was left-handed, brushed his cheeks with his left hand.
Two days without shaving, and without any wish to do so. Grizzled,
troublesome, bristly stubble.

Lingering in that pose he felt against his lower lip what remained
of one of those old calluses from his days as an acrobat, a bump of
dry and whitish tissue, nearly thirty years old.

Every morning the manicurists filed and cut, spread unguents,
softened Cary's hands, hands that every woman in the universe would
have wanted under their skirts or busy unbuttoning their blouses,
but the callused tissue was beginning to grow again, a memory of
his previous life, the past of Archibald Alexander Leach.

Hands on the floor in hundreds of somersaults, friction on the
ropes for a thousand vaults, luggage transported from one town to
the next, hundreds of little theatres and music halls, putting on
make-up, jumping. Bob Pender and his Knockabout Comedians.
Tightrope walkers, clowns and conjurors, every evening and matinee
facing the working classes of the kingdom.

Pender said, 'Come on, boy, you've got to earn your keep. There's more to the theatre than just walking on your hands!'

From the wings, while the extraordinary magician David Devant was performing on the stage, Archie gazed enraptured at the eyes of the younger members of the audience, which quivered in the flickering limelight. Archie read those eyes, the surprise, the dreams, the temporary escape from a life of shit and work. Eyes of young people already cheated of their own futures, but prepared to react with a shrug of the shoulders and a fuck it, in their slightly worn out Sunday best, not stiff or formal, but cheeky and sniggering in the queue for the tickets, children once more at the sight of the flying acrobats and an illusionist's sleights of hand.

The eyes of the little boy from Bristol who had, one fateful afternoon in August 1910, been hypnotised by the mimes and stunts of Bob and Doris Pender, so much so that he wanted to follow them, to be an actor, to leave an elusive father and the void of a vanished mother. In the Empire and in the Hippodrome the lights go down . . .

The ragged-trousered Englishman had crossed the Atlantic to accomplish a titanic enterprise: to climb the highest mountain as though faced by a hillock, a pathetic hump, a slope, moving one foot behind the other without bothering to think.

Cary Grant.

How astonished he had been, in the late thirties, the man of the new century. Astonishment went hand in hand with awareness: who had never yearned for such perfection, to draw down from Plato's Hyperuranium the Idea of 'Cary Grant', to donate it to the world so that the world might change, and finally to lose himself in the transformed world, to lose himself never to re-emerge? The discovery of a style and the utopia of a world in which to cultivate it.

Meanwhile there was an Austrian dauber out there winning a career and followers, whose speeches hit the hearts of the *Volk* 'like hammer-blows', and a distant clang of weapons heralded the worst: the clash of two worlds.

Against the world of Cary Grant, the dauber had finally lost with dishonour, in a puddle of blood and shit.

Without a doubt, the Russian winter was partly responsible, but one thing was certain: the New Man, at least for the time being, wouldn't be having to tuck his trousers into two-foot-high leather boots to march the goose-step.

The New Man, if there was such a thing, would be reflected in Cary Grant, the perfect prototype of *Homo atlanticus*: civil without being boring; moderate, but progressive; rich, certainly, even extremely rich, but not dry, and not flabby either.

Even some of the most vehement enemies of capitalism, of America, of Hollywood, were willing to concede that the baby was one thing, the bathwater quite another.

Cary Grant, born a proletarian and with a ludicrous name to boot, had defied fate with the ardour of the best exemplars of his class. He had denied himself as a proletarian, and now he was bringing dreams to millions. If one individual could achieve it, there was no reason why the rest of the working class shouldn't have it as well.

Cary Grant was a living demonstration of the fact that progress existed, and had been going in the right direction at least since Cro-Magnon man. Socialism would crown this impressive series of results with social justice, harmony among human beings and the liberation of all creative energy. In a classless society, anybody could be Cary Grant.

Well, not really. That's what a few intellectuals might have claimed. Neither the proletariat nor the bourgeoisie really gave a damn about historical materialism. Simply speaking, they admired Cary Grant and they wanted to be like him.

That day Archie Leach turned fifty. The two last years had been the worst.

And how hard they had been for Cary! Three box office flops in a row. The decision to retire from the screen. A holiday in the Far East with Betsy, which hadn't been sufficiently restorative. The exhausting quest for palliatives, yoga, new reading matter, the perennial intoxication of self-improvement but without the moment of truth, without setting foot on-set. A difficult relationship with Archie, who also used his body and came to get it back in periods of crisis and disorientation. A difficult relationship with Elsie, who had made a surprise reappearance in his life fifteen years previously.

As to Betsy, she was madly in love, she did her absolute best to keep his spirits up, she had hypnotised him to stop smoking, quite the best wife he could have had. But it wasn't enough. It was never enough.

After an interminable year and a half, he was touched by the cautious desire to return to acting, casting complicit glances at the audience, having the opportunity to improvise those wonderful one-liners. But that desire had to do battle with the effects of a long depression, with a lack of interesting scripts, and above all with Archie's disgust at the inroads being made by Joe McCarthy and his henchmen. A sense of guilt and embarrassment for his own indifference, for not protesting, for not defending the free world as he had done fifteen years before in the war against the Germans.

For Archie, the Americans were now their own Germans. Chaplin in exile. The best writers on the blacklist.

Cary was a long way from being a radical, let alone a communist, but how could he bear all those intrusions into people's privacy, their political ideas: 'Have you ever been a member of such and such a party, such and such a union, such and such a circle . . . ?' What had come over everyone? Either you were good at your work or you weren't, you were a good set designer, or director, or actor, or you weren't. If the jokes were funny, if the love scenes were exciting, if the story had a beginning and an end, in that order if possible, then nothing else mattered.

For at least a year Archie had returned to brooding over Frances Farmer, for whose fate everyone felt responsible, even Cary, and especially Cliff.

After a few weeks Frances had come back to see them. They had had heart-rending conversations with her, which left them devastated. No, not the Frances of '54, exhausted by the mental hospital. It was the Frances of '37, the new, wild and beautiful actress, the girl who didn't believe in God, the girl who had been to Russia.

'You know, Cary, I don't get you. Everything you do, the way you move, the way you speak in that accent that isn't English and isn't American . . . I can see it, you work hard on your character . . . No, not your character in this film, I mean a character you're going to be playing every day for the rest of your life. I feel you've nearly got it, but . . . there's one thing that doesn't convince me, you know?'

She talked like that during the coffee breaks on *The Toast of New*

York, she turned to look at Cary, but it was Archie she was talking to, a cocoon about to pop.

'I imagine they expect the same of me, my mother expects it, Hollywood expects it but . . . I won't do it. Why not just be yourself?'

The poor girl from Seattle. They had broken her into tiny pieces, all of them together: the producers, the politicians, the police, the gutter press, the bloody psychiatrists . . . and of course Cliff. The great playwright Clifford Odets, good friend of Cary's, intellectual prick. He had seduced her with his big words, sound causes (a long way from home and with McCarthy still to come), the bust of Lenin on his bedside table, quotes from books. He had seduced her and dumped her, abandoned her to the vendettas of Hollywood, to the gossip columns of Hedda Hopper and Louella Parsons, to a bitch of a mother who would have her locked up.

In a madhouse, just like Elsie.

Archie couldn't find peace, and he made Cary feel guilty as well.

Just as she had been seventeen years before, the same blond hair, the shaved eyebrows, the body that hadn't yet been raped, draped in a kind of shroud. She came back to them smiling, but reminding them that they had not once spoken out against her persecutors.

Chapter 7

'You see, in Italy, it isn't the Italians who make the decisions, that's
what it is, I'm telling you. If it was up to me, I'll tell you where I'd
send the Allies . . . Oh yeah, you can say that we lost the elections
in '48. Course we did, with all the moolah that the Americans have
given to the Christian Democrats and all the southerners following
the priests. Down south that's the way they like it. It's what they're
used to: taking things easy, isn't that right, Walterún? You tell us,
you were born and bred down there.'

Walterún scrutinises his cards, perplexed, ignoring Melega's
question. When political questions arise Walterún hardly ever intervenes, so much so that some people cast doubts on the soundness
of his convictions. It's all slander, of course, but it's true that it is
difficult to discover what he thinks about a pile of important questions, such as Italian Trieste, Germany or the coming of television.

Today the main topic is Trieste, or rather it is Mauro Melega, the
best *boccette* player in the whole bar, who is talking in his usual voice,
too loudly, forcing everyone to listen to him, even if some of us,
heaven alone knows, might like to concentrate on their own affairs.
Then you know how it is: it starts with this and that and you end
up talking *urbi-et-orbi* even about serious things, and in the end you
can't even remember how you started.

'Those southerners are all Christian Democrats out of conven-
ience, because everybody knows that the Americans and the priests
will always give you a present, whether it's a bar of chocolate or a
pair of shoes doesn't matter: thanks and shut up. The Yanks and the
Vatican are in charge in Italy, all because we, the only ones who
know what's best for Italy, aren't in government. We're always the

ones who have to do everything for everybody. Look what a prize bollocks they made of Trieste at the end of the year. They rise up against the Americans and the British, they want to drive them out, and they're right, the poor things, you can't have strangers in your house all your life. But the Allies are worried that Tito will take Trieste, and they don't trust the Italians. Moral of the tale: they haven't let go for ten years. And the people of Trieste are getting well fucked over.'

Walterún lifts his head from his trump cards and stretches his neck: 'Go on then, explain to me that story about Tito that I keep forgetting. How come he's a fascist? I mean, he's a communist, but really he's a fascist?'

Melega sighs, with the face he makes when he wants to say, 'another ignorant southerner': 'Right, listen carefully, I'm only going to say this once. Not everyone who claims to be a communist is a real communist. Otherwise we'd already have taken over the world! Tito, for example, goes along with the Americans, he acts the whore, he'll go with anyone. He wants to make socialism, but he wants to do it according to his rules, the way it suits him, he won't listen to anyone, least of all the Russians, who had their revolution before he did. But what I say is that if someone got things right before you did, you pay him some attention, don't you? It means that he's got more ex- perience! But the Slavs are horrible people, you can never trust them, gypsies the lot of them, worse than the southerners. But we're the only ones standing guard, so we don't end up in that situation.'

Then, because he's about to hit the jack, Melega leans over the billiard table and is silent for a moment, concentrating on the game. Turning his back on the door, he fails to notice that Benfenati, from the Section, is here on his usual visit. After scoring his point, he is about to continue with his speech, particularly the insults directed against gypsies, southerners and tramps, but Bortolotti manages to save him: 'Benfenati's here, Mauro,' he says loudly. 'Why don't we ask him to explain this business about Tito?'

Melega just manages to bite his tongue; he rolls his eyes like someone who has just escaped a danger, throws back his head and greets the new arrival. He has Bortolotti to thank for avoiding a slanging match, and us too, because no one could have saved us from a lecture on Gramsci and the southern question. Because Benfenati isn't a bad person, quite the opposite in fact, and also a very good comrade, sure, but he has this one shortcoming, which is that whatever people are talking about, he has to stick his nose in and tell you the Party line on it. Now that's absolutely fine if you're talking about Tito's fascism, for example, everyone's interested, but other times he does it just for the sake of chatting and once he goes off on his little lecture, you're never going to bring the subject back to football or some actor's divorce or whatever. Some people say he does it just because that's what he's like, he always wants to be top of the class, while others swear that it's the Party that's taught him to be like that, 'activism starts in the family, in the place of work, in the bar . . .' Or something of that kind.

'. . . and after the war Tito had the Russian technicians shadowed when they came to give him a hand with the reconstruction, see what I mean? Fine example of international solidarity among the workers! And then there's the fact that he's a nationalist, he treats the Soviet Union like any other bourgeois state, and on top of that he's arrogant, ambitious, presumptuous, typical of the counter-revolutionary Trotskyites.'

Bottone nods, convinced, this Tito strikes him as a scoundrel, while Garibaldi, as usual, decides to be bloody-minded.

'Ok, so at the end of the day you're trying to tell us that the Yugoslavian communists became fascists because Tito and Stalin didn't get on, is that it?'

'No, Garibaldi, don't put words in my mouth! There are serious ideological reasons, and besides . . .' He raises his hands and hooks the index finger of one into the thumb of the other: 'First, in the Yugoslavian Communist Party there are no discussions, woe betide anyone who dares to criticise, the rulers aren't elected, there's a police check on militants and a real Turkish-style despotism. Second,' and his index fingers meet to form a cross, 'Tito says that the peasants are the most solid base of the Yugoslav state, in the face of Lenin and the proletarian hegemony. Meanwhile, in the countryside, he doesn't do anything Marxist, and one day he allows the little private farm to generate capitalism, the day after that he's acting the demagogue, hoopla, all of a sudden he wants to sweep away all the wealthy peasants, nationalise the land, like that. Thirdly' – his whole hand engulfs his middle finger – 'he'd bring the communists in the Free Territory of Trieste over to his side, if it weren't for the fact that there's someone there like our old comrade, who –'

'Oh Vidali, Vidali . . .' Just for a change, Stefanelli, who's playing with The Baron against Melega and Bortolotti, shakes his head, which always seems to mean something like 'Oh, if you only knew,' or 'poor innocent creatures', but no one really knows what it means.

Melega walks around the table, takes aim and throws the bowl. He obviously wants to talk, but he doesn't dare to while Benfenati's around. And in fact, the moment Benfenati says goodbye to everyone and heads for home, Melega comes into the main bar with his finger pointing and his cowboy look. 'All I want to say is that as far as I'm concerned Togliatti just has to say, "Come on, then!" And I'll be off. I'll get out my Sten gun and pick them off one by one. Round them all up: Christian Democrats, Americans, Yugoslavs, bang! Only language they understand.'

Garibaldi's booming voice thunders from the card table. 'Wasn't the last war enough for you? Do you want to have another one?'

Melega turns towards him and waves his index finger in the air like a sabre. 'Don't you come the pacifist with me, Garibaldi, I know how many fascists you killed in Spain. And it was the same thing here: if we communists hadn't taken up arms in '43 and hadn't killed loads of fascists and Germans we'd all be talking English right now! They didn't give us free rein because the time wasn't right. Do you know what I mean? They're bloody lucky the time wasn't right!'

'Listen,' says Bortolotti with an irritable nudge of his elbow, 'could you throw that bowl before I die of boredom?'

'I'm coming, I'm coming.'

Melega turns around to study the billiards, and Walterún immediately stretches his neck towards Garibaldi and speaks quietly so as not to be heard in the other room. 'Oh, Garibaldi, perhaps I shouldn't say this, perhaps I'm getting old, but is Tito really a fascist communist? It's just that I've always thought you were either a fascist or a communist. So what's going on exactly?'

'Shut up and play, all this talk's really getting on my tits.'

Chapter 8

Naples, 21 January

You couldn't trust anyone, that was all there was to it.

Getting the trucks out of that inferno of carts and humanity, a pack of ravenous stray dogs, incomprehensible cries flying from one side to the other and the stench of fat mixed with the sweetish smell of rotten fruit. Get the load on and off we go, no dawdling, no stops, him in front and Palmo following along behind, twelve hours without interruption. A place like that had nothing whasoever to do with stories of the war, his war. Or rather they did, indeed they did, you just had to look around, all the navy insignia, all those soldiers, but in a different way that he still had to understand. They had told him it was like Calcutta, and he had nodded. But who'd ever seen Calcutta? Certainly not Ettore, who was sure to have seen plenty of chaos, shit and gunfire, but that Mediterranean Calcutta, Naples, affected him, and Palmo made him anxious. What the hell sort of people were wandering around in there? Time to get away quickly, smiling and friendly, but quickly. He didn't even have any sweets or chocolate that he knew of. All those children jumping and shouting and charging madly about on those wooden carts cobbled together with iron wheels, it all worried him, something insidious like that illness that had carried off part of his family and lots of his mates, that not even the Thompson gun stowed safely away under the driver's seat could pacify.

American cigarettes, refillable Ronson liquid gas lighters, various brands of whisky, and junk watches that the shysters on the Via Emilia could sell to some poor suckers. That was the cargo that Ettore took on in Naples, covered with bales of hay and quantities of sack-cloth. It was the first time they had taken two vehicles, tarpaulined great things, of wartime vintage, that gave off more smoke than the volcano up there ahead of them.

Mustn't be distracted.

The man that everyone, deferentially and submissively, called Vic, orchestrated that chaos almost without moving, in a dark-blue double-breasted suit that made him look even squatter than he was, a basalt block with his hair slicked back with brilliantine and a bouffant pompadour. Soon, Vic would give him a nod of the head and they would be moving, with him in front and Palmo behind, towards the port exit.

He gave a honk of his claxon in the middle of the hubbub, and for a moment he saw Palmo's unintelligent expression falter, just for a moment, before he poked his big moon face out of the window.

'When they let us out, stay right up my arse and don't stop, ever!' Ettore boomed, while Palmo nodded without a great deal of conviction.

After several long minutes and two more cigarettes, the man everyone called Vic finally raised his right arm, and with three crisp movements of the hand he indicated that the cargo was on, telling them to turn around and head off along the internal road running along the shore towards the exit. A few hundred metres in a column, at walking pace, behind other lorries, carts pulled by emaciated horses, women offering fresh water, fruit and all kinds of fried food. Then the little monkeys, dirty and pestiferous, who went on jumping and cavorting all over the place.

At the start of the Via Marina, the long road running along the docks that was to take them out of the city, the chaos was at its most intense, with passing trams and a mad scramble of carts and horses, and when a gap opened up, Ettore resolutely drove into it, setting off towards the clear road.

Behind him the screeching brakes of Palmo's lorry and a series of excited cries announced the shit he had been most afraid of.

The little boy lay contorted under his back wheels, or rather between the wheels and the cart on to which he had been dragged by his mates, screaming like a lunatic, while another boy clung to the windscreen, shouting, 'You've killed him! You've killed him!' and all of a sudden people were crowding around them.

When he saw Palmo, purple in the face, getting out of the vehicle clutching his rifle, he knew they were done for.

'Christ alive, Palmo! Stay here, don't get out, Palmo! For God's sake!'

But Palmo was out already, and from that moment it took only a few seconds: the little boys to send Palmo flying, the one who can't have been more than twelve has leapt for the steering wheel, another three or four have gone for the cargo, and all of a sudden there's this gap behind the truck, which means they can reverse quickly and flee, despite the shots fired into the air by a furious Ettore.

One of the monkeys in the gang hadn't managed to get away. He wriggled about as Palmo came back, cursing, towards the lorry, rifle in hand and the little pest held firmly by the arm.

Ettore could only watch, from less than fifteen metres away. If he'd got out, they'd have had his lorry as well.

'You are a moron, Palmo,' he said the moment he had got on board with his writhing snake, who was yelling, 'Lemme go! Lemme go!'

Ettore struck him with the back of his hand. He shut up.

'Now what are we going to do?' asked Palmo, panting agitatedly.

'We'll head back to the docks, kill someone and get ourselves killed.'

Ettore didn't intend to do either of these things, but he was pissed off, he'd said it to frighten Palmo and that little bastard. They'd pinched his lorry, Christ almighty! What was he going to tell Bianco?

'*I'm sorry, goombah.* Those fuckin' brats, they're devils, they are . . .'

'Listen, Yank, I'm not leaving without the rig and the cargo, and I know I'm not going to come out of this looking too great, and neither is my colleague, but first we're going to have ourselves a bit of fun as well.'

'Listen, my friend. I'm going to see what I can do. But you're not to fuck things up. Put your gun away and tell your associate to let the boy go, it won't do anybody any good, there are too many others around. Otherwise we'll have the Military Police on to us.'

Ettore looked at him grimly. 'Don't you think I know that the police around here see what they want to see? I want the lorry. Without the lorry, there's going to be a bloodbath.'

Victor Trimane snorted a few times, troubles every fuckin' day. He adjusted his tie, glanced around and nodded at someone in the crowd around them.

He swapped a few words with a small, thin guy who waved his arms around a lot. First he shook his head, then, with a look of resignation, he appeared to be convinced. As the man walked away, Vic said loudly, 'Tell him Steve Cement and I will be coming later on. Tell him, Antonio, and be quick about it!'

He turned towards Ettore with a strained smile.

'My friend, as you can see, we're going to sort everything out right now. You just wait here and don't do anything stupid.'

Then he walked over to Palmo, freed the little boy from his grip and sent him on his way with a kick in the arse.

Ettore lit himself another cigarette. He had to wait and hope that things would be ok, that they weren't pulling a fast one, he and that cretin of a colleague he'd been lumbered with.

Palmo stood next to him, silent and red in the face; he was trembling and still hadn't put down his rifle.

Ettore handed him a cigarette. 'Smoke this and put the gun down, quickly.'

An hour later, Antonio reappeared at the wheel of the lorry, among the shouts and yells of a crowd that hadn't stopped commenting on what had happened.

Ettore felt lighter, but the lorry was lighter too.

Standing by the empty trailer, he looked quizzically at Vic.

Vic shrugged. 'What the fuck am I supposed to do, my friend? They're animals, that lot. Poverty turns them into animals. We can't give them all a job. They won't even let us work. Listen to me, you got off lightly. You got your rig back, and believe me, you're lucky there, this lot have dismantled aircraft-carriers, they've sold whole American liners. Listen to me: I'll give you a little compensation. I'll give you another five cases of cigarettes and one of whisky, so we don't leave the lorry empty. And you go home happy and with Don Luciano's blessing. Ok, goombah?'

Ettore looked at the tip of his shoes, with his scorching cigarette between his lips. He just had to play his part, and he'd be ok, because although he was furious he had no other option. The lorry was the basic thing.

He looked up, holding the American's eyes for a few seconds. He nodded to Palmo, who was still walking around the lorry to check that it was all there.

'Let's go.'

They headed back to Bologna, to Bianco.

Chapter 9

A late-nineteenth-century town house converted into apartments. Via San Mamolo, an affluent district at the foot of the hills. Behind the massive front door, the smell of bourbon-scented tobacco and disjointed fragments of jazz from upstairs.

Pierre bounded up the stairs and found himself right in front of him on the landing, tall and still slim, pipe gripped between his lips and an absorbed expression.

'Sorry I'm late, *professore*, my brother wouldn't leave me alone.'

'That's fine, Pierre, catch your breath and make yourself comfortable while your tea cools down.'

Renato Fanti led the way down the corridor. Long and narrow, it led through a glass door to the sitting room. That one room, with its floral-patterned sofa and dark furniture, was about as big as the Capponi brothers' whole flat. Pierre couldn't stop admiring the elegant furniture, the embroidered curtains, the library crammed with books, the old upright piano that no one played. On the oval table sat a steaming teapot and raisin biscuits, as they did every Friday.

'This is Darjeeling, one of the best teas in the world. It's produced in India, at an altitude of 1,800 metres,' Fanti explained. Every week, a different variety of tea.

Pierre filled the cups and added a cloud of milk, in the English style. Before the lesson there was always time to catch up with the latest news.

'Have you read about the Djilas trial? Unbelievable, isn't it? A month ago they make him president of the Yugoslav parliament, and now they're dismissing him and throwing him out of the Party.'

'I don't read the paper very often, you know. But I've heard people talking about it a lot,' and he pointed behind him at the big and very cumbersome radio. 'There are strange things happening in Yugoslavia, that's true. What does your father have to say on the subject?'

'My father . . . my father doesn't say anything. He knows Djilas, as a matter of fact. He might have something to say about it, but I haven't heard from him for almost a year. He should have dropped us a line at Christmas, but there was nothing.'

Fanti noticed Pierre's expression. 'A month's delay could be down to the post, couldn't it? Yugoslavia seems close, but you can never tell. That's why I prefer pigeons.'

'But you see,' replied Pierre without looking up, 'it's a whole collection of things. The last letter arrived in March, just a few lines, bad news . . . Then nothing for ten months and now this business about Djilas.'

'Was your father on his side?'

'Well, yeah, something like that, although over the past few years he'd got up a few people's noses. He said he'd been fired, he said people got riled at seeing an Italian getting important jobs to do.'

The professor tamped down the tobacco in his pipe. The flame from his lighter revived the embers, and his lips smacked as he took rapid puffs.

'Don't you think he would have come back to Italy if things had got really bad?'

'Well, you see, things here aren't that much better, in fact they're no better at all.'

'What do you mean?'

'Well, at the end of the day he's a "traitor", you know? On the Yugoslavian front in '43, he quit the army, he killed an officer and joined the partisans. Here in Italy they'd stick him in jail. At least if he had the Party on his side, he might be able to manage for a few years, but no, he's a "Tito-Fascist", as they say, his comrades over here are leaving him there to rot.'

The jazz stopped, and the needle clicked at the end of the record. Fanti got up to turn it over, and after a moment's hesitation the Count Basie Orchestra started up again. Outside it had started snowing.

'As to the Party,' the professor continued, 'Togliatti and Tito will soon make peace, now that Uncle Joe has gone. This Djilas business demonstrates as much: Tito wants to go back to the Russians, so he's abandoning everyone who criticised the Soviet Union.'

'To put it briefly: my father has never been on the right side,' Pierre observed with a half-smile. He swallowed down his last mouthful of tea. He took from his satchel some pieces of paper and the pen that Angela had given to him. A lick of his finger as he looked for his most recent notes.

'Here we are.' Then, in English, '*We go to the cinema and after we have a drink*, I've underlined *after* but I can't remember why.'

'Because it's a mistake: you should have said *and then we have a drink*. Write it out correctly, you'll find it easier to remember.'

Renato Fanti had a perfect command of English. He had lived in London for more than ten years, and only came back in '47 after Italy became a republic, three years after the death of his wife. Now he taught at a scientific secondary school, but before the war he had been a professor of literature at Bologna University. They had met at evening classes. Pierre had taken them to get his lower secondary school diploma. He had immediately been struck by the suave and rather unconventional gentleman. He knew the world, cinema and music. He had strange, almost manic, interests. And he taught courses like this because he was passionate about them, certainly not out of necessity. That was why he appreciated Robespierre's desire to distinguish himself, to know things, to embrace life.

Pierre remembered the moment on the course when Fanti had talked about *A Streetcar Named Desire*. His astonishment at finding that someone else knew the film, and the day he had given him a ticket for *Rashomon*. Then the idea of English lessons, and the discovery that the professor had lost his wife just as he had lost his mother. The same illness: tuberculosis.

Down at the Section they didn't approve of his friendship with the professor. An anti-fascist, certainly, who had been removed from the university because he loved American literature too much and the blackshirts too little. But they called him bourgeois, and a political cynic.

Certainly, Fanti wasn't a comrade, and he wasn't a member of the working class either. He sided neither with Moscow nor with the imperialists. Perhaps he was an anarchist, who could tell, it was almost certain that he didn't vote. Where books were concerned, he wasn't scared of the alleged ideas of the authors, and he remained a great admirer of John Fante even though the communist newspaper *La Rinascita* said he was halfway to being a Nazi.

Once he'd finished Dos Passos, he would have to ask the professor to lend him something by Fante.

Chapter 10

Bologna, Sunday, 24 January

She leaned forward between the front seats, and pointed the driver towards the tree-lined avenue on the right.

The trunks of the poplar trees disappeared into the pile of snow on the sides of the road, and the car wheels splashed muddy puddles on the side windows. Angela had put on her high-heeled shoes specially, hoping to use them as an excuse to persuade Ferruccio not to go for a walk.

The usher recognised Signora Montroni the moment he saw her come in, and immediately sent for the nurse who looked after her brother.

Angela wasn't very fond of Villa Azzurra, but at least it wasn't a mental hospital. After the war, in the first few months of '48, Ferruccio had been given two weeks' respite in a psychiatric hospital. The memory of that place still made her shiver. Screams, bodies trapped in absurd positions, lakes of piss on the floor, smells that would turn your stomach. Until one day she had gone into her brother's room and found him strapped to his bed with belts. It had taken three orderlies to keep her from untying them. Another few moments and they would have confined her as well, because she wouldn't stop weeping and crying. The next day she had persuaded her boyfriend, Odoacre, to assume legal responsibility. Ferruccio had come home.

'So, how are things?' Angela asked the nurse, as if reading from a script. She asked him the same question every time she came, and she knew the reply as well. 'Everything's fine, Signora Montroni, we're making progress.'

'. . . he's having a bit of trouble sleeping, he wakes up, he wants to have his breakfast at three o'clock in the morning, he insists on having cigarettes, then during the day he settles down and hardly creates any problems.'

'He settles down.' 'He doesn't create problems.' A way of saying that his new tranquilliser was working. They were very pleasant at the Villa Azzurra, and Ferruccio, Dr Montroni's brother-in-law, was treated with the greatest respect. And Marco, the nurse, was a fine person, you could tell that he was fond of Ferruccio. But there was nothing to be done: in there, 'being well' meant 'not creating problems'. If her brother changed and hit someone, that meant he was ill. If he spent all day in the garden, at three degrees below zero, staring at the clouds, then everything was fine, he was well.

'If he's not on the swing near the fountain, we'll find him under the cypress tree, on his usual seat,' said the nurse, opening the glass door giving on to the park.

A few old men were defying the cold. They were walking along the avenue of statues on the arms of their children or grandchildren. An elderly lady with half her face wrapped in bandages was engrossed in some unlikely gardening work, while two men sat chattering on a stone bench, beneath a yew tree sprinkled with snow. As she passed them, Angela noticed that they were talking to themselves.

'Hi! Got a cigarette?' said Ferruccio without turning round, when the crunch of dry leaves announced the arrival of his sister.

'Hi, Fefe,' Angela put her arms around his shoulders and kissed him on the cheek. 'Come on, the taxi's waiting for us outside.'

'Are we going for a walk?'

'I'm not wearing the right shoes, Fefe, we'd at least have to stop by at the house.'

An arm swung through the air to dismiss the suggestion. 'No, no. Let's stay here, then. Let's stay here.'

'But you're here every day, I'm sorry, always shut up in the building,' Angela objected, and then realised why her brother was so reluctant. 'Odoacre isn't at home, he had to meet a friend, he's gone out.'

'Have you got a cigarette?' asked Ferruccio, rising to his feet, and miming the gesture of someone smoking. Angela handed him the pack.

'Can I keep it, really?'

Angela gave a resigned nod. It always took a while before Ferruccio let himself go. At least an hour or so, then he became distracted, lost his thread, stopped asking for cigarettes, or asking the time, or why on earth you had come to get him. Once that was over it was like being with a normal person, apart from the fact that sometimes his replies were a little off kilter, and he tended to change the subject without warning.

The taxi driver had gone to sleep. Angela knocked on the window, and he gave a start as though he had been woken at the dead of night. He raised his hand in apology and hurried out to open the door.

'I told my wife, I told her not to give me fried food when I've got to go to work, but she doesn't understand. Sooner or later there's going to be an accident and then, no, well, that is, that's all we need, when I drive I'm wide awake, but God almighty, I'm losing customers.'

'Have you got a cigarette?' Ferruccio began the moment he sat down.

'A cigarette? Yeah, of course, why not?'

'Fefe, why do you need a cigarette?' Angela intervened. 'I just gave you a whole pack!'

But the driver had already passed a Chesterfield over his shoulder, and Ferruccio had pounced on it straight away. The good thing was that he didn't smoke. Every Monday, in Villa Azzurra, he did the rounds of the rooms, offering cigarettes to the patients, to the nurses, to the doctors. They all smiled at him, they thanked him, and he felt happy.

'Why did you come and get me today?' he asked again.

'Because it's Sunday. Don't I come and get you every Sunday?'

'Yes, but last time your friend came too.'

'Teresa? She can't come every time.'

'Can't she? Shame, I really like your friend. You must tell her. She's nice, you know. As far as I'm concerned you can stay at home if you're busy, send Teresa to see me, we can go to the cinema, drink some hot chocolate, and I'll be fine, really fine.'

He was almost shouting, very excited at the idea. Angela would just have been irritated by his speech if she hadn't known that Ferruccio had a precise reason for saying these things. And it wasn't that he preferred Teresa to her. In fact, he knew very well why it was that Angela sometimes left him with Teresa on Sundays. And because he didn't much care for his brother-in-law, he was pleased that his sister was enjoying herself a bit.

'So you'll tell your friend, yes?'

'What?'

'That I really like her. You've got to tell her.'

'Fine, Fefe, I'll tell her as soon as I see her.'

They sat there in silence for a few minutes. A dense group of people were chatting in front of the church of Santa Maria dei Servi, while others, beneath the portico, made their way to mass. Little boys were throwing snowballs under the skeletal lime-trees in Piazza Aldrovandi, while their parents laid siege to a patisserie. When they reached the towers, the taxi turned left into Via Castiglione.

Odoacre's house was beyond the lower tower, where the road widened, allowing a glimpse of the keep of the old city walls. Beyond that boundary, the road climbed into the hills, a refuge for the very rich, in their luxury villas, and for unmarried couples, locked in their cars or lying in the grass.

Angela paid the driver and ran to the door, while Ferruccio was already blocking the path of their neighbour from the floor below to ask for his umpteenth cigarette.

The sun was peeping through the clouds, and it was less cold. She thought that she might still have time to change her shoes and take her brother to the Margherita Gardens. A Sunday without a stroll was not going to put him in the best of moods. And it wasn't just that he needed to walk about and get some fresh air; for that, the park at Villa Azzurra would have done, and it was right on his doorstep. But without taking a nice walk among other people, how would Fefe ever collect the forty or fifty cigarettes he needed to hand out on Monday?

Chapter II

*Statement given on 25.1.1954 to Police Commissioner Pasquale
Cinquegrana by Salvatore Pagano of unknown parents, suspected of
the theft of an expensive television set of American manufacture from
the military base of the Allied forces in Agnano, Naples*

Fine, I get you. You're saying someone saw me down at the base.
Agnano, I mean. The Allied base in Agnano. But what does that
mean? They might just have made a mistake, you know how it is in
the dark, you think you've recognised a friend and instead it's someone
completely different. There, that's what must have happened. What
do you think? Loads of people can tell you I was at the party. I told
you about the party last time, Epiphany party. At the Santa Teresa
orphanage. Sure, giving presents to the little souls, why not? You can
ask Sister Giuliana, if you want, it wasn't dark there, she looked me
right in the eyes, and we talked. And Sister Maddalena was there as
well, you can ask her too. You're not going to tell me that two nuns
are going to lie to you, they're the brides of Christ, you know the
sisters, all prayers and good works, they don't know what a lie is, or
rather, don't get me wrong, they do *know*, but they think that if
someone lies the Madonna weeps, really, that's what they used to
say, you know what happens if you tell lies?

They brought me up. The nuns, I mean. Sister Giuliana and Sister
Maddalena together. You can check, up until the age of thirteen I
lived in the Santa Teresa Children's Home, because in the end my
mother had barely enough money to live, poor thing, and with her
job, if you get me, a child was a heavy burden to carry. As to my
father, well, I won't say anything about him. Brothers and sisters? I
expect I had a few of them as well, but no one's ever told me.

So there you are, when you go to the nuns, ask them, ask them
if I'm a criminal, as you put it. They'll tell you no lies, you know
that. Salvatore Pagano? He's a good lad, that's right, always around
the horses, at the betting, but of course he is, he's got a living to

earn. Because the nuns aren't so keen on betting either. If someone bets too much it makes St Teresa weep. That's what they used to say. Every sin has its weeping saint, and the more serious the sin the more important the saint. But I'm sorry, I was talking to you about the nuns. Salvatore Pagano? He's never stolen anything, that's what they would tell you, apart from the odd sweet and, all right, maybe the odd cigarette and once, but just once, a bottle of wine from the cellar, but a television, that's too much, and where would he put a television? No, no, Totore is a good lad, that's what they would tell you.

And then, look, to prove to you that I really mean it, like in the confessional, apart from the sweets and the cigarettes and the bottle of wine, that time, but only that one time, ok, there was one other thing. And I don't think the sisters would tell you this, because they were also, in this case, you know what I'm talking about, right? And this is really the most serious thing that I've ever done, my intentions were good, I can assure you of that, a decent thing, yes, sir, because the sisters would never have let me do it otherwise, I was still living half with them at the time. Yes, half, in the end, half in half out, in the daytime I was left to myself, and in the evening I went back to them to sleep. I was thirteen at the time.

I told you, didn't I, that there are some friends, not many of them, and other ones as well who just know me as Totore 'a Maronna? No, no, don't worry, I'm not changing the subject again. It has something to do with this serious but decent thing that I did a long time ago, that thing with the nuns. Right, so I was telling you, that's what they called me, Totore 'a Maronna, because I, not on my own, right, but with other people, I made the Madonna weep. Because some lies were told, you say? That's a manner of speaking. No, I've never made those Madonnas weep by telling lies. They really did weep. That is, not really, it wasn't a real miracle, it was a lie, but they were weeping, goodness me, haven't you worked it out? I'll try and put it more clearly, ok: those people I was with, they used to help some other people, some very important people, big nobs. Those big nobs went around loads of different villages around Naples, places like Acerra, Marano, Afragola, they talked about their stuff, they did propaganda, they told people about their plans. And when these people, and almost everyone was still there, down below the stage, and those big nobs were talking up on the stage, then we would turn up. That is, the other people and me. And it's not as if I had to do a lot, they would send me into the church in the village, along with the parish priest, he was with us as well, and after a while I had to run out like a madman saying I had seen the Madonna weeping, that it was a miracle, quick!, an old woman who was with me had fainted with fear. And those other people who were with me had put a water pump inside the little statue of the Madonna, and she really was crying, that is, not really, it wasn't a miracle, but in the end it looked as though she was crying. But other times you didn't have to, it was enough for the people in the village to see the boy and the little old woman saying yes, the Madonna had wept, they had seen it with their own eyes, while that big nob was saying that we had to vote for him, put your cross on the cross, otherwise no Madonna, no Italy, people would come who ate babies and . . . Don't you want to hear this story? Do you know it already? Fine, fine, that's all I'm going to say, I told you it was pretty serious, but I wanted to tell you everything, like in the confessional, but it was those people who really introduced me to the nuns and told me that in the end there were lies and lies, and that was a lie for a good end, you must have told white lies yourself, this was one of those, and it was good because by telling them we saved Italy in '48, me and those others . . . And fine, you're not interested, I'd worked that out, I'll stop in a minute, but that was why some of my friends, but not many, and others as well, call me Totore 'a Maronna – Salvatore of the Madonna. I kind of prefer Kociss.

But if you don't want to hear this story, I'll tell you once again that I really have nothing to do with this business about the American television. And that stuff with the Madonna really is the most serious thing I've ever done.

The 5,000 lire, you say? What 5,000 lire? I had it in my pocket? Well, yeah, of course, 5,000 lire, but it's mine. And you think that if I'd sold someone an American television they'd only have given me 5,000 lire? That television was worth twenty times that, at least. But it seems strange to you that someone like me is going around with 5,000 lire in his pocket. And fine, I already told you that the nuns don't like it, but I bet on the horses. May Saint Teresa forgive me, and whenever I win, I make some money. And you know how it is,

I'm always at the racecourse, and you can make a killing up there, you do your bit, you place a bet for the gentleman who wants to sit comfortably where he is, and that's how you make a bit of money. But not as much as that, 400 or 500 lire max. I won those 5,000 lire. At the Sunday Grand Prix, I think we had three, I bet on Monte Allegro, everyone said Ninfa was going to win, and instead it was Monte Allegro. You know, Agnano is my second home, or perhaps my first one even, and I really know horses, and Ninfa had had bad colic the day before, while Monte Allegro was in great form. The totaliser had him at 10–1, you can check, and I bet all my savings on him, 500 lire, that's exactly what happened.

A big bet, commissioner. Never seen so much money in all my born days!

Chapter 12

Palm Springs, California, 30 January, afternoon

Seated on the Chippendale, facing Cary, was Sir Lewis Chester Kennington, a senior MI6 officer who had arrived from London a few days previously. Next to him was Henry Raymond, American director of the same organisation. Stiff, in their perfect grey suits. Combed wool, grey pinstripe, two buttons, waistcoat, probably Anderson and Sheppard, and their shirts had the unmistakable cut of Turnbull and Asser on Jermyn Street. Each of them shod in a pair of black Oxfords. But the ensemble was worn with an impersonality typical of the English, who are more concerned with perfect camouflage inside their office walls than they are with looking good.

Sir Lewis, about six feet tall and about sixty years of age. White hair combed back, a neatly trimmed black moustache.

Raymond was perhaps ten years younger, and three or four inches shorter. Soft red hair, parted on the right. They both had the affected accents of members of the upper classes, and very clear eyes, the kind that tend to look washed out and insincere in black and white.

Cary had dark eyes that could 'burn through the screen' and communicate any emotion you liked.

The FBI agent, fair-haired, medium build, a little over thirty, had introduced himself as 'Bill Brown' and remained standing beside the marble fireplace. Athletic-looking, unbuttoned blue jacket, magenta shirt, a tie with a skewed knot, sunglasses (frame too heavy for his features). He had said only a couple of words, but Cary had immediately recognised a Texan twang, like that of his friend Howard Hughes.

Pouring a trickle of milk into his tea, Sir Lewis said, 'Mr Leach, you must have been wondering what Her Majesty's Government wants of you.'

Cary, an American citizen since 1942, nodded and said nothing. Over the past few days he had been feeling too low to be curious. No one had called him 'Mr Leach' for over twenty years.

Sir Lewis, choosing an adulatory register, referred to the 'past services' that he had rendered for His Majesty, as he was then, and the patriotism he had shown during the war, for the benefit of the Crown.

'Your assistance has been extremely precious, Mr Leach. The gratitude of Her Majesty and all the rest of us goes far beyond the honour conferred upon you.'

'. . . a few years too late,' concluded Cary. He had received the King's Medal only in 1946, officially for having given the strife-torn motherland his entire salary from *The Philadelphia Story* and *Arsenic and Old Lace*.

Raymond was caught off guard. 'I'm sorry?'

Sir Lewis began: 'Of course you understand that we were waiting for some pretext, a different reason for awarding you the King's Medal without disclosing the role that you played, and the role played by other valuable informers.'

'Gentlemen, it is not my intention to deliver pointless polemics, let us be clear about that. I was not annoyed at the time, let alone in the year of grace 1954, but my friend and collaborator Alexander Korda was made a baronet in 1941. Or am I mistaken?'

Who was speaking, Archie or Cary? The spark of memory had relit the flame of his wounded pride, bringing with it a resentful curiosity. What did MI6 want from him? If they were there, in his house, in his drawing room, asking him a favour, well, they had a nerve!

'Mr Leach, we hope that you do not doubt the deep gratitude –'

This time Cary exploded. 'Gentlemen, let's forget about it. We can return to the issue in a moment: I already wanted to enlist in '39, as David Niven did, but Lord Lothian told me I would be more useful in Hollywood, from where I would report on Nazi sympathisers in the cinematographic industry. Why not, there were Nazis all over the place, even my second wife used to socialise with them, and my Spanish teacher was an Axis spy, not to mention that awful Countess di Frasso. Have you any idea how many interminable parties with unpleasant people I had to endure between '39 and '43? I have done my part, even when that damned Hoover and the whole damned FBI were trying everything they could to embarrass me: what's this Englishman doing on our territory? Couldn't we dig out the Nazis all by ourselves? Then I point out to Sir William Stephenson that Errol Flynn is keeping company with German agents and, as a British subject, he is guilty of high treason. My God, did I point it out! And what does MI6 do? Nothing. And in fact, for the whole of the course of the war, Flynn is acting the hero on the screen, and I have to put up with the barbs of the London scribblers, calling me a coward because I didn't join up like David Niven! Then, when the war was over, you give me that damned medal and I, who have among other things become an American citizen, am supposed to be on cloud nine, isn't that right?'

Who was speaking, Archie or Cary?

'One second, please,' Sir Lewis interrupted in the patient but irritating tone of a primary school teacher. 'Let's reflect for a moment about what it would have meant to accuse Mr Flynn of high treason or espionage: there would have been a long and tortuous trial, vulnerable to enemy disinformation, and who would have been in the dock? A man adored by women all over the world. We risked turning Flynn into a martyr.'

'That's true,' Raymond went on. 'If you might allow me to give one more . . . contemporary example, the same thing might happen with those suspected of "anti-American activities". It's terribly risky having all those trials to identify a handful of Bolsheviks. In Great Britain we prefer subtler, less noisy tactics, but the United States is still such a naive and superficial country –' Then he turned towards Brown and added, 'With the greatest respect, of course.'

Brown remained impassive and gave no indication that he had understood a single word. Probably, Cary thought, he didn't even know what a 'Bolshevik' was.

'If, on the other hand, we had left Mr Flynn a free man, as we did,' Sir Lewis continued, 'his well-known impulsiveness would sooner or later have led to the discovery of other elements of the spy network, and in the event his reckless movements in Mexico turned out to be terribly revealing. As to your unpleasant experiences with British public opinion, Mr Leach, things could have been worse. It

is our duty, should it become necessary for the security and prosperity of the Crown, to expose our real or suspected agents to public
opinion as a diversionary tactic. Please remember that in order to
protect the intelligence work of your friend Mr Coward, we circu-
lated the rumour that MI6 had relieved him of his duties because
of his lack of discretion. It was the only way to keep the Germans
from trying to infiltrate.'

'As to Flynn,' Raymond continued, 'there were other ways of
getting rid of him, and that's all I'm saying.'

Sir Lewis turned to Raymond with ill-disguised annoyance. At
almost the same moment, Raymond and Brown saw Cary Grant
raise his left eyebrow in an expression of surprise already seen on the
big screen. In the few moments of unease that followed, Cary thought
quickly. *How could I not have worked it out?*

In 1942, Flynn had been arrested on accusations of raping underage
girls, with reference to four incidents that had taken place on his
yacht, the *Sirocco*. The two accusers, known as Betty and Peggy,
were no younger than twenty-three, they had been deflowered long
before Flynn got there, and they were more than consenting, but
during the trial the prosecution had had them dressed up as little
girls, with tiny shorts and plaits in their hair . . . Flynn had been
found not guilty, but the rapist label had stuck to him. That had
been the start of his decline as an actor and a man, the alcoholism,
the drugs, the self-destruction.

An MI6 operation.

Cary was disgusted: *Subtler and less noisy tactics!*

'Gentlemen, I don't know what you want of me, but I think this
conversation has gone on too long, and –'

'Mr Grant,' Sir Lewis began, showing him the palms of his hands
in a gesture of surrender, 'yes you're right, we're about to get to the
point.'

At least they'd finally stopped calling him 'Mr Leach'. They had
worked out that there was little to be gained from mentioning loyalty
to the Crown. 'Mr Grant, the NATO governments need your help
in a delicate matter of international importance. It may seem para-
doxical, but we are approaching you as an actor and an . . . elegant
man.'

Raymond pursed his lips, trying to keep from smiling. Cary's eyebrow arched again, and remained in that position for much of the next hour. Raymond's face exploded into a joyful expression, as though his shares in the Union Pacific Railroad had just risen by twenty points.

Chapter 13

The shining shoes sank into the mud and the smell of shit and stables rose up from below. Some makeshift fences planted in the slime in the midst of the dung-heaps, men wandering about among buffalo and cattle, about twenty cars parked not far away, and the buzzing of the flies often louder than the mooing of the cattle. The livestock market in Marcianise, near Caserta.

Zollo eyed the moron's convertible. Only a son of a bitch could come to a place like this in a luxury car. Zollo complimented himself for leaving his own in his garage at home. Trimane called his attention to a well-dressed man – hat, scarf, coat – in the middle of the crowd of yokels and livestock breeders. He couldn't make out his face from where he was standing, but he was the one.

They came down from the hill where they had been lying in wait, cursing the mud that stained the hem of their trousers. They reached the dirt path leading down to the village. A few hundred metres further, they found the Fiat 1900 borrowed for the occasion. They got in. Trimane lit a cigarette.

He said, 'So, you see this road?'

'Well, yeah, I see it.'

'In Italy the roads are not good. If there's no mud, there's dust, if there's no dust there are holes, if there are no holes –'

'There are always holes, Vic. *E niente* highways.'

Zollo peered into the rear-view mirror to see if anyone was coming. He wanted to get things over with and head back to Naples. The silence of the countryside made him strangely agitated.

'No good roads, no good cars. Just carts.'

'Jesus! Tin cans on four wheels, they make more noise than a tank, more stench than a gas can, and in the summer you'd think you were in a goddamned oven.'

The backwardness of Italy was another of Lucky Luciano's favourite subjects. When he had been pardoned for unexplained meritorious wartime service, and sent across the ocean, Salvatore Lucania had expected something more from his country of origin. For Stefano Zollo, the effect had been no different. He had often heard it said that the Italians had brought organised crime to America, and yet even from that point of view the old country seemed rather antiquated. Would anyone in New York have been dumb enough to slap Don Luciano? One such person, in America, had already ended up in the bay of the Hudson River, with a pair of snugly fitting concrete shoes. A clean and secure system for the concealment of corpses, which had won Zollo the nickname of 'Steve Cement'.

The only good things in Italy were the climate and the women. But even that was only partly true, as was demonstrated by the freezing January they had just endured. The women were, indeed, very beautiful, but, as Don Luciano said, they were stay-at-homes, and their clothes were designed for concealment rather than display.

'What do you think, Vic, Marilyn or the Italian actresses?'

'Well I'll say this, my friend, the Italian girls certainly have tits! When I got here, there were posters showing a girl all covered with mud, a peasant, wearing short short pants and a tight sweater. I found out her name, too . . . Mango, Mogano, can't remember.'

Behind him there was the sound of an approaching car. Victor checked the mirror and nodded. The moron's convertible. Steve got out and grabbed a big wrench from under the bonnet, which was open to look as though they had broken down. He wrapped it up in a copy of *Il Mattino* and went to stand by the edge of the road. The moron and his friend were laughing their heads off. They had clearly done some good business.

Zollo took a step forwards.

He stopped with one hand raised, the newspaper gripped in the other, lined up along his body.

The moron's car slowed down and stopped abruptly.

Zollo approached the passenger.

Zollo said, 'Could I have a word?'

The man looked at him quizzically.

The wrench came down twice on his head, hard. Despite the hat and the paper, Zollo heard the sound of the skull cracking. The man's friend heard it too, and as soon as he gave a sign of wanting to react, he saw Trimane, standing beside the Fiat 1900, aiming a gun at him.

'If you know anyone else who's planning on slapping anyone, tell them what happened to your pal.'

Zollo took a step backwards and the car, skidding in the mud, set off again.

Trimane got moving and Zollo joined him.

'Let's stop off at my house, Vic. I've got to change these filthy bloody shoes.'

Chapter 14

Bill Brown cleared his throat. It was only at that moment that Cary noticed his moccasins, brown penny loafers that clashed with everything else he was wearing. To tell the truth, the whole outfit was a disaster: his trousers and black socks were too short, and revealed the hair of his legs. Christ almighty, was it really possible that Uncle Sam was sending his men about the place dressed like that? Didn't the FBI agents all wear black suits, white shirts and black ties? Perhaps that Saturday was Brown's day off and they'd called him in at the last minute. But not even during one's leisure hours should anyone be guilty of such a lack of taste.

The American took off his dark glasses, tried to assume a solemn expression and said, 'Mr Grant, before my colleagues . . .' Cary noticed horror and a sense of superiority in the eyes of the two Englishmen. 'Before my colleagues continue, it is my duty to ask you a few questions in the name of the United States Government. First of all, what do you think of the country that has granted you citizenship? Do you consider yourself a good American?'

'Do you?' Cary fired back.

'I would like you to answer my question, Mr Grant,' Brown repeated.

Sir Lewis and Raymond stared at Cary. Their faces showed irritation with the presence of the American and an urgent need to explain the reason for their visit. With vague nods, they made it clear that they had done their best to spare him the third degree, but they were guests of the local government and had to let Brown get on with his job.

Cary tried to avoid vulgar expressions. 'What is this, another of those investigations you're so fond of? You're expecting me to plead the Fifth Amendment, *in my own home*, to allow you to conclude that I have something to hide, that I'm not "anti-communist"?' The two Englishmen could almost see smoke issuing from the actor's ears. 'Brown, just as I let you in, I can also throw you out. You're already standing up, you just have to put one foot in front of the other until you reach that damned door.'

'Mr Grant, I'm asking you this because it is a well-known fact that your friends include Clifford Odets, a writer with socialist sympathies, who financed the Spanish communists during the civil war –'

'Financed *the Republicans*, agent Brown. They weren't all communists. There were fascists on the other side, did no one tell you?'

'Mr Grant,' Brown went on, 'in an FBI report from 1944 you figure on a list of people linked in some way to communists.'

'Mr Brown,' Raymond intervened, 'we consider it a matter of fact that, while it may have been expressed in more colourful terms, Mr Hoover did not look kindly upon Mr Grant's activities as a representative of the British Crown. It is the firm conviction of MI6 that the Federal Bureau of Investigations deliberately exaggerated –'

'Raymond,' Brown exploded, 'I don't like being interrupted, ok? I didn't interrupt your solemn blather, so just shut your mouth and let me finish! Your Mr Grant has been directly involved in the production of left-wing films, and last year he even went so far as to defend Charlie Chaplin!'

Cary rose from his armchair and took a few steps towards the federal agent.

'Mr Brown, this is official. I'm throwing you out of my house. If you want me to add a kick in the pants, I will be delighted to oblige, and given that you've said you're –'

'Gentlemen, please!' said Sir Lewis, while the two Englishmen got to their feet to separate the combatants.

'So you're going to kick my ass, are you? You just try it!' roared Brown.

'Thanks for the permission, but I think I'd rather knock a couple of teeth down your throat,' replied Cary.

'Gentlemen, some civil behaviour, for heaven's sake! We are here to discuss a mission . . .'

The two Englishmen finally managed to re-establish a semblance of calm.

Sir Lewis straightened his jacket, before solemnly announcing, 'Mr Brown, Mr Grant's assistance has been formally requested by the British government. MI6 has incontrovertible proof of Mr Grant's democratic loyalty, and is willing to convey the relevant documentation to your agency so that Mr Grant need not be subjected to any awkward investigations, which would, during this phase, interfere with the interests of the United Kingdom and also of *your* government, which I shall inform about the present incident. I assume personal responsibility for the decision to remove you from this house, and I wish that to be specifically mentioned in your report. If Mr Hoover is not satisfied by such guarantees, he can always send an official protest to London.'

'What do you think you're doing? Cary Grant is no longer a British citizen, and –'

'For God's sake, will you just go before I lose patience? Get out!!!' shrieked Sir Lewis, without parting his lips any further than he did when speaking normally, almost without moving his facial muscles. Cary was stunned, but not stunned enough to miss an opportunity to dismiss Brown in an appropriate fashion: 'While you're at it, tell Edgardina to stop circulating rumours about *my* alleged homosexuality: he's a fine one to talk!'

Sir Lewis settled back down on the sofa, while Raymond walked the cursing Brown to the door.

'Why is MI6 showing up with one of Hoover's men?' asked Cary.

'As you yourself have pointed out, Mr Grant, J. Edgar Hoover has had it in for you ever since he first felt his jurisdiction being invaded by your intelligence activities, and by ours. Furthermore, you are friends with well-known liberals, and you have defended Mr Chaplin, who is perhaps the single individual most hated by the head of the FBI. As you have said, Mr Grant, Hoover is a squalid nuisance, and his bureau is more like the Gestapo than anything else I have ever seen. Even President Eisenhower holds him and his methods in profound contempt. Such things would be unimaginable in England.'

'In fact, the gentlemen of the old school are exerting pressure and settling disputes in very subtle and graceful ways. Even down to using those "underage girls" of easy virtue . . .' said Cary with a wink.

Sir Lewis stopped for a second, and began again with some difficulty. 'This is different, Mr Grant. Errol Flynn was *effectively* a Nazi sympathiser, and we discovered as much thanks to you. The way we confronted him may strike you as underhand and unpleasant, but Flynn was a traitor, as well as an idiot. On the other hand, many of the people blackmailed or ruined by Hoover have *never* sympathised with bolshevism. For four years, the FBI has unofficially supported Senator McCarthy, supplying him with documentation about the private lives of politicians and intellectuals. Except you can have too much of a good thing: McCarthy is not as popular as he was. Hoover doesn't want to end up in the dirt with his old chum, he's trying to distance himself from him, but at the same time he wants to demonstrate that American life really is infiltrated by reds. Once they learned that MI6 planned to contact you, the FBI intervened, presenting themselves as the agency best suited to putting your Americanism to the test. MI6 protested, but Hoover is very powerful.'

'So now you're going to have problems.'

Brown was heard cursing in the entrance hall, son-of-a-this and son-of-a-that.

'Nothing we can't handle,' Sir Lewis replied. 'In spite of everything, any set of scales you might wish to employ could tell you that the Commonwealth is weightier than Hoover.'

'Well said.'

Raymond came back into the drawing room and went and stood by the mantelpiece, where Brown had been until a few moments before.

'Let's speak about us,' said Sir Lewis. 'Mr Grant, do you keep yourself informed about the world political situation?'

'Er . . . if you're referring to the fact that the Korean War is over, yes, I have heard about that. And I also know that Joe Stalin died last year,' Cary replied sarcastically.

'I hope I'm not abusing your patience. I fear that the preamble may go on for some time. I will try not to be too verbose, and leave you some documents in which you will be able to find anything that I have omitted. May I continue?'

'I must admit that at last you are arousing my curiosity, Sir Lewis. Forget tea, can I interest you in something stronger?' Cary reached out from his armchair and pulled the drinks trolley towards him. 'Scotch? Brandy? A martini?'

Having served the two Englishmen and himself, Cary was all ears.

'Yes, the Korean War is over, but the Cold War continues, and I can assure you that it has never been more intense. The West risks losing strategic territory, the Soviets are very aggressive, and they are waging obstructionist battles in every area of diplomatic confrontation. The unfortunate execution of the Rosenbergs, here in America, less than six years ago, has given an increasingly bitter tone to communications and led to reciprocal accusations. Furthermore, you will be aware that the Soviet Union has had the H-bomb for two years. A global balance of terror has established itself, and there are at least four crucial, thorny questions on the table, upon whose diplomatic solution the fate of the whole planet depends. Does that sound too high-flown?'

'Well, who isn't afraid of the atom bomb?' replied Cary.

'Indeed. And unfortunately, even in the country of which you have become a citizen, there are people who are threatening to use it at the drop of a hat. The Berlin Conference has been under way for a week, involving the United States, the United Kingdom, the Soviet Union and France. On the agenda are the war in Indochina, the partition of Korea and the rearmament of the German Federal Republic. Let's leave Korea out of the picture, because we might say that the fever there is subsiding. The most explosive situation is in Indochina, where the French colonial army has been placed in serious difficulties by Ho Chi Minh's communists. As far as the German problem is concerned, the Federal Republic is sure to amend its constitution to allow the reorganisation of a national army, and become a NATO member by the end of the year. You can imagine the repercussions in the Kremlin.'

'I suppose they'll say that a new German army would call various Nazi lunatics back into service,' the actor mused.

'That is actually one of their favourite topics. But Germany no longer poses a threat: the Allied administration, the Marshall Plan and the territorial division have stabilised the situation. Indeed I would go further than that: the anti-communism of the German military cadres is a precious resource, because the Federal Republic is now one of our bastions along the Iron Curtain.'

'So you're saying that in order to oppose the Russians, Europe is placing its trust in people who were wearing swastika armbands until just the other day?' asked Cary.

'*À la guerre comme à la guerre*, Mr Grant. I repeat that there is no risk of a Nazi revival, while the Russians have the H-bomb and are conquering new territories. The admission of the Federal Republic into NATO is a crucial act within the context of the Cold War.'

Cary interrupted him: 'You've hinted at *four* crucial questions, but you've said that in Berlin they're discussing three.'

'I note that you are an attentive listener,' Sir Lewis said with a slight smile. 'The fourth has to do with the city of Trieste.'

'Trieste in Italy?'

'That is precisely the point: at the moment, Trieste is not Italian territory, but neither has it been annexed by communist Yugoslavia. Its official title is the "Free Territory of Trieste". For nine years the administration has been in the hands of the British and American military police, the Italian and Yugoslavian governments have not yet reached an agreement, and recently the city has been the scene of bloody clashes. MI6 is firmly convinced that, even before the rearmament of the Federal Republic of Germany, East–West relations depend on future agreements concerning Trieste. As you must be aware, Yugoslavian communism is a thing of its own. Yugoslavia doesn't obey Moscow's rules, and was therefore "excommunicated" from the Cominform in '48.'

'The Cominform?'

'That's the consulting body of all the communist parties in the world. All, that is, except the League of Yugoslavian Communists.'

'And why did the Russians dismiss the Yugoslavs?'

'For their refusal to submit to Stalin's authority, and for making unorthodox foreign policy decisions. In other words, Yugoslavia is outside the logic of the Eastern and Western blocs, and is deserting the Cold War. For example, it has remained entirely indifferent to the conflict in Korea. You see, between '41 and '45, the Yugoslavs freed themselves from the Italo-German occupation without any help from anyone. It was the Yugoslavian Communist Party that led the struggle. In short, the Yugoslavian communists carried out their socialist revolution all by themselves, and for that reason they don't need to kowtow to Moscow. Besides, they already have a supreme leader, Marshal Josip Broz, known as "Tito", a partisan hero and a great military strategist. Once the war was over, the two personality cults could not coexist: it would not be possible to venerate Tito *and* Stalin.'

Cary elegantly crossed his legs without crumpling the line of his trousers, and gave a slight nod. 'My colleague Sterling Hayden talked to me once about this character Tito, I think he knew him personally during the war.'

Sir Lewis allowed himself a faint smile. 'We will get to Tito's personality shortly, it's something that concerns you more than you can imagine.'

Cary refreshed the glasses.

Raymond sipped his scotch and folded his arms as he waited for his superior to continue.

Sir Lewis started talking again, extremely calmly. 'I don't want to bore you with a detailed technical description of economic and political issues, Mr Grant. You need only know that when we speak of Tito's Yugoslavia we must not think of the Soviet Union.'

Cary's face assumed an ironic expression, as though he were preparing to utter the punchline of a script: 'So you're telling me, Sir Lewis, that there are *good* communists?'

Raymond blushed with embarrassment and looked at Sir Lewis, who didn't turn a hair. 'I wouldn't say anything of the kind. But certainly there are communists who may be useful to our purposes. Tito is one of those.'

The MI6 officer paused, waiting for Grant to say something, but Cary remained silent, sipping his drink.

'The United Kingdom enjoys a state of privileged dialogue with the Marshal. You should be aware, in fact, that during the war contact was made with the Yugoslav partisans, with a view to sending aid to Tito. And Washington tried something similar as well: as you just mentioned, Mr Grant, some officers with American links, including your colleague Hayden, have established contact with the Yugoslavs. But over the past few years the work of the McCarthy Commission has made any form of approach towards the communist countries utterly unthinkable. Let alone thinking of exploiting for the purpose individuals who have had dealings with them during the war. I am aware that Mr Hayden has had problems with the Commission just because of his war record.'

Cary snorted. 'Let's drop the euphemisms, Sir Lewis. Hayden was interrogated by McCarthy as a communist sympathiser, he was accused of un-American activities, and it was impossible for him to go on working in Hollywood. That's a little more than "having problems", don't you think?'

Sir Lewis nodded irritably. 'Without a doubt. But what matters is that the United Kingdom does not have a McCarthy. We have a different margin of manoeuvre.'

'To do what, Sir Lewis?' asked Cary, tired of the endless preamble.

Sir Lewis exchanged a glance with Raymond, who nodded and said, 'To bring Yugoslavia on to our side.'

Cary Grant's left eyebrow reached an altitude it had never touched before, not even on the big screen.

'But didn't you just say that Mr Tito was a communist, or am I mistaken?'

Raymond sought his superior's agreement again, and said, 'Certainly. And no one is about to try and make him change his mind. But a country such as Yugoslavia could be subjected to . . . *blandishments*, enough to make it prefer us to the Russians. It would be a matter not of interfering in the political system of the country, but of establishing firm economic and diplomatic relations. The process has already been under way for a number of years, a commercial partnership already exists, and Her Majesty herself has received Tito in Buckingham Palace.'

Raymond broke off at a nod from Sir Lewis and let him continue. 'You see, since the death of Stalin, a few things are changing in Russia. In other words there is a real danger of rapprochement between Moscow and Belgrade. As far as we are concerned, however, to open up a dialogue with Yugoslavia would be to build a bridge with Eastern Europe. To encourage Tito's choice of autonomy, to give him international credit, would suggest an escape route for the other satellite countries of the Soviet Union as well.'

Cary coughed gently a number of times. 'Erm, gentlemen, this is all very interesting, but the obvious question is, "Where do I come in?"'

Sir Lewis straightened his back. 'In essence, Mr Grant, we are suggesting that you help us to change the attitude of Western public opinion about Tito's Yugoslavia. It will not be necessary to persuade people that the Soviet Union is not hell on earth, but simply that not all socialist countries are. Or rather, in particular, that Yugoslavia is not. In order to accomplish this, we need to give the world a new image of the country, its leader and its history. And we must be the ones to do it, because at the moment the Americans are still trying to come up with the best way of eliminating McCarthy and his inquisitors.'

Cary smiled, with ill-concealed irony. 'That is what is called plain speaking, Sir Lewis. And now, before I return to my reading of the Greek myths, would you please tell me what sort of help you are asking of me?'

'We would like you to make a film on the life of Marshal Tito and the Yugoslav Resistance. A film that would draw attention to the anti-Nazi character of the partisan struggle, rather than its communist connotations, and exalt Yugoslavian national pride, the collective effort and, not least, relations with the Allies.'

'And you think a film will be enough?'

Sir Lewis crossed his fingers, leaning back in his armchair. 'Films can be very useful, Mr Grant. I don't know whether Hollywood was ever a "hotbed of reds", as Senator McCarthy maintains, but certainly until the United States joined the war it was a circle of Nazi supporters. Errol Flynn, Gary Cooper, Walt Disney, Howard Hughes . . . From the point of view of the war effort those people were just as dangerous as Hitler's troops who were invading Europe. Because cinema is the dream factory of the free world, Mr Grant, it is its conscience and its imagination. If Hollywood had, at that time, decided to make the democratic world look fondly on Hitler, it could have done so. That's why your work has been so useful. Now we would like to use one of those dreams, Cary Grant, to win an important battle in the war that is currently under way: the Cold War. To put it briefly, Mr Grant, we are asking you to serve the cause of the free world once again, just as you have in the past.'

For a few moments Cary was uncertain whether or not to start laughing, but in the end he chose his most incredulous smile, and stretched out in his armchair, holding his elbow with one hand and his chin between his thumb and his index finger. 'Once again you astonish me, Sir Lewis. I wouldn't miss the ending of this story for anything in the world.'

The secret service officer was unmoved by the irony. 'Now Mr Raymond will talk to you about Marshal Tito.'

The underling cleared his throat, brushed invisible crumbs from the sleeve of his jacket and began. 'Josip Broz, known as "Tito", is a singular and without a doubt an interesting character, Mr Grant. And hard though it might be for you to believe this, it was he who first mentioned your name.'

The Cary Grant trademark smile was all that the actor would concede.

Raymond went on. 'Tito genuinely admires you. He has seen your films and he thinks most highly of them. When we aired the hypothesis of involving an Anglo-Saxon producer in a film about his life, he made it quite clear that he would be flattered by your involvement. And it was the Marshal himself who suggested the character that you would interpret. In 1943, two English officers were parachuted into the mountains of Yugoslavia with the task of linking up with Tito. They joined forces with the Resistance and for a few months they shared the fate of the partisans, so much so that one of them was killed during a German bombing raid. Should you accept our offer, we would suggest that you interpret the role of the surviving officer, who is also available to work on the screenplay.'

Cary raised a hand. 'One moment, Mr Raymond, kindly explain. Who would be the producer? Who would be the director? What is the budget for the enterprise?'

It was Raymond's turn to cough. 'That still remains to be determined.'

The actor looked away for a moment, before suddenly turning back to stare at Raymond. 'In other words you're suggesting that I take part in a film for which you have as yet found no producer and no director, for which you don't know the budget available and for which there is as yet no screenplay.' He rolled his eyes. 'What the hell has been happening in England while I've been away? Have the alcoholics taken over?'

The two MI6 officials lowered their eyes in embarrassment. Sir Lewis was the first to break the silence. 'You see, Mr Grant, for the time being this is a hypothetical project.'

'You can say that again.'

'We haven't actually come here to offer you an engagement. That isn't our job. But Marshal Tito has asked to be able to meet you. Let's just say that he has imposed a few preliminary conditions on the whole enterprise.'

Cary's frown forced Sir Lewis to explain. 'That's why we're here. It certainly won't be MI6 that offers you an engagement, but perhaps MGM will in due course. We would like you to meet Marshal Tito as an ambassador for the Western cinematographic industry. It is clear that if Tito had not expressed this wish, we would never have been so bold as to come and disturb you, Mr Grant.'

Sir Lewis let Raymond speak. Cary wondered on what basis the two of them had divided their roles, or whether it was a casual arrangement.

'MI6 can supply the logistical support to enable you to go to Yugoslavia. Obviously you would be travelling incognito: the Russians must know nothing about the meeting, or they could undertake unpleasant countermeasures. Besides, no one is going to want to divulge your name without being certain of the project going ahead.'

Cary had to confess that he was fascinated by the absurdity of the situation. For a moment he thought that at any second David Niven might jump out of the next room to reveal the joke with one of his quips.

'To avoid arousing suspicion,' Raymond went on, 'we thought we would employ a double, Mr Grant, who would, in your absence, allow some photographs of himself to be taken from a long way off, in the company of your wife, to keep the glossy magazines happy. To do this, we would take advantage of the fact that your withdrawal from the cinema and the Hollywood party scene gives us ample room for manoeuvre.'

'A double?'

Raymond took a photograph from the briefcase and passed it to Cary, who looked at it for a few moments.

'You can't be serious! This person is supposed to stand in for me?' Cary exploded into liberating laughter. 'This balding, unshaven fop is supposed to look like me? *Be* me? Gentlemen, you must have had a few drinks too many!'

'Obviously there will have to be some retouching –'

'But he looks nothing like me!'

'Make-up can work wonders, Mr Grant. An actor like yourself knows that.'

'Wonders? They'd have to photograph him from the top of the Empire State Building to make people think that's me!'

With a hint of self-importance, Sir Lewis reassured him. 'This is our job, Mr Grant. When our agents informed us in 1943 that Hitler had a plan to assassinate Winston Churchill, we engaged a certain George Howard Foster, known in the world of impressionists as the Great Foster, to impersonate the Prime Minister at various public occasions. No one ever noticed the difference.'

'So who's this guy? Is he a comedian as well?' asked Cary, still looking at the photograph.

'No. He sells second-hand cars in Montreal. His name's Jean-Jacques Bondurant. He sometimes impersonates you at parish festivals and in Christmas pantomimes.'

Cary laughed again.

'And when is this "mission" supposed to be taking place?'

'In the spring. We would fly you to London in a military plane, and from there on to Yugoslavia.'

There was a long pause. Sir Lewis appeared to be meditating on what to say. In the end he found the right words. 'Mr Grant. The last message that Admiral Nelson delivered to the fleet before the battle of Trafalgar was: "England expects that every man will do his duty."' He sighed and added, 'I would ask you to give our proposal serious consideration. It would be an inestimable service to the cause of the free world.'

Cary smiled and reflected that the tone of the phrase was too pompous. Rhetoric entirely in keeping with a grey officer of Her Majesty's Secret Service.

Chapter 15

Strips of daylight filtered faintly through the half-open shutters. Brando's flat was on the first floor and the window, overlooking the footpath, was far from private. In any case, Angela would have been worried at the top of Bologna's massive Torre degli Asinelli.

'But if your husband asks you which scene you liked best in the film, what are you going to tell him?'

Pierre gathered up the clothes scattered on the floor, and turned around to hand her her blouse. Angela was slipping on her stockings. He went over to her and started kissing her on the neck and caressing her.

Angela put on her skirt and sat down on the edge of the bed.

'I've never asked you why you and Nicola didn't go to Yugoslavia too.'

Pierre didn't like talking about it. But there was no point trying to hide things from Angela. 'You know,' he began, 'my brother was already grown up, he had a job, he'd been in the Resistance in Italy, he's not the kind of person who likes change. I was just thirteen. My aunt Iolanda had brought me up from the age of five, I was fine with her and I had started working in a factory as well. My father didn't know whether I would be happy in Yugoslavia. With Aunt Iolanda they thought I would make my mind up when I was bigger, and that was ok too.'

Some women's laughter reached them from the street. They had stopped just underneath the window. Angela suddenly froze and fell silent. The tenants of the building might grow suspicious if they heard unfamiliar voices in Brando's flat. The women were almost shouting. They burst out laughing again, and then their voices moved away. Angela relaxed and repeated the question.

'Why didn't you go and find your father?'

'Oh, you know!' Pierre spread his arms out. 'I've been setting money aside since I was little. But I wasn't given a passport. And then there's the fact that we haven't heard from him for almost a year.'

Angela realised she had touched a raw nerve. 'How do you mean?'

'He used to write, we stayed in contact, often, but there was something else as well, that sense that you've still got at least one of your parents. He asked questions, he took an interest in us. Then, all of a sudden, it stopped.'

'Do you think something terrible's happened?'

'Listen, if he was dead, surely he would have had a friend who would be willing to tell his sons, don't you think? I don't believe he's dead, but I'm sure he's having problems of some kind.'

All of a sudden the fridge started humming.

'My husband and his friends say that Tito is a traitor.'

'Of course they do, he's the only communist who quit Stalin.'

'Did your father ever meet him?'

'You bet! He was made a hero of the people by Tito in person.'

The darkness erased the outlines of the room. In the light from a match, Pierre's face lit up for a moment, then all that remained was the glow of his cigarette. Short days. Halfway through the afternoon the sun disappeared, the streetlights spread a yellowish light through the fog and bicycle dynamo-lights were switched on.

'I've really got to go now.'

'When will we see each other again?'

'Don't ask, Pierre. Odoacre may be going to Rome on Tuesday, I don't know.'

'Fine. If you can, send Teresa to tell me about it. We'll have to be able to tell Brando so we can have his flat.'

They set off towards the door and Pierre helped her on with her coat. He kissed her and stroked her hair, and they exchanged a long kiss, almost like one in a film. Then Angela passed through the door and he heard her going down the few stairs to the door. Through the gap in the shutters he saw her passing quickly, her handbag clamped under her arm. He bade her a silent goodbye, turned the light on and tidied up the bed.

Before he left, he went into the bathroom and used Brando's brilliantine to slick back his hair. He looked at himself in the mirror. What kind of situation had he got himself into! The young wife of the great and meritorious comrade Montroni.

It was less cold outside, and the snow was melting into dirty slush.

Chapter 16

Statement given on 1.2.1954 to Police Commissioner Pasquale
Cinquegrana by Salvatore Pagano of unknown parents, held on a
charge of stealing an expensive television set of American manufacture
from the military base of the Allied forces in Agnano, Naples

Excuse me, but this time I really don't understand. What's all this about a slap? Yes, of course I know Don Luciano. Who doesn't? I've already told you that Agnano is my second home, almost my first one, and Don Luciano goes there too, and everyone knows him, you can't help it, go and talk to the jockeys, the bookies, the people in the bar, the waiters. They all know him. And you're saying that someone's supposed to have slapped him, on the day when I was there too, the 3rd of January, when I won those 5,000 lire with the bet on Monte Allegro. Are you absolutely sure? Look, apart from anything else, this business has nothing to do with that other stuff about the American television, nothing at all, and if I knew anything I'd be happy to tell you, but unfortunately I didn't see anything of the kind, and I didn't hear anyone talking about it either, and people would have been talking about something like that in Agnano, you can be sure of that. And who's going to give Don Luciano a slap? Everyone loves him.

A slap? Listen to me, if someone slapped Don Luciano he certainly wouldn't have lived to tell the tale, if you follow me. Do you not see that? Ok, look, I only know Don Luciano by sight, as you might say, and he's a really great bloke, but there are some other people who criticise him and say that he does terrible things, just because he's a foreigner, that is, he is Italian but he comes from New York, and it's really easy to take against him. Then his friends, the ones who help him get by, they got annoyed, in fact they got really furious, because they love Don Luciano. And in the end, if anyone really did slap him, those guys don't like it, and you know how these things go, in fact maybe they go and get him, the low-life, to tell him to

stop doing it, to tell him that this thing has caused them a great deal
of grief and maybe he gets on his high horse and who do you think
you are, and who's your mother, and who's Don Luciano. Then off
you go, maybe you come to blows rather than being able to talk
about it calmly, and the man on his own takes more than he gives
because there's more of them. Afterwards, he doesn't come and talk
to you, number one because he started it, he gave the slap and
provoked the people who came to talk to him. Secondly, because
he's now furious as well, and if he has friends he sends them to speak
directly to Don Luciano's friends, not to you, and they try to resolve
the matter in a gentlemanly fashion.

I understand, yes. Don Luciano's friends, as you put it, have already
gone to the low-life who slapped him, but rather than talking, you
say they were heavy-handed, a wrench, you say, crushed his head.
And why are you coming to tell me all this, when I'm only here for
the business about the American television?

Do I know Stefano Zollo? I told you, at the racecourse everybody
knows everybody, the people who come here regular. But maybe
'know' is a bit strong, you know what somebody's name is, and what
somebody looks like, and when you meet them, well, what's up,
what's wrong, take care, and off you go. Zollo, yes, I think I know
him, big guy, but I'm not sure. And that is all I know, I assure you.

Cassazione? Ok, him too, another of those people you see in
Agnano, he does odd jobs just the same as me. He had 5,000 lire in
his pocket as well? Obviously he had placed a good bet too. No,
that's a lie. Don't believe a word he says, let me warn you. Do you
think this guy Stefano Zollo is going to go round handing out 5,000
lire to everyone because we've placed a bet for Don Luciano? He
makes things up, he gets everything muddled, you see he won the
money with a bet that wasn't all that clean and he doesn't want to
tell you. Remember they call him that, *Cassazione*, because one day
he says one thing and then the next day he says the opposite, he
changes his mind, like the judge in the Court of Cassation, you see,
when he says another judge made a mistake and they have to do the
trial again. In the end he's his own cassation, he does something then
he undoes it, he says something and then he contradicts himself, he's
famous for that, ask around, you don't need to pay him any attention, never, you'll catch him again tomorrow and he'll tell you he

was given the 5,000 lire by Princess Soraya, that pretty lady, as a handout, and the next day he'll tell you he prayed to St Gennaro and, lo and behold, there they were in his pocket, by a miracle.

No, I've never worked for Don Luciano, I swear, he's far too important, he'd never trust someone like me to place his bets. And a gift of 5,000 lire? Don Luciano isn't a millionaire! He's lucky with the horses, but that's all. Ok, he did bet on Monte Allegro that day, you're very well informed. So you can see that he knows his horses well, too, maybe a friend who's a jockey told him that Ninfa had had a bad case of colic. I couldn't have been the only person who knew something like that, rumours go around, you know how it is.

But excuse me, didn't you want to know about that television?

Chapter 17

The maid set the tray of Wedgwood cups and the teapot down on the little table, waited for a nod and withdrew in silence. The tea was the only ingredient of a traditional breakfast to have survived Betsy's new alimentary convictions. Rather than bacon and eggs, orange juice, and toast with cherry jam, there were oat flakes, bran, soya bean sprouts, and a vegetable drink based on celery, carrot and banana. Quite honestly not even the tea was the same, because the old Earl Grey had made way for a greenish Chinese variety from Hong Kong. At first Cary had welcomed the novelty enthusiastically, as he always did, trying to find out everything he could on the subject. Subsequently his interest had abated, and the crisis peaked when the crazed blender, rather than producing a carrot juice for his friend David Niven as he intended it to do, sprayed the whole kitchen with orange pulp.

Betsy Drake glanced up from her morning paper and looked at her husband in his blue pyjamas and indigo silk dressing gown, shaking his head as he flicked through some typed pages.

'Something wrong, darling?'

'No, nothing. I get the feeling that even old Hitch isn't feeling so great. This script isn't one for him.'

'What's wrong with it?'

'I can't make a comeback with something like this. For pity's sake, a captivating little story based on a novel by a certain David Dodge. A retired thief in a hotel has to demonstrate his own innocence by catching the man really responsible for a series of thefts. A beautiful girl tries to put him to the test with her jewels and falls in love with him. In the end he finds the guilty man and marries the girl. But I don't know . . .'

The tea was too hot. The bean sprouts were tasteless, the bran was utterly unappealing, and just looking at the vegetable glop made his gorge rise. Cary got to his feet and started pacing back and forth. Even dressed like this, he could turn up at the newsagent's without anyone passing remarks about his elegance. Betsy couldn't remember ever having seen him coming out of his bedroom in anything less than a dressing gown.

'I have a sense, my darling, that you don't know what it is that you really need.'

Without stopping, he expressed a thought out loud. 'I can't make a comeback with this stuff, God damn it!'

'But listen, starting over would do you good, I'm sure of it.'

'Sure it would do me good. But what with? They've also suggested I take part in a film about Tito, the President of Yugoslavia. What do you think?'

Betsy opened her eyes wide and straightened her back, surprised. 'Who on earth wants to make a film like that? Clifford?'

'No, MI6.'

'M what? What is it, a new studio?'

The sofa's soft cushions attracted him. Cary sank into them, arms at his side and legs outstretched.

'Military Intelligence.' He said the words in a serious voice. 'The British secret service. And the CIA and the NATO governments. Two Englishmen were here the day before yesterday, secret agents of Her Majesty, not the fascinating spies you might imagine, they were like a couple of bank officials. They want me to go and see Tito in Yugoslavia, to discuss a film about his life. They've also given me a lot of documentation about the man.'

Betsy sipped her carrot juice as though it were medicine, waiting for her husband to continue. Pressing his eyes with his fingers, trying to concentrate, Cary went on. 'A film about Tito. In Yugoslavia. Something that will present him as a hero in the eyes of the West. Turn him into an acceptable ally. He expressly asked for them to give me a part, and he's very keen to meet me. You see? And the film doesn't even have funding, a screenplay, a director. Nothing at all.'

'But they must at least have told you —'

'Let me finish, this is the good bit. Before going to Yugoslavia I would have to stop over in London, so I'd be away for a few weeks. But they don't want people to know what's going on, so I'd have to travel incognito. And do you know what brilliant idea they've come up with to make sure that my cover isn't blown? A double, a man they say looks like me, a French Canadian with a ludicrous name, who would come here to impersonate Cary Grant. Can you imagine?'

There was a good minute's silence. Then the sound of newspaper being folded, and the wheeze of the armchair as it was freed of Betsy's weight. Now it was her turn to pace.

'I don't understand, honey, spell it out for me. They want a stranger to come and live in our house?'

'That's what I thought too, Betsy. But they're not as crazy as all that. This man, this individual they say looks like me, wouldn't be here all the time. He would come every now and again, show his face, go out and buy some aftershave and come back home again, take you for a walk, make everyone think that Cary Grant never moved away from Palm Springs.'

Betsy handed her husband the glass of vegetable juice; she wouldn't let him leave it there. There was something tempting about the secret service suggestion. Admittedly, it wasn't the kind of come-back for Cary that she'd been hoping for, a film to restore his self-confidence and his desire to work. Neither would it win him back his success and his audience. But there was something *active* about it, meeting new people, seeing new countries, getting away from home for a couple of months. A little holiday for her as well: Cary was becoming increasingly nervous and depressed, and it was Betsy who paid the price.

'Obviously I told them you would never accept such a situation. "Your wife will understand, Mr Grant," they kept saying, over and over. Ludicrous, I said, going out with a stranger, someone who's supposed to look like me, while I'm far away, and not even for work, but on an utterly unbelievable special mission. Can you imagine?'

The maid leaned against the door and Betsy beckoned her in.

'Just leave the bean sprouts, Jenny. At least eat some bean sprouts, darling.'

She waited until the maid had gone, and tried to resolve her last perplexities.

'I still don't understand why this thing has to stay such a secret.
You'd only be a famous actor visiting a head of state.'

'It's not as simple as that. Listen: this fellow Tito is a communist, but he's not working with the Russians. So the British want
to bring him over to their side. Except that for the time being they
don't want word to get out, they aren't all that sure what's going to
happen. Most importantly, they don't want the Russians to find out
about it.'

A bowl full of bean sprouts took the place of the empty glass of
vegetable swill. Cary looked at his wife, looked at the bowl, looked
up again to say he didn't want any, and found a fork in front of him.
He picked it up and started choking them down.

'"Your wife will understand, Mr Grant." Ridiculous, isn't it?'

'Yes, darling, the mission may well be ridiculous, but in the end
so are all things political. We can only understand them up to a
certain point. On the other hand, couldn't you do with a distraction? Something that isn't acting, but isn't brooding at home all day
long, either. If you have to go to London, well, maybe you could
use the opportunity to pass through Bristol to see your mother. And
apart from that, you would meet an important, interesting man who
would treat you with the greatest possible respect. You'd be doing a
favour to America and everyone else. It doesn't seem all that un-
acceptable to me, quite the opposite.'

Cary automatically arched his eyebrow. 'But what about the
doppelgänger? This French Canadian who's supposed to be the image
of me?'

'Don't tell me you're not curious to meet him. At least to see if
he really is the spit of you.'

'If that's why, then there's no doubt about it. They showed me a
photograph, and if I'd asked them to let me have it, you could judge
as well. A stocky man with no sense of posture whatsoever.'

Betsy stopped walking back and forth and joined her husband
among the cushions on the sofa.

'I confess, darling, that I really am curious about it. Basically, I'd
get used to it. The occasional stroll with a stranger, what could be
wrong with that?'

'I'll think about it, Betsy, I'll think about it. The secret agents reckon it would take just a little make-up to turn a used-car salesman into Cary Grant. It would take a damned sight more than that: showing him how to walk, how to dress, how to smile. I'd have to give him a few lessons. Otherwise it would be a disaster. He doesn't look a bit like me. Not a bit!'

Chapter 18

Around lunchtime the Bar Aurora is always half empty. Not many of us stay there to eat. Maybe there would be more of us if Capponi bothered to serve up something other than the usual old mortadella sandwich, I don't know, maybe a nice plate of pasta, but he says you need a special licence to cook, and Benassi won't have anything to do with it because it would be too expensive. Anyway, even if he did, everyone with families would rather go home, tagliatelle made by your wife is always going to be better than anything Pierre throws together. So, at about one, you usually see the bachelors, the child-less widowers, and people like La Gaggia or Brando who have a shop a stone's throw away and don't fancy going all the way home.

But after an hour, an hour and a half at the most, the bar starts livening up again, like a cat after its nap, a few yawns and it's ready to go. First arrival is Bottone, with his son Massimo, on a motor scooter, wobbling slightly on the pillion seat. Massimo is one of the people who took part in the 'Ten Thousand Kilometres on a Lambretta' competition, the one in which a Bolognese student, who rode into the desert and then all the way to the North Cape, was placed third. Massimo got as far as Paris, met a girl, and forgot all about the competition.

Bottone is already sitting next to La Gaggia and shuffling the *tarocco* pack, when Waltcrún and Garibaldi turn up. They live in the same building and still ride bikes. Then the rest come in dribs and drabs, all in an exact sequence. The only unpredictable one is Melega, because if he has some news he wants to deliver, he waits until the bar is full to make more of an effect, and, if not, he's always among the first to arrive after work.

'So what do you think?' Walterún suddenly begins. 'Now that Scelba's back, there's not going to be much to smile about.'

On the other side of the table, La Gaggia pulls a face and tries to change the subject.

'D'you hear what happened on Friday? They interrogated that girl who knows all about the death of Wilma Montesi.'

'There are some good ones going around about that,' comments a tram driver, cup in hand. He only ever comes here to drink coffee.

Walterún insists on the accuracy of his news. 'I'm sure you're right, but, mark my words, if the murderer of the Montesi girl turns out to be a big shot, that's Scelba finished.'

Our emigrant's shin takes a sharp kick under the table. La Gaggia shakes his head nervously, and tries to nod towards Bottone, who still hasn't dealt the cards. He is trying to point out to Walterún that the issue of Prime Minister Scelba is something to be saved for later on, for when they're playing, as though he were a joker to be pulled out in an emergency, because once this subject comes up Bottone will start going on about the atom bomb again and the game will be over. But Walterún just won't get it.

'That bloke isn't a Christian Democrat, he's a fascist, he's the kind who solves problems with a truncheon! You remember the time they tried to change the election law? What a shock that was!'

'Why, is Fanfani any better? With that Hitler 'tache of his?'

'But they do say Fanfani's more left-wing,' the postman butts in, sipping his glass of bitters.

'No, no, let me tell you,' Bottone's voice shuts everyone up. 'They're not more left-wing and less left-wing, they're all exactly the same.' He pauses for a moment, and La Gaggia attempts the impossible.

'Quite right! For example, that guy Fanfani knew stuff about the Montesi case —'

'The only good Papist is a dead Papist!' Bottone again, red in the face, thumping his fist hard on the table. 'Fanfani, De Gasperi, Pella. But Scelba is in another category, a much bigger one. They're the ones who were delighted with Benito before the armistice, and then afterwards they were all anti, and now they're back doing their thing again. There aren't enough bullets for them all, you'd need something else.' He starts machine-gunning with his finger. 'And if

I had a button to set off an atom bomb to wipe them off the face of the earth before they even noticed, I'd press it, boom, you can count on that.'

All that happens is that Bottone ends up with eighteen cards and has to deal again. La Gaggia shakes his head dolefully, and Walterún tries to apologise.

'What's this about Fanfani knowing things, Gaggia?'

A glance across the table, reproof for having woken up too late.

'Well, it seems that this girl who knows everything, the one they interrogated, told Fanfani a few things back in December, on her parish priest's advice.'

'Priests, priests . . .' Stefanelli nods mysteriously, knocking back his chaser as well.

'Hey, Gaggia,' Garibaldi says as he throws down a king of cups. 'I don't get it, I really don't. How come this girl Anna Maria went to Fanfani rather than the cops?'

'How the hell should I know? She probably thought they were important matters, and pretty much everyone was involved, aristocrats, politicians, people at the highest levels. Because forgive me, if you knew things as big as that would you go and tell the cops?'

'Oh no, certainly not. But I wouldn't go to Fanfani either. I'd go straight to the editors of *L'Unità* and put the cat among the pigeons.'

'Well, I don't know, Fanfani was Interior Minister, they must have thought he was better.'

The bar door opens all of a sudden, and everyone turns round and stops talking. It's an unusual time for anyone to show up, and Melega and the others are still at work. The bald pate of Adelmo Castelvetri pops into the bar, gleaming like its owner's leather shoes. His clothes, on the other hand, show signs of wear: jacket frayed at the elbows, colours a bit faded, one button different from the others, but he still manages to look stylish, at least as stylish as Pierre on the evenings when he dazzles everyone at the dancehall. He's a queer customer: everyone expects him to turn up in the bar at some point during the day, but he's one of those people who doesn't have a fixed time, he just shows up all of a sudden, and because of that habit of his many people wonder what exactly it is that he does for a living; he can't be more than forty, a bit young for a pension. He doesn't have a private income, Bottone knows his father and says it isn't possible. But he does have money, he can afford expensive clothes and he's got a scooter as well. In fact it seems as though money comes and goes from his pockets in waves; he'll turn up in a new suit, then he'll wear it every day for a few months, and he'll tell you it's more lived-in that way and he likes it better. But no one believes him, and in fact the most mean-minded among us say he's involved in shady dealings. And no one can agree on what those dealings might be, some people say it's petrol-smuggling, others that he's simply a conman. And what about him? He claims to be an agent and a – how does he put it? – business broker, always there to give everyone advice on how best to use their savings, how to exploit them, what to buy and where, the best deals of the moment. And we can't really say that he cons us that often, although it's true, his nickname, Gas, comes from that scam he did in gas for lighters, which left lots of us 3,000 lire the poorer. And Garibaldi, who invested more than everyone else, took that very badly and has never let him forget it.

'So, Gas,' he begins all of a sudden, 'weren't you telling us to stock up on watches, telling us that if you buy them at ten today, in a few years you sell them on for at least fifty?' The tone is accusatory. All other conversations stop abruptly and everyone listens.

'Ah, calm down, now,' he says defensively, his first glass of red wine already poured, 'that depends on the type of watch, it doesn't work for all of them, otherwise . . . you have to be able to tell which is which.'

'You're right there, you know, the other day in Vergato someone paid 50,000 lire for a piece of junk worth a thousand at the most. But maybe in a few years he'll be able to sell it on for 100,000, what d'you think?'

'Careful, Walterún,' Bottone intervenes before Castelvetri can reply, 'you lot should be able to make 121, because we played pretty well on the Big One.'

While Walterún sets down his point cards, and Castelvetri approaches the table to give a more thorough account of his views on watches, the door opens again, and in comes Melega with the latest news.

'Have you seen Montroni? Is anybody still going to criticise him for working in the Villa Azzurra?'

'So, what's he done?' Bortolotti asks immediately.

'Haven't you read *L'Unità* this morning? Has anybody read it?'

He has everyone's undivided attention. Melega picks up the newspaper from the bar and flicks through it, licking his fingers. 'Listen to this: "Dr Odoacre Montroni, vice-secretary of the Bolognese Federation, director of the Villa Azzurra Clinic, has organised a team of young voluntary medics who will join him in launching a programme of free vaccinations in our province. 'There are many small hamlets and villages,' explained Montroni, 'remote from the main towns and most ambulances. In many of them there is a risk of infection,'" etcetera etcetera.'

'Is there a photograph?' asks Garibaldi, who has trouble reading without his glasses.

'Montroni's a good comrade, of course,' Capponi observes from behind the bar.

In the billiard room, between the clicks of the balls, you can imagine Stefanelli nodding. 'Eh, Montroni, Montroni . . .'

The copy of *L'Unità* passes from hand to hand, amidst general chatter. And there is a photograph, Montroni with his little glasses, sitting behind a big desk covered with pieces of paper.

'Well?' Melega continues provocatively. 'Where's everyone who used to say that a doctor who's a comrade shouldn't work for a private hospital? Are you still there? Hey, Walterún, you used to say that a communist doesn't make money out of people's health, off you go, what a comrade, Odoacre Montroni!'

Walterún doesn't reply, he's not as young as he was, so he doesn't tear into Melega, because if he was that bit younger he would have to leap up and have his say so as not to lose face. He turns towards Garibaldi and shakes his head. Bottone comforts him in a whisper. 'We're old, Walterún, don't take it to heart. Not long ago if you wanted to be a comrade you had to go to Spain to get rid of the fascists, but now . . .'

And you can be sure that if it wasn't for Melega, who is strutting stiffly around the room, Bottone would be happy to drop his atom bomb.

Chapter 19

Less than a quarter of an hour after the start of the film, Pierre started to come out with a long stream of malevolent comments. Angela dug an elbow into his ribs, asking him not to make a spectacle of himself, saying that in there they were hidden from everybody. To tell the truth, there weren't many people in the cinema who weren't sniggering or calling out coarse comments in dialect, and throwing around lupin seeds, liquorice and banter, all well chewed.

Angela was embarrassed. Pierre was aware of that, but he could do nothing about it: the film was terrible, boring, stupid and reactionary as well. Two hours down the drain, because Brando had caught the flu at the last moment, which meant that they couldn't use his flat. They had nowhere else to make love, and Angela had suggested, 'Why don't we go to the cinema?' Fine, just to make her happy and just to be with her, then in the darkness of the Imperiale they could kiss and touch each other, sitting in the back row was enough to avoid indiscreet glances, and they would leave before everyone else.

But Angela had insisted on going to see *Siamo Donne*, of all things, because she'd been told she looked a little like the actress Alida Valli. Pierre couldn't see it himself: Angela was more beautiful, with dark eyes and black hair.

Actresses playing themselves in everyday life. Wealthy, successful women pretending they missed the 'simple life' and *envied* the poor. Pierre couldn't contain himself.

'But this guy Zavattini who wrote the film, wasn't he a comrade? What does that mean: "we were better off when we were worse off"?'

At the beginning, a girl called Anna was shown arguing with her mother and going to Cinecittà for a competition called 'Four Actresses, One Hope'. Hundreds of girls from all over Italy were competing for four parts in a major film, which, as chance would have it, was this very same film, *Siamo Donne*.

Clearly the directors wanted to tug on the audience's heartstrings. There was a girl from Mantua, by the name of Emma. It was her first visit to Rome, a note that was struck a few too many times: she missed her dad, she had never been so far from home, etcetera.

'Oi, I've never been there either. Hardly anyone I know has ever been to Rome. So why does someone who's never been to Rome have to be an innocent, somebody you have to feel sorry for? And that's nothing like a Mantuan accent, either.'

Angela had been to Rome. With Odoacre, on their honeymoon. Odoacre went there at least two or three times a year, for the Central Committee. It almost turned Pierre's stomach to hear talk of Odoacre, and he was mentioned in the bar day in and day out, worse luck: Montroni such a great comrade, Montroni has two great bollocks this size, and so on. The more time passed, the more cause for annoyance there was. He loved Angela, she certainly loved him, and the situation was getting difficult. If they had made love this afternoon, he might have tried to talk to her clearly about it, ask her what she really thought about things, how she felt, what she thought was the right thing to do. Instead they had come to the Imperiale.

What was that word that Fanti used to use? Oh, yes: 'alienation'. In the first episode Alida Valli was feeling awfully alienated, poor thing, she never had time to do anything that made her happy, because she was forced to go charging from one posh party to another, meeting millionaires, what an effort it must have been, and how she complained, how unhappy she was in the world: she envied her masseuse, she envied the families of the proletariat, and so on and so on, until someone in the first few rows shouted, 'Well go and work in a factory, then, off you go!' and other people had suggested other trades typical of the 'simple life', from tomato-picking to tree-grafting, from labouring to street-walking.

The second episode was absolutely meaningless, it was unwatchable. It was directed by Rossellini, about whom Fanti had expressed a strong and clear judgement: 'a dotard'. Ingrid Bergman was chasing a chicken that had eaten her roses. Pierre had seen hundreds of chickens, and never one that ate roses. Bergman called, 'Come, come, little one, little one!' caught the chicken and hid it in a chest of drawers, and then the owner found it and left her looking ridiculous.

'What does that mean? What sort of nonsense is all this?'

Angela replied that she didn't know either, and added, 'Pierre, if you like, we can get up and go, but we've paid for our tickets, at least let's try and see the other two episodes. But if we're going to stay here, please try and control yourself.'

Third episode, bad to worse: Isa Miranda, overacting like mad, had the audience splitting their sides. Same tune as before: my life is empty, I am denied so many simple little pleasures, I'd be better off doing another job, but there's no going back now, and then there was a little boy too, who had hurt his arm and was forever going 'Ayayayayayay,' and from the middle rows someone had shouted, 'For Christ's sake kill him somebody, put him out of his misery!'

Finally Anna Magnani appeared and got into a taxi carrying a sodding lapdog. Pierre would cheerfully have strangled her with his bare hands, the kind of woman who makes working people waste their time and doesn't pay an extra penny for the fucking dog.

Pierre's tone changed, and he murmured to himself in a low voice choked with indignation: 'Go fuck yourself.' It was his final comment. Pierre and Angela got up and sneaked out of the cinema. Anna Magnani hadn't even finished singing.

In the centre of the city they never walked side by side: Angela was on the other side of the street, one of many things that left Pierre feeling bitter. Even from the opposite arcade you could see that she was sulking. At the end of Via Indipendenza, Pierre crossed over to her.

'Listen, I'm sorry, I'm not blaming you. We've been unlucky: Brando caught the flu, we chose a rotten film, and ok, I wanted to be with you, but on our own. In the end my nerves got the better of me. I'm sorry.'

'Pierre, you talk too much,' said Angela, looking round. Another habit imposed by circumstances. What got on Pierre's nerves more than anything else was that she was always giving sudden starts and jumping away, every time she heard footsteps in the corridor, keys in the lock, car horns down in the street. The atmosphere suddenly worsened, passionate kisses were interrupted by a return to reality.

Angela took his hands. She never did that in public.

'I know it's not easy. It's even harder for me, can't you see that? Oh, and I nearly forgot, we've had a piece of good news.'

Pierre looked at her. Angela smiled at his surprise.

'At the end of April Odoacre is going to be away from Bologna for at least two weeks, at a conference. We'll have as much time as we like to be together, just think, more than we've ever had before! Are you pleased?'

Pierre nearly kissed her, right there, in front of everyone. Angela looked up a little and brushed the tip of his nose with her lips. Then she broke away from him and smiled again. 'I love you so much! Well, bye, I've got to go, but promise me you'll call me the day after tomorrow, I'll be alone in the house all afternoon.'

'I promise,' said Pierre. Angela headed for home ('Odoacre's house', as she called it), in Via Castiglione. Pierre thought that, however you looked at it, half a kiss on the nose wasn't a fuck. He decided to go and have a hot chocolate, then he would go and see Brando. He already had his line ready: 'You may be sick, but I'm the one who's taken the medicine.'

Chapter 20

Bologna, Cirenaica district, an hour and a half later

'I've got a temperature of thirty-eight and a half, my bones ache, I've got stomach pains and diarrhoea, I won't be able to go to work for who knows how long, so just try and imagine how much I care that you haven't been able to fuck Montroni's wife today!'

Brando spat into the chamberpot at the end of the bed, and then continued: '. . . and by the way, if someone sees you going in or out of my house, the sky will fall, listen to me Pierre, it's time to call it a day, he's the big boss, everyone speaks well of him, if you're caught no one, I mean no one, will be on your side, your brother will come after you with his Bren gun, and what can you offer Angela? She was an orphan, she was on her own with a brother you could hardly call normal, Montroni saved both their lives, he actually took the spastic in, and he's looking after him at his own expense, whereas what are you? A part-time barman and the only thing you know how to do is a *filuzzi* pirouette! Then there's the fact that Angela and Montroni have been married for so long, and you're not as young as you were, and even I don't want to act like an idiot any more, fuck, do you see yourselves hiding away in my house as though I had nothing to do with it, do you think things can drag on like that for ever? Pass me my dressing gown, come on, and let me make myself a cup of coffee. And wipe your mouth, you've got a chocolate moustache.'

Pierre smiled and did just that. Brando had been feeling peevish already, and Pierre's remark had merely unleashed his anger. In his patched pyjamas and his worn-out slippers, sitting on the edge of the bed with his tousled curls falling over his eyes, and at least three days' worth of stubble, Brando no longer looked much like the actor, and more like an old beggar.

Yes, Brando wasn't entirely wrong, but he didn't like it when people referred to Ferruccio, Angela's little brother, as 'spastic' or 'abnormal'. That was just Brando's way, he enjoyed making fun of mad people, cripples, invalids. Perhaps it was because he was a barber – with all those hours spent listening to dull chat, recriminations and endless moaning – perhaps it made you a bit jaundiced, and if you were like that already, who knows what you would turn into. On the Via Libia, a few metres away from Brando's shop, there was a fruitseller with no hands, he had lost them on the Russian front, and now he had claws instead. With the help of his wife he managed to do all the work, carry the boxes, weigh the fruit, put it in the bags, count the money and give out change, holding the coins tightly between the two claws and pouring them into the customer's hands. He was a fine person, and no one had ever heard him complain, but Brando had taken one look at him and nicknamed him 'Houdini', saying that if he was put in handcuffs he would be able to free himself in no time at all. Every now and again, when he was cutting someone's hair, he told sniggering imaginary anecdotes about 'Houdini', saying that he always had blood pouring out of his nose from scratching himself with his claw, and nonsense of that kind. Yes, Brando could be unbearable. But he was a friend.

Ferruccio was the same age as Pierre. Ten years before, his and Angela's mother had been killed in an air raid. He had survived by a miracle, after being trapped under the rubble for hours, clinging to that life-less body, feeling it grow cold and stiff. Angela hadn't been there, she had gone to get some flour with the ration card.

Her father, who had been recovering in a sanatorium for some time, had died of TB a few months later. Ferruccio had never recovered from those tragic events. He became anxious over trifles, he was afraid of thunder, once he had even hit Angela, and then there were also long periods when he never got out of bed and refused to talk to anyone. By day Angela worked, cleaning in Sant'Orsola Hospital, in the evening she returned to the little council flat and found herself alone with Ferruccio again. Sometimes he was totally distant, at other times quick to anger. It was a bad dream from which she was unable to awake.

One day, at the end of '47, she had met Odoacre, who had by that time been a respected doctor for a number of years. Always an anti-fascist, of liberal family, during the Resistance he went secretly to treat injured partisans. After the Liberation he had joined the Communist Party and immediately become a member of the Federal Committee of Bologna.

Odoacre had a very fine way of life. A distinguished 38-year-old, and still a bachelor. Angela was a beautiful girl in poverty. He had started to court her, until their engagement and marriage in '48, shortly before the elections. In the house in Via Castiglione, they had put poor Ferruccio in a little room on the ground floor. But Ferruccio didn't like Odoacre, he responded badly to him, held his mouth when he was there, sometimes growing incandescent with fury, calling him 'a criminal', and saying that just because he had money he thought he could take advantage of his sister. Odoacre never lost patience, he tried to reason, to calm his brother-in-law, and sometimes he was successful, but there were some terribly uncomfortable moments for Angela. Before she too lost her mind, Odoacre had sent Ferruccio to Villa Azzurra, in the district of San Lazzaro, and from that day onwards he had taken care of him.

That had happened early in 1950. From then on, Ferruccio left the clinic only on Sunday, when Angela went to collect him and bring him to the cinema or take him for a walk. At Christmas and during the summer, Ferruccio stayed with Angela and Odoacre, for as much as a week or ten days in a row. His outbreaks of rage had grown rarer, because Odoacre gave him some new medicine with a complicated name, a very modern tablet that calmed him down.

Over the past three or four months, Angela had spent only two Sundays a month alone with her brother, because she spent the others with Pierre. So as not to arouse Odoacre's suspicions, she went to pick up Ferruccio in a taxi, and then left him with a friend, Teresa Bedetti, who was for Angela what Brando was for Pierre, a friend and accomplice. Ferruccio had problems with his nerves, but he was not unintelligent, far from it. He knew everything, and he was also happy that Angela was cuckolding her husband. For some reason, he went on hating him, although he never attacked him verbally. On the other hand, Teresa, like Brando, didn't really agree with what was happening, but she was also a friend.

Ferruccio went to the cinema with Teresa, and then they met up later and, all together, prepared the story they would tell Odoacre.

*

'Oh, Brando, it's not simple, you know. I really love Angela. It's easy
for you to make judgements from outside, but I know she doesn't
love Montroni. It's gratitude on her part, and also it's as you say, lack
of choice. But what should I do, just give her up like that, without
saying anything?'

'And what would you say? You have no prospects. If you had the
money you'd go to San Marino, but in Italy divorce isn't even legal,
and you know what they say about women who have separated from
their husbands.'

Brando dipped his bread into some milk, sitting at the table on
which Pierre and Angela had once made love. Pierre was standing
by the window: outside it was already dark.

'But even Togliatti married one woman and lives with another!'

'Togliatti, Togliatti, what's he got to do with it? Angela isn't going
to leave Montroni, she's not going to just dump her brother, and
she's certainly not going to starve just because you satisfy her in bed
and Montroni probably doesn't.'

'But they can't even have children! She's told me that Montroni
is sterile . . .'

Brando said nothing. He ran his hand over his prickly chin. Pierre
bit his lips and felt like an idiot. He shouldn't have revealed such a
private detail. Brando was no different from the others, no different
from the comrades in the Section or people like Melega: he respected
Montroni, he put him on a pedestal, he considered him to be
untouchable, and he really was, insofar as a big shot in the Party in
the most left-wing city in Italy can be untouchable. That reference
to his sexual life was sure to have wrong-footed or horrified Brando.
Certainly no one had ever imagined Montroni in the intimacy of
his bedroom; he was always so stylish and distinguished, perhaps a
little gloomy, and he never showed his teeth when he smiled. Hard
to imagine him in his pyjamas, or remember that he, too, like all
ordinary mortals, shat and pissed every day.

It was Brando who, embarrassed, broke the silence: 'Pierre, I repeat:
you should break it off before something serious happens.'

Pierre looked into the distance beyond the window.

All he saw was a long black expanse stretching out ahead.

Chapter 21

His eyebrows were too thick, they almost met in the middle, and the cleft in his chin wasn't very pronounced.

Jean-Jacques Bondurant strode across the drawing room. A forced smile, his right hand plunged into his pocket, he looked like a commercial traveller on his first business appointment. He tried to appear casual, as he would have done in the parochial little theatres of Montreal, but the Palm Springs house wasn't the same thing. Neither was his audience.

Cary watched him walk as far as the library, on the other side of the room, and rose from the sofa to stop him.

'Forgive me, Mr Bondurant, but with that walk you wouldn't even look like a Cary Grant reconstructed from hearsay evidence. And sooner or later you'd have to throw your shoes away.'

'What? My shoes? Mr Grant, I don't understand.'

He spoke with an impossible accent, sharp and nasal, and the collar of his jacket covered his shirt collar.

'You see,' Betsy interrupted, despite her observer's role, 'to walk like my husband, you have to try and think like him. One major point: don't ruin your shoes. The Grant method: avoid bending your feet.'

Bondurant's arched eyebrow was almost perfect, the same scatter-brained expression as the original. Thin those eyebrows out a little and no one would notice the difference.

'My wife means that you shouldn't take your foot off the ground in two moves, heel then toe, but both at once, heel and toe at the same time. It stops your shoes wrinkling in the middle.'

Cary Grant's walk: the prototype of casual elegance, a prelude to

a thousand flirtations and other kinds of triumph. The double tried
out a few different ways of walking, then came back to stand beside
his model. His legs stiff, but agile and slender, flexible at the knee.
Major point: the shoes. It wasn't easy, he had to think about his feet
without looking at them, glancing smugly around.

Betsy clapped her hands and encouraged the Canadian. 'Fine, Mr
Bondurant, you're a fast learner.'

There was something overdone about the hand in his pocket, and
his face was a little pale.

The double smiled. Bondurant's smile.

'You're going to need a bit of training, Mr Bondurant. I suggest
you work on your walk.'

'Certainly, Mr Grant.'

'Fine. Now satisfy some of my curiosity, Mr Bondurant. What do
you think about your English?'

'What? My English?'

'Your accent. Do you think you'll even manage to speak like me?'

The arched eyebrow performed its task. He would have to
remember to use it sparingly.

'I've been told I should hardly open my mouth. Just be seen, go
for walks, ask for the paper, say goodbye to your wife as I leave the
house. No one would notice the difference.'

The people in MI6 must have been crazy. Fine, the newspaper
and the walk. And what if someone approached him for an autograph? And what if it was a journalist? What would the double do?
He certainly couldn't claim an infection of the vocal cords, that would
only attract people's attention, would prompt photographs and newspaper articles. Justifying his curious pronunciation by saying that he
was preparing for a new character would be even worse. Curiosity
about Grant's return to the big screen would be multiplied ten times
over.

Cary drained his glass of Scotch. His double looked around in
embarrassment. The knot of his tie was wider than it should have
been, and his toupee didn't hide all of his receding hairline.

Problems for Her Majesty's Secret Service. If the trick was discovered, they would come up with something. That wasn't for him
to worry about. In fact, if Bondurant did his job properly, no one
would think that Cary Grant had lost his style, that he had let

himself go, wearing badly cut jackets and shoes that wrinkled in the middle.

'What you're wearing, Mr Bondurant, is that one of Cary Grant's suits?'

'What? No, Mr Grant. And how could I have got hold of one of your suits so –'

Seeing that her husband was getting into difficulties, Betsy interrupted Bondurant to avoid their relationship taking a turn for the worse. 'No, no, you misunderstand. My husband was asking whether the suit you're wearing was chosen to make you look like him, or whether it's a suit that you wear regularly.'

'Oh, I see. Of course, of course. They told me I would have to give some thought to my wardrobe. Of course. They just told me to follow your advice to the letter, without worrying about the expense, that they would take care of that.'

Cary held back a nervous twitch, and took some folded sheets of paper from his pocket.

'I've listed here the characteristics that your suits must have, Mr Bondurant. I would ask you to follow this advice very carefully. I've already informed Sir Lewis Kennington of MI6 that I will not move an inch out of Palm Springs without first personally checking all your suits.'

For the third time, Bondurant's eyebrow arched, wrinkling his forehead. His hands were not well manicured, and he wore a horrible gold ring. Cary felt like a director who had had an actor imposed on him by the producers for a part beyond his capabilities.

'Get up, Mr Bondurant. I'll show you what I mean by "control" of a suit.'

Grant's double put his glass down on the table and got to his feet. He was at least two inches taller than his model.

'You'll find it all written on the sheets I've given you, but, just by way of example, there are three aspects of your attire that are incompatible with being Cary Grant.'

He turned around to the double and gripped the collar of his jacket between two fingers.

'The collar of your shirt must always protrude from your jacket by about half an inch,' he went on walking around, and came back to stand in front of Bondurant. 'The knot of your tie should be tighter, like this, and must always hide the top button. Finally, your shirt sleeves should be longer, the cuff should rest on the beginning of the thumb.'

The lesson in elegance had restored Cary's mood. He crossed his arms and studied the double with his torso leaning over to one side, like a sculptor looking at his own work.

He had a little mole beside his nose, and the enamel of his teeth was yellowing slightly.

'Fine, Mr Bondurant. I think that with a little exercise, remembering all the advice I have given you, and avoiding opening your mouth, you will manage to deceive the whole district. Get in touch as soon as your wardrobe is ready, so that we can have a look at it.'

Betsy got up from the sofa as well and held out a hand to Bondurant.

'Don't be afraid, Mr Bondurant. Even if it's usually my husband giving me advice about the way I dress, I'll try to advise you as best I can.'

Their pleasantries were interrupted by the ringing of the telephone. Betsy went to get it as her husband walked his double to the door.

'Oh, Alfred! How are you? I'll pass you to Cary right now, he was just saying goodbye to a guest.' She put the receiver to her chest and called towards the door, 'Darling, it's for you. Alfred!'

Cary strode back into the drawing room, arranging his tie as though he were about to meet someone.

'Hitch! . . . Yes, not bad. Are you well? . . . Mhm, yes, I've read it. Look, I'm not entirely convinced. But I don't think it's anything to do with the script. It's a good story, although I'd have liked a little more suspense. No, it's the fact that I don't yet know if it's time to relaunch myself . . . Of course, no, absolutely, you're the only one who might be able to convince me, I've always said as much . . . Em, I also have a few things to sort out. I'm going to be busy until the end of May. Yes, yes, the usual things . . . Oh, I don't deny that the Côte d'Azur is an attractive location. Yes, we could go to the casino . . . Yes, that's it . . . It isn't the only attractive thing? What else is there, don't be mysterious . . . Oh, my . . . Yes, yes, really fascinating, yes . . . Of course, I've seen her in *Mogambo* . . . Yes, you told me she was making a film with you, yes, two of them, that's right . . . Extraordinary, isn't it? . . . Oh, you're piquing my curiosity, you really are . . . Ok, listen, I'll think about it, yes . . . I'll give you an idea in about ten days, ok? But nothing before June . . . Yes, fine, speak to you soon.'

He stood there with his hand on the receiver, too many thoughts running through his head. MI6, Yugoslavia, his double, the Hitchcock film. The active life wanted him back. Maybe he was really starting to need it. Two months away from home, a rather unique job, then back on to the set. Yes, it could work. Hitch's favourite actress, absolutely beautiful, a sure thing. The return of Cary Grant and the definitive success of Grace Kelly.

'Good news?' asked Betsy, interrupting his reflections.

Cary realised he had been leaning on the telephone all the time.

'Neither good nor bad. Old Hitch is trying to persuade me: the Côte d'Azur, his new film, *Rear Window*, which is sure to be a hit, the casino in Monte Carlo, the usual things.'

Well, not usual exactly. Grace Kelly exerted a fascination that was out of the ordinary. Cold and magnetic at the same time. If he had been Clark Gable, in *Mogambo*, Cary would have had no doubt about whether to choose Grace or Ava Gardner.

Hitchcock had scored an extra point. He knew Cary very well, and he knew Archie, too. He knew how to needle them both.

Chapter 22

Zollo had other things to think about, but he couldn't do it. There was no way you could think when Don Luciano decided to be hospitable, because his words flowed without interruption, one sentence after another, finally enveloping your mind until you found yourself following them whether you felt like it or not. The boss didn't talk like ordinary mortals: it only looked like talking for talking's sake; in fact his words were weighted and carefully chosen. Mixed in with all the idle chatter there was a certain amount of wisdom and a good dose of *savoir faire*. He monopolised the conversation without being rude, and flattered his interlocutor by skilfully forcing him to follow his train of thought.

'Italy is a country where everything is yet to be done, my friends. Every now and again I feel as though I'm in the wild west. Like a prisoner, yes. Everything is yet to be built, there are great opportunities for anyone with the wit and the balls. As to myself, what do you expect, I'm a poor pensioner now who can't make it to the evening without an afternoon nap. But for those with fresh blood, there's enough to keep everybody busy. In Naples the people are hospitable. Now that there are more Americans than Italians . . . Sailors, officers, doctors, journalists. I feel as if I'm at home! The Italians, pal, may not speak foreign languages, but the Neapolitans do, they speak the lot! You know the history of this city? You don't? Everyone's passed through here: the French, the Spanish, the Piedmontese, the Germans and now the Americans. The Neapolitans aren't used to being on their own. There's always someone at home, always different people, different languages, new faces. And they have a very curious way of doing things, everything out in the street, everything in public. I lead a reserved life – who do you think is going to come and talk to an old man? – but I see everything from my armchair. I see it out on the terrace and from up there I watch the life of Naples passing below. Better than Cinemascope!'

Lucky Luciano sank into the back seat of the convertible Plymouth and talked, smiling generously at the girl sitting in the front, who couldn't help turning around, craning her neck, to nod at what the old man was saying.

Young Anastasia looked like a fop sitting on hot coals, only laughing at the jokes or asking the occasional question about Italy. Every now and again Luciano gave him a slight nudge, when the innuendo got a bit near the knuckle. But without overdoing it, barely touching him, as though they had been friends for a long time. He never missed the opportunity to observe on the intimate relationship based on friendship and esteem that bound him to his uncle Anastasia. All very knowing. No overstatement.

'There are hidden jewels in the city, you know? Churches, squares, palaces. History passed through here, my friends, and if anyone with a will decided to rebuild the whole thing, the tourists would come flocking, just from the States. Here in Italy, they call this place 'Africa'. But I say they don't know what they're missing, because if you take a moment to sit down and wait, you don't really have to go and discover this city, Naples will come and find you! It'll come and meet you and claim you as its own.'

Zollo gripped the wheel with both hands and said nothing. Every now and again his eyes fell on the girl's legs, when a slightly tighter bend ruffled her skirt. Lovely legs, at least. The Anastasias knew how to live. The young nephew was someone to be treated with great consideration. And then here was the idea of the excursion to Pompeii. At least it was a nice day.

But Zollo had never liked the countryside. When you're born in Brooklyn, and you do your growing up between one sidewalk and the other, you don't feel at ease among the dunghills. Apart from a few trips to Chicago, he had never left New York until the day when the oldest member of the Anastasia family had decided to 'give him' to Luciano, who was setting off for Italy. He had had no complaints, he needed a change of air as it was, especially since that Jewish attorney had got it into his head to have the Hudson River dragged. That fucking rabbi had managed to make one of the dockers sing, and when he had done that, he had hidden him in the devil's asshole and placed him under strict protection. The wretch had also given his name: 'Steve Cement has sent a good lot of people down to the bay, half a dozen, maybe more.' Not that the shlub had been able to do it. Even if they'd locked him up in some kind of armoured fortress, guarded like Fort Knox, no one had stopped him drinking lemonade laced with strychnine. But now the die was cast, the time had come for good old Steve to go into the icebox, at least until the balance of power had been resolved. When you thought about it, his story was not unlike Don Luciano's. Then he had waited for the call to come from the Anastasias, but it hadn't come, so now he had stopped hoping it would.

'So, I've got my shop, and I'm fine as I am. But if I was a bit younger, there are plenty of things here that need doing, isn't that right, Steve? And no shortage of pretty girls to date! Not as lovely as you, miss, but the Neapolitan girls can look after themselves as well. *Procaci*, isn't that the word? Pert, sexy. I like it: *procaci!* I'd forgotten that word in America, and it came right back to me here. It makes you think of prosperity, the generosity of nature. It's a nice word to say: *procaci*. It sounds good, it feels good in the mouth, don't you think? Italian is a language that flows like a river. It's a language that needs time if you're going to speak it properly. It's a language with a history. Like this city. Like the whole country. *You* can still get by with Italian, but your children may not speak it any more and that's a shame. Because American is a good language for business, for ordering a beer. And that's it. But here the words have a special meaning: they fill the mouth. *Procaci*, you hear that? They're not just for getting things with, you say the words for the sake of saying them, you say them for the pleasure of speaking.'

Zollo couldn't make up his mind. He didn't like Italy. It was a backward, uncivilised place. Beautiful women, sure, but they had no notion of real femininity. They looked like peasants dressed up for a party. Not a patch on the girls in New York. Those were classy women, he remembered very clearly: the nightclubs, the luxury bordellos. In New York they did things with style: fucking, and having people clipped. Not in Naples: shouting, yelling, dramas about nothing. He couldn't bear it. He felt as if he was the victim of a script in which everyone had a part to play and he didn't get so much as a line. And yet he was obliged to move about on the gigantic stage set of the city. Every day he felt himself sinking, wrapped up in that slow rhythm that opposed any form of dynamism. Stefano Zollo deserved something better, he was convinced of it. Basically he had always been good in his field. Clean, orderly. He'd never made any mistakes. Not one. Once he'd made a pair of concrete shoes for somebody, and the guy had asked him to take 500 dollars to his girlfriend, because he hadn't had the chance to say goodbye. And he had done it. He could have stuck it in his pocket, spent it on a nice present for one of his girls, but he hadn't, he'd gone to the address and given the woman the money. He'd just said, 'From Sal. He's had to go on a long journey in a hurry.' Nothing but that. Impeccable. And stylish. He'd always insisted on it.

Naples was a stranger to discretion. In Naples people shouted. Rows and shouting over the slightest thing. All that arguing over crumbs: unbearable.

So a few months ago he had decided to take some action. He had had enough of just mulling, brooding, changing his plans every month, every week. This time he had had a really good idea. And like many good ideas, it needed patience and perseverance, and it was also extremely risky. But at the age of thirty-five Zollo had worked out that he was willing to take that risk, if he wasn't to suffocate on that pestilential gulf, working as a driver for an unrepentant old gangster. So he had decided to go for broke.

He looked in the rear-view mirror to check that the other car was still following them, then he turned right towards the dig.

From the other car climbed, in order, Victor Trimane, a girl of Neapolitan high society who had joined them for the occasion, and one of young Anastasia's dandy friends with his girlfriend. They walked along the path leading to the Roman city, Luciano at their head with his host. The site was officially shut, but no attendant would object to a visit from Don Luciano and his friends.

'You see how much space there is, my friends? And the streets.

You see these big stones between one side of the street and the other? They were like our pedestrian crossings, exactly the same. So that you could cross the street without getting covered with mud. And the wheels of the carts passed in between them. Not a bad idea, is it? The ancient Romans knew what they were up to. Pompeii was a holiday resort, the wealthy came here to relax, to get away from the big city. Good weather, the sea nearby, good soil for wine and olives. The Romans liked the good life, my friends, they knew how to choose their places.'

One of the girls came up beside the old man. 'It must have been horrible when the volcano went off and covered everything up.'

Luciano crossed his hands behind his back. 'That's the fascination of Pompeii, my dear. Time stopped here. All of a sudden. And no one touched anything. Just as it was. Look at this: this was a tavern. They kept the wine in these holes and sold it by the glass, like this.'

Luciano made the gesture of picking up a glass of wine from the cavity that opened up along the little low wall.

'How civilised! Imagine this street full of people, slaves carrying things, litters and carts. And the vendors shouting. Further off there was the Forum, where the notables talked politics and business.'

The little group advanced into the middle of the ruins.

One of the girls stopped by a crossroads. 'What's this writing?'

'That's an advertisement.'

The girl looked perplexedly at the old boss. 'Like a commercial?'

'For the oldest profession in the world, my darling.'

The girl blushed, while the two young Americans looked up in curiosity. 'It's a whorehouse. Satisfied customers put up posters for the bordello.'

The two drivers followed on a few steps behind. Zollo lit a cigarette and glanced around him.

'You know, Vic, I've never liked these old crocks.'

'You don't need to tell me, goombah.'

Luciano led the way towards the house of Priapus, after putting his arm around young Anastasia. 'Well, my friend, the Romans sure knew how to enjoy life, not like us, constantly thinking about business. They took over the world without exhausting themselves. And those cathouses of theirs had to be very professional, very properly run, you know. They didn't ruin their hands doing housework, you can be sure of that.'

'They were still whores,' observed the young man.

'Yes, yes, but that's not the point.' Luciano folded his hands behind his back once more. 'The fact is that the level of civilisation in a society is measured by the *women*. That's why I sell electrical appliances. It's a civilising mission,' he guffawed.

Anastasia shook his head. 'I don't get it.'

'Let me explain. What's the difference between American women and the women here in Italy?'

'Affluence?'

Luciano gave a sly laugh and spoke in an undertone, as though revealing a major secret: 'Electrical appliances.'

Zollo studied him with a certain admiration. There was something brilliant about him. A raging torrent, but not overstated. Amazing, if you thought that he didn't need to speak to order someone killed, direct the trafficking of drugs from the Mediterranean to the Pacific, or throw all the races for the coming month.

'American dames', Don Luciano went on, 'have electrical appliances to do their housework for them. That's why they have the time to take care of their appearance, to read magazines, to keep up with fashion. They're that bit freer, my friend, and that's why they're more beautiful and intelligent. That's why they turn your head. Italian women, on the other hand, are housekeepers and mothers seven days out of seven. Then on Saturday evening they get dolled up and try to convince their husbands that they've married a fine lady. But they're a bit pathetic. It's not their fault. Italian men want a good child-rearer at home, a housekeeper for the whole week, and then they demand that she turn into Silvana Mangano, or even Marilyn Monroe. So it isn't long before the husbands get fed up, and the wives feel unappreciated and stop looking after their appearance. Moral: they get fat, they lose their figures, by the age of thirty they're ready for the scrapheap. And nobody's happy!'

Zollo was flabbergasted by Luciano's reasoning: he had never thought about it before, but it was all true. What irritated him was the air of parochialism and recently scrubbed dirt that hovered around Italian girls. Their attempt to look like screen goddesses. And their obtuse and ignorant husbands were even worse. It made him shudder to think about it. He felt sad all of a sudden.

The attendant wanted to keep the girls out of the house. Luciano made a barely perceptible gesture, and Zollo slipped his hand into the inside pocket of his jacket. His hand brushed the wooden handle of the 'alternative', before taking out, with the tips of his fingers, the banknote he always kept ready for such occasions. As he was handing it to the attendant, he recalled old Anastasia saying, 'You'll never have another choice in life, Steve: pay or shoot. You've got to know how to do both, otherwise you'll never be anything but a lousy little guy, however much scented brilliantine you can put on your head.'

Women were forbidden to see the enormous member of Priapus, the god of sexual potency, and the lewd frescoes on the walls. The two girls cackled, pretending to be shocked, while the young Americans exchanged whispered wisecracks.

Zollo remembered the legs of the girl he had glimpsed in the car, and noticed a sudden twitch in his trousers. He cursed the base instincts that clashed horribly with his mood, and turned his back on the group, pretending to light a cigarette, in the hope that no one would notice the hardness of his cock.

Il Resto del Carlino, 17.2.1954

INCIDENTS IN ROME AND MILAN
DURING DEMONSTRATIONS DISPERSED BY THE POLICE
Six hundred far-left activists arrested in the capital
where the mounted police broke up communist demonstrations
– Two commissioners injured by rocks and many police officers
injured –
One demonstrator killed

Il Resto del Carlino, 18.2.1954

The Scelba cabinet appears today in Parliament
UNDER WAY: THE COMMUNIST MANOEUVRE
TO STIR UP THE MASSES AGAINST THE GOVERNMENT
The left plan to undermine the new Prime Minister
despite his moves to combat poverty
Speculating on the incidents they THEMSELVES provoked
they are trying to create schisms in the governing body

Serious incidents in the province of Caltanissetta
FOUR PEOPLE KILLED BY THE CROWD
ESCAPING A POLICE CHARGE
In Mussomeli the forces of law and order
are forced to use tear-gas

Il Resto del Carlino, 20.2.1954

After the four-party conference
A COMMON DECLARATION
BY THE THREE WESTERN MINISTERS
The governments reaffirm that an attack on West Berlin
will be considered as an act of war against the Allies

L'Unità, official organ of the Italian Communist Party, 28.2.1954

After the capitulation of the Armed Forced Minister
THE AMERICANS ARE BECOMING ASHAMED OF
'TRADERS IN FEAR AND BLACKMAIL'
Bitter attack by Gen. Lehman on the 'inquisitors' of the Senate
and the Chamber of Deputies

L'Unità, 7.3.1954

Grave courtroom accusations from Anna Maria Caglio
SENSATIONAL REVELATIONS OF CONNECTIONS
BETWEEN UGO MONTAGNA, PICCIONI
AND THE CHIEF OF POLICE
After the death of Wilma Montesi
Miss Caglio went to the Ministry of the Interior
with Montagna and Piccioni
After their discussion Montagna said:
'I have sorted everything out'

L'Unità, 7.3.1954

Sensational document on the corruption of the clerical regime
THE POLICE CONFIRM THE ACCUSATIONS AGAINST MONTAGNA,
HIS SORDID PAST AND HIS RELATIONS WITH OTHER FIGURES

Il Resto del Carlino, 11.3.1954

MONTAGNA IS A PREVIOUS OFFENDER
FORMER SPY FOR OVRA AND THE NAZIS

L'Unità, 12.3.1954

MCCARTHY TO BRING CHARGES AGAINST
THE SCIENTIST EINSTEIN?

L'Unità, 14.3.1954

EINSTEIN CALLS ON THE AMERICANS TO REFUSE
TO COOPERATE WITH THE TRIBUNALS OF THE
INQUISITOR MCCARTHY
Thomas Mann and Bertrand Russell
applaud the great scientist's courage

Chapter 23

Pierre often dreamed of his mother. She spoke to him in those dreams, but her words vanished the moment he woke up. When that happened, he was in a bad mood all day, irritated at having lost an important detail. Her face was not the one in the family photograph that showed him as a little baby with an arrogant expression. His memories were not enough to give her a proper shape; she looked blurred, in black and white, against a sepia background. And yet she was telling him something, he was sure of that. But what?

Pierre was six years old when his mother died of tuberculosis. Her second pregnancy, the one that had led to his birth, had tested her beyond endurance. Perhaps, as Fanti said, a secret sense of guilt gave form to the memory, based on the little that had stayed in his mind. An extreme attempt to make her survive.

He remembered her smiling, a modest and angelic smile, watching down over him, murmuring a phrase, something to calm the impetuosity of a precocious and agitated child. Nothing but a sensation.

Rosa Montanari was a slim and very beautiful woman. She came from a poor family in Solarolo. She had married Vittorio Capponi in 1920, when she was only eighteen. Pierre's father, first a day-labourer and then a worker from Lugo, born in 1901, was a veteran of the 1919–20 riots, the 'Two Red Years', and bore carved into his flesh the marks of the destiny that he had chosen for himself: the blows of the agrarians, membership of the newly born Communist Party, the name of his first son, who had arrived a few days after the death of Lenin and been called Nicola in honour of the great revolutionary. Except, Pierre reflected, Nikolai hadn't been Lenin's real name. That was Vladimir Ilyich Ulyanov. And Joseph Stalin also had a very long and complicated name that no one could remember. To pass into history your name has to be simple, short and incisive.

Robespierre was born in 1932, registered as 'Piero' on the fascist register. It was a bad time for the family. His father hadn't taken the Fascist Party membership card, and he would pay for his choice to the bitter end. Poverty persecuted the Capponis for a decade, with few moments of respite.

Rosa had died in 1938. Pierre remembered very little of those times; his father with his head in his hands and Nicola running upstairs. That was all.

From time to time that memory came back in Pierre's dreams. When he awoke he fantasised, wondering how his life would have been if his mother had survived. From that day onwards, Nicola had locked himself away in a funereal silence. His character had changed, he had become confrontational, with a terrifying temper. Vittorio had wept for days, cursing God and swearing at the heavens, crazed with grief. That much he remembered clearly.

During that same period, one evening a drunk had sung the praises of Stalin in the village square. The fascists pounced on him, seven against one. Vittorio hurled himself into the scrum and knocked someone out, but he was overcome and beaten till he bled.

So Pierre learned to hate them.

A few days later, Vittorio took Pierre and Nicola aside and, with his black eye still half closed, he outlined the most categorical and incisive teaching of his life, something that would always be associated with the figure of Vittorio Capponi. He pierced them with his eyes: 'Never stand and watch.'

Then the Capponis moved to Imola, to the apartment that Aunt Iolanda had found directly opposite her own. It was thanks to her that the family managed to keep its head above water. She took care of everything, without poking her nose in where it wasn't wanted. She dedicated herself heart and soul to her nephews, without confusing them with the children she didn't have. She supported her brother without acting as his wife.

Father and sons treated her with great affection, and she treated them with attentiveness and pride. She was the only person Nicola ever confided in. Vittorio involved her in all important decisions, and Pierre did everything he could think of just to please her.

When, in April 1941, Vittorio Capponi was called up as a reservist to fight on the Yugoslav front, the presence of Iolanda ruled out any chance of exemption; it was true that his sons had lost their mother, but the elder boy was working, and their aunt 'catered to their every need'.

The nephews' needs did not keep Iolanda from doing her part in the fight against fascism. On 29 April '44 she went down into the square with the women of Imola; on 13 May she tended to those who had been injured in the bombing; a few months later she hid two partisans and let Nicola follow them into the mountains.

He was twenty years old. He had endured the abuses of power for too long. He could no longer stand and watch.

Pierre didn't see him again until the war was over, limping, thin as a rake, a steely glint in his eye.

One day in 1945 a letter arrived from Yugoslavia, and Pierre discovered that his father was a war hero. Shortly after arriving in Croatia, Vittorio Capponi had killed the vice-commander of his unit, and joined the Yugoslav Resistance. After 8 September 1943, he had recruited hundreds of Italian soldiers to the the ranks of Tito's army. He had taken part in the liberation of Zagreb, and received a medal for military valour from the Marshal in person.

Shortly afterwards, Pierre, Nicola and Iolanda hugged him for the last time.

He came back undercover, like a thief, hiding for two nights in the cellar of an old friend.

He risked serious punishment in Italy: charges of insubordination and homicide. Furthermore, he was a member of the Yugoslavian Communist Party, there was a country to build, a socialist country, a revolution to take to its conclusion. He couldn't pull out.

Pierre listened in as Vittorio and Iolanda discussed his future. If they had asked him he wouldn't have been able to decide whether to go with his father or stay in Imola. For that reason alone he let them choose on his behalf. Nicola chose to stay.

Pierre stayed too. Yugoslavia was too risky. His father promised to see him at least once a year. He never came back: too dangerous. They went on writing to each other, in the rhythm that the post allowed: a letter every five or six months.

Pierre and Nicola clung to those letters, which brought them news of their father in the broadest terms: he had been given an important job, he had remarried, this time to a Yugoslav partisan, and he had opted to stay with Tito even after 1948 and the break with Stalin.

The last two choices poisoned Nicola's blood. The world could clear off as far as he was concerned, and he never wanted to hear his father mentioned again.

In the meantime he had been offered the job of manager of a bar in Bologna. Nicola Capponi was a war invalid and a hero of the Resistance, and the Party had put pressure on comrade Benassi to let him manage the Bar Aurora. So Pierre, too, was able to leave his workshop, say goodbye to Aunt Iolanda, and move to the city.

Pierre sat down at the table. Gas was savouring his vermouth, lost in his thoughts. He stared quizzically at the boy. Then he worked out that he wanted something. His businessman's sixth sense allowed him to read other people's minds. At least, so he thought. He stretched out on his chair and snapped his American lighter a few times. The smoke from his cigarette twirled over his gleaming bald head.

Pierre remained serious, he hadn't come to buy lighters.

He said, 'If you talk to anyone about it, I'll track you down and break your legs.'

Gas smiled and puffed out a series of smoke rings.

'I am bound by the rules of professional secrecy, you should know that. Without discretion, no trust. Without trust, no business. I would shut up shop before you knew where you were.'

He was always satisfied when he was able to rattle off his maxims of business philosophy.

They stared at each other again for a long while.

Then Pierre said, 'How would you go about getting into Yugoslavia?'

Gas nodded to himself thoughtfully, taking another few puffs, as though he had been asked an existential question.

'As an entrepreneur I can point you towards the right people. But I would have to warn you that these characters don't stand any nonsense. Not the sort of people you want to get on the wrong side of, if you catch my drift.'

'I mean it.'

The man's bald pate shone beneath the neon.

'Cavicchi's fighting the day after tomorrow. In the Sala Borsa. Go there and ask for Ettore. Tell them I sent you. If there's anyone who can give you a hand then he's your man, but I can't guarantee anything.'

Pierre got to his feet. 'This vermouth's on me. And let's hope something comes of it.'

Chapter 24

*From the statement of Salvatore Pagano to counsel
appointed by the Public Prosecutor's Office for Naples High Court,
Dr Carlo Ercolino, dated 10 March 1954*

Thank God, Mr Lawyer! Thank God you've come, I thought I was
going to snuff it in this hell-hole!

And what am I supposed to do, Mr Lawyer, how can I stay calm,
it's hell in here, it's been more than two months now, you can't have
any idea what life's like in this place. Mr Lawyer, there are more bugs
on my arm than there are whores in the whole of La Sanità, and
you know how many whores there are in La Sanità, *mamma mia*!
And the stuff they give us to eat, don't even get me started on that,
with all due respect, they give us *shit*, Mr Lawyer, the dogs in the
street wouldn't eat it, and neither would the whores of La Sanità if
you ask me, what a situation!

And me as innocent as an altar boy, Mr Lawyer, can you imagine?

Yes, yes, it's fine, forgive me, I know, I know, I'll calm down, but
in here you can forget how to live, then the cold, fucking cold in
here it is, with a threadbare blanket and half eaten up by bugs,
mamma mia, what a situation, but I'm calmer now, I'm sorry, but
let me tell you one more thing. You must be a great man, yes, a
great man, don't run yourself down, because only a great man could
take on the case of a poor wretch without a lira like Salvatore Pagano.
Because let's be clear about this, Mr Lawyer, I haven't got a lira, you
must have worked that out.

Your duty, you say? You were appointed by an office? Well, what
of it, doesn't matter a damn, you're a great man anyway, people like
you must live for a hundred years, accidents permitting.

You say we've got to get a move on, what have you got to do
with it? Of course, sure, you must forgive me, but I don't understand anything any more, because in here time is the only thing

I'm not short of, in fact I've got far too much of it, it just won't pass.

Yes, fine, you tell me that you're aware of this nonsense about the television set, I'd like to know why me of all people, what have I got to do with anything like this, believe me, I've explained it to him, I've fallen on my knees and bawled my eyes out, Mr Lawyer, but he doesn't believe me, not a word of it.

Who? What d'you mean who?

Mr Lawyer, Commissioner Cinquegrana, who else, the one who's decided it's got to be me, who's made up his mind that I'm going to end my days in here, on the word of some bastard or other, some great son of a bitch, with the greatest respect, of some *cackhead* who's decided to get on my case. Because I'm ruined now, that much is clear. I've explained, I've told the commissioner everything, absolutely everything, including the story of the Madonna in 1948, no, don't put your head in your hands, Mr Lawyer, I'm not going to tell it to you, don't worry. I told him I was with the nuns in Santa Teresa, giving some little presents to creatures less fortunate than myself, then just a few hours with my Lisetta, I'm mad about my Lisetta, even if she does drive me round the bend every now and again, and now I don't even know where she is, she came to see me a month ago, and there's an end to it. But there you go, my words mean nothing to him, they go in one ear and out the other, that's what I say. Commissioner Cinquegrana, I mean.

What did I want with a television? If it was just that, you'd be better off asking Don Luciano, with the greatest respect, and that other guy, never heard of him, the one who was killed stone dead, what do I know?

You say we're supposed to be thinking about the television, well, fine, let's think about it. You say down at the station they're insisting that they saw me that day near the American base in Agnano, that they're sure of it? Damn and blast it, Mr Lawyer, damn and blast it, I'm nothing but a poor wretch!

Why? Well, how can I put it, bad luck follows bad luck, as they say, the dog bites the beggarman.

You say I have to speak more clearly, that you don't know where I'm taking this? Well, ok, then, damn it to hell!

My misfortune is that on that day round about there I actually did go to bring my Lisetta . . . No, no, Mr Lawyer, don't put your head in your hands, don't lose your rag. I was going to tell you, wasn't I? I walked her to Vergini all the way with the pedal cart, bloody hard work it was, Mr Lawyer, you'd never believe it, but I'd do anything for Lisetta, and maybe that's my downfall. Lisetta had to get to the American base, and I went with her, with the cart, and there's an end to it.

To do what? Me? But I've told you, oh, you mean Lisetta. What are you getting at, exactly, Mr Lawyer?

Chapter 25

What with washing the glasses, fixing the tap and grinding the coffee, Pierre had made himself late.

He rummaged through his pockets to be sure he had the ticket, jumped on his bicycle, and headed off at a lick in the direction of Via Ugo Bassi. He wasn't the only one in search of a decent seat. At the last Cavicchi fight, there had been such a scrum that the riot squad had even left people with tickets standing outside.

An agitated crowd pushed its way towards the entrance of the old Sala Borsa. Pierre leaned his bicycle against the wall and threw himself into the midst of it, resolved to get in whatever the cost.

Franco Cavicchi, known as Checco, the colossus of Pieve di Cento, was an idol to Pierre. His favourite boxer. Big as a mountain, determined and generous. Every day he rode sixty kilometres on his bike to get to Bologna, to the legendary Sempre Avanti gymnasium on Via Maggia, a club of glorious socialist origins.

Three riot cops were already complaining that the hall was full, and trying to get people to stop pushing.

Pierre stuck his elbows into the ribs in front of him, and with two blows of his hips he managed to get a fair way forwards, amidst general protests.

He was alone. The other musketeers had been put off by the price. Pierre wouldn't have missed the great Cavicchi for anything in the world. And Ettore, the guy with the truck, would be there, and he'd be able to give him some advice on how to get to Yugoslavia.

Now he'd made it to the door. The cops, six of them now, were pushing on the sides of the crowd in a pincer movement to cut off the people at the back. Just as Pierre was sure he was in, they lined up.

'That's enough, you lot can go home, no one else is getting in.'

Shouts and insults from the dozens of people excluded. Pierre recognised the riot cop who had beaten him up on the procession for the victims of Mussomeli. Without thinking twice, he took a few steps backwards, braced himself against the people behind him, and then charged, head down, to break through the blockade. Taken by surprise, they tried to catch him, but it was too late. One of them took a blow from the knee, the other a hand in the face, then Pierre was swallowed up inside, while an almighty row erupted in his wake.

He found a place to sit on the higher benches. The bloke beside him was eating enormous quantities of pumpkin seeds. There was a carpet of shells around his feet. Between one seed and the next, he spoke to him.

'Have you seen how many people there are? It's a far cry from the basketball! It's a good thing they're getting a move on with the new stadium, but for Cavicchi, not for Virtus.'

'If it goes on like this,' added Pierre, 'they'll need more than a local stadium. He'll be European champion in two years.'

The first fighters of the evening entered the ring. Bernardi came from Ferrara. There was, amidst a chorus of whistles from the locals, fallout from the football-based hatred between Bologna and Spal Ferrara. Malavasi, on the other hand, was born within the city walls, but many people remembered him wearing the uniform of the fascist Black Brigade. The insults of the comrades were all directed at him. The referee for the clash was Signor Cinti from Ancona.

Clash? Depends what you mean. After the first two rounds, 'Pumpkin-seeds' started to complain to Pierre.

'Call this boxing? They're rubbish, them two.'

Pushing, hugging, jerking, no real punches to speak of.

By the time of the fourth, after two cautions for fouls from the referee, the crowd started whistling. They shouted that the Ferrara boxer would have been better off 'breeding eels', and someone asked if he could get up into the ring to teach the fascist a lesson. So the match, while it languished in the ring, spread into the ringside seats.

A short, squat bloke, red face like a baboon's arse, came over to Pierre with a menacing look.

'And as for you, my handsome lad, you go and tell people in your bar that Malavasi tried to fight and the other guy didn't.'

'You call that fighting?' said someone a few inches away from his nose. 'Bullets are too good for you fascists.'

The right hook thumped into Pumpkin-seed's cheek in a flash. He hadn't been the one talking, that had been someone with huge great shoulders, far too big for that short-arsed wanker of a fascist. Pierre threw himself at the troublemaker, whacking him in the jaw with his elbow. The man fell back with Pierre on top of him, while the fray began all around them.

On the other front, the referee stopped the fight. Renato Torri of Sempre Avanti took the microphone to ask the audience to be calm, threatening to interrupt the evening immediately.

At the thought of losing Cavicchi, Pierre loosened his grip on his adversary, abandoning himself to the arms that were trying to pull him away. He took a hefty kick in the stomach, just as he was moving away. He replied with a spit, aiming at the little guy's bald head, and then he too was immobilised and carried away, still bellowing.

'You're Pierre from the Bar Aurora, aren't you? Brother of Nicola Capponi?'

The guy who had threatened the fascist was standing behind him. Pierre straightened up and replied, 'Yes, that's me. And who are you?'

'I'm Ettore. I believe you wanted to speak to me.'

Cavicchi's arrival was greeted with an ovation. Pierre forgot to applaud. 'Shall we do it now, or wait for them to finish?'

'Let's wait,' said Ettore. 'We'll see how Checco gets on, and then go and get a drink.'

The first round ended with the German Wiese on the ropes. Cavicchi was burying him beneath an avalanche of punches, waiting for the right moment to land one of his famous left hooks. Filled with admiration, Pierre watched the fluent and devastating action, trying to plan what he was going to say, his head filled with awe and fisticuffs.

In the interval between the fourth and the fifth rounds, he turned to say something to Ettore, but Ettore had already moved away, and was engaged in intense conversation with two men.

As the bell sounded, he looked towards the ring once more. His excitement was mounting. Not because of the boxing match, which was dominated by Cavicchi, but because of the business with Ettore, and its possible consequences. Would he find a way to get to Yugoslavia? And where would he lay his hands on the money to pay for the journey? Would it be very dangerous? And what about Angela? If he stayed away for a while, would it bring them closer together or persuade her that it was better if they parted? And Nicola? What would he tell him?

Wiese's trainer didn't ask himself quite so many questions, and threw in the towel in the sixth round.

Pierre realised he had missed something. He looked around. Ettore was beckoning him over. A gap opened up, and he joined him.

As they walked along the street they exchanged a few words, just to choose where to go.

The restaurant beneath the city towers was rather crowded, late as it was. They found a corner table, tiny and somewhat discreet, sat down and ordered two brandies.

Ettore sat back, lit a cigarette and took two drags on it.

Pierre cleared his throat and decided to get straight to the nub.

'I need to go to Yugoslavia, and Gas, Castelvetri, says –'

'Calm down, now,' Ettore interrupted. 'I don't like getting involved in stuff I don't know about. We always have a chat first, and if you're ok you'll win, I'll be that much happier to help you.'

A few tables away, a girl laughed loudly, above the gabble of voices. The arrival of the waiter helped Pierre out of his embarrassment. He gripped his glass, turned it around in the palm of his hand, sniffed his brandy and took a sip.

Ettore started talking again. 'Your brother was in the 36th, wasn't he?'

'That's right, in Kaki's company.'

'And what about you?'

'Not a bit of it,' said Pierre, his throat burning. 'I was little more than a child. I'm twenty-two now, but if I'd been at least sixteen in 1944 I'd have gone, sure, it's a family habit.'

'It's one that I have too, but a bad one if you're as young as that. It's not worth risking your life at the age of sixteen.'

Pierre looked Ettore right in the eye. For a moment he felt as though they were alone in the restaurant. He leaned forward and lowered his eyes. 'My father said you shouldn't always stand and watch.'

A couple of people at the nearby tables glanced over at them.

Pierre lifted his elbows from the table and leaned his chair against the wall.

'Your father was in the mountains too, wasn't he?' asked Ettore.

'Yes and no. He ended up fighting in Croatia, with the Italian army. Then his company mutinied and went over to Tito's side. My father fought with the Resistance there, between Zagreb and the coast, and then he decided to stay, because socialism had triumphed there, and also they'd given him some important jobs to do.'

He said these words quite openly. But Ettore wasn't the kind of person to start arguing about whether Tito was a fascist or a comrade, whether or not he was a traitor. He sat there in silence, drained his brandy and lit another cigarette. Pierre did the same. They talked about other things for half an hour. The illusions of the partisans and the directives of Togliatti, Bologna football team and Cavicchi. When Ettore started talking about his father again, Pierre realised that it was time to move on to business.

'I've always longed to hug my father again,' he began, 'but there are too many obstacles in the way: the journey, the money, the documents. For many years I've made do with his letters. Then there was silence, then nothing for months, and now mine have started coming back. So I made up my mind: I've got to go, find out what's happened, find an answer to all those questions. That's why I turned to you.'

'A journey, perhaps undercover.'

'Exactly.'

'It's risky. If they get you, you'll spend a few years in jail.'

'Only fools end up inside,' Pierre announced, trying to look tough.

'Then perhaps you're about to do something foolish.'

'Fine.' Pierre tried to smile, but managed only to raise a corner of his mouth. 'So let's say it's worth the trouble. As it was worth the trouble for you, my brother, my father and everyone else to do your duty when the time came. Sometimes it's worth it.'

Ettore reciprocated, a full smile that vanished as suddenly as it came.

'You wouldn't be the only one taking a risk, and other people's risks have to be paid for.'

Pierre stared at him. He wanted to ask him if he'd passed the test, but he held back.

'How much?'

'Let's not talk about it here,' Ettore interrupted, seeing the waiter come over. 'I'll get Gas to let you know when we can meet to talk about it in greater detail. And have no illusions: I don't even know if we'll manage to get the thing organised. Try not to think about it, and you'll find out more in ten days' time.'

The waiter approached and asked if they wanted anything else. Ettore ordered two more brandies, saw the worried grimace on Pierre's face and said, 'This one's on me,' and narrowed his eyes, which were irritated by the smoke.

Although perhaps it was a gesture of complicity.

Chapter 26

Friday, in the Bar Aurora, pools coupon day. In Bologna, especially in the centre, there are some bars where you turn up, pick up your pools coupon, sit down at a table somewhere off to the side and start filling it in. You can't do that in our bar, it's something only outsiders do, because in our place everyone gets involved, it's a communal ceremony, and to do it well you need the good luck of many and the experience of a few.

Luck, as you know, is something you either have or you don't, but there are things that can help, like the people who have been wearing the same tie to the ground ever since Bologna beat Inter. And if you point out that two easy goals slipped past them at the last home game, they'll tell you that without the tie we'd have let in at least twice that number, and there's no way you'll get them to think any differently.

In the same way, the pools coupon shows up at one on the dot on Friday. While the rest of us are writing away, the few people who aren't interested can just get on with playing billiards or chatter away without bothering anyone, but no one's allowed to play *tarocchi*, *tressette* or *scopa*, because they're all games that depend on chance, and at coupon time the Bar Aurora's lucky star must on no account be distracted. Which amounts to saying that, on this point too, we communists are opposed to private property.

'What do you think, Melega, shall we put two on Triestine–Juve?' asks the Baron, sucking the tip of his biro.

The expert flicks through his notebook, then delivers his verdict. 'Juve aren't playing Hansen, who isn't that great anyway, and nobody's won in Trieste in the past season. I reckon they'll draw, two crosses max.'

The Baron considers for a moment, then lowers his head and writes. Others nod and mark their X by the game. Walterún is still undecided. Pierre, leaning on the bar, tries to put two and two together, because everyone is doing his own coupon and writing whatever he wants, but he's in charge of the bar coupon, the communal one, the one we're going to buy the television with if we win. We've all agreed on that.

'So what do I do, do I put an X?'

'Go on, go on,' urges Stefanelli, the other expert.

And because no one objects, the draw meets with general agreement.

In the Bar Aurora, every subject has its expert. Where the football pools are concerned, it has precisely two: Melega and Stefanelli. They're the kind of people who read *Stadio* every day and write down important information in a little exercise book so that nothing slips past them. They know which players have been injured and which are in good form, they know the results of the games of the past twenty years, and they can tell you that if team A is playing team B, they haven't beaten them in years. Usually they pretty much agree with each other, but plenty of times they don't. And a few months ago there was a bit of a bust-up between those of us who agreed with one, and those of us who supported the other, and Capponi, to calm everyone down, decided to play an extra column. We did eight of the thirteen, and that was that.

'Are you finished with that coupon?' asks La Gaggia, poking his head through the door, his hand still on the handle.

'We haven't done the reserve and C Series matches,' Melega, eyes on his notebook, calls back with a gesture.

'Ok then, I can tell you those, you'll never get them. They're 2–1, I can feel it in my bones.'

'Oi, Gaggia, aren't you supposed to be tidying your shop?' protests Bottone, given that La Gaggia never shows his face before two on a Friday, and his excuse is that he has to put all his tools away and finish his work as a shoemaker, but the real fact is that he doesn't care for football, he doesn't know a thing about it, and some people say that it's because he's a jinx, that he'd be happy to come but no one else wants him there, and all three things could be true.

'I bet you haven't even opened the paper yet, you animals!' A glance around, no one protests, and he tries to go on: 'Big news on the Montesi case: they've opened a parliamentary commission to inquire into the morals of the deputies.'

'Hmph, what's Montesi got to do with it?' asks Garibaldi, after giving an X to Sanbenedettese–Arstaranto. 'Why can't they leave that poor girl alone?'

'I agree,' another man chimes in, but he can't get his words out before La Gaggia silences everyone with an impatient glare, as though we were a pack of ignorant schoolboys.

'What's she got to do with it? Are you pulling my leg? It looks as though two of them killed her, with drugs, and one, Montagna, is a little pusher who's thick as thieves with politicians, and the other, Piccioni, is the son of the Social Democrat minister. And as chance would have it, the police have hushed it up until just now, they've tried to make everyone think it was an accident. And now that's it, final straw, they've got to clean up, time for all the politicians' dirty tricks to come out into the open.'

La Gaggia breaks off with an air of satisfaction, waiting for us to share his enthusiasm. But many of us just scratch our heads, until Walterún says, 'I don't get it. It all looks to me like one huge great mess. Who killed that poor girl?'

'Are you listening to me or not? They did it, Montagna and Piccioni, they gave her some drugs so they could fuck her, and the heads of the Chamber of Deputies tried to hide everything, but they couldn't, and now all the politicians' dirty tricks are floating to the surface!'

'Well it's about time,' observes Bottone. 'And you, Garibaldi, what do you have to say about this Montesi business? Are we going to get them this time?'

Old Garibaldi has already set aside his coupon, and is sitting at the table flicking through the newspaper, as though he didn't give one fig about the Montesi girl.

'You lot are kicking up a fuss about four fat rich perverts, while important things are happening in the world. Things that will change history, unlike the Montesi girl.'

'What's happened?' asks Pierre from behind the bar.

'What's happened is that Ho Chi Minh has decided to send the French packing once and for all!'

'Really?' asks Bottone in disbelief, putting on his glasses to read the microscopic letters of the newspaper. Even the most inveterate pools devotees look up from the table and listen attentively, because on Friday, at this time of day, no one has read the paper yet.

Garibaldi nods seraphically. 'Yes, sir. The Vietnamese have attacked the general HQ of the French forces.'

Bottone reads out loud: 'On 10 March Vietnamese troops laid siege to the entrenched camp of Di Ben –'

'Dien Bien Phu, you ignoramus! It's where the French army is based,' Garibaldi corrects him. 'This time we're going to send them home with their tails between their legs, General Giap isn't an idiot, he's a skilled warrior, a hero of the people.'

Walterún is still trying to read the article over the shoulders of Bottone, who explodes, 'Those Vietnamese may be small, but they're pretty wicked, aren't they? They might look like puny little shrimps, but they won't let anyone push them around. Good on them!'

The tram driver Lorini intervenes to have his say, as he pays for his coffee. 'It's because they're so small that they can come at you from all directions before you even notice. While the French, big and fat, make easy targets.'

Garibaldi raises his eyes to the sky and shakes his head. 'The sort of bollocks I have to put up with. What does the size of the Vietnamese have to do with anything?' Then, as though explaining a history lesson, he says, 'It's because the French are all Foreign Legion mercenaries, they're all people who fight for money. While the Vietnamese are fighting for their country, to free it from colonialism, just as we fought against the Germans. So were we tiny as well?'

Pierre finishes tidying up the cups on the bar. 'Then let's drink this coffee to the health of Comrade Ho Chi Minh.'

'To his health!' says Bottone, raising his cup.

'If the communists win there too,' says Garibaldi after taking a sip, 'we'll have taken the whole of Asia. The Soviet Union, China and Indochina.'

We nod emphatically.

'And what about us?' asks Walterún.

'We'll come after them. One thing at a time, for Christ's sake!'

Bottone's abrupt riposte brings the political debate to a close. On Friday, no subject can hold his attention for long, the Americans could drop the bomb and after a few observations we'd be talking football again.

And sure enough, Melega and Stefanelli are already playing billiards, and the crack of the balls drowns out all discussion of the fate of Bologna FC, which, with Atalanta on the team, has to make up for its 3–1 loss to Palermo. Capponi does the weekly accounts for the owner, Pierre checks the level of liquid in the bottles, and the *tarocchi* players argue over a trick.

Chapter 27

'I can't leave Odoacre.'

Angela broke the silence that had engulfed them after they had made love. Neither of them had spoken for several moments. They had stayed there, reading each other's thoughts, with no need to say anything.

Pierre shook his head. He had never asked her to decide, but she knew that the clandestine nature of their relationship was beginning to oppress him. How long had it been? Five or six months. Yes, it was getting oppressive, it wasn't easy for her, it was madness, but it was also a breath of fresh air, joy and passion. Odoacre hadn't the faintest idea what passion was. He was kind, attentive and old. It wasn't just his age, it was his character, he couldn't have been any different as a young man. Generous, altruistic, serious, always devoting himself to some good cause or other, always sure of what he was supposed to be doing.

'Angela, I'm in love with you.' Pierre's voice was tired.

She didn't have the courage to look him in the eye.

'I'm in love with you and I'm fed up with all this.'

'I know, it's as though we're living in hiding.'

'No, not just because of the two of us. It's because I can't see any future for me. Any future for us. Sooner or later we'll have to stop seeing one another, before we fall too much in love, before we miss each other too much when we're apart. We're fighting a losing battle. But I wonder if it's right.'

Pierre's eyes stared into the void. He ran a hand through his hair. She lit a cigarette and handed it to him.

'Life isn't fair, it isn't a polka, it's hard. It's been hard for me, and if I hadn't met Odoacre, who knows where I would be today.'

God almighty, how many times had she repeated that same old story? He'd had it up to there with Angela's resignation, but Pierre had no answers.

He said, 'Is this really all there is? Is there nothing else? Is this supposed to be enough? Working and waiting for Sunday?'

'And what do you suggest?' exploded Angela as though telling off a child. 'Are we rich? That man Renato Fanti tells you all sorts of fine things, but it's easy for him, he comes from a good family, he's travelled, he's been abroad, he can speak languages. What are we, Pierre?'

'Dupes, that's what. Everything's fine. The rich are fine, the poor are fine, it's fine to work like mules, it's fine for the riot cops to crack our heads open when we take to the streets, it's fine if two young people who love each other can't tell anyone.'

'You and I can't change the world, Pierre. Even if I leave Odoacre and spit on everything that he's done for me and my brother, what do we do then? We'd have to leave Bologna, everyone would chuck stones at us. And I'd be called a whore for leaving Dr Odoacre for the Filuzzi King. A pauper working as a barman. Where would we go?'

Angela realised she had raised her voice, and all at once she fell silent. She stroked Pierre's head, but he remained impassive.

'There's something strange about you. Something I don't get. We have to make the best of these moments, we mustn't think about horrible things. I know we'll have to stop seeing each other sooner or later, but until then hold me close and let's try to be happy. Please.'

Pierre stubbed out his cigarette and hugged her, felt her hot breath against his chest, kissed her face, then saw her tears.

'Don't cry. When the time comes I'll disappear without a fuss. I may go away.'

'Where?' she asked with a sniff.

'I don't know yet. Perhaps to Yugoslavia, where my father lives.'

Angela studied his face. 'You really want to leave?'

'There's this business about my father, my letters have started being returned to me. And since the age of thirteen I've wanted to see him again, and see a country that isn't like this one, a socialist country, a place where we've won.'

'Odoacre says Yugoslavia is a social-fascist country.'

Pierre couldn't bear to hear Montroni's name mentioned any longer. 'Well I don't know, at least they've had a revolution there. And anyway I don't trust what Odoacre, Benfenati and all the others say. As far as they're concerned, whatever the Party says is true. You have to see with your own eyes to judge. My father is no fascist, and yet he's stayed there. That might be a reason, don't you think?'

Angela nodded gloomily. 'This is what Fanti tells you, isn't it?'

'No, Christ almighty, it's what I think!' He leapt to his feet, then faltered and stopped in the middle of the room, paralysed by his thoughts. He walked towards the window, and peered through the half-open shutters.

She studied the thin shadow that stood out against the blades of light filtering through.

He spoke with his back towards her. 'I want to see something different, Angela. When I think that my life is going to be spent between the ballroom and the Bar Aurora I can feel myself dying. At the demonstrations, when I get a kicking, I don't feel like a hero. My father, my brother and everyone else have fought for a good cause, but people my age have nothing but stories about partisans and weapons that are left to rust in cellars, nothing to do but dream of the revolution that never comes. What are we supposed to do? Find a good job, a nice girl to marry, have children, wait till we're old enough to have people listen to *our* stories, that time we fought the riot squad? I can't see myself at the age of seventy playing *briscola* with Brando and Sticleina. I'm sorry. I don't want to end up like the guys in the bar.'

Angela felt a thump inside her, like something breaking, and her eyes filled with tears once more.

Pierre went on. 'Thinking about the revolution, taking up arms. All those things that other people have done in the past, during the war and before, when we were children. But when they brag to their friends, they know they've lost. I've got a Party card as well, but I don't want to see the world through the eyes of Montroni or the editor of *L'Unità*.' He turned to her. 'I want to go and see and judge for myself. I want something else.'

Angela wiped her eyes. 'I was starving before I married Odoacre, and Ferruccio . . . you know. Life isn't like it is in the films, you don't bump into Cary Grant on the train, he doesn't fall in love with you and take you to America. Go to Yugoslavia if you want, then come back and tell me if it's that much better than it is here.'

Pierre went over and hugged her and held her tight. They settled into the sofa, and he cuddled her gently, trying to make her go to sleep. 'Shhhh. Let's pretend we're two hares in our lair, and it's snowing outside and very cold and we've got loads of food set aside for the winter, and we're going to keep each other warm with our fur.'

As he talked and ran a hand through her hair, he heard her breathing more heavily.

She was right, there was something strange about him. And it certainly wasn't easy to understand.

His father, Yugoslavia, the Tito fascists.

Sleep finally extinguished his thoughts.

Chapter 28

Jean-Jacques Bondurant forced himself to look at the screen.

He was having trouble keeping his eyelids open, he was sweating, *Nom de Dieu!* If he had so much as arched his eyebrow, his toupee would have fallen over his eyes. God, it was hot in there.

Now he ran the fingertips of his right hand over his forehead, keeping his thumb pressed into the hollow of his temple to prevent the imminent migraine. Just before he did that, he ran his index finger across the damp zone above the top of his nose. Until the previous day, a tuft of hair had connected his eyebrows. 'Thin it? Thin it? It's going to take more than a little bit of retouching!' the beautician had told him.

Even stranger was the flat surface left by the removal of his mole. He was having trouble getting used to it.

What else? His teeth had been whitened, his gold ring removed (with some difficulty) . . .

If anyone had seen them there, sitting side by side, two replicas of a single face in the shimmering light: Bondurant, exhausted by the interminable matinee of Cary Grant comedies; Grant very attentive, his arms lying loosely on his thighs, his buttocks perched on the edge of the little sofa. But there was no one else there in the sitting room.

At that moment, in the black-and-white film, a third (younger) version of Cary Grant sat with legs crossed and arms folded, a beatific smile on his face, the expression of a man savouring his own triumph to the last drop.

'Freeze!' One of the two full-colour versions, raising an arm, the one who wasn't perspiring.

A frozen frame, one of the scenes from the denouement of *The Awful Truth*, 1937.

'You try that now!' Cary ordered his double. 'But first of all compose yourself, for heaven's sake! You're drenched in sweat!'

Bondurant mopped himself dry with his handkerchief, and straightened the hairpiece on the top of his cranium.

'There's no need to be so agitated, I've told you you're making progress! Keep at it, I want to see you in this pose, the same smile, the same air of self-satisfaction.'

Bondurant crossed his legs, took his elbows in his hands, then arched his spine backwards and tried to imitate the smile.

'We're not quite there, Mr Bondurant. The attitude is missing. In fact I'll go further than that: the feeling is missing. I'll try to put you in the right frame of mind. You're forty-three, isn't that right?'

Bondurant nodded too vigorously, and had to rearrange his *perruque*. Grant noticed and exploded: 'Christ almighty, where on earth did they find that little wig that does nothing but slip around all over the place? In a joke shop?'

He took from his pocket a black leather-bound notebook, scribbled a note, then continued. 'Let's get back to us: in your forty-three years of life, has there ever been a moment when you've said to yourself, "The worst is past"?'

In what sense . . . Oh! Of course! *Le plus gros est fait!* He had understood. Grant was referring to a moment of complacency, in which *il se la coula douce*.

'But yes, of course, when the war was over and I returned from the Italian front.'

'Fine, Mr Bondurant. When you got back to Montreal I expect they threw a party for you, or am I mistaken?'

'Of course, and I was delighted. I saw my fiancée, Charlotte, again for the first time in five years.'

'Fine. Shut your eyes.'

Bondurant did so.

'Imagine you're at that party. You've just been dancing with your Charlotte. You're sitting down on the edge of the dance floor. In your chest you feel the warmth of the community congratulating you. You've done your duty. Finally you feel a certain lightness after years that seemed they would never end, you think of the days to come. Your whole body is filled with expectation, and the ambition of a happy life.'

While Grant spoke, the double breathed deeply. A new smile started to form.

'That's good, Mr Bondurant. Now, from this position of strength, think about Hitler!'

'Pardon?' Bondurant opened his eyes again.

'That's right, Hitler. You've won the war, Mr Bondurant, and the Nazis have lost. You're alive while that son of a bitch with the moustache is dead. The good people have won, and you've made a contribution to that. You and Charlotte have blue skies above your head, Hitler and Eva Braun are six feet under. You're part of the future, you've dreamed of the enemy, and you're happy, yes, Mr Bondurant, you're happy, touch the sky with a finger. The war is over. The bad people have been defeated. I want to see you smile, because you have the right! Who more than you? You're at that party, and you're smiling!'

'Oui, je suis aux anges! Zut! Je suis aux anges, et je souris!'

Bondurant opened his eyes in triumph. The war was over. Hitler was gone.

Grant was staring at him.

Not bad.

'Fine, Mr Bondurant. As my wife said, you're a quick learner. And now it seems appropriate to me to show you a sequence from *I Was a Male War Bride*, in which . . .'

Bondurant fell back on to the sofa. How long was this going to go on?

Chapter 29

He chose a bar on the other side of the city. Perhaps it was a pointless precaution, but neglecting the details wasn't a good habit to fall into. Experience tells us that it's the insignificant things that trip you up. He had known so many clever men who had been ruined by blunders. One word too many to a prostitute, a fuck that would have been better postponed, a forgotten ticket in a jacket pocket, a worn tyre that had popped. You would have bet on them 100 per cent, but they had all made one small mistake. And found themselves staring into the blue lights, or keeping company with the fishes at the bottom of the bay. He had caught some of them out himself, surprised with themselves for having coming up with such shrewd and meticulous plans. And then they'd been fucked over a detail. Perhaps it was the universal law of chance, which applied to anyone who put all his eggs in one basket, knowing that he risked losing. That there wouldn't be another chance.

Zollo went in and ordered a coffee. Then he asked where the phone was.

The barman pointed to it.

He picked up the receiver and dialled the number.

A young woman's voice said, 'Hello?'

'I need to make an international call.'

'Where to?'

'Paris.'

'Please give me the number.'

Zollo read out the digits, giving her time to jot them down.

*

In a bar in rue des Abbesses, in Paris, the phone rang three times before a fat, sweaty man picked up the receiver.

'*Allô?*'

The clear voice of the operator said, 'A call from Italy. One moment, please.'

An Italian-American accent butted in: 'Lyonnese Toni, please.'

'Toni? *Attendez, monsieur.*'

The fat man set down the receiver on the bar and walked through the gloomy bar, rubbing his neck. He opened a door at the back and entered a little smoke-filled room. Four people were sitting around the circular table. The green top was scattered with *fiches* and cigarette burns. Cigarette butts spilled from two glass ashtrays.

The fat man turned to one of the gamblers. 'Toni. *Téléphone.*'

An emaciated man, a cigarette dangling between his lips, eyes half closed, replied with a grunt. He looked at his cards: two aces and two eights. The dead man's hand. *Merde.* A glance at the pile of *fiches.* He was already 10,000 down and it was his turn to call. He picked up everything in front of him and put it in the middle of the table. He folded his cards together and got to his feet. His exhausted muscles responded after a delay: it must have been about ten in the morning. They had been playing for twelve hours.

As he headed for the telephone, he was seized by a coughing fit that left him breathless. He spat into his handkerchief, and when he folded it up it was full of blood He heard the men in the other room exchanging useless comments. 'That lunatic should look after himself', 'If he goes on like that he's going to pop his clogs', 'He should stop smoking like a Turk.' Hypocritical fools. After tapping a load of money out of him, they worried about his health.

He went behind the bar, poured himself a generous shot of brandy, then picked up the phone.

'*Ouais?*'

'Lyonnese Toni?'

'*C'est moi.*'

'Zollo.'

'*Zollò*, it was high time to hear from you.'

Apart from his pronunciation, his Italian was good. He'd consorted with more immigrants than an Antwerp whore.

'Still interested in this deal?'

Toni gulped down the brandy and felt it burning his guts like red-hot iron.

'Sure. The way the poker's going, I'm going to have to make it up somehow.'

'How do you mean?'

'*Rien*, nothing. When do you think you'll be ready?'

'In two months. I'm going to need all the money. Clean.'

'*Pas possible. Non.* I haven't got that much. But if I have a sample of the goods, I can get it valued by a guy I know who's interested in the whole deal. He's willing to pay the figure you're asking.'

There was silence at the other end of the line. Toni felt he could hear Zollo thinking.

'*Zollò*, no one buys blind, you know that. This person trusts me. Give me a sample and I'll let you have the money.'

'I'll be in Marseille in about two months because of Luciano. And he'll have the sample.'

'Not in Marseilles, too dangerous, the walls have ears.'

'Where, then?'

'Cannes.'

Another silence.

Then: 'Ok, Cannes in two months. But tell your friend the price stays as it is. I don't want any nonsense.'

'Don't worry, I told you, he's loaded. If it's good stuff, he'll pay.'

'I'll call you on the same number in exactly twenty days.'

'*Bon*, I'll be here.'

The communication was interrupted.

Lyonnese Toni drank down a second glass, and returned to the poker table.

Someone had matched his cards.

He set down two pairs.

The other man put down three tens. Of course.

Toni repressed a cough, the taste of blood in his mouth. His ashen face contemplated the cards without any particular expression. He remembered why they called it the dead man's hand. History related that when a glory-hunter fired into the back of 'Wild' Bill Hickok's head, he was sitting at the green table holding a hand of two aces and two eights. God knows why he had turned his back to the door.

Toni got up, slipped on his jacket, put the money on the table and went out without saying goodbye to anyone. As he raised the shutter and the light of the morning burned his eyes, he heard them talking in low voices.

'He hasn't got long to go', 'He should get some treatment', 'He can't go on like that'.

Bloody jinx. He walked along the street and disappeared behind the first corner.

Chapter 30

Bologna, 23 March

The warehouse stood right next to the building site for the new hospital. When it was finished, it would be the biggest in Europe.

The entrance was obstructed by the trailer of a lorry. Pierre slipped into the narrow passage between the lorry and the wall. It was hot inside, with a smell of damp and petrol. Two boys not much older than himself were unloading big tin drums and lining them up against the wall.

'Hi,' said Pierre. 'I'm supposed to talk to Ettore.'

'Ettore? He was here until ten minutes ago, then he left, but he should be back soon.'

'Can I wait here?'

'Make yourself comfortable,' replied the younger of the boys, and without stopping his work he pointed to a chair at the back of the shed.

Beside the chair, two men were talking and studying some pieces of paper. Pierre preferred not to disturb them and leaned against the wall. He lit a cigarette to kill some time, but felt like a halfwit when one of the men pointed out that the drums contained fuel and smoking near them wasn't the best idea in the world.

He stubbed out the cigarette against the wall and slipped it back into the pack. He couldn't stay long, he had left the bar on an insignificant errand, and Nicola had got out on the wrong side of bed that morning.

The boys seemed to be tireless, and were still hard at work around the lorry. From the little that he knew, everyone who worked with Ettore had a partisan past, and those two must have taken up arms before the age of eighteen. The hardest of them came from the 'Red Star', the others had been later additions. Gas said there were about fifteen of them in all. The boss was called Bianco, but he was sick, and now he followed the business from a distance, having been replaced by Ettore on the ground.

The two men studying the papers raised their voices. Raised voices, harsh words. The men doing the unloading stopped halfway between the lorry and the wall, glancing towards them. One of the two had grabbed the other by the jacket, and was shouting in his face. 'You'll pay for that, you son of a bitch, you'll pay me the lot, right now!'

The drums rolled to the ground, the noise bouncing off the ceiling.

The one who had been grabbed by the jacket wriggled free. The boys went and stood next to him. The other man was training a pistol on him.

'Tell your mate to come over here too,' Pierre heard him say, but without giving him time to finish, he dashed towards the lorry and climbed underneath it, wriggling towards the exit on his elbows.

When he re-emerged, clutching the back mudguard, he found himself looking at a pair of legs and a pointed gun. He felt something like the blow of an enormous weight around his heart, and hid his head under his arm.

'Come out quietly,' a voice whispered. 'No nonsense.'

Pierre did so, stiff as a piece of salt cod. The voice went on speaking. He didn't understand the order, but he seemed to recognise the voice and raised his face.

'Oh, it's you,' Ettore said. Then he curled his index finger to beckon him over. 'What's happening in there?'

'I didn't know,' Pierre replied breathlessly. 'Someone wanted to be paid, and drew a gun.'

'Is he alone?'

'Yes, he's alone.'

'Where is he?'

'On the other side, towards the back.'

Ettore moved the palm of his hand towards the floor, indicating to Pierre that he should wait where he was, and disappeared behind the corner. In less than two minutes Pierre heard his voice booming around the shed, followed by a shot. Two.

A moment later he saw a head peeping out from underneath the lorry. It wasn't Ettore, nor was it one of the boys, and the man was holding a gun. There was no time to gauge his expression. He kicked him right in the face, so hard that he almost turned him over. He heard Ettore's voice again, behind him this time, calm as ever.

'Well done, Pierre. I hope you didn't kill him.'

He handed the gun to the other man and bent down under the lorry. The face of the guy who wanted to be paid looked like a burst watermelon. He was bleeding from an eyebrow and from his mouth, and his nose was smeared over his right cheek. His other cheekbone was reddish-purple. He was still breathing.

'Palmo, Beppe, take him away,' Ettore ordered once he had risen to his feet. 'Wait for him to recover, and tell him we're through with him, and I don't want to see him again.' Then he smiled, turning back to Pierre. 'Well, you showed up at a good time. Come on, let's go for a drive.'

The 1400 was parked across the way, under an acacia. They got in. Ettore started the engine and set off with a faint squeal of tyres on the gravel. He drove towards an area of the city dominated by railway tracks, barracks, warehouses and vegetable gardens. It was as though urban expansion towards the plain had been somehow obstructed there, and the remnants of the city ran in two streams of asphalt and bricks parallel to the railway tracks, along Via Emilia in one direction, and out of the Porta Lame in the other.

'Good news,' began Ettore with his cigarette dangling from his lips. 'I've found someone who can take you to Yugoslavia. I've got a load that's supposed to be setting off towards the end of the month, from Ravenna.'

'Ravenna?' Pierre's eyes turned towards the driver. 'By sea?'

'Yes, in a boat, it's safer and shorter.'

'Why?'

'Travel by land has been risky, relations between the Italian border guards and Slovenian customs officers aren't as good as they were immediately after the war, when there were communists over there, or rather friends of the communists from over here.' He broke off for a moment to wind down the window. 'On the boat it's different, the guy taking care of the cargo will take care of you too, just as if you were one of his cases, he'll unload you in a safe place, he'll even drive you to the first village, and then say goodbye.'

'And how much would it cost me?'

'Without a discount, almost 200,000. But after what's happened, I can offer you half that, documents included.'

Pierre whistled between his teeth and turned to look outside. A Lambretta parked against a hedge, in the middle of nowhere, declared the season of love on the grass reopened. If he had had a motor scooter like that, he and Angela would really be able to enjoy themselves, without doing everything on the sly, in constant fear of passersby and neighbours. But he couldn't afford a Lambretta, and he couldn't afford such an expensive journey, either.

He ran a hand over his mouth. 'Where am I going to get 100,000 lire?' he whispered to himself.

'What do you mean?'

'A hundred thousand lire is too much. If I turn my pockets inside out I can just about manage 50,000.'

'Fifty thousand?' Ettore widened his eyes and dismissed the idea with a nervous gesture. 'You thought you were going to cross the Adriatic for as little as that? Who put that idea in your head? Was it that fool Gas?'

'No, Gas has nothing to with it, I just thought . . .'

He felt a bitter taste filling his mouth, like a childhood memory of being forced to drink that disgusting cod liver oil, followed by honey, of course, although the honey was never a match for the taste or, even worse, the smell. Silence roared in his head like the engine of an aeroplane. After a few minutes, Ettore spoke again.

'Listen, there is one way of getting the price down.'

'Let's hear it.'

'Your bar has a spacious cellar, doesn't it? Fine. Let's say that the minute you get back from your trip, you rent it to me for six months. Wait, let me finish, I don't mean you won't be able to use it any more, I just need enough space for a few boxes, where no one's going to be poking their noses in. And that's enough. What do you think?'

'Depends. If we did it that way, how much would I have to pay?'

'Let's say that your 50,000 might be enough.'

'And what's in the boxes?'

Ettore changed gear and studied Pierre to see if he had the right to ask the question.

'Cigarettes,' he replied finally.

'Fine. If my brother finds out he'll kill me, but I'll think about it, ok?'

The silence that followed was very different from the earlier one. Pierre leaned his elbow on the lowered window, slid forwards on the seat and closed his eyes to concentrate. If he accepted, he would have to do it in such a way that Nicola's suspicions weren't aroused. Ever. Otherwise, goodbye Yugoslavia, goodbye money, goodbye everything. A passing train blanked out any further thoughts.

'Are we taking a drive just to talk, or are we going somewhere?' he asked when the rails had grown quiet again.

'I'm taking you to see Ghigo, the guy who's taking care of the documents. He'll get you a false passport with an entry stamp for Yugoslavia. He's a sound bloke, he works in watches.'

'Watches?'

'Not your good stuff. Junk.' He took a drag and threw away his cigarette. Ghigo's scam was worth relating. 'He's the king of junk,' he went on with a chuckle. 'Last week he pulled this brilliant trick on a geezer from Vergato.'

Pierre's attention was hooked already. 'He stops the mark in the street, right, and he says, "Excuse me, I have a case of very valuable watches here, and they haven't yet been through all the necessary customs procedures. Do you know where I could fill in the requisite forms?" The man stands there looking stupid, while an accomplice of Ghigo's comes over and says, "I heard you talking about watches. I need to buy one, can I have a look?" So Ghigo opens the case and shows him, and his friend pretends to be interested, like these are really precious watches. "They're worth an arm and a leg,"' says Ghigo. '"But because I haven't paid border tax, I can keep the prices low: 50,000." The other man acts as though he's about to pay up immediately, but he hasn't got enough money. So he turns to the mark: "Can you lend me 30,000 lire? I'll go to the bank with this guy here, and I'll be back straight away. As a guarantee I'll give you this watch, which is worth 50,000. Is that ok?" The fool's wife tries to stop him, but he says the gentleman is clearly

on the level. He lends him the 30,000, the two men go off and
don't come back.'

'And how much was the watch worth?' asked Pierre, amused.

'Not more than a thousand. I think they make them in Bulgaria
or somewhere down there.'

Pierre smiled. At the worst, he'd found a way of getting hold of
the 50,000.

Chapter 31

General Ivan Alexandrovich Serov tried out the sofa in the big office. The afternoon light came faintly through the window, the Moscow spring trying to defeat the frost: it had been a hard winter.

He still didn't feel at ease. In particular, he couldn't see why a single person needed such a capacious office. Elegant surroundings. Too much so, he thought. He would get rid of some of the fripperies. The heavy curtains could be used to warm up the army rather than gathering dust by the window. And the ornaments would go first, he'd always hated them, pointless, cumbersome objects. With all that iron you could forge weapons to defend the revolution, and the wood could be burned in the soldiers' bivouacs. And the porcelain vases? A better use could be found for the porcelain, too.

Basically that was why he had been put there. To restore order and clean up. He would start with the small things. Ornaments and knick-knacks.

The 'economic' vision of things was the strong point of his career and his political training. A sound practical sense at the service of the greatest ideal. If the ideal was the dynamite, the practical sense was the fuse. During his years at the Ministry he had never got used to working behind the scenes.

Having grown up on the battlefields, he knew the cold of Belorussia and Poland, and the lead of the Nazi bullets. He didn't need frills and furbelows to direct the deportations from the Caucasus, to put down the pockets of White Russian resistance in Poland, coordinate Ministry activities in East Germany.

He studied the paintings on the walls. Lenin stared at a vague point on the horizon. His determined gaze inspired a profound trust in human destinies. He had seen the Little Father only once, when he had marched through Red Square with his regiment at the age of eighteen.

May the 1st 1922: he turned his head towards the stage, along with all his comrades, and he saw him, small, fur hat protecting his bald head, flanked by the traitor Trotsky and Comrade Stalin.

Now Stalin looked down at him from the wall opposite, with an 'amused' expression. His moustache hid his mouth, it was impossible to tell whether or not he was smiling, but it seemed to him that he was: the wise, angelic smile of someone who has understood everything. He remembered the day of the funeral, the yelling masses, the women tearing their clothes and striking themselves on the head.

He wept too. The first time in years. He hadn't even shed a tear in Berlin, in the spring of 1945, at the sight of the red flag hoisted over the Reichstag. And yet he had been moved. The victory crowned years of hard work, hunger and death. He would carry that moment with him, the big flag flapping in the wind, until the end of his days. And Stalin's funeral. An infinite sense of loss, a vague sense of panic: the Leader was no longer there. That day the question rose up from the back of his mind, the same question being asked by the members of Central Committee: 'What now?'

'Now.' General Serov immediately knew what would happen. Only the strongest survive. And the patient. A lesson he had learned while fighting Hitler: a good general must always know when to retreat, to allow the enemy to advance, to tire themselves out, and then to strike them mercilessly until they are destroyed. That day, as he stared at Stalin's coffin, he banished his tears and started thinking.

Only a year had passed since then, enough to make some calculations and decide who would be promoted and who would stay where they were.

The struggle for succession had been resolved in a few months. 'Stalin's dauphin', Malenkov, versus 'Stalin's best friend', Beria. He himself had known how to wait and choose his moment. Anyone who had set out to rout his adversaries and win hands down had been dragged into the mud. Same mistake as Hitler: *Blitzkrieg*. A strategy that doesn't pay off in the long term. Any self-respecting Russian should know that.

As Minister of the Interior, Beria planned to change everything, trampling over Stalin's corpse while it was still warm. Bloody lunatic. From the first moment, when he was called in to receive his new instructions ('No more purges of Jews from the Party, no more trials, we've got to start everything over from the beginning'), the general understood that this fool would not get far. He stepped aside, to watch the wolves tear him to pieces. At the head of the pack he found his man, the cleverest one, who would destroy all the rest of them: the future Party Secretary, Nikita Khrushchev. The general didn't think twice before joining the conspiracy to eliminate Beria and the 'Caucasian' clan. It was a matter of survival.

It was easy to imagine Beria's deputy in the Ministry of the Interior, Sergei Kruglov, being bought for a couple of roubles, just to take the place of his boss. But the general didn't trust him to stay in the saddle. What was certain was that before going into action, Khrushchev would make sure he had the support of the army. So he sent an explicit signal to Marshal Zhukov, Deputy Defence Minister and an old associate from his Berlin days. So he went in search of conspirators.

In June, Khrushchev won the support of Malenkov. The end of the 'Caucasians' was not far off.

When Khrushchev gave the order to arrest Lavrenti Pavlovich Beria, on charges of 'moral decadence' and 'espionage in the service of foreign powers', the Moscow police rose up in his defence. Marshal Zhukov sent armoured cars into the city to restore order. That day civil war broke out. The general stayed in his office at the Ministry, waiting for events to run their course.

The traitor Beria was sentenced, and it was clear to the general that within a few months Khrushchev would make a clean sweep. The day after Beria's elimination, Khrushchev handed the Ministry to Kruglov: a reward for doing over the boss.

Kruglov was an arriviste bureaucrat, put there to keep the Services quiet while the cards were being dealt again. The general could tell that this was his big opportunity. At the age of only forty-nine he would be able to make it to the top. Take it or leave it. He had to take a gamble.

Discrediting Kruglov was the riskiest manoeuvre of his career.

As a man in a position of trust, the general had access to

information about the spy network abroad. He needed only to spread the news of a coming purge of the agents in the 'hot' countries. The Yankees, diligent as ever, would do the rest.

In January, the Tokyo resident defected; in February, so did the one in Vienna; in the same month, the agent in charge of an important mission in West Germany went over to the CIA the moment he crossed the border from the Eastern Zone.

Kruglov found himself being pensioned off without even knowing what had happened.

The rest followed of its own accord. Recent history.

In early March, after the commemorations for the first anniversary of Stalin's death, Malenkov had severed the Services from the Minister of the Interior, to reconstitute them as an autonomous organ directly dependent on the Council of Ministers: The Committee for State Security. The man in charge would be the loyal and incorruptible General Serov.

He had reached the top.

Sitting at his desk, in absolute solitude, he was willing to bet that sooner or later that fat *muzhik* Khrushchev would oust Malenkov too.

Better to concentrate on the task at hand. He opened his folder: the headed paper on which the documents were written was fresh off the press. The coat of arms stood out clearly: the shield, to defend the revolution, and the sword, to strike the enemies of the country. The three letters at the top of the page, solid, crisp capitals, in perfect harmony with his vision of things.

KGB.

The photograph showed a young man, almost bald, pointed chin and strong jaw. The general read the data carefully.

Andrei Vassilyevich Zhulianov; born in Kiev in 1924, into a family of shopkeepers; marked out at secondary school as a student with a particular gift for languages and sent to the Foreign Languages Faculty in Kiev; military service in the Second Desanniki division from 1942 to 1945; reached the rank of sergeant-major; medal of honour for merit on the field; joined the Soviet Communist Party in 1945; active in the Military

Information Service with the rank of captain from 1945 to 1948;
special praise for three undercover operations in West Berlin
between 1946 and 1948; admitted to the Higher Political School
of the Ministry of the Interior in 1948; perfect knowledge of
English, German, French and Serbo-Croat; partial knowledge
of Italian; joined the Ministry for State Security in 1953. Personal
characteristics: higher than average intelligence; exceptional dedi-
cation to the party; good general knowledge; excellent knowledge
of the classics of scientific socialism; unmarried; judo, wrestling
and pistol-shooting.

An interesting candidate, without a doubt.

Andrei Vassilyevich Zhulianov looked at himself in the bathroom
mirror, to check every detail. Six foot one, fourteen stone, square
shoulders, broad chest. He checked that his nails were clean. He was
wearing a woollen jacket and matching tie. He had been told that
the general was a scrupulous observer, he had to be neat and tidy,
and there must be nothing superfluous. The only detail allowed him
was the Party badge on the lapel of his jacket. He polished the gilded
hammer and sickle with his sleeve, gave a long sigh and went out
into the corridor.

Being called in by the head of the newly born KGB was not something that happened every day. There had been a few changes at the
top levels over the past few weeks, and the wind of change was in
the air for everyone. Some people had already disappeared, to end
up shuffling paper in obscure and marginal offices. Others had been
given the opportunity to put long years of study to the test. The few
women working in the Ministry had been excluded from operational
duties. It had been the first order from the head of the Committee.
The women's action in the field would be limited to the role of 'bait',
to extort information and unmask infiltrators or double agents. But
no network would place any trust in agents of the female sex. The
general's mistrust of women was well known. Jews received similar
treatment.

As he climbed the stairs of the building, banal phrases came to
his mind, to be dismissed immediately: 'If my mother could see me
now . . .'

Everyone in the Ministry knew that a personal summons from the President of the Committee meant a big job was a possibility. The department's director had given him to understand promotion was in the air.

After the end of the war, opportunities to shine had been few and far between. He had exploited them to the best of his ability. In Berlin, when the fame of General Serov instilled reverential fear in him, he had won the praise of his colonel. Military counter-espionage was satisfied with the way he had behaved on several occasions at least. But his gifts for learning languages had removed him from active service and transferred him to the Ministry's Higher Political School. Six years had passed, during which he had devoted himself chiefly to study, perfected his knowledge of languages and improved his memory.

His memory. As he had been able to understand since he had been transferred there, the bulk of the Ministry's activity was devoted to the accumulation of information. Hundreds of thousands of files, cards, profiles, personal data. On everyone and everything. Obtaining and storing information, that was the real power of the Ministry, now the KGB.

The secretary admitted him without a smile, checked his card and told him to wait in the antechamber, after which she slipped behind a door and left him on his own.

He waited five minutes before the secretary appeared and told him to go in.

A wide, rather gloomy room. Heavy curtains kept the light out. At first he could discern only a black outline behind the black mahogany desk. A table lamp lit a man's hands.

General Serov said, 'Step forward, comrade.'

Zhulianov walked over to the desk, clicked his heels and gave the military salute in homage to their old times in Berlin.

The general did not reciprocate. 'Sit down.'

From close up he was frightening. A young-looking fifty, skinny physique, slightly grizzled air, hard features, as though sculpted from rock. But the most striking thing about him was his eyes. Grey and impassive, they stared into his own. He remembered the advice of the head of department, and he did not look down.

The two men said nothing for several long seconds. Zhulianov was motionless, not making a single gesture, not even swallowing. The test had begun.

Then the general said, 'Comrade Zhulianov, from this moment you are transferred to the First Central Directorate, Subdirectorate S.'

The 'illegals', thought Zhulianov, containing his emotion.

'You've been chosen for a level-4 mission. On the basis of your curriculum vitae I think you are the most suited to the kind of work required. It is an extremely high-risk job, and one of very great importance. You are not obliged to accept, but your dedication to the Party and the country lead me to suppose that you will not let us down.'

Zhulianov absorbed the information while trying to remain calm. This was his big opportunity.

The general continued without taking his eyes off his face, his every reaction would be recorded: 'Level 4 provides for the possibility of losing your freedom and your life. The same risks that you have already run while fighting against the German invaders, and infiltrating yourself into West Berlin after the war. The mission's success will contribute to the preservation of peace and the defence of the Soviet Union against its enemies.' A pause. 'I don't think you need any further information in order to make a decision.'

Silence again. Zhulianov waited. The general's expression did not change. He added, 'You have twenty-four hours to make your mind up.'

Zhulianov understood what he had to say.

'That will not be necessary, Comrade General. I accept without reservation the task that you wish to assign to me, in the interest of the Soviet Union.'

'Very good. The details of the job are contained in the folder that will be handed to you at the end of this meeting. You will have to learn them by heart. Meanwhile bear in mind that you will have to travel to a hostile country to kidnap a subject against his will. The subject's safety will have to be guaranteed at the risk of your own life. If conditions appear too risky for the safety of the subject, you will have to consider the mission suspended. But the Committee will do its best to ensure that this does not occur.'

Silence again. Zhulianov felt pride swelling his chest, but made an effort to give no sign of it.

The head of the KGB handed him a blue folder.

'We will meet again next Tuesday. By then you will have to have memorised the contents of this dossier.' No gesture of farewell. 'The Committee places its trust in you, Comrade Zhulianov. You may go.'

Chapter 32

Bologna, 2 April

The grey Crombie came to just below his knees, and distinguished him from all the Bolognese who were out walking in long overcoats or wrapped up in double-breasted mackintoshes with very tight belts. There were also old men in black cloaks, but they didn't count.

Fanti wore black leather gloves and a characteristic, very English bowler hat. Grey corduroy trousers and a pair of low-sided boots. No one else in the city dressed like the professor, although that in itself did not make him look like an eccentric, at least not in the eyes of people unfamiliar with his way of life. You would have mistaken him for a distinguished foreigner passing through, perhaps an Allied officer in civilian clothes. But when he went up to the pigeon-house dressed like that, and you saw him on the roof, from the street or from the building opposite, going into the cage in his English coat, exposing his expensive hat to the birdshit, and plunging his hand into the grain box wearing those gloves that must have cost at least 5,000 lire, well, you'd have thought, this really is an odd geezer, a very peculiar character indeed.

Winter was over, he no longer had to break the layer of ice to give the pigeons something to drink. The professor lifted the birds out of their little rooms and into the cage, opened the shutter, liberated the flock and started waving his banner around to send them into the sky, like a conductor performing an *andante maestoso*.

What a sight! As they wheel, each pigeon displays first its back, then its belly, a completely different colour. Multiply the effect by several dozen, and you end up with a shifting wave, the light breaking on it and fragments shooting off in a thousand different directions.

In the flock there were pure and piebald plumages, black, dun, powder-blue, almond, bronze . . .

Fanti was a pigeon-fancier, one of 3,000 in Emilia Romagna. He had fifty individuals, from *triganini modenesi* to pedigree doves (chosen by Manifardi and Corradini) and homing pigeons. Every day he fed them a kilo of vetch mixed with corn, maize and millet.

He had been a pigeon-fancier since he was a boy. When he moved to England, he had not given up his hobby, and had in fact become an important member of the International Federation of Homing Pigeon Fanciers, founded in 1881.

He had gone mad at the last fair and market held in Bologna, spending 300,000 lire on a slender female, with a bright-grey back tending to indigo, *sgurafosso*. Very elegant. Her name was Eloisa, and she had made the journey from Indochina to Italy in two months. Two hundred kilometres a day, 'a remarkable accomplishment'. That had happened on 6 February – the purchase, not the flight, which had occurred some months before. Fanti was in correspondence via homing pigeon with various friends in England, France and Ireland, but he had not yet put Eloisa to the test.

When he was in his pigeon loft, Fanti fell into a sort of trance. Standing beside him, on the roof, was Robespierre Capponi. A promising, restless pupil . . . He was saying something to him . . . *Zara . . . bicycle* . . . To Zara on a bicycle? No, can't be that . . . *the watch . . .* 10,000. Fanti nodded, said 'mhm' from time to time, but his mind was elsewhere: his eyes narrowing slightly, he stared at a tiny black dot to the north-west, in the middle of a patch of sky not occupied by the flock. A small object with a globular outline, then, as it got closer, bigger and arch-shaped. *Lend me* . . . The approaching object was Bertram, one his homing pigeons. Pierre broke off. Fanti stretched out his hands, and the bird allowed itself to be caught.

How do pigeons find their way home? Many people think they somehow take their bearings from the sun in some way, but they make their way home without any difficulties on foggy or cloudy days. According to some people, pigeons are sensitive to geomagnetic fields, taking their bearings from those when the sky is overcast. An interesting hypothesis. It was probably a combination of magnetism, the position of the sun and familiar landscapes. 'Pretty impressive for such a small bird, don't you think?'

A message from his friend McCullock, who was inviting him to spend the summer at his home in Arklow on St George's Channel.

Pierre started talking again, a couple of phrases, then silence once more. Fanti became aware that Pierre had hooked a question mark into the Celtic fantasies in which he was about to lose himself.

'I'm sorry?'

'I said, since you agree, and since you're even encouraging me to leave, will you lend me the 30,000 lire? I'll pay you back little by little, but I will pay you back.'

'I've encouraged you to do what?' Fanti thought he must have been speaking out loud, and perhaps Pierre had misunderstood his stream of consciousness, imagining that it was somehow connected to what he was saying himself.

'What do you mean, do what, *professore*? Set off for Yugoslavia in search of my father! You were just saying it was important to take risks, to go, to free yourself, break through the mist to reach your destination. I've sold my bicycle and my watch, I have 10,000 lire set aside. All I need is 30,000 to get across the Adriatic. But have you heard a word I've said to you?'

Fanti sighed, took off his bowler and smoothed his hair. Having called back the pigeons and lowered the shutter of the cage, he turned towards Pierre, with his hands in his pockets and a thoughtful expression on his face. 'Be patient, my boy. You'll have to tell me everything all over again. Let's go down to the house. Fancy a cup of tea?'

Chapter 33

Information always reached the Ministry first hand. The Committee had inherited the entire network.

A few years previously the moles working inside the British secret service had been discovered. According to rumours circulating in the corridors some of them had 'gone back' to Moscow, and the ones who had remained 'outside' had taken precautions, scaling down their own activity. Be that as it may, there were people around who had worked behind enemy lines, renouncing the love of their homeland to serve the cause of socialism. No one apart from the big bosses knew who they were, but Zhulianov felt great admiration for them. Now he too had his part to play in the intricate machinery.

The material he had in his hand came from London. Ten typed pages containing the information he needed.

It wasn't a question of kidnapping an enemy agent, a scientist who wanted to change flags or an agent who had to come back. Nothing of the kind.

The subject of the kidnapping was one of the most famous actors in America, actually a naturalised Englishman. Zhulianov remembered all the films he had been shown to perfect his accent: dozens, hundreds of films in which the American bourgeoisie displayed its own decadence and moral corruption for all to see without the slightest concern for modesty. Family dramas, betrayals, comedies of error, ostentatious luxury. And the dreary war films in which the Russians never even made an appearance. As though they hadn't been the first to stop Hitler, while the Anglo-Americans were playing at naval battles. The first to enter Berlin, when the Allies were still wading through the Rhineland bogs.

But it wasn't the fault of the actors. Parts in the big American propaganda machine, luxury employees who had bartered their dignity for wealth and glory. In the Soviet Union, the cinema was at the service of the people. In the capitalist countries the people were at the service of the cinema. Millions of workers, wits so dulled by Hollywood comedies that they forget their exploited status and rush to spend their money at the box office.

'Cary Grant' was on top of the documents, along with his physical description and distinguishing features. The directives were clear: Zhulianov would be in command of a four-man squad of well-trained and well-motivated soldiers. His task was to identify the target, intercept him and transfer him on to a Bulgarian merchant vessel en route for Malta. The hostage was then to remain on board the ship for seventy-two hours. After that, he would be released outside the headquarters of Military Intelligence in La Valletta.

Andrei Zhulianov thought of his old mother, in Kiev. She would be proud of him.

Moscow, the Lubyanka

The general looked out of the big window. Cars drove across the square in front of the building, under a fine rain.

This mission was a new step forward in his career. Khrushchev's trust was well placed. He was beginning to understand how the squat Ukrainian's mind worked: many things were changing, and Soviet foreign policy would never be the same again. They needed practical, trusted people. People like him. He allowed himself a faint smile as he watched the headlights shining in the Moscow evening.

Khrushchev wanted to renew relations with Tito. Yugoslavia was a strategic country, the heart of the Balkans, in the lee of the West, with hundreds of miles of coastline. But Khrushchev also knew that Tito was ready to go with the best bidder. It was important to make him understand where Yugoslavia's best interests lay: with the Soviet Union and its brother nations. The fall of Djilas, even more critical of Moscow than Tito, seemed to be a first sign of rapprochement. They needed to press the point.

Having read the report from London, General Serov had immediately set about informing the Secretary and the Prime Minister. MI6 was bothering one of the greatest actors in Hollywood just to persuade that whore Tito to become a friend of the West. They were turning themselves into movie impresarios: a film about the Yugoslavian liberation struggle! They would sell their mothers' arses just to stay a step ahead of the USSR. But they hadn't reckoned with Nikita Khrushchev, the bear dressed as a lamb. And they hadn't reckoned with General Ivan Serov.

The disappearance of Cary Grant will be like an earthquake for the Western secret services, and it will discredit the Yugoslavians, turning their idyll into a nightmare. Imagine their faces when they lose contact with their 'artistic ambassador'. Accusations being thrown around, insults, people with their heads in their hands, even threats of war. Seventy-two hours of pure panic. Who knows what they'll come up with? Maybe nothing: Cary Grant's ambassadorial work is a secret operation, those oafs won't be able to justify themselves. Then, all of a sudden, Mr Grant reappears safe and sound in Malta with the best wishes of the KGB. A strong and clear message in the ears of MI6 and the CIA. Don't try anything like that again.

Marshal Tito's only option will be to force his best smile and shake hands with Nikita Khrushchev.

Let the enemy advance, then strike him mercilessly until he is destroyed.

Chapter 34

Dear Nicola,
    I've left. I'm going to Yugoslavia in search of dad.
    I know what you think. Dad has made his life, and we've got to make ours. It isn't because he went over to Tito that you can't forgive him. You think badly of him for abandoning us here when I was thirteen and you were twenty-one. You know as well as anyone that if he comes back he's going to face a severe punishment. And then you don't like the fact that he's remarried either, you only told him once but I can still remember, 'It's as though our mother had died again.'
    And I don't like the fact that dad stayed there any more than you do. If he's remarried it's up to him, it's nothing to do with us, and I also think that if he hasn't come back, then this guy Tito can't be a criminal, because our father wasn't a criminal. I miss him, even though I've only seen him once in thirteen years. In fact that more than anything is why I miss him. We used to listen to the bulletins from the Slavic front together, on Aunt Iolanda's broken radio. Then one day you left as well, and I stayed with our aunt, both of us waiting. I want to find him, I'm doing it for you as well, because I know that deep down you're worried too.
    Don't worry. I have the documents, I've already got the border stamp, I'm in with people who know what they're doing. If everything goes well I'll be home in a month.
    Your brother,
    Pierre

Chapter 35

The shack was lit by an oil lamp. Pierre didn't mind the smell, which reminded him of petrol pumps, mingling with the saltiness that impregnated the pine forest.

He had had to come on foot, and he hoped it was the right place, because his legs hurt and the evening was cold.

City life had made him unused to the sounds of the countryside. He found himself given a start by the rustle of animals scratching about beneath the maritime pines. But there was also the tension.

The canal flowed blackly, placidly. Fishing nets hung from the bottoms of the pile-built huts, looking like flabby bellies. He pulled the clean shirt out of his travelling bag and wrapped it around his head so as not to be eaten alive by the mosquitoes, which went on buzzing around in search of an opening.

His footsteps echoed on the gravel path.

The door opened with a creak, and a dark figure appeared, barely lit by the lantern. It seemed to be leaning on a stick.

'Who is it?'

The tone wasn't friendly.

Pierre stopped. 'Friend.'

'What do you want?'

'I'm looking for Robinson.'

'Come under the light.'

Pierre pulled the shirt away from his face, and stepped in front of the door.

The man was small and thin, with black eyes and a hooked nose. He wore a tattered felt hat and a hunting jacket. He was leaning not on a stick, but a rifle.

'Are you the bloke from Bologna?'

Pierre tried in vain to wave away the cloud of mosquitoes that was attacking him. 'Yes, that's me. Are you Robinson?'

The man gave a little grunt, which Pierre interpreted as agreement. 'I've been waiting for you for two hours.'

'I didn't think it was so far. I've had to come from Ravenna on foot.'

Pierre noticed that the man was entirely immune to the mosquitoes. 'How come they don't bite you?'

The man didn't move. 'Bitter valley blood. They like sweet city blood.'

'Can I come in? They're eating me alive.'

Robinson studied him for a moment longer, then nodded to him to follow him in.

Inside it was bare: camp bed, table, three chairs, cauldron on the fire and rolls of fishing nets in the corners.

'The money.'

'Ettore didn't tell me I'd have to pay you first.'

The expression on his face didn't change. 'You're the one who wants to go.'

Pierre thought he didn't have much choice. He opened his wallet and handed him the money.

When he had finished counting it out, the smuggler slipped it into a pocket in his jacket.

Pierre felt cramps in his stomach. 'Haven't you got anything to eat? I'm starving to death.'

The man looked at him as if he'd said something ridiculous, then handed him a plate that looked very much like the only one available.

Pierre served himself from the cauldron: bits of something dark and indefinable.

'What is it?'

'Eel.'

It tasted of brackish water, but he was too hungry not to eat.

Robinson started fussing about with some petrol cans, completely ignoring him.

When Pierre had finished his eel, Robinson picked up the plate and said, 'We leave in two hours.' He pointed to the camp bed. 'You can sleep a bit. Tonight we dance.'

'How long is it going to take?'

He shrugged. 'We'll get there tomorrow evening. It's dangerous by day. If we get there before, we'll wait till it's dark.'

The longest sentence he had come out with. He looked annoyed at having used so many words.

Pierre lay down on the camp bed and felt his leg muscles stretching until he groaned. But he knew he wouldn't sleep, the emotion was too intense, his heart was thumping.

His father had crossed this sea as well, many years before, never to return. He was going in search of him.

He was agitated but satisfied. He was risking the most hazardous enterprise of his whole life. Leaving the country, going to an unknown place, among unknown people, but with a goal. Whatever happened, this journey would mean something. Fanti said that journeys meant change. And if he said that, when he was so well travelled . . .

He felt different, amidst the pine trees and the mosquitoes, and with this grim-looking character Robinson. Ettore had told him he smuggled between Italy and Yugoslavia. Smuggling what? Cigarettes? Petrol? Maybe he was heading into difficulties that he wouldn't be able to get out of. It didn't matter. He felt alive, for the first time away from the bar, the dance hall, the life assigned to him.

He had said goodbye to everything he loved. Angela had told him not to go. 'You're crazy, Pierre, if they put you in prison there, you'll never get out.' She had reminded him about Odoacre's conference, a fortnight all to themselves, at the end of April. 'Now of all times you had to decide to leave!' But she hadn't been able to give him a real reason to stay. She couldn't, when she was so stuck in her own life: her husband on the one side, her brother on the other. And Pierre in the middle. 'I love you, Pierre. I will always love you. Even when you decided to stop seeing me.' To stop seeing her. He was in love with Angela. Every time he had thought of putting an end to the relationship, his stomach had tightened and he hadn't been able to do anything.

'You men deceive yourselves, and for your self-deceptions you destroy everything. I can't leave my husband, you know. Love is a luxury for the rich. And you and I aren't rich, Pierre.' But perhaps everything would change now. After his journey, he would be a different person. Stronger. Perhaps he would also find the strength

to say goodbye to Angela. As he tossed and turned on the filthy
camp bed, Pierre thought that this journey would give him the
strength to clear the situation.

It wasn't flight. It was like the *Odyssey* that his father had told him
as a child, on those long evenings by the fire. His father was Ulysses,
he had left all those years before to fight a war that wasn't his, and
had never come back. And Pierre was Telemachus. That was how
the story began: a son setting off in search of the father he had never
known.

Someone shook him and he started awake.

'It's time to go.'

Robinson had two guns on shoulder belts: the rifle and a
Thompson submachine-gun, like the one that Nicola had in the
cellar.

Pierre leapt out of bed and picked up his case.

Robinson picked up one of the two cans. 'You take the other one.'

It was heavy, but he pretended it wasn't. He followed the man out
of the shack.

They walked in the dense darkness, along a path that ran through
the pine forest.

When Robinson stopped, Pierre nearly crashed into him with all
his weight. He kept his balance, and managed to glimpse a little inlet
in the canal, where it widened to reach the sea.

The boat was smaller than he had expected. He was frightened,
and about to confess that he couldn't swim. He held his tongue. It
wasn't the moment to show that he was afraid. They climbed aboard.
As Robinson started the engine, Pierre looked towards the sea. The
night showed him nothing.

Chapter 36

Nothing.

Spasms shook his stomach and his throat, but by now there was nothing left to come out.

Robinson, sitting solidly at the stern, by the engine, didn't react; the spray licked at him as he bobbed with the rhythm of the waves, but he kept hold of the rudder. Every now and again he consulted the compass, then went back to staring straight ahead once more, as though he could see the route ahead of them.

Pierre wiped his mouth with the sleeve of his coat and thought that if he could get through this crossing, everything else would be a stroll in the park. He gritted his teeth and anchored himself more firmly in his seat.

He would have liked to speak, not to think about his nausea, but the boatman wasn't the right person.

He decided to try anyway, shouting over the noise of the wind. 'Why do they call you Robinson?'

Silence.

He thought he hadn't heard him, but when he was about to raise his voice, the reply arrived from stern: 'Because I look after myself, like Robinson Crusoe.'

The tone was less dry than usual. Perhaps the boredom of the journey was getting to Robinson as well.

Pierre decided to try again. 'Ettore told me you were a partisan. Were you in the 28th?'

'No. But I lent Bulow a hand.'

'Were you in the Battle of the Valleys?'

The reply came back sharply: 'I took them into the valleys.'

'Seriously? Did you get a medal?'

The wind carried away his reply.

'What?'

Robinson raised his voice. 'What would I want with a medal?'

Pierre didn't know what to add. He said, 'My brother was a partisan as well. Up by Imola, in the 36th. He got a silver medal.' Silence. 'Did you kill any Germans?'

Robinson raised his hand with four fingers raised. Talking made Pierre feel better, his nausea had subsided.

'And how was it?'

Silence again. For a moment Pierre thought he had asked the wrong question.

But the other man said, 'They killed my brother.'

'And did you shoot them with that?' He pointed to the Thompson gun wrapped in the tarpaulin on the bottom of the boat.

Robinson shook his head. He rummaged under his jacket, then something flashed between them, landing on the seat, just beside Pierre.

'With that,' Robinson said, running his thumb along his throat.

Pierre shivered and pulled the knife from the wood, feigning indifference: his stomach was tight, but not with nausea. One of the knives they use for gutting and cutting up fish.

Killing a man in cold blood. Once, as a child, he had seen a pig being slaughtered. It squealed like a human being, and it took five people to hold it still. The most impressive spectacle he had ever witnessed. Perhaps death was what distinguished him from men the age of Robinson and his brother: having had to kill, and seeing people die.

He wrapped himself tighter in his coat, and did his best to banish the image of those four Germans squealing like pigs while Robinson butchered them one after the other. He decided to concentrate on his own stomach.

'Do you see those lights?'

'Yes. Is it a village?'

Robinson nodded.

It was pitch-dark. Pierre thought that if there were rocks, the boat would shatter.

Eventually he glimpsed something. It was the coastline, less than a hundred metres away.

Robinson switched off the engine and started to row.

When the lights of the village were far enough away, he switched the engine back on and guided the boat in a southerly direction.

The engine was turned off again. Pierre glimpsed a brighter strip along the coast, perhaps a beach. A light was shining from the shore, it flashed twice.

Robinson replied with the electric torch, after which he fixed the oars in the rowlocks and started rowing with all his strength, until the keel scraped on to the sand.

It was a little beach trapped among the rocks. The mountain wall descended steeply to the sea. Pierre felt absolutely tiny.

He put on the rubber boots that Robinson handed him, and jumped out, drenched to the marrow.

Three men joined him to carry the boat on to dry land.

When they were all on terra firma, Robinson swapped a few jokes with the smugglers. Pierre couldn't understand a word. Then he saw that they were opening a case and illuminating the contents with their torches: cigarettes. Sticks of every brand.

As they loaded the cases on to the boat, Robinson whispered, 'Give them a hand.'

Pierre picked up one of the boxes, helped by one of the Slavs, and loaded it on board.

When he had finished, Robinson threw Pierre's bag on to the dry sand. He passed an envelope to the Slavs, then took the lid off the can of petrol and refilled the tank.

One of the men offered Pierre a cigarette, and he accepted it. A very strong flavour of black tobacco.

Robinson's voice forced him to turn around. 'These men will take you up to the top, to the village. They'll understand if you talk to them in Italian. I'll be back in exactly a month. If you don't see me coming, find a spot around here, and come to this beach for three nights. If I haven't come by the third night, then go away and come back the following month on the same date.'

'But I haven't enough money to stay here for two months!'

Robinson shrugged. 'You haven't given me enough money to risk my skin.'

Pierre didn't know what to reply. He was there now, take it or leave it.

He helped push the boat back into the water.

He saw Robinson rowing towards the open sea. The night gradually swallowed him up, like an ink stain.

Chapter 37

The port of Naples was a vast marina for military vessels. Nato Command for Southern Europe: all orders for the Allied bases from Portugal to Turkey came from here.

Zollo watched the city moving away beyond the parapet. Luciano had been right: choose this city as a retreat. Who would ever have imagined that the biggest drug-trafficking operation in the world would have its nerve centre right in the backyard of the Allied armed forces? And the great thing about it was that not a single gram of heroin came out of Naples. At least not wholesale. It came from the Middle East through the Balkans. From there it reached Sicily and Marseilles, where it was refined and cut for the first time. Then New York, America.

Luciano, the brains, the big *capo*, touched nothing, saw nothing. Every so often he collected his takings and received emissaries from the American families. The racecourse served as a public relations office, and provided him with an army of freelance office boys.

And then there was the betting and the cigarettes, but that was all just small change. A top-up. Luciano sold electric appliances.

A long way from their days in New York, when a spruce dandy, with a little dog in his lap, rained sweets on the poor children of the district. The days of rackets and brothels: whores to suit every pocket, from the poor man to the Wall Street agent. 'Lucky', who had, in a single night, eliminated the competition with bursts of machine-gun fire. But transforming exile into one of the most profitable businesses in the world had been a masterstroke. Zollo couldn't help admiring the old snake.

Turning bad luck into profit. Resurgence. That was the example to follow.

The ferry manoeuvred its way between torpedo boats, destroyers and battleships, heading for the open sea.

The trip to Sicily would be instructive, even if it promised to be a trip to the zoo. The island where his parents were born was inhabited by cavemen, but it had the most efficient refineries in the market. He was going to inspect them. Their journey passed through Yugoslavia: bought goods. Finally Marseilles.

The plan was starting to take shape. Luciano had assigned him the task of checking the Sicilian bases, and overseeing the buying and selling of the heroin: a sign of absolute trust. Zollo was counting on this for a hefty pension.

As he prepared to go undercover he ran through the details of the plan once more. A matter of time and quantity. On his previous trips he had already set aside twelve kilos. He had found a safe hiding place for them. Even if someone discovered them, they could never be traced back to him. Otherwise, Luciano would eat him for lunch. The opportunity had presented itself by chance: no one would find the packets where he had put them. A meticulous skim: about one kilo every fifty. He had done it well. One more job, the last one, the most consistent, and he would be guaranteed whisky, sun and women until the end of his days. He would leave them all standing, and disappear for good, bye-bye everyone, from Steve Cement. He had also thought of faking his own death: a terrible car crash. There was no shortage of places to vanish into.

He had contacted the buyers, in France. This last trip took it to fifteen kilos. A skilful hand would double that and turn them into a mountain of money.

But who would ever suspect him? Steve, general dogsbody to Don Salvatore Lucania, aka Lucky Luciano. Impeccable Steve. Clean-Work Steve. No, no one imagines anyone cheating Luciano while standing elbow to elbow with him, right in the lion's mouth. If they had had an inkling, the blame would have fallen on those swinish Slavs.

He came downstairs and walked into the restaurant. As the barman poured him a whisky, he contemplated his image in the mirror behind the bar. His eyes were black holes in his pale face: his face said that no one would stop him. He raised his glass and, all alone, toasted a better future.

Chapter 38

Gramovac. A miniature village in the hills behind Split, eight kilometres from the capital, the road that Vittorio Capponi cycled down each morning. Pierre had walked it on foot, an hour and a half through pastures, vines and twisted olive trees.

Just as his father had described it to him. Poor but dignified houses, twenty at most, red-tiled roofs and dark olive green window frames. The church, tiny, in bright stone, a simple arch supporting two bells on top of the façade. On the other side of the little square the only sign of life, two old men sitting by their front doors. Voices roll faintly up the street. The café looks like someone's house, a cross between a bar and a village shop. Above the door, words painted in red.

Pierre would have liked to roll up under the oak tree that shaded the square and sleep for hours, after his sleepless night, exhausted from his journey, his stomach still drunk from the waves. But the tension wouldn't leave him in peace.

Now the old men were watching him. A man came to the door, adjusting his beret. With the right music and a couple of six-guns, he could have been in *High Noon*. But noon had passed some time ago, and the only reason for Pierre's hesitation was a linguistic one: Professor Fanti had assured him that everyone in Split understood Italian, and yet it seemed strange to address these people as though they were strolling along the Portico del Pavaglione. Not that there was anything strange about them: shirt, trousers, shoes, all normal enough, perhaps tailored in a way that would raise a smile in Bologna. And yet the sky seemed to have a different blue, and unimaginable smells seemed to carry on the air.

'Hi,' he said finally, after crossing the little square. 'I'm looking for Vittorio Capponi . . .'

The wrinkles deepened on the man's tanned face. Eyebrows, head, shoulders and arms: his whole body said no, the name meant nothing . . .

'What did you say?' asked one of the old men.

Pierre smiled, Fanti had not been mistaken. 'I'm looking for Vittorio Capponi, where is he?'

'Cappone? I don't know, don't know him.'

Don't know? Twenty houses in the village and they don't all know each other? The old man spoke Italian, but he must have been a bit befuddled. Or perhaps he came from a nearby hamlet where there wasn't even a bar, and he had come here for a chat and he'd never seen Vittorio Capponi; his father worked in Split, he had never set foot in the bar. Pierre rummaged in his jacket and pulled out the piece of paper with the address.

'Where? *Dove?* Where?' he asked tapping the paper with his hand and holding it out to the man with the beret. The man beckoned him to follow and set off under the beating sun. A herd of sheep cut across the main street, a fast white torrent driven by the cries of two grimy small boys, and slipped into a narrow side street. The man with the beret stopped at the next junction and pointed to a house halfway down the alley. Pierre thanked him with his voice and his eyes, and the man muttered something in reply, plunged his hands into his pockets and turned back towards the café.

There was no one home. Nothing strange about that: everyone would be at work at that time of day. Nothing to worry about, he would wait, he needed to sit down, just for a moment, even on the ground or on a rock, as long as it was fixed and motionless.

He leaned his back against the wall, his knees between his arms. After a few minutes his chin bounced on to his chest a few times, his eyes closed and his brain switched off.

He hadn't eaten since the previous evening. The Slav smugglers had changed him a little money, but Pierre had only been able to think about the quickest way of getting there, walking, then a few kilometres by coach, then walking again. He still had some money, about 2000 or 3000 lire, and his stomach was protesting, no longer distracted by vomit, nausea and tension. They were bound to sell something edible at the café, but he preferred to stay put now that he was there, outside his father's house. He would rather wait.

Before long he would see him appearing at the crossroads riding his bicycle.

An hour passed, perhaps more. A sunset dense with clouds and mist. The shadow at the top of the alley might be someone. No bicycle, but that was a negligible detail. Pierre leapt to his feet, more because he couldn't stop himself than in order to attract attention. The man had a big knapsack over his shoulder, and was holding a bunch of keys. He glanced fleetingly at the stranger, walked past him and stopped at the next door along.

'Excuse me.' Pierre took a couple of steps towards him. 'Excuse me. Do you speak Italian? I'm looking for Vittorio Capponi, he lives here, do you know him?'

'Caponi? No, I don't know, sorry,' the man replied, strangely embarrassed. 'I not here long, not know much.'

Pierre pointed to the house with both hands. 'Here, his house, Vittorio Capponi.'

'No, sorry, don't know.' The man with the knapsack pushed open the door and slipped inside. Pierre didn't get his foot in the door quickly enough, and it closed. He knocked two or three times. 'Excuse me, just one moment.'

In the faint light of the only street lamp, three faces appeared at various windows. One of them withdrew the moment Pierre glanced up. The others stayed there.

'Excuse me, do you know where Vittorio Capponi is? Where is Vittorio Capponi? Does he live here?'

The heads swayed in unison, like puppets in an animated clock. Then the second face disappeared as well. Pierre turned to the only one remaining, a woman.

'Vittorio –'

He didn't get to finish before the woman shook her head again.

Pierre felt rage welling up inside him. He turned around all of a sudden and banged a fist against the door. He cursed. He went and sat down disconsolately once again, but he couldn't sit still, he started pacing back and forth like an animal in a cage. His knuckles were bleeding. Every minute weighed an absolute ton.

Darkness fell, along with cold and another shadow. This one too just glanced at him and kept on towards the end of the street.

Pierre caught up with the shadow and touched it on the shoulder. The woman turned around in alarm.

'Excuse me, miss, I'm looking for Vittorio Capponi, does he live her?'

'Not here,' replied the woman. 'He gone.'

'Gone? Where to?'

The woman started walking again at a brisk pace. 'Where I don't know. He gone.'

'When? When did he leave?' Pierre noticed that he was holding her by one arm and relaxed his grip.

'Two or three months.'

'Why, what happened?'

The woman stopped and crossed her hands over her chest. 'I'm sorry, I don't know that.' Then she started walking again, and Pierre gave up following her.

He went back towards the house, while a deluge of thoughts swept through his mind.

Gone.

Pierre tried to put his ideas in order, to organise his information, think about what was to be done. He crouched down again to calm himself, but it didn't work for long. Then he was on his feet again, pacing back and forth in front of the door, his bones frozen and his head in flames. A letter marked 'return to sender', his departure from the village, the eloquent silence of his neighbours. Two months' absence. January: the expulsion of Djilas from the League of Yugoslavian communists. It all added up. But there had been no sign of Vittorio Capponi since long before that, since March, and even then there had been just two lines on the death of Milena, and then nothing. What had happened? Only one way to find out: stay in Gramovac, keep on asking, pick up a scrap here and there, assemble the mosaic, find a gap in the wall of silence by continuing to ask, plead, even threaten. He could try to get into the house, force the door or a window, try to find something that would help him understand, a scribbled address, any kind of clue. But he had to be on his guard. If his father had problems with the police, he would have to be very careful. He couldn't overdo it, make an awful scene, sit down outside the door for too long or frighten anyone. An Italian with a false passport and a counterfeit border stamp didn't want to go attracting attention to himself.

He had done enough of that already that evening. Trying to get into the house straight away wasn't the best idea in the world. Too many eyes watching him from the windows. He thought he could feel them. He decided to make himself comfortable there and try to sleep. The last time he had slept had been thirty-six hours ago, and his exhaustion didn't help. He sat down, stretched his legs out on the pavement, his case between his back and the wall. He tried to breathe more and more deeply.

'What is it?'

Eyes suddenly wide open, mouth too, as he was woken by a hand tugging his jacket.

'I am friend of Vittorio Capponi. Who are you?' whispered the white-haired shadow.

Pierre ran his hands over his face a few times, as though washing it with imaginary water. 'I'm his son,' he said finally.

'His son? Really? Are you Nicola?'

'No, I'm Robespierre.

'Ah, Robespierre, of course. Finc, Robespierre. It big pleasure to meet you. Come, come.'

Sheltering Pierre under his coat, he all but dragged him towards the shaft of light that crossed the cobblestones a few metres away.

'Come in, quick. This my house. Come in.' He pointed him to a chair and made him sit down. A faint light fell on the table. The room was small, in semi-darkness: a chest of drawers, a washbasin, a gas cylinder, a bed.

'Here. Take it.' The man put a glass on the table and slid it towards Pierre. 'Drink, is good, against the cold.'

It was a strong and rather bitter grappa. Pierre downed it in one and the glass was refilled. The man was older than his father, he must have been over sixty. When he turned to pour himself some grappa, Pierre saw that half of his face was disfigured by a burn.

'Souvenir of the war,' he said, brushing his scars with his fingers. 'Bad memory. I'm Darko, I know your father very well, we great friends, look.'

He opened a box behind him, and after rummaging about in it for a moment, he took out a photograph. The man without a scar, standing in front of the carcass of a deer with his arm around Darko, was his father.

'Can you tell me where he is, why he left?' asked Pierre, to choke down the lump in his throat.

'He had to go away. Problems with political idea, you know?'

'Yes, yes, I understand, but where is he now? How would I find him?'

'Calm now, Robespierre, I'll explain everything. He now in Šipan, near Dubrovnik, 200 kilometres from here.'

'And how do I get there? Is there a coach, a ferry?'

Darko poured the third glass, then he turned back and a piece of cheese, half a loaf of bread and some black olives appeared on the table.

'*Uzmi jedi, moj sine.* Eat!'

Pierre didn't need to be asked twice. He stretched his hands out to the bread and repeated the question. 'How can I get to Šipan?'

'Wait, Robespierre, let me think.' He sipped his grappa calmly, as though hoping to draw inspiration from it. 'Listen. Tonight you can sleep here, ok? Tomorrow morning, very early, I must go down to Split, with my cart. If we're very careful, I can take you with me. At the market in Split we ask friend with lorry if he's going to Dubrovnik, this much better than coach. Then from Dubrovnik you ask someone, some fisherman, to take you Šipan, because no ferry, understand?'

'I understand,' said Pierre and his stomach rebelled at the mere thought of another crossing. 'Thanks, Darko. I don't know how to thank you. Everyone else here was afraid to speak. You weren't. How come?'

'If someone was looking for me, Vittorio he do the same. I saw you asking and I knew you were friend. Then when you said the son, then I had to help.'

Pierre ate some cheese and a few olives. He wondered if Šipan would be his destination, or just another stage on the journey. He devoured every last crumb on his plate and asked again, 'What else can you tell me about my father? I've had no news of him for months now. He hasn't written for a year, and my last letter was sent back to me.'

Darko got up again, disappeared out the back door and reappeared a moment later with a wooden box in his hands. He opened it on the table and pulled out some newspaper cuttings, which he gradually spread out in front of Pierre. He picked up the last one. It was written in Italian. Signed by Vittorio Capponi.

'Article by your father for Italian newspaper in Zadar. These two also by your father, for other newspaper, in Slavonic language. And these others, they are by Milovan Djilas, for the *Borba*, the Party newspaper. You know Milovan Djilas?'

Pierre looked up from the article. 'I know he's a dissident, that he was expelled by Tito.'

'That's right,' Darko replied. 'At October last year he start writing these articles. At December elected as President of Skupština. Two weeks later, trial begin against him. Not expelled, that is Stalin's thing and Tito does not want, but forced into self-criticism.'

'And what about my father?'

'Your father write that Djilas says many true things. Others not, but many are right. Then towards the end of January they come and take him to Split. No trial, for him: they say he expelled, enough of his work, he must not express his ideas any more, better he go away, far away, where no one know him. They treat Djilas better than anyone less important. Djilas too famous, must be careful. Luckily he does self-criticism, otherwise much worse for his comrades.'

Pierre read a few more lines. An Italian translation of Djilas's article 'New Contents', with the addition of a brief commentary. He reached the end, while Darko put another piece of cheese and some more bread on the table.

'What happened then?' Pierre asked when he had finished reading.

'Afterwards? Your father stayed on his own, people stopped talking to him. No work, and in Split no one wanted him. He was afraid they take him to Goli Otok, the prison camp for friends of Stalin. One day he tell me he want to die. Then instead he leave. Fishes, looks after sheep, and can live on partisan pension. But I don't know much, he phoned one time, then nothing.'

Darko bowed his head and ran the back of his hand over an eye. 'He was my only friend,' he said in a breath. He tried to go on, but all that came out was, 'Sorry.'

Then he picked up the articles, quickly closed the box and disappeared once more through the back door.

Chapter 39

Naples, 17 April

It was a relief to walk along the road, in the sunlight, amidst the hubbub of the people, and the shoving and the shouts. After three months in jail, Salvatore Pagano, known as Kociss, only wanted to run. Three months they'd kept him in there! In that dirty, disgusting prison, full of stinking murderers, and Commissioner Cinquegrana firing questions at him, and the television, and the money, and Don Luciano, and this one and that one. Now, finally, he breathed, he looked at the sky, and the women. He thought about all the things he would do. Three months of recuperation. He had the money, they hadn't been able to take it from him. Honest earnings. With that money he would get a present for Lisetta, a nice present, and at that point she would be sure to let him have what he was after, on a silver platter. Because he hadn't given her name to the commissioner, no, he hadn't done that. No names. The policeman had yet to be born who would make a fool of Kociss. But he had got scared in that nick. Pretty damned scared. It was as if they wanted him to tell them everything, as if he was a big player, as if he knew things. Absolute silence. He'd given them nothing. What would the commissioner think if he knew the truth? Neither nuns nor charity that night . . . Oh heavens, yes, he'd been giving presents to the little orphans, then he had taken his bike, the one with the platform on the front and gone to see Lisetta. What a woman she was!

He stopped by the window of a clothes shop, and saw a beautiful red dress. She'd look like a dream in that. He saw his reflection in the window: he could do with some new clothes too, what with these rags he was wearing . . . But that could come later. First he had to sort out the most important thing, otherwise he would have put in all that effort for nothing. But the thought of Lisetta wouldn't leave him alone for a moment, he wanted to stop someone in the street and tell him what she was like, and then if he got annoyed, just hand him one of Don Luciano's banknotes, easy, now, easy, my friend, I'll pay you for your time.

Ah, Lisetta. He really did like her. Apart from her job, but what are you going to do, no one's perfect. When she asked him a favour, with those green eyes of hers and all that hair, and her mouth, and so on, he couldn't say no. Like that evening when it was cold, and she had asked him to come with her to the American base. And then – once he'd left the orphans – take the bike and go and pick up Lisetta. And pedal, with all that perfume and her hair flapping in your face, pedal away, nearly killing yourself as you take a bend, and her skirt sliding up, and her leg dangling from the platform. It was really driving him out of his mind. Nothing to be done. Lisetta was Lisetta.

He crossed the street without looking and someone beeped his horn. Pagano replied with a loud and liberating insult and strode on.

That evening he had worked out where she was going. To make love with that American officer. She only had to bat her eyelids and he started chucking the money around like he was King of Catalonia. He was due something too, for the journey and the effort. But it was his own fault if he hadn't had his compensation. Because once he had got to the base, with all that cycling and the perfume and the legs and the hair, and what Lisetta was going to do, he had said to himself, 'Kociss, you've got to have some kind of payment for all your effort, and for your broken heart as well.' And while he was thinking those things, the payment had appeared before his very eyes, as though the Madonna had been reading his mind.

Great brute of a thing it was, would it fit on the platform? Wouldn't it bring him and the bike crashing to the ground? And would the tarpaulin be big enough to hide it? And what if the Military Police showed up? Would they shoot him? Don't be crazy. He had to hurry. Someone might come. They would kick seven shades of shite out of him.

In the end he had been encouraged by a man dressed as a general, pinned to the wall in a photograph, right in front of him. He was smiling. And he was giving the thumbs up, as if to say, 'Ok, son, go ahead!' He was right, he would have to be paid. He had taken it. For Lisetta.

The stink of shit was still the same. But he was happy to smell it. The stables of Agnano were his home. He heard the voices of the stable boys greeting him, 'Kociss, you're back!' 'Where've you been?' 'What you been up to?' But he didn't really hear them. He waved a greeting, but his head and his legs were heading straight to the back of the stables, to the storeroom where the harnesses were kept. One thought in his head: compensation. He walked through the building and came out by a little door at the back, finding himself in a service passage. The shed was covered by climbing plants, and the door could hardly be seen. He found it closed with a steel padlock, and his heart started thumping. He appealed to a few saints for assistance. Before there had just been a rusty chain. The thought of someone cheating him of his compensation put him in a cold sweat. He started walking around the construction in search of a way in: who the fuck had been able to get in there? There was nothing inside but junk and cobwebs!

Nothing, not even a little window. There was nothing for it but to crack open the padlock. He went back to the store, took a pickaxe and a hammer and went and positioned himself by the shed door. A glance around: no one. Off we go. Four dry, precise blows. It fell to the ground with a thud.

He went in, letting in enough light to make out the things inside.

He saw the pile of old saddles, still intact. He felt as though he had been reborn. He dismantled the mountain of leather. Someone had moved the tarpaulin. But underneath, thanks be to the Madonna, the television was still there. Right where he had left it.

He just had to clean it up a bit and it would be as good as new.

He would make money with this. Real money. Bollocks to Cinquegrana and the American army.

Transporting it was a bit of an enterprise. Who knows what had happened to the bike. A rusty old boneshaker, which had transported tons of shit in the past, was the only means of transport at his disposal. He leaned against the tarpaulin and gripped the television. It was one hell of a weight! It seemed to weigh twice as much as it had when he had taken it. Jail had softened him, what a pain in the arse. He had had it up to there already. But his compensation had arrived. Now he faced the final torture: the miles he would be taking the great brute of a thing, all the way to Gigino on the Vico Vasto.

Chapter 40

In the early afternoon mist, Pierre spotted a dark line on the horizon.

He pointed and said, 'Šipan?'

The man looked up from the tangle of his fishing net and nodded.

That morning, Darko had woken him while it was still dark. A cup of milk and honey sat steaming on the table. Pierre had washed away his sleep in the cold water of the basin and hurried to get dressed.

The cargo was already on board, covered with an old military cloth. Cheese, to judge by the smell.

The motion of the truck had rocked Pierre to sleep. Once they reached Split, Darko had woken him again.

The journey had taken less than an hour.

Pierre narrowed his eyes and looked again. The reflection of the sun on the water was dazzling. He was sorry he had never learned to swim, because the island looked so close. But perhaps that was just an illusion.

He leaned towards the fisherman and touched his shoulder. 'Do you speak Italian?'

The man's head rocked to left and right. He pushed out his chest and pointed to someone sitting on the wharf a little way off.

The lorry driver's name was Stjepan, and he was going to Mostar with a cargo of fish. The turn-off for Mostar was on the coast road, ninety kilometres north of Dubrovnik.

Darko had suggested the alternative: 'You wait till tomorrow and go with Milos, no problem for him, he has to get to Albania, or else set off now with Stjepan, then find someone else.'

Pierre didn't want to wait: he had hugged Darko and climbed aboard the lorry.

Over the next half-hour he had not taken his eyes away from the window. The road ran parallel to the coast, through an imposing chain of mountains high above the sea, and the barely discernible line of an island. He had never seen anything like it.

'You come from Italy?' Stjepan's voice had broken the silence. He spoke Italian more or less as Darko did. 'Learned in war,' he had added.

There had been twelve Italian deserters fighting in his partisan battalion.

'Vittorio Capponi?' A pause to ransack his memory. 'No, I don't remember.'

The second fisherman was fiddling with a net as well.

'Do you speak Italian?' Pierre asked again.

The reply was more than affirmative.

'I *am* Italian, from Rovigno.'

Pierre smiled. 'Oh, good. I'm from Bologna, my name's Robespierre. I'm looking for a passage to the island of Šipan.'

'Are you a tourist?' His expression was diffident.

'No, I've got to meet a relative I haven't seen for years.'

He didn't want to be too explicit about his father, but a generic 'distant relative' tended to put people at their ease.

The fisherman studied him for a moment, then struggled to his feet, putting one hand on the ground. 'Come on. I'll take you to someone who lives there.'

The place was like the valleys of Comacchio, but wilder and dense with trees. A maze of water and land. Lakes, canals, hidden inlets. A stagnant bog and a river.

They always had the sea ahead of them, and yet another island breaking up the horizon.

'*Neretva rijeka*, the Neretva river,' Stjepan had said in reply to Pierre's unspoken question. 'I was born nearby, in the village of Bacina. You know, during the war, here, there were fascists. They want to put my family in the *Lager*. An Italian save us.'

Pierre hadn't had to ask twice, and soon he was hearing stories about the man they called 'Diavolo' – the Devil – the army in Abyssinia, Albania, Greece and finally Bacina, the Italian army base.

'He helped everyone. He spied for our partisans. He warned you when they come to put you in the *Lager*. He carried bombs and guns.'

In the long run, he had been discovered and imprisoned. Then Stjepan and some others had got the guards drunk, and he had escaped barefoot, his wrists tied together, joining the rebels the following morning.

'*Smrt fašismu . . . Sloboda narodu!*' the lorry driver had concluded, pulling up to the right.

The road branched. The signposts said Dubrovnik 94, Mostar 57, Sarajevo 193.

The journey had taken a few hours.

The two men muttered something to each other.

The Istrian said, 'Frane's leaving at eight for Šipanska Luka. He can take you. You have money?'

Pierre rummaged in his bag. 'Not much,' he replied, and took out the roll of notes, still intact from the day before.

'Half of that will be fine,' commented the Istrian.

'About 1,000 lire?'

'Fine.'

An hour passed. Pierre had started walking.

The lorries were in a hurry, they showed no sign of wanting to stop, and three out of five were taking the road for Mostar. Only two cars had passed, one a police car, and fortunately Pierre had noticed in time, had lowered his arms and sat on the roadside looking uninterested. No sign of a motorcycle. Bicycles passed by, laden like donkeys, full shopping baskets hanging from the handlebars, and often with a passenger sitting sideways on the crossbar. Some people travelled on foot.

Walking, Pierre covered five or six kilometres an hour. He had calculated his speed years previously, when walking along the Via Emilia between Bologna and Imola. A bet that he had lost with the musketeers, and those thirty kilometres to pay as a forfeit. The rest of them drove along behind him in a friend's car, laughing their heads off at the new Zatopek.

In a few days, he might get as far as Dubrovnik. It would take at least two. The sun, having just emerged from the mountains, began to grow warm.

Pierre returned to the wharf at a quarter to eight. He had eaten and slept, lying in the meadow just outside the village.

Frane saw him and waved. He sorted out the last few tangles and hoisted the anchor. The blue-green fishing boat was ready to set sail.

Another two hours had passed, three lorries, two tractors and a cart driven by some bastard who wouldn't stop. Pierre's gestures were growing more disheartened and less enthusiastic.

But the third car of the morning had stopped anyway.

'Grüss Gott,' the woman had said by way of greeting. 'Wohin gehst du denn?'

Pierre didn't know a word of German, but giving the reply 'Dubrovnik' had struck him as fair enough.

The woman had said something and nodded to him to get in.

'Wartest du hier schon lange?' her husband had asked with a big smile. To which Pierre had felt obliged to explain, in English, 'Sorry, I don't speak German.'

But the Austrians spoke English.

Tourists on their honeymoon. From Vienna to Greece. A nice, rather eccentric couple.

Pierre had told them the story of his distant relative, adding a few details, and the newlyweds were delighted. Not least because Pierre, in the confusion of the moment, had used the English word 'parents' when he meant relations.

When they reached the village of Slano, the woman had spread out a map and shown Pierre that the island of Šipan was a stone's throw away, much closer than Dubrovnik. If he was after a crossing he would be better off searching there rather than elsewhere.

Pierre had been persuaded, although Darko had talked about Dubrovnik. He had asked them to wait for him, and headed straight for an old fisherman who was sorting out his nets.

Some church bells had been striking one.

The journey had taken half an hour.

*

Pierre heard the engine starting. He looked after the wake of the boat, as far as the coast, which was gently getting further away.

Halfway across he felt as though several hours had passed. They had been on the sea for fifteen minutes.

That sensation was reversed immediately afterwards. A faint gleam of houses emerged from the darkness of sea and sky. For a moment he forgot everything, Gramovac, Darko, Stjepan and the two Austrians. He forgot the visions of water and land that had accompanied him so far. He forgot Frane.

Telemachus was going to meet Ulysses.

Chapter 41

The cheesemonger had smiled. Behind him, the man at the fish stall had confirmed the idea, slicing the air with the side of his hand: *'Ah, talijanski drug!'* The woman selling vegetables had tapped her finger to her temple with a strange expression on her face. Finally a customer had nodded, paid quickly and dashed off to point towards a paved alleyway leading up towards the church and the hill overlooking the bay. He had waved his hand up and down a number of times, as though stroking the top of the mountain. Pierre deduced that the 'Italian' lived on the other side. With a similar gesture, fingers climbing over an obstacle, he made it clear that he had understood. The guy nodded and repeated his gesture from the start.

After the first bend, the alley turned into a path. It climbed steeply between the last bright houses, passed the drystone walls of the tiny gardens and plunged into the dark green of the gorse bushes.

Pierre started sweating. His suitcase wasn't the easiest kind of luggage to drag all the way up there. He kept switching hands, and wiped his forehead with his shirt cuff. The night spent on the wharf had left a sticky deposit all over his body. He had slept enough to set off at a marching pace the moment he arrived, but the fact that the village was deserted had made him postpone his departure.

His mind was blank. His eyes looked at the sea, but didn't enjoy the view. They looked for a house in the middle of the wild-west cacti and the mastic bushes. He couldn't distinguish individual sounds, there was just a single droning noise in his ears, a dissonant chord of birds, cicadas and the wind. He changed hands again. He took a deep breath. He couldn't smell anything. Just the weight of the suitcase on his fingers, sweat trickling behind his ears and the pain of his feet, crushed by shoe leather.

The path reached the top. Pierre saw the green scrub descending uninterruptedly to the sea. He saw the ruins of a building that had once been a church. He saw bare patches of land dotted with white sheep. He saw a brighter plot of land in the midst of the shrubs and the holm oaks, and a stone house on the edge of the plot.

He changed hands again and braced himself for the descent.

He didn't hear someone shouting, '*Stoj!*'

All he heard was a sudden bang, like a gunshot. A cloud of dust rose up in front of him.

'*Stoj!*'

Pierre looked towards the ruin, at the goats, at the house. He couldn't see anyone. For a moment he didn't move. Then he put down the suitcase, took a few steps forward, waved his arms above his head and shouted, 'Don't shoot, don't shoot!'

The dust rose a few inches to the right of his leg, and fragments of bark spattered from a shrub.

'I'm called Robespierre Capponi, I'm the son of Vittorio Capponi, don't shoot! I'm looking for Vittorio Capponi!'

He picked up the suitcase and resumed his descent. No one fired.

A minute later he heard the voice, and saw the barrel of the Mauser that had greeted his arrival.

'Hands up. Don't turn around.'

Pierre did so, without breathing.

A hand took his suitcase from him. He heard a hinge opening. The barrel of the Mauser was still fixed on him.

'What are you doing here?' the voice said again.

'I'm looking for Vittorio Capponi,' Pierre said clearly. 'I'm his son.'

'Don't try to be clever, my son is in Italy, tell me what you're doing here.' The barrel of the gun against his back stressed the importance of the answer.

This was not how Pierre had imagined it, the meeting between Telemachus and Ulysses.

'It's me, dad,' he said finally in a desperate voice. 'I'm Robespierre, it's true.' He tried to turn round but the Mauser replied that this wasn't quite the moment. 'I've come looking for you, I didn't know

where you'd got to, I was worried about you, really, if you don't
believe me, ask me some questions, something that only you and I
could know, anything you like.'

'I don't feel like playing games. You could have learned all kinds
of things about me. Aren't I right?'

'No, go on, dad, please . . . Listen –'

'Fine,' said Vittorio, interrupting him, 'our song. The one I sang
to put you to sleep.'

Pierre was completely taken aback. Fanti said he had no ear for
music, but it was just a question of training. Angela always stuck
her fingers in her ears when he sang.

He began. Simple, childlike music, the words in dialect.

After the first two verses, he realised that he could turn round.

Vittorio Capponi was holding the submachine-gun with both
hands. He looked hard into Pierre's eyes, and didn't move. His grey
beard contrasted with his tanned face. He had long hair down to his
shoulders. His face was hard, his eyes bright. He looked like a hermit,
the shepherd king of some remote Balkan tribe.

Pierre stopped singing.

It wasn't how he'd imagined it, Ulysses and Telemachus.

He opened his arms, ran forward and threw his arms around his
father in a nine-year hug.

Vittorio Capponi took his hand off the barrel of the Mauser,
lifted the gun upwards, and stood there, unsure what to do with the
weapon.

'. . . then a fisherman brought me over here, I slept under the canopy
of the market and the moment I woke up I asked around to see if
anyone knew where you lived.'

Pierre had run through the whole of the journey in a few minutes.
His memories flashed by as though in a film, from Ravenna to Šipan,
his deal with Ettore, the letter to Nicola, the meeting with Darko.
Everything.

His father had listened without interrupting, chewing wild fennel,
his eye fixed on the goats. He was still holding the Mauser in one
hand, and stroked his beard with the other.

They were sitting there, not far from the path, under a maritime
pine with a twisted trunk. There was a smell of resin and dry grass.

Pierre had expected to be welcomed into the house. A table, a chair, something to eat, but after the gunfire nothing surprised him. Knowing how to be with other people is a matter of training like everything else. It didn't look as though there were many visitors around here. Vittorio Capponi had lived in Šipan for almost three months. He'd probably fallen out of the habit.

Pierre tried to fill the silence and check his thoughts. 'I made my decision on the spur of the moment. Yes, to cut a long story short, I'd been thinking about it for ages, but difficulties were always coming up. They seemed insuperable to me, and perhaps I'd never have done it if hadn't been for that letter that never came, and the last one I sent you, to the old address, the one that was returned to me.'

Pierre looked at his father again, as though waiting for a reply to an unvoiced question. He felt it deep down in his throat, a dim awareness suppressed until then by the impetuosity of his quest. *Why did you stop writing, dad? Why haven't I heard from you for over a year? Why?*

His thoughts ran through his brain faster than the ticking seconds. He saw his father's eyes again, just as he had seen them the last time, in Italo's cellar, in the faint candlelight. Proud, determined, prepared for anything. Their colour darkened by the shade of his beret. Ready to say 'farewell', and to linger inside you for ever.

He saw Nicola's face again. His eyes had changed, too. Now, on the few occasions when he talked about their father, there was no way of telling what light flashed there. He looked away, staring obliquely at the floor.

He stretched out a hand to his father's shoulder, and chose the easiest among a thousand questions. 'What's up, dad, aren't you feeling well? Aren't you pleased to see me? What is it, has something happened?'

Vittorio Capponi lolled his head, took a deep breath and finally looked Pierre right in the face.

Nine years later, on a remote Dalmatian island, he saw those eyes again.

Filled with exile and resignation.

Chapter 42

'Of course I'm pleased to see you, Robespierre,' Vittorio began without smiling. 'But I'd rather you'd stayed at home and spared me all this.'

'All this what?' Pierre insisted.

Vittorio struggled for words. His pronunciation and his way of expressing himself betrayed the fact that he had been used to speaking a foreign language for a long time. 'This crap,' he said finally. 'This rock where I'm forced to live, shooting at anyone who turns up. This poor thing that I've become.'

'But dad, what's happened to you, will you tell me? Why have you kept us in the dark for so long?'

'And what was I supposed to tell you?' Vittorio's face darkened. 'Last year I buried my second lifelong companion, she died slowly before my eyes . . . What else is there to say?'

Pierre got up, so as not to reply straight away.

'You could at least have dropped a line or two,' he said. 'No more than that, just a couple of lines. After Milena died I wrote to you twice: you never replied.'

'Haven't I hurt enough people already? I came here to live far from you all, I've never made it back, I've written twice a year, and now I'm supposed to burden you with my troubles? You knew something, didn't you? Politics was going badly, life was going badly, things in my head were going badly, but a father doesn't weep on his son's shoulders.'

'And instead you don't give a sign of life for more than a year?' said Pierre. Then he regretted it. But it was too late to turn back.

'I just don't feel I'm alive, Robespierre. Do you want me to tell you everything? Fine. It's as though I'm dead. So I thought it was better for you to forget. Death is contagious, a dead man's letters make you die inside.'

Pierre felt the blow. He swallowed hard to check his tears, but neither operation was entirely successful. Vittorio seemed to do the same, then he started talking again. Pierre listened to him in silence, still walking, slowly, around a white stone that protruded from the grass.

Things had started going badly in the early fifties, with the first elections of the workers' councils in the factories. As far as Pierre could tell, this was still an experiment, but in essence the state was granting workers the chance to take control of the reins of the companies where they worked. His father had been keen on the project. He said that self-management was the only way forward for true socialism. So, as a member of the union, he wanted to put his name down on the electoral list for the workers' council in his factory.

'They knew we were enthusiastic about it, but they played dirty: they gave me a promotion, a job that didn't interest me, in an office in Split. I had to take it and give up the election. That was the start of it all.'

After that there was a succession of little signs. The 'Italian comrade' started getting 'awkward'; his compatriots were accused of being spies for the Cominform, relations with Italy were becoming increasingly tense over Trieste, and a generous helping of racism completed the picture. The partisan war was a faded memory. The 'hero of the people', Vittorio Capponi, was becoming a foreigner once more, while official blessing was still being bestowed on the internationalism of the workers' movement.

'No, Djilas didn't give me much help. Friends? Did I write that we were friends? Well, not really, that was just to help you understand. The fact is that I didn't mind some of his ideas, particularly when he attacked Party bureaucracy and accused the Central Committee of being rather undemocratic and very, what's the word, *Mafioso*, is that right? The problem is that he was one of the four most important people in the country, he drove around in a Mercedes, with a chauffeur, he frequented the smartest drawing rooms, hunts, big ceremonies. He dreamed of devoting himself entirely to theory and literature, but he had important political jobs, and in the articles in the paper you would have thought he was attacking himself.'

Milena had passed away in March the previous year. A lingering death, a horrible illness. Pierre understood that the illness had been fatal for his father as well. He had thought he would be able to pick himself up by throwing himself headlong into politics. Milovan Djilas wrote his critical articles for the Party newspaper, and Vittorio had followed his example in a few local or Italian-language dailies. It had been a time of hope and enthusiasm. Then, all of a sudden, disaster struck. Djilas had been released from all his positions, and forced to engage in self-criticism. His most fortunate followers had had to leave their jobs and politics. In most cases they had been removed from their villages, from their friends and family.

'And it hasn't stopped there. They're turning up the heat. People are saying that sooner or later, the moment the Western press stops taking an interest, we'll be taken to the concentration camp for members of the Cominform, unceremoniously thrown out of the country. That's why anyone who walks down my path finds themselves staring down the barrel of a Mauser. I'm just waiting for them to come. Every day. But it's no way to live, always on the alert, always anxious. But you see, I can't trust anyone, and I've had to sever my connections with my friends as well, to keep them out of it.'

'With Darko too, isn't that right?' Pierre intervened, kicking a pine tree.

'With him too. I'm alone. In the village they think I'm mad. They're ignorant enough not to know why I've come up here. They buy my cheese, and they're afraid of the Mauser and the dogs. That's our relationship. Just that.'

Vittorio drew himself to his feet. He brought a hand to the small of his back, and stretched himself. 'The damp is killing me,' he observed with resignation. Then he slipped two fingers between his lips and whistled loudly. From a low bush there emerged a sheepdog that Pierre hadn't noticed before. It came bounding down the slope, and stopped in front of Vittorio, to have its muzzle stroked. His master complied, then held his arm in front of him and allowed the dog to snap at it playfully. He picked up a leather bag and slung it over his shoulder. The moment his back was turned, the dog charged up the hill, barking at the goats to get them to assemble.

'What's his name?' asked Pierre, enthralled by the dog's skill at corralling the herd.

'Radko,' his father replied, clapping his hands to impose an about-turn on a ginger ram.

Radko seemed to understand that he was being talked about, and came down to sniff the new arrival.

'He seems more sociable with strangers than you,' commented Pierre, at the sight of the dog's joyfully wagging tail.

'Sure. But you have to see what he turns into if you try even to raise your voice at yours truly.'

Pierre put it to the test. Radko immediately started snarling, his fangs bared, crouching and ready to jump.

'Ok, ok, I was joking.'

He raised his arms in the air, to demonstrate his innocence.

Radko went back to his master, who had been walking in the dusty path. He joined him, darting ahead every now and again.

Pierre watched their progress, in the noonday sun, against the background of a choppy sea.

Chapter 43

Something had changed, inside. He was upset, bloated, he'd lost his perspective on things. Blind. And mute. Not deaf, he could still hear properly. Perhaps it was the accumulated damp of that dusty hovel, or the dust itself, or the rough hands of that guy who had shaken him like that. Perhaps it was a depression caused by the unforgiving nature of his surroundings. But once everything was sorted out he could get going again. He would be able to get out of that insalubrious place, which was unworthy of him: you had to have confidence. Full stop.

What was the president always saying to his men? 'On the wings of our products and of technological progress, borders will be eliminated. You will be at home anywhere in the world!'

Exactly. That was how it would be. Although, logically, you had to allow for the initial backwardness of the people that the latest models reached. It was all a matter of time and habit.

He felt like a pioneer. The Pilgrim Fathers' route retraced to dispense a new Word, to display the new miracle. Endangering his own safety at the clumsy hands of four troglodytes was the smallest possible stake for such an important game.

The president got it right: 'When you go around the world, be proud to be Western. Bear the message of your country proudly. You will find your place.'

He was a McGuffin. He had a mission.

'Gigino, Ciro Stecchino dropped by, he says his girlfriend's dying to have one, he's going to come in tomorrow and talk money, keep it for him, set it to one side, he really wants it.'

You see?

Chapter 44

He was in a terrible mood.

He hadn't had a minute's sleep. The military plane that had brought him from the United States was the most uncomfortable crock it had ever been his misfortune to travel in: poor air pressure, noisy, freezing. It had landed at the military airport near London, just long enough for a piss, and had set off again straight away. This time it was a Bentley with all mod cons, right into the heart of Essex, to the country home of Sir Charles Tilston Bright. He hoped he would at least be able to shower.

The English countryside was soporific. Cary didn't agree with those who said it was boring. Certainly, it lacked the variety of a mountain vista, or even the romantic touch of a coast over the sea, but if you made an effort there was a certain fascination in the succession of identical ploughed fields, cottages and rows of trees. There was the possibility of something happening, especially when the fog came down like the dry ice that conjurors use to make their performances more spectacular. Any kind of situation could come out of the top hat, even a secret meeting between a famous Hollywood actor and a head of British intelligence with an interest in a film about Marshal Tito.

He was awoken by the ticking of the indicator, and saw the bonnet of the Bentley heading towards a metal gate and entering the drive of a little Victorian-style villa.

A gale swept the landscape, raging against the doors of the car and tearing at the hat that Cary was tempted to let it have, feigning an accident just to get rid of it. He turned up the collar of his coat and followed the chauffeur to the back of the building. The front door was locked.

They passed through several rooms that not a single ray of light penetrated, before the chauffeur threw open a door and, standing in the doorway, stiffly announced the guest.

'Mr Kaplan has arrived, Sir Charles.'

Cary took a few steps forwards. The room was tastefully furnished and filled with a pleasant smell of wood and tobacco. The man who must have been Sir Charles Tilston Bright came towards him, extending his hand. Cary looked at him and had to admit that the man had a certain style. A relaxed gait, a sincere smile, clear, deep eyes, wearing classic weekend-in-the-country clothes, down to a neckerchief that puffed elegantly from his pullover.

'Welcome to Wilford, Mr Grant. And welcome back to England. Have you been away for long?'

'Since the last time I visited my mother,' Cary broke in. He wasn't in the mood for nostalgic observations about the old country. He could leave that to retired colonels.

As they made themselves comfortable on their little sofas, Sir Charles gave a slight cough: 'Forgive me, but we haven't told the chauffeur your identity. Apart from me and my closest collaborators, everyone else thinks they are dealing with George Kaplan, an agent returning from the United States with important information to pass on to us.'

'A sensible precaution,' replied Cary, 'and my compliments on your house, Sir Charles, it really is enchanting. Although, to be honest, after ten hours on that infernal aeroplane, I would have been just as comfortable in a garage.'

Sir Charles laughed loudly, perhaps out of embarrassment, or perhaps because the humorous approach was one with which he was unfamiliar.

'Thank you, Mr Grant, the cottage has been in my family for over a hundred years, and I try to keep it cosy. Now I'll leave the choice up to you: I imagine you must be very tired from your journey. If you wish to go up to your room, you need only ask, otherwise we can discuss the matter at hand right away, and relax later on.'

Cary took another close look at the man sitting opposite him. He ran a hand over his rough chin, and slackened the knot of his tie. Better to find out straight away what death he was going to die

'Since we're here, Sir Charles, I'd prefer to find out more about how I'll be travelling. Once I know that, I'll find it easier to sleep.'

Sir Charles poured three fingers of Scotch into two elegant glasses and handed one to the actor.

'Well, Mr Grant,' he said finally, sniffing the whisky, 'I know you want to go and see your mother in Bristol, but I imagine that there might be some other requirements of which I have not been informed. I would proceed as follows: first I will explain your itinerary as it currently stands, and then we will set about satisfying any requests you might have.'

Cary nodded to him to continue.

'As regards the visit to your mother, it is important that you should be extremely careful. You are well known in Bristol, and so is your mother, and the journalists in the provinces are always chasing after news.'

'I can', Cary interrupted him, 'reassure you on that count. To avoid being mobbed, I have stipulated a pact with the local press. They leave me in peace and in return, before I go back to America, I will undertake to see the journalists who wish to interview me. Of course I have no intention of doing any such thing on this occasion, but at least my mother's house will not be besieged by photographers.'

'That makes everything easier, Mr Grant. We had thought about organising the meeting in a hotel, but as I understand it that will not be necessary.'

'For pity's sake! My mother couldn't bear to meet me in a strange place, it would make her impossibly nervous.'

Sir Charles relit his pipe, taking long puffs, and offered Cary a cigar. He suddenly felt that Betsy was very far away. Having smoked three packs of cigarettes a day before his wife helped him to stop, he suddenly yielded to temptation. The pungent taste of cigar combined on his tongue with the aroma of the Scotch.

'Sadly you will have to travel by car to Bristol, there's no way round it. We can't allow you to use the civilian airport, and the military airport is not near enough to the city. Do you think you might ask your mother to be careful not to give too many details away if she mentions your visit to anyone?'

'I don't think that will be a problem. If I started talking about Marshal Tito and Anglo-American interests in Yugoslavia she'd stop me after the first three words. I'll find a way to satisfy her curiosity without revealing anything about the mission.'

'Good,' Sir Charles smiled enthusiastically, 'very good. Then let's deal with everything else. The important thing, Mr Grant, is that you should reach Trieste by the end of the month. As long as we stick to that, you will be able to organise your time as you see fit, with the one reservation that you should stay abreast of your schedules, and avoid public places and public transport. Over the next few days you will have to acquaint yourself with the details of the mission. You will leave for Trieste from the airport at which you landed this morning. Once you have arrived there, you will be driven to the border, where one of our functionaries will be waiting for you. He will accompany you as far as Dubrovnik. From there, the Yugoslavians will bring you to Tito's secret residence, about which I know little: it is a pleasant place, in all likelihood an island, in the south of the country. Obviously one of our agents will be with you at all times, our best man, you will meet him tomorrow. And that is all.'

'All right, Sir Charles,' replied Cary. 'If it isn't a problem for you, I'd like to set off for Bristol tomorrow. I would spend the night there and come back here the following day.'

Perhaps it was Archie who had spoken. Perhaps it was the approach of an adventure, of the unknown. Archie Leach, so close to home, was trying to escape.

'And now,' Cary continued, rising to his feet, 'if there's nothing else, I would very much like to get some rest.'

He held his hand out to Sir Charles, who shook it firmly. The chauffeur, reappearing in the doorway, asked Cary which suitcases he wished to unload.

Outside, the wind had subsided, but the usual fog was coming down. Cary had taken out an overnight bag, just enough for a change of clothes. Then he reached towards the front seat, where he had left the leather folder containing Hitch's screenplay.

As he did so, he noticed a strange book on the dashboard. *Casino Royale* by Ian Fleming. He picked up the book and closed the door.

'Is this yours?' he asked the chauffeur.

'Yes, are you interested in it? Take it, I finished it while I was waiting for you at the airport.'

'Thanks, I haven't brought anything to read apart from work. Is it any good?'

The driver shrugged. 'It made me angry. If only our lives really were like that: beautiful women, gadgets and fist-fights. And to think that the author is one of us. A commander in the Naval Intelligence Department, it says there. But to pass the time . . .'

Cary smiled. A novel by a former secret agent. The most appropriate reading matter he could have found.

Chapter 45

General Serov and I have fought together, did you know that, Comrade Zhulianov? You will have to pass on my greetings when you return to Moscow. Cigarette? Of course.

The head of the Military Secret Services in Vienna maintained a superficially friendly tone, just enough to avoid creating a bad impression.

Having responsibility for the Eastern sector of the city, I must advise you against walking around the city. We are still at the front here, there are spies everywhere, and the Americans are always trying to infiltrate us. For your own safety, and for the purposes of secrecy, it would be better if you stayed in your hotel, Comrade Zhulianov.

He immediately noticed that people lowered their eyes as he passed, then turned surreptitiously to peer at his back. Everyone looked at him, but it was General Serov's shadow that they saw cast on the wall.

I will ensure that you want for nothing. If you need anything at all, my assistant will be at your disposal.

The hotel was an old *Jugendstil* building that had been requisitioned by the army. The officers and the diplomatic corps lived on the floor where he was staying.

For reasons of security, Comrade, as you well understand.

He couldn't blame them for their circumspection, but at the same time he felt uneasy, he imagined them all there with their ears pressed to the walls of the old room. And perhaps that wasn't so far from the Schwindsuchtstrasse. He remembered the motto of his professor at the High School: 'Only friends have bigger ears than the enemy.'

He put his few clothes in the wardrobe, changed his shirt and went downstairs.

The other man already sitting waiting for him. They shook hands. The man introduced himself as Kaminsky. They ordered two coffees.

He looked like a post office clerk. A fat man with a receding hairline and heavy-framed glasses. Secret agents were like that. In that job, the less conspicuous you were, the better it was for everyone. Zhulianov had known a few of them in Berlin. 'Vague stains on an urban landscape' was what his colonel had called them. Grey, apparently pointless lives that would never arouse suspicion. No sentimental bond, no friendships beyond the cordial relations of good neighbours, walks in the park, stale dinners and a larder full of tins.

Kaminsky spoke in a low voice, articulating his words, eyes fixed on his steaming cup.

'I've been asked to give you the coded orders,' and from under the table he handed him a large yellow sealed envelope. 'Inside you will find the new documents as well, a railway ticket and a boarding card. You will have to travel to Venice by train. There you will embark as an ordinary seaman on the *Varna*, a Bulgarian merchant ship. Did they give you a password in Moscow?'

'Yes.'

'You must use it only at the moment of embarkation, with the commander of the vessel. He will ask you for it as you hand him the second envelope. If anyone else does, no matter who they may be, kill him and consider the mission abandoned.'

He said it with absolute calm, almost indifference.

'Is that all clear?'

Zhulianov said that it was.

'Fine. My task finishes here. Goodbye, and good luck.'

He got to his feet, they shook hands and he set off with short, quick footsteps.

He hadn't even touched his coffee.

He spent the evening locked up in his room studying. So much to commit to memory: a new name, date of birth, a brief biography, the details of his itinerary. It took him two hours. On the Bulgarian vessel he would meet the other components of the mission: three exiled Yugoslavians with an expert knowledge of the region. Some hard men who, in 1949, had escaped from Goli Otok, where they had been interned as supporters of the Cominform. They had reappeared in Bulgaria, and the Ministry had picked them up in passing. Memorising the biographies took him another two hours. The years of training at Politics School made the task easier.

He still didn't have the details of the mission itself. They must be inside the envelope he would give the commander of the vessel.

He gathered together all the documentation and burned it in the fireplace, one page after another.

Then he got dressed, performed three sets of press-ups on the carpet, and went to bed.

He had a long day's train journey ahead of him.

Chapter 46

Bristol, 25 April

The greatest density of piliferous follicles per square centimetre of facial epidermis is recorded on the upper lip. The least, on the cheek. The type of beard and the frequency with which it requires to be shaved depends in part on anthropometric factors. Put bluntly, some races are hairier than others. Caucasians, vulgarly called 'white', are the most hirsute. Amongst these people, the beard reaches its maximum density at the age of about thirty-five.

Within film-going memory, Cary Grant had never displayed a beard longer than a twelfth of an inch. Among the sixty or so films in which he had appeared, the ones in which he did not appear perfectly shaven could be counted on the fingers of one hand. Each of those films coincided with a return of Archie Leach and his searing proletarian sarcasm. It's difficult to cope with your traumas when you're busy spying on Hollywood's Nazis.

In *The Talk of the Town*, 1942, the Caucasian Grant – at the peak of his own piliferous productivity – played the role of Leopold Dilg, a trade unionist unjustly accused of homicide, who escapes prison and hides in the home of a fastidious law professor.

And after that came *None But the Lonely Heart*, 1944, practically a session of self-therapy. The head-to-head clash between Cary and Archie, as orchestrated by Clifford Odets. The story of the unemployed cockney Ernie Mott and his bitter, belated reconciliation with his mother after years of separation. ('Did you love my old man?' 'Love is not for the poor, son. No time for it.')

And then in the unsmiling city of Bristol, escorted by Her Majesty's grey-suited servants, once again there are two of you.

Two, because you're 'Mr Grant', the one who is obliged to camouflage himself lest anyone recognise him, but you're also Archibald
Alexander Leach, the one paradoxically free of camouflage, author-
ised to breathe, you're the one singing silently to yourself the words
of *Anything Goes*:

> 'The world has gone mad today,
> and good's bad today,
> and black's white today,
> and day's night today . . .'

You're the one walking the streets of your birthplace, preparing to
see Elsie once again.

Your mother.

Elsie, who still calls you both 'Archie'.

Elsie who talked to herself, washed her hands repeatedly, stripping
off layer after layer of skin with a hard-bristled brush, and asked
everyone and no one where her dancing shoes were.

Elsie, whom your father Elias had placed without your knowledge
in a psychiatric clinic. The Country Home for Mental Defectives,
in the crumbling suburb of Fishponds, the terminus of one of Bristol's
tramlines.

You were nine years old. 'She's gone to the seaside, to Weston-
super-Mare, for a few days' holiday.'

When did you work out that she wouldn't be coming back? When
exactly did you conclude that your parents had separated, that your
mother had abandoned you? . . . *Archie?*

Elsie, just one pound a year to keep her in a state of filth, non-
existent hygiene, aggressive nurses.

Elsie, twenty pounds in all, until the death of her husband and
the letter dispatched by an English lawyer.

Elsie, alive. Fifty-seven years old.

December 1935.

Migraines, nightmares, the ghost of your father trying clumsily to
justify himself. Stinking breath, worms in the throat of the man who
died of cirrhosis of the liver. 'You can't ask other people to be transparent, Archie. Even you aren't transparent.'

Dodging journalists. A few months before, at your father's funeral, you fell into the hands of a clutch of reporters. Then the meeting: 'Mother. I'm here.'

She remembers you in short trousers, Archie.

She doesn't recognise you, Cary. She doesn't know you're a famous actor.

'Archie, my boy . . . Is it really you? Have you missed your old mum?'

A life annuity. Finances administered by the office of Davies, Kirby and Karath in London. A house all to herself, where you can go and see her. No servants, though: 'I can manage fine on my own, my darling, I don't want people buzzing around me telling me what to do, and you see, keeping myself busy keeps me alive, my love.'

And here she is now, in 1954, in Bristol, in the strangest days of your life; you open the door and see the little old woman sitting at the end of the corridor. Will she recognise you, under a quarter of an inch of beard, and wrapped up in a grey duffel-coat? When you take off your hat (Cary *hates* hats!) your old mother's face lights up with surprise. She gets up with a little start, throws up her arms and shrieks, 'Archie! Son! I'm so happy to see you!'

The world has gone mad today.

A few hours after saying goodbye to his old mother, Cary – booked into a small hotel in Swindon under the name of 'George Kaplan', his bodyguards' rooms on the same floor – sought sleep by reading this man Fleming's little book. The protagonist was a bold and arrogant secret agent on a mission to the French town of Royale-les-Eaux. MI6 had given him an unlimited budget: stratospheric sums to bet at baccarat, extremely generous tips distributed to the hotel concierges, glass after glass of vodka.

> *For a few moments Bond sat motionless, gazing out of the window across the dark sea, then he shoved the bundle of banknotes under the pillow of the ornate single bed, cleaned his teeth, turned out the lights and climbed with relief between the harsh French sheets. For ten minutes he lay on his left side reflecting on the events of the day. Then he turned over and focused his mind towards the tunnel of sleep.*

Cary looked up: around him, peeling, faded wallpaper. Bubbles had formed, distorting aeroplanes and small smiling women. There was a small, almost invisible hole in the pillow. Every now and again a feather came out. The light from the lamp was too faint. The only window looked out on to a little alleyway with no distinguishing features. Outside it was raining.

The plot was about espionage and games of chance. Bond had to trap a communist double-agent, Le Chiffre, by setting a trap for him in the Casino Royale.

Bond liked to make a good breakfast. He consumed half a pint of iced orange juice, three scrambled eggs and bacon and a double portion of coffee without sugar. He lit his first cigarette, a Balkan and Turkish mixture made for him by Morlands of Grosvenor Street . . .

Paragraph after paragraph of pointless details, depicting a lifestyle that struck Cary as brash and fake:

Bond's car was his only personal hobby. One of the last of the 4$\frac{1}{2}$-litre Bentleys with the supercharger by Amherst Villiers. It was a battleship-grey convertible coupé, which really did convert, and it was capable of touring at ninety with . . .

Cary closed the book, put out the light and 'focused his mind towards the tunnel of sleep'.

Frances Farmer arrived at two in the morning. Archie and Cary dreamt of her locked up in the lunatic asylum in Fishponds, but tranquilised by American paramedics, rednecks to a man, not even shouting, then alone, her knees in a puddle of urine with saliva and cigarette butts floating about in it.

'Archie, my son . . . Have you missed your old mum?'

A crowd of people screamed from a single throat: a nine-year-old child coming home and being unable to find his mother, a famous actor meeting up with his mother after twenty-one years of separation; an English proletarian imprisoned in the body and the myth of the most stylish man in the world; an ex-actor racked with doubts about his future; the double of a certain Jean-Jacques Bondurant; a

Caucasian with a terrible nostalgia for the invention of King C. Gillette; a secret agent involved in a bizarre diplomatic enterprise; a paranoid schizophrenic persecuted by ghosts; and last of all, one 'George Kaplan'.

The little hotel was filled with voices and hubbub. The bodyguards, in their shirtsleeves, burst open the door but stayed out of the opening, then dived on to the floor of the room, revolvers at the ready. When they saw that Cary was (apparently) alone, they got back up, and one of them asked, 'Is everything all right, Mr Kaplan?'

Cary, in a pair of dark-blue pyjamas with two or three white feathers stuck to it, and a beard almost half an inch long, looked at them and replied, 'Yes . . . It was just a bad dream. Forgive me.'

When they had gone, Cary got up, brushed down his pyjamas, took a needle and thread from his jacket pocket and mended the hole in the pillow. He sat down on the bed and opened Fleming's book again. Chapter 6 was called 'Two Men in Straw Hats'.

Chapter 47

The communist agents were described as utter imbeciles, incompe-
tents with shady attitudes, and recognisable from a hundred yards
away.

James Bond walks along the footpath. On the other side of the
tree-lined avenue, two strange figures leaning against a plane tree.
They are dressed alike: dark, 'rather hot-looking' suits (how could
you fail to notice a detail like that, from only a hundred yards away?)
and straw hats decorated with a black ribbon. They are both wearing
cameras around their necks, although one of them is carrying his in
a red case, the other in a blue case. Bond makes his way towards
them, wondering what sort of attack he's going to have to deal with.
Red-man nods to Blue-man, who takes out his camera, kneels down
. . . and is ripped apart by a terrible explosion. The impact sends
Bond flying and blows down the two nearest trees, the others escaping
with scorched foliage. All around, the stench of roast mutton. The
two figures are reduced to scraps of flesh. The explanation comes a
few chapters later: two Bulgarian hired killers. Their instructions: to
unleash a smoke screen from the blue case, while the red one was a
bomb to be thrown at Bond. Protected by the smoke, the assassins
were to make their getaway unharmed. In actual fact, *both* the cases
were bombs, the goal being to eliminate Bond and leave no witnesses
alive.

Scratching the dense bristles on his cheeks in disbelief, Cary had
reread the whole section out loud, for the benefit of his escort.

'Who does this guy Fleming think he's kidding? First of all, there
have been no reports of any bombing attacks by Soviet agents in
Western Europe; secondly, a sequence of events of that kind is

extremely unlikely; and last of all, if every enemy operation were to conclude with the elimination of the perpetrators, there would be no enemy left!'

'Well said, and in any case Soviet agents aren't like that, and neither are agents working on Her Majesty's service: this man Bond is a dandy, and his conduct on the mission is thoroughly reprehensible. Besides, MI6 would never burden the Commonwealth Exchequer with the budget of such a bizarre mission, set entirely in the world of gambling.'

They were as boring as a conference of Flemish podiatrists.

This conversation had taken place in the truck bringing him to the little military airport from which they had taken off for the Free Territory of Trieste.

On the plane, Cary put aside the novel, and concentrated on the files.

Many of the pages of this compendium on the Yugoslavian war of liberation dwelt on the German Fifth Offensive against Tito's army (the encircling of the freed territories of Montenegro and Hercegovina, May–June 1943).

The Axis forces consist of eight divisions, a total of 120,000 well-trained men, including groups of artillery and armoured units, plus a squadron of Luftwaffe bombers. Tito has 15,000 poorly armed soldiers, starving and exhausted, plus another 4,500 injured men in the field hospitals, many of whom are dragging themselves around with open wounds bared for want of bandages. The partisans – including the wounded – are fighting desperately, always hand to hand, running along rough mountain paths in broken shoes. Finally the remnants of two divisions break through the lines, sacrificing almost two thirds of their effective forces, including some of the best officers.

The Fifth Offensive had been defeated. It was one of the most epic and unbelievable chapters of the whole war. No one should have been surprised that they wanted to get a film out of it, but Cary was perplexed about the role he was supposed to play.

The outline mentioned the 'participation of British personnel' in breaking through enemy lines. To Cary, such 'participation' seemed relatively insignificant, at least from the military point of view. The British mission consisted of six men, including Major William Stuart and Major F. W. Deakin. They had parachuted into Tito's head-quarters on the night between 27 and 28 May.

In response to Stuart's question, 'Where's the front?' Tito had replied, 'Wherever the Germans are.' Stuart had said, 'And where are the Germans?', to which Tito had shot back, 'Everywhere.'

On 9 June, during a German bombing raid, Stuart had been killed and Deakin had been injured in the foot. On the same occasion a piece of shrapnel had wounded Tito in his left arm, and another had killed his dog Lux.

Who were they suggesting he play, Stuart or Deakin? There wasn't much to go on in either case, unless the scriptwriters were going to rely on fantasy. Who knows, perhaps they would introduce an imaginary character, to inflate and glorify the 'involvement of British personnel'. It seemed like a lunatic idea . . .

. . . Until he moved on to the long historical and biographical section on Josip Broz, otherwise known as 'Walter', 'Zagorac', 'Novak', 'Rudi', 'Kostanjsek', 'Slavko Babic', 'Spiridon Mekas' and above all . . . Tito. Pseudonyms and false names adopted during his long periods underground.

There were various photographs attached to the seventy pages. All of the pictures taken during the war showed Tito in uniform. A hard expression, features sculpted from marble. Bolt upright, every inch the part. With his arm in a bandage. Thoughtful, smoking a Bent army pipe, slender and curved. With his glasses on, studying topographical maps. Meeting his senior officers. With Winston Churchill in Naples, in 1944. With Stalin the following year.

The photographs from the period after the revolution were very different: Tito was almost always shown in the peace and tranquillity of his own various residences scattered around the country.

On the Brioni islands in June 1952: half-length portrait. Pale suit (beige, perhaps; linen, at a guess) with a narrow lapel, very probably two-buttoned. A lighter-coloured shirt with a tab collar, a tie with a large polka-dot pattern knotted in a tight triangle, (and probably without a loop, given that he wore a tie pin). An unmistakable Panama hat on his head. A sardonic smile, a smug expression directed at the lens. A cigarette smoked with a long holder. He looked a bit like a gangster, but he showed a certain style.

What the document said: the leader of Yugoslavian communism

was proud to have done it on his own. He would never have author-
ised any narrative strategies that took a sixteenth of an ounce of merit
from him and his soldiers.

What Cary thought after reading the file: he liked the sound of
Josip Broz.

What he concluded after an hour of free association: he and Tito
had a great deal in common.

Above all there was his obvious interest in matters of grooming
and clothes. According to the file, Tito had personally designed the
uniform of the Yugoslavian national army. There was also an anecdote: on 25 May 1944, just before the Normandy landing, the German
Oberkommando had unleashed its final attack on Tito's general staff,
which had its headquarters in Drvar, in Bosnia. The officers had
made it to safety, but the Germans had stolen a very stylish uniform
designed by Tito, to be worn on the day of victory. The high-ranking
officials of the Reich must have been *au fait* with their arch-enemy's
dandyism, since they had displayed the uniform as a war trophy in
a gallery in Vienna.

And then there was the fact they had both become famous with
a name other than their given name. They had both passed through
different identities. Cary for his work, Tito . . . for the same reason.
Wasn't he a 'professional revolutionary'?

And also: they were both well known for having indefinable
accents.

Cary was born in Bristol, he had spent his adolescence travelling
all around England, he had disembarked in New York (where he had
socialised with people from all over the world), he had travelled all
around the States on long theatrical tours and finally he had pulled
up roots and moved to Hollywood, the centre of a multinational
community of deracinated artists, refugees, the mentally stateless. All
that before the age of thirty. His English intonation was a synthesis
of all those experiences.

Tito was twelve years older, and of Croatian origin, but he had
been an officer in the Austro-Hungarian army on the Russian front,
and had been taken prisoner in 1915. After the Revolution, having
joined the Bolsheviks, he had fought against the White Russian
armies. Returning to Croatia in 1920, he had pursued underground
political activities. Between 1928 and 1934 he had been in prison. He

had spent most of the next few years in Moscow, during the time of the great 'purges', which he had survived by the skin of his teeth. Then there was the return to Yugoslavia, the war of liberation and the assumption of power. As a result he spoke a strange mixture of Croatian, Serbian and Russian. He had excellent German, and could get by in French and English.

But what fascinated Cary the most was the perpetual quest for independence, both personal and national. During the days of the Fifth Offensive, when Major Stuart had told him that no RAF planes would be covering the breakthrough, Tito had said, 'It's better that way. We'll do it on our own, and after the victory, we won't have run up any debts with anyone.' The next thing he had done had been to break with Stalin and the Soviet Union, provoking a real schism within the communist camp.

Cary, for his part, had been Hollywood's first freelance actor. From the thirties onwards he had freed himself from the grip of the studios. The first actor to win 10 per cent of takings. Cary discussed contracts in person even though he had both an agent and a lawyer-manager.

He was mulling over all this on the back seat of an official AMG car, while his new escort (the changing of the guard had occurred when they touched down at the tiny airport) showed him the city of Trieste, the sole concession to any form of amusement before crossing the border and placing him in the hands of one Major Alexander Dyle. The envelope also contained a file on him, but he hadn't yet got around to . . .

'One moment, gentlemen!' exclaimed Cary, reading his own name in a newspaper headline. The paper was the *Daily Telegraph*, which the bodyguard sitting next to the chauffeur was perusing.

'Is anything wrong, sir?'

'Could you lend me that newspaper for a moment?'

'Exclusive interview with CARY GRANT: *Now I am a happy man!*' was the headline. The various subtitles combined to form this message: 'A year after his retirement from the cinema, we asked the world's most famous British actor a few questions – in his Palm Springs residence: "I am devoting myself to my wife" – But there are some who swear: soon he will start acting again.'

For a few fractions of a second, Cary feared the worst: Bondurant in the hands of a journalist! Would Raymond and Betsy have dared to do such a thing? Reading on, he realised that the article and the so-called 'exclusive interview' were a collage of old statements, repeating inaccuracies that had been corrected at the time. The writer, one Paul Moorish, had not been to the house (he supplied no descriptions), and nor had he met his lookalike. A diversion that screamed 'MI6' from the first line to the last. There was also a photograph . . .

'Good Lord! Put me in contact with your superiors straight away!' he erupted from the back seat, as he realised that the photograph did indeed show Bondurant, with an eager smile and the wrong sort of tie.

A regimental tie! Under no circumstances should you even dream of wearing such a tie unless you belong to the club or institution announced by the colours. It was a black and white photograph, but the tie appeared to have its origins in the Royal Pioneer Corps. Typical gaffe by a sloppy yank. In an English newspaper. 'His' face!

So, for a moment, Cary stopped thinking about Tito and devoted himself to reprimanding Her Majesty's servants over the telephone, climbing the hierarchical ladder three steps at a time until he spoke to Sir Lewis in person and threatened to abandon the mission if any similar lapse of style should come to light.

Chapter 48

Outside it has been raining for hours.

He loves the smell of wet grass and mud and moist air and gleaming tarmac, in which you can see your reflection where it is smoothest. He loves it: people passing with their umbrellas low above their heads like so many vampires and the water roaring along the gutter and the light from the streetlamps dripping on to the street.

He would like to get up, now, open the window, bring in all that good smell and send out the lysoform, bleah, awful, you sniff two drops of it and you'd think you had two litres in your stomach.

And the lysoform calls to mind the bad things, the ones you should never think about, no, it's better not to think about it, come on, let's go for a walk. Yes, yes, a walk. Do you want a cigarette? Because when you were a child that was what she used, poor mum, lyso-form, down into the hole to drown the monster that jumps out to bite your willy. Die, you horrible thing!

We would really need to open the window, to let the monsters out. But forgive me, if the lysoform dissolves the monsters, then they can't be here in the lysoform room, not at all. And then where are they? Oh, forget it, his monsters are inside, better not to talk about it.

You'd like to get up, but you can't. Why not? Well, you know that when you get agitated you've got to go to bed. But nothing happened, did it? Say it, say it, nothing happened. Nooo, what on earth is supposed to have happened! If he's just a bit worked up, that happens every now and again, now let's give him this special medicine and it will pass.

He gets agitated every now and again, you know? But he never broke a nurse's nose. Do you think so? He hasn't been calm since they stopped giving him the medicine.

Can you break a nurse's nose? Can you have breakfast at night? What does a friend of mine say to me if I grab his snack from him? What happens when I have my impulses? Give me an example. Well, you know you're not supposed to grab Giorgio's snack from him, you know that.

Do you want a cigarette?

Don't grab other people's snacks. Under any circumstances. At night you sleep and you don't get up and you don't go to the kitchen to make coffee, because it puts you in a terrible state. You mustn't give cigarettes to Davide, no, under no circumstances must you ever do that again. Too much cold water hurts and if you drink it in such a hurry I'm never giving you any more. There are rules here, you know.

Fine, rules, nothing has happened. But now you're getting me up to send the monsters away?

The nurse walked quickly, spurred on by the nervous tapping of the heels behind him.

After three-quarters of an hour talking to her husband's locum, Angela was not even any calmer, let alone satisfied by the brief statement that she had had to sit through. 'A sudden thing, we really weren't expecting it, until just the other day everything was going swimmingly . . .'

She would happily have talked to Marco, who had known Fefe for a long time and understood his reactions better than anyone else. But Marco was on honeymoon and wouldn't be back for a week.

As they walked down the corridor, Angela tried in vain to calm herself down, by digging her nails into the leather of her handbag and inhaling great gulps of lysoform.

Ferruccio had been put in a different room, on the third floor, a room all to himself. Angela knew very well what that meant. Odoacre, on the phone from Rome, had reminded her, to avoid nasty surprises. 'Just for today, they've assured me. To keep him from hurting himself, more than anything else . . .'

It was Odoacre himself who had given her the news, and even the fact that they had warned her in advance hadn't gone down well with her; it made her feel useless. Fine, he was the leading physician at the clinic, he followed Ferruccio's therapy in person, he was the head of the family and all the rest, but who cares, a sister should have the right to know before anyone else, isn't that right?

That was why, when her husband had promised to come home that very evening, leaving the conference and his illustrious colleagues, Angela had had an impulse of pride: 'Just stay in Rome,' she had insisted, 'you don't need to put yourself out, I'm thoroughly capable of looking after my brother on my own.'

Then she had changed her mind. She knew Odoacre, she knew how fond he was of his work, and Fefe wasn't as serious as all that. If he came back, it was to be close to her. For her, not for Ferruccio.

'Hello, Signora Montroni. Come through.'

The old servant wrung out the floor cloth, dropped it into the bucket and bowed slightly.

'Hello, Sante,' Angela replied distractedly.

'I heard about your brother, I'm really sorry.'

'Never mind, let's hope it's only temporary.' Angela hated small talk, but Sante was always good with Fefe, always available and patient, and his interest was sincere.

'Yes, let's hope so, he's seemed strange to me lately, and on Monday he didn't even bring any cigarettes.'

'Then he must have been in a sorry state!' Angela tried to joke, but it didn't work terribly well.

Just before the first door, the nurse turned towards her. 'Signora –' he said in a voice filled with compassion.

Angela nodded her head, an exaggerated, insistent nod, to spare herself what was to come: 'It's ok, thank you, I know the procedure.' Then she hid her face in her hands, because 'knowing the procedure' gave her no comfort whatsoever.

The door opened. Ferruccio was lying on the bed, staring into the distance, his blanket tucked up around his neck. The three straps were barely visible: around his chest, his waist and his ankles. Angela tried not to think about them, to empty her mind of the bad memories and walk towards him with a smile.

'Hi, Fefe, I've brought you some cream puffs.'

'Yes, that's fine. Can you open that window a bit to let the monsters out?'

'What monsters, Fefe?'

'Oh, forget it, his monsters are inside, you know? Better let them stay there.'

He always talked about himself in the third person when he wasn't well, and parroted the phrases he had heard other people using about him. Angela sniffed the air and immediately worked out what was wrong.

'Won't you be cold with the window open?'

'No, no!' shouted Ferruccio as he concentrated all the strength in his body on shaking his head. 'Don't worry about the cold. Open it, open it.'

'Fine,' Angela conceded, and walked across the freshly cleaned room to the window.

'Nothing has happened, has it?' Ferruccio asked again, and without waiting for a reply, he went on talking: 'No, no, not a bit, absolutely nothing! He's just got himself a little worked up, it happens to him every now and again, but a nurse's nose, now . . . What do you think? Since they stopped that medicine of his, he hasn't been calm at all. Not at all.'

The bag of pastries still lay untouched on the chest of drawers.

'Aren't you eating your cream puff, Fefe? I brought it specially for you!' Ferruccio turned to look at it, Angela called herself an absolute cretin and approached the bed to feed him.'

'Slowly, now, ok? Don't be in such a rush!'

'What does Marco say to me if I eat too quickly? Well, Ferruccio, you know that's not all right, you'll swell up, and if you go on like that I'll take it away from you.'

Despite the rule, Fefe devoured the cream puff in three mouthfuls.

Angela checked her watch. Almost midday. She gave herself another five minutes. Ferruccio mustn't get too tired.

In the taxi she tried to hold back her tears. But she couldn't stop the thoughts writhing around in her head like snakes. She tried again, a long, deep breath. Hugging Pietre would have done her good, or even just talking to him on the phone. Damn him for wanting to go to Yugoslavia to find his father, to see the world! It *would* have to be during that famous 'fortnight without Odoacre'. A fortnight just for the two of them. Now, with Ferruccio's relapse, Pierre could have been near them. But he would have started cursing his luck, his own powerlessness, his poverty, their hopeless affair. No, come to think about it, Pierre wouldn't have been much help, except to spend a night giving vent to the sadness she felt inside.

She realised she thought of him as a little boy. He was fascinating, handsome, she still remembered the first time their eyes had met, at the dance hall. He had that barely perceptible smile of a screen idol, his hand in his trouser pocket, his brilliantined kiss-curl that flopped around as they twirled on the floor. The Filuzzi King. All of a sudden she found the whole thing ridiculous. Pointless.

The black hole in her thoughts became a chasm. She felt old, as though she had lived her life twice. She was Ferruccio's mother by necessity. She was the mother of Pierre, also an orphan, in pursuit of adventures to show that he was a match for any mysterious father. Perhaps in a way she was even older than Odoacre, who had not known hunger and poverty, who had not brought up a mad brother, without a penny, without anything. That was why he had picked her up off the street, giving her a decent future. She immediately regretted thinking anything of the kind. Odoacre had left the conference, he was coming back to be close to her. He really loved her, she was the one who was betraying him. She felt bad, remorse gripped her by the stomach, a shiver ran through her. With her last breath, she begged the driver to stop. She opened the door and threw up on the pavement.

Chapter 49

By the time they had reached Jablanac, Cary was certain of it: Major Dyle was an idiot.

Certainly, what he had read about him in the MI6 dossier had not made him warm to him particularly. Only a major idiot could manage a career like that without going under. But other factors had intervened, clothes first and foremost, then the affected upper-class accent, the chicken's-arse mouth and the over-active Adam's-apple.

On the other hand the major wasn't entirely to blame if Cary was in such a twitch during those April days. He had set off in the hope that Archibald Leach and Frances Farmer would leave him in peace for a while.

There were other bores, too, plotting in the shadows.

On the journey from Trieste to the border alone, the AMG car had had a flat tyre, nearly knocked over a cyclist and had only avoided a head-on collision with a truck by a miracle. On the pitted Italian roads, Cary had had discovered, at the age of fifty, that reading in a car made him sick. He had thrown his guts up in a stinking ditch, not even managing to save his shoes from mud and vomit.

It was at that very moment that his nerves had started to go into a tailspin.

He had begun reading the Dyle dossier the day before, in the hospitable calm of a Trieste café, over a steaming cup of black tea. He had persuaded his escort to leave him alone for a few hours, long enough to take a walk, to have a bit of peace. He was in such a dishevelled state that no one would recognise him. They had agreed on discreet and remote surveillance. Remote, but not too much so. The delicate pier-glass reflected a clear image of the two Englishmen whose task was to follow him everywhere, busy downing a beer at three in the afternoon.

In 1947, during a communist uprising in Greece, Major Alexander Dyle had asked Marshal Tito to close the Macedonian border. No communist was to escape the repression. Slaughter, mass executions on Churchill's orders. The kind of solution that Cary found revolting. You didn't have to be a communist to see it as carnage. When you've won, you've won, you don't have to be merciless. What was the Latin quote? *Est modus in rebus*, or something of the kind.

He had sipped his blended Assam tea, resolving to deliver that opinion to the major in person when he met him face to face. That happened the following day, on the border between zones A and B of the Free Territory of Trieste. Major Dyle, a British official on Yugoslavian soil, had come to take delivery of Cary, to bring him to Dubrovnik.

He was wearing an old and uncomfortable-looking deerstalker hat in mouse-grey tweed.

He had a ludicrous moustache.

He was pompously smoking a pipe curved like a saxophone.

He didn't stop talking for ten minutes at a stretch, and, with minimal pauses, for the remaining three hours.

Cary was not well versed in the study of physiognomy. To claim that the facial features revealed anything about a person's character struck him as an exaggerated hypothesis, supported by large numbers of idiots with idiotic faces and refuted by too many criminals who looked like gentlemen. Anyway, he had a technique for recognising imbeciles. More than a technique, a sixth sense. Infallible. Based on a simply elaborated concept of 'external appearance', which was not limited to the face, but encompassed the manner of speaking, the choice of clothing, the gait. Out of a sense of indulgence towards his fellow-man, he hesitated to attribute 100 per cent certainty to his diagnoses.

With Dyle, he restricted himself to a probability of 70 per cent.

The information in the file added another 20 percentage points.

Some 150 kilometres, 180 minutes and thousands of words were more than enough to supply the remaining 10.

The umpteenth confirmation. A moron.

Fortunately, thanks to this talent, Cary immediately sensed what a terrible blunder he had committed in bringing the discussion round to Greek communists, Tito and the style of the victors.

After travelling 160 kilometres, just past Jablanac, Cary pretended to go to sleep, but this childish ploy was not enough to silence the major. He merely redirected the flow of his logorrhoea towards the driver, the innocent victim of bombastic pronouncements on international politics.

The big dipper started getting faster, his nerves were whirling now.

Cary regretted the meditation courses recommended by Betsy; he had never gone beyond the introductory lesson. If he couldn't actually have slept, he would at least have closed his eyes, breathed deeply, relaxed his limbs. And fixing his mind's eye on a point above his lip where the breath brushes the skin as it leaves the nostrils, he would have avoided drowning in the muddy torrent of crap issuing from the major's mouth.

That area of the body, just above the lip, a meeting point, etc., was currently covered by annoying bristles. Raymond had dared to suggest a false beard: 'Mr Raymond, I gave up being a circus performer thirty years ago, and I have no intention of starting again now.'

He would have given all the banknotes in his wallet to be able to concentrate amidst all that confusion.

As a conditioned reflex, Cary stretched out a somnambulant hand along his duffel-coat to find the pocket in which . . .

Empty. No comforting bulge.

His hand darted towards the other pocket and rummaged around in it. His fingers gripped a piece of paper.

Cary opened his eyes wide with a start and unfolded the sheet in front of his nose.

Major Dyle fell silent.

Cary turned the paper around to read it. An incomprehensible language. Italian. A large title in the middle, in block letters. Then, one line under the other, something that looked like the lines of a poem, some scribbles, words crossed out with a stroke of the pen.

'What is it, Mr Kaplan? You seem concerned.'

'I am, Major. It would seem that this is *not* my duffel-coat.'

'It's not yours?' exclaimed Dyle in an over-the-top performance of astonished stupidity. 'Whose is it, then?'

'I couldn't begin to guess. Does this scrap of paper give you any clues?'

The major put on a pince-nez and concentrated on the ornate handwriting. He was the kind of person who overemphasises his every attitude, like B-movie character actors. If the situation called for astonishment, Dyle was the most astonished man in the world; if he was expected to concentrate, his forehead immediately developed five or six profound wrinkles; if his role required him to demonstrate affability, the only way to switch off his natural charm was to knock his teeth down his throat.

'It looks like Italian,' he said after a great deal of effort. 'The headline says *Povera Patria*, "Poor Fatherland". Does that suggest anything to you?'

'It suggests that someone must have swapped my duffel-coat for his, and it must have happened in Trieste, in that café in the centre, what was it called?'

Cary clearly remembered going into the establishment, ordering his tea and paying straight away, yes, and the waiter had asked for his duffel-coat, which was slung over the back of the chair, to take it to the cloakroom. And then? Then nothing, he hadn't used his wallet again: he hadn't had to pay for anything else, and they had been waved through customs because their car belonged to the *corps diplomatique*.

'Stop in the first village, Howard,' ordered Major Dyle, 'and find a telephone.'

Then he turned back to Cary, still calling him Kaplan for the sake of the driver. 'Could you give me a description of your duffel-coat, Mr Kaplan?'

Cary pursed his lips, the big dipper accelerated: 'My duffel-coat is *identical* to this one, Major, the swap was caused precisely by their similarity to one another. Doesn't that seem likely to you?'

'Oh certainly, Mr Kaplan, that's elementary.' Sherlock Holmes grumbled to himself, then continued: 'And your wallet? Could you describe it to me? Do you remember what was in it?'

'A plain leather wallet, long and flat. Inside: my passport, two hundred-dollar bills, a bit of loose change in lire, and . . . I don't remember anything else, Major.'

'Fine, Mr Kaplan, forget it ever happened. With the help of our agents in Trieste, it will be as though you never lost your wallet. And please note that I am not saying this out of national pride, or to give you some kind of pointless reassurance, you see –'

'Could you pass me that piece of paper for a moment?' Cary asked with perfect timing. If he let him loose on that subject he'd be off again, at least half an hour's tirade on the efficiency of His Majesty's agents. Then he had noticed something. On the back, someone had reproduced a signature hundreds of times. The handwriting looked the same as the poem. The signatures were almost identical, with small variations here and there, as though to the writer were trying to find the most elegant way of writing his name.

Cary narrowed his eyes and tried to decipher the scribble. Then he asked for confirmation.

'This is an interesting piece of information, Major. Your friends won't mind having a name to start off with, will they? What do you think it says?'

Dyle studied the piece of paper as though it were the Rosetta Stone.

'Hmm, let's see, Carlo . . . Carlo Alberto Rizzi, I would say, yes, that's it, Carlo Alberto Rizzi. There's no doubt about it. Things are looking up, Mr Kaplan. By this evening, we will have found your wallet.'

In the meantime, the Triestine poet Carlo Alberto Rizzi would search fruitlessly for a patriotic poem in the pockets of his duffel-coat, finding instead a leather wallet, 200 dollars and the British passport of Mr George Kaplan.

Chapter 50

A mixture of fish, naphtha and sweat. The smell of the port. Since he had learned to walk, he had grown up on the docks, cadging a few cents from the longshoremen and listening to the sailors telling their fantastic tales. The smell of grim and boastful men, trawlers, barnacles clinging to the piers of the bridge. Even when he had had his first fuck, the youngest whore he had been able to afford. And that smell was still there as he weighed down the feet of those poor bastards, deaf to their pleading and the promises of all the wealth in the world.

He climbed down from the ship, feeling sick. It wasn't seasickness; he was disgusted with the endless shit jobs he had done in his life. To discover that what he was best at was settling other people's scores in exchange for decent wages, a clean suit and a matching tie. His tour of the Sicilian refineries had been enough to stir old grievances in his belly: now here he was in a lousy little harbour frequented by the worst kind of human scum that the asshole of the world could shit on to the earth. Another job for Steve Cement.

Just one thing kept his mind alert: determination. The last task was completed. Lyonnese Toni was waiting for him in Cannes, to buy *his* drugs.

Walking towards the three shady figures at the end of the bar, he thought about what Luciano had said: 'I commend myself to you, Steve, I want everything done just as it was before. And if they balk at the price, tell them to fuck off, and their mothers too. And take care, ok?'

The three faces showed a complete set of all the things that a blade can do to a human face. Only their sloping moustaches partially hid the damage. They were wearing stinking jackets and sailors' berets made of rotten wool. They emanated *that smell.*

He stopped in front of them and looked straight at them without batting an eyelid.

'Bulatovic.'

The man in the middle nodded to him to follow him. Zollo walked behind them.

They escorted him to a tavern with the sound of music and laughter coming from inside. About thirty men were crammed into the place, and an old man was wheezing away on the accordion in a corner at the back. Some of the patrons were soldiers, with long beards and uniforms loosened because of the heat. The smoke from cigarettes and hubble-bubbles created a dense fog, and beyond it Zollo could just make out the one who was supposed to be his man. On previous journeys he had dealt with intermediaries, but this time the packet of heroin was a very big one: the boss himself had bothered to come here to receive it.

Mikhail Mehmet Bulatovic was sitting at one of the smoky tables. Two ugly great brutes were standing behind him. The three guys from before were actually rather pretty in comparison.

Bulatovic was wearing a suit at least twenty years out of date, and was badly shaven, as though his tough skin had put up furious resistance to his razorblade. The kind of character that Zollo deeply loathed. A megalomaniac bumpkin who thought he was the Tsar of all the Russias just because he had some cop in his pocket and sold drugs at the head of a gang of cutthroats. No rules.

These were the kind of people who kept the wheels of the international drugs trade in motion. Tens, perhaps hundreds, of provincial little Caesars in pursuit of cash and glory.

Bulatovic nodded to him to sit down on the other side of the table. Murderer's eyes, grey and expressionless. Zollo had never seen eyes like them. He held out a rough hand and took his seat. He was offered a glass of brandy which he barely sipped.

One of the men from the port said, 'Mikhail don't speak 'Talian, says it fascist language. I do, I made war against 'Talians. You speak, I translate.'

'I want to know where to pick up the goods, and where to deliver the payment.'

This was quickly translated.

Bulatovic uttered a few words.

'He says the day after tomorrow in Dubrovnik. At the docks. You check the goods, then you pay.'

Zollo nodded.

'He say also that you in great danger here. Mikhail has many enemies, people who want to get their hands on his business. You understand? He got to keep everyone in their place. He spend money to pay soldiers, and to defend your way of life. If he don't check everything, his enemies kill you for ruining his business.'

The usual shitty stuff. The tribal elder had stepped forward, just to tighten the rope.

Zollo got to his feet.

'Tell him the price is the same as it was the other times. I'll look after my own back. *Ok?*

The guy translated and Bulatovic went on staring at him for a few seconds, as though weighing something up.

Zollo felt like a cavalryman defending his scalp against the Indians.

He turned on his heels, not wild about the idea of turning his back on these people. Before he left he spat on the floor.

As he walked towards the ship he wondered how long it would take for them to come after him. The tavern door closed behind him.

And here they were.

He stopped and calmly lit a cigarette.

It was the two bodyguards.

They were clutching .45 calibre Lugers. Scrap metal.

He didn't like trials of strength. They were just rhetorical gestures to show whose cock was the hardest. But that was how these people were, they spoke an ancient language.

He drew his Smith and Wesson, complete with silencer, and shot them both in the left kneecap before they had time to take aim.

He finished them off with a flurry of kicks and the jack-knife he kept in his pocket.

By the time he got back to the tavern his jacket was creased and he had a bloodstain on his sleeve. Bulatovic and the interpreter sat

petrified at the table. It was the same colour as they were; they looked
as though they were part of a single wooden sculpture.

Zollo walked over to them, his face unchanged.

The drugs dealer heard a *plop* in the glass in front of him.

As his brandy turned red he saw two ears floating in it.

Zollo murmured, 'Now you know who's hardest.'

He turned to the interpreter. 'See you in Dubrovnik.'

This time he looked over his shoulder as he left.

Chapter 51

It happened five years ago. Kardelj, who had had dinner with me that evening, was clarifying the issue of Leninist theory in Yugoslavia, and rejecting the accusations of 'Trotskyism' issuing from Moscow. The mirror spied on us from the end of the corridor, our lookalikes copying our every move, perhaps preparing to reproach us. Here we were, well fed and clothed, so unlike the days of the *konspiracija*. Was it just vanity that dictated the stance that would consign us to history? We discovered (at dead of night it's inevitable) that there was something monstrous about the mirrors. Kardelj said the mirror is an infernal machine, because it separates the individual from the community, stimulating his petty-bourgeois narcissism. I replied, 'So how do you trim your moustache, by leaning over puddles?' adding that, on the contrary, the mirror *unites* the individual with the community, and its admission into proletarian houses has cemented class pride, that sense of decorum thrown back in the bosses' faces, 'We have been naught, we shall be all! We can be, and we are, more stylish than you are!' It was thanks to that decorum, to that pride, that the war was won.

Here I am. In a week I will be seventy-two. My temples are greying, I have a hint of a double chin, but I still get by, I have a young and beautiful wife. Stalin is dead, I'm alive. And I'm no longer an *ilegalac*. When I look in the mirror, I don't miss those days. How could I? Two wars, prisons, fights, flight and privations. Lepoglava, Maribor . . . I haven't had so much time to read since then. I still remember the smell of each book, the paper with its different colours and typefaces, every single copy brought into the jail. I used to read wearing pince-nez glasses that made me look like an intellectual. Me, a worker, the son of dirt-poor peasants.

And now I'm at the wheel of the new Yugoslavia, I'm wearing a new panama hat and in twenty minutes I'm going to be meeting Cary Grant. The coffee pot is hissing, the coffee is ready. Will he be one of those people who hold up their pinkies when they hold the cup? And what if he wants tea? No, he's an American now, Americans drink coffee. The first American I ever met . . . when was that? At the Lux, in the shower, almost thirty years ago. Tell him about that?

White suit, sky-blue shirt, indigo tie matching my socks.

That interview in *Life* magazine, when we went to the UN. Lovely photographs, but Bebler and Djilas said I looked like a 'South American dictator', that I would have to be less 'showy' or I would repel Western public opinion. Strange, just a few weeks previously I had been talking to Kardelj about mirrors.

They're stubborn, they don't want to understand. They've never saved to buy the feathered hat of the gymnastic association. In Kamnik (what would it have been, 1911?) and Vienna, the dancing school, fencing school, skiing. Taking care of every detail, always improving your own way of doing things. In 1913 I became regiment fencing champion, I was admitted into that big tournament, I came second and made such an impression that I was sent on a course for junior officers. Small steps along the way that brought me to see the October Revolution and become a Bolshevik. Could I have led *our* revolution without a presence appropriate to the task? Small steps, and that hat.

One day even Djilas will understand: the League of Yugoslavian Communists governs this republic with the consensus of the people who founded it, a mosaic of races, religions, traditions. At the top you need rituals and certain roles. Without rituals and shared symbols, without a guarantor of the community's cohesion, we would be finished. Every detail of my public face is a symbol, it must transmit the message: 'I am everything *and you are everything along with me!*' The perfect cut of my uniform gives concrete form to the pride of the workers.

Stalin looked as though he was being choked by his jacket collar. The first time I saw him, he looked painfully clumsy. I cut a fine figure even in Buckingham Palace, a real man among bloodless dandies and doddering old fools. Bringing a breath of revolution and

a brave new world to Buckingham Palace. Isn't that a titanic enterprise as well?

Stalin. I'm the only person who can say I contradicted him in
public. Other people did it too, of course. Except that they didn't
live to tell the tale. 'And what are we going to do now?' everyone
asks me. After a long time the first shy signals are coming in from
Moscow. Djilas is raising a cloud of dust. Serov's spies in every corner,
in all likelihood. The British are suggesting a film. Very peculiar. A
strange way to familiarise the West with our form of socialism. And
then I say: bring me Cary Grant.

Ten minutes away.

Will he be bothered by smoke?

Enter Cary. Clean-shaven, finally, and wearing a suit sent from Palm
Springs for the occasion. This is the Cary Grant everyone knows,
the one Tito imagines he knows, nerves of steel, intent on wiping
out a network of Nazis in *Notorious*. Tito expresses himself in passable English, apart from the occasional *faux ami*: he says 'anaemic'
instead of 'enemy'. Cary doesn't correct him. As usual when acting
the generous host, Tito makes the coffee in person. Cary looks on
with amusement. A few mentions of Trieste, the coat recovered in
no time at all by the AMG agents. And who is this character Rizzi?
A poet. Ah. Tito talks about his first visit to Trieste. He was eighteen,
he arrived on foot, eighty kilometres from Ljubjana. He was stunned
by the sheer size of the harbour. He felt lost.

Grant asks Tito about the schism with Stalin, adding, 'That took a
bit of nerve, he looked like one of the bad guys in a Disney film!'
Tito laughs and thinks about the wicked witch in *Snow White* interrogating her mirror. He thinks about Kardelj, about Djilas, about
decisions that were so hard to take. He thinks about Moscow, about
the purges, about the ever emptier floors of the Hotel Lux. Then he
rewards his guest with a few anecdotes. Just after the war a team of
Russian film-makers turned up here, also wanting to make a film
about our Resistance. They were really a bunch of boozing whores
and scoundrels, they got drunk day and night, they caused trouble
over the merest trifles, on a number of occasions our police were
called to sort them out. The film was an obscenity. Our war emerged

from it as a secondary conflict, a diversion to keep the Axis busy while the Red Army got on with the job. And in fact it was we who broke first the Duce's back, then the backs of the Germans. Your Churchill understood that after the Fifth Offensive, although if he'd worked it out earlier many of the comrades would still be alive. Oh, it's true, you aren't English any more, or rather you're English and a nationalised American. He should have said 'naturalised', but Cary doesn't correct him. He feels good.

Today we've got information suggesting that members of the crew were spying for Stalin. It was an initial attempt at destabilisation. They've always been afraid of us. Tito finishes, so to speak, with an allusion to his knowledge that he can take care of himself, even when there seems no immediate need to do so. You're better off not owing anything to anybody. Grant sips his coffee, which is very good, and delights Tito with details of his conquest of artistic and economic independence. People admire Tito, they really do. And what about this film? Tito smiles, lights a cigarette and raises a quizzical eyebrow. No, it doesn't bother me. You know, I managed to give up, thanks to my wife. I used to smoke, of course I did. Thanks to your wife? What did she do, if you don't mind my asking? Did she threaten you with not . . . ? The two men laugh. No, no, she hypnotised me. Really? But does it work? I can guarantee it. Your wife is a hypnotist? Well, she tried it and it worked. You know, she subscribes to these oriental disciplines that are so much in vogue in California, less so in Yugoslavia, I would guess. Tito blows out a smoke ring. I'll set up a commission of doctors. If they can prove to me that hypnosis works, then perhaps one day we'll make it part of our public health system. If it exists, the people have a right to it. Cary arches his eyebrow. At the end of the day, we *are* in the East.

You know where I met my first American citizen? In Moscow, in the shower. In the Hotel Lux, where foreign communists stayed. The hot water wasn't on all the time, and when there was any it ran out almost immediately. Moscow isn't Palm Springs, it was absolutely freezing. To wash ourselves, we showered in pairs. That was how I met Earl Browder, the great leader of American communism. He stood for the presidency if I remember correctly. I don't know what happened to him in the end, but I'm sure he isn't getting on too

well with that oaf McCarthy. Oh, Stalin took good care of him.
What? They killed him? Not physically, but in 1944 he declared that
capitalism and communism could coexist, and lost his post as Party
secretary. Two years later the Cominform called him a 'deviationist'
and expelled him from the Communist Party. I don't know what he
lives on now. I see him as a precursor of what we're trying out.
Browder was in favour of an American way towards socialism.

I saw you in that film where you were dressed as a woman. Which
one, the one with the leopard or the one with the male war bride?
The male war bride. Really good fun. And the one with the Nazi
wine cellar. *Notorious*. Terrifying. You know, my secret services gave
me a file on you. Don't worry, nothing compromising as far as I'm
concerned, quite the reverse. You've served your country and the anti-
fascist cause in a sector of such crucial importance as entertainment.
Cary holds his breath. What I was about to say: in the photographs
you wear exceptionally well-tailored suits. I have some too, you know.
We working-class children have to acquire elegance. Doggedly. Ever
alert, as though we were at the front. At the end of the day this is
war as well. Cary is almost moved. He thinks about his childhood
in Bristol. He thinks about the mother he thought was dead and
who came back from the grave. He thinks about his time as a sandwich board man on stilts, in New York. Just to say it isn't a silly
question. You don't wear a belt. You don't wear braces. You haven't
got a pot belly. How on earth do you hold your trousers up? Cary
laughs. Tito laughs.

They mention that the Italian tailor and fashion house takes its name
from the Islands of Brioni. Strange, isn't it? I don't know why. You
know, I think we have a lot in common. I know it's strange, we've
had very different lives, and yet . . . Cary expounds his views. Tito
surprises him: *konspiracija* and cinema have forced them to adopt
different identities. Let's try and count them! I have been Josip Broz,
Georgijevic, Rudi, John Alexander Carlson, Oto, Viktor, Timo, Jiricek,
Tomanek, Ivan Kostanjsek, Slavko Babic, Spiridon Mekas, Walter and
finally Tito. I have been, to cite only a few: Archibald Alexander
Leach, 'Rubber Legs', the magician Knowall Leach, Max Grunewald,
Cary Lockwood, Jimmy Monkley, Jerry Warriner, the palaeontologist

David Huxley, Sergeant Archibald Cutter, the pilot Jeff Carter, the
newspaper editor Walter Burns, Leopold Dilg, Ernie Mott, Joe
Adams, the millionaire C. K. Dexter Haven, Johnnie Aysgarth,
Mortimer Brewster, Cole Porter, the agent Devlin in *Notorious*, Mr
Blandings, who wanted to build his dream house . . . To come here
I have assumed the identity of 'George Kaplan'. What I don't know
is who I would be expected to play in the film, if it should happen.
Why did you decide to leave the cinema, Mr Grant?

   They chat like old friends. Have you stopped drinking, too?
Certainly not. Then I shall have them bring a brandy from these
islands, an aperitif. This evening you will dine with me, have you
told them that?

Cary realises that Tito has not the slightest interest in the bizarre
suggestion being put forward by MI6. His game is one of tempor-
isation, waiting to see what's happening in Moscow, keeping a foot
in both camps. He goes to dinner with Her Majesty, and the heretic
Djilas is immolated on the Moscow altar. A strategist, a political
animal following the trail, scenting the smell of death: every time
Stalin is mentioned, a light in his eye goes out for half a second. He
hears something. The patter of feet dancing on the tyrant's grave? In
any case, the idea of the film is a load of crap. That or a huge joke.
Tito and Cary Grant converse amicably. Can you imagine a more
surreal scene? Nothing means anything, apart from the fact that I
am here and I feel good. What? Oh, sorry, I was thinking out loud.

Treacherous eyes follow smiles and slaps on the back. Who can tell
that the film isn't going to happen? Elsewhere, people are waiting
for reports.

Chapter 52

Two in the morning. President Tito left Mljet less than four hours ago. The garden of the villa is so quiet you would think you could hear the tide lapping in the distance.

The shadow emerges furtively from the back door. It creeps past boxwood bushes and palm trees, before crouching down between the hedge and the statue of Hermes, which is smothered in climbing plants.

On its knees, a little case. The shadow opens it carefully, takes out a pair of headphones and puts them on. Expert fingers fiddle with slides and dials. A faint hiss comes from the headphones. Eyes stare alertly at trembling gauges and decipher each oscillation. One hand works delicately to position the circular antenna and the telescopic aerial. The other picks up a receiver and brings it to the shadow's mouth.

'Fish in the sea, Varna, fish in the sea . . .'

The long-wave beep pierces eardrums. The shadow repeats insistently: 'Fish in the sea, Varna.'

Broken words. Whistles. A sound like wind in a microphone. The hand adjusts the circular antenna. Indistinct phrases. Thumb and index finger stroke a dial.

The shadow whispers into the receiver: 'It doesn't matter if the trawler comes here. There are more fish in the sea around Šipan, repeat, Šipan, Mediterranean zone, uninhabited, landward side. Tomorrow morning, time unspecified, at least three swordfish, maybe four. The tuna has migrated, only sea bass and swordfish. Roger and out.'

The shadow throws back its head and blows a mouthful of tension at the stars.

It slips off the headphones, closes the case and lightly makes its way back across the park.

The prow of the dinghy scrapes on to the sand, impelled by the last stroke of the oars. Four men jump into the sea and pick it up before dropping it on the beach.

Andrei Zhulianov glances nervously around. He has never liked changing plans at the last minute. Even when the changes seem to make everything easier. He would rather have a big risk calculated down to its tiniest details than a linear action filled with unpredictable possibilities. Mljet was a big risk. Šipan looks easier, but they're still going to have to improvise the whole thing.

The map of the place, found on the *Varna*, doesn't add a great deal. A nautical chart of southern Dalmatia. Like trying to find a restaurant on a globe.

Zhulianov glances at his watch. Four o'clock. Better act immediately.

First of all, unload the dinghy.

Then hide it.

Finally, find a good observation point, to sight the yacht arriving from Mljet.

Don't let all that confuse you. In one rucksack, all the scuba-diving equipment. In the next, binoculars and telescope. In the third, the instruments. Never forget, I'm looking for a place to hide the dinghy.

Three hours later, twenty or thirty metres along the beach and just a bit more to the east, Pierre will wake up in his father's bed after a night spent tossing and turning. The first sun of the morning will fill the room, with the promise of a hot day, ideal for swimming.

Pierre will reach the window on bare feet. He won't be able to keep from thinking about Bologna, the day he left, still cold, damp, wrapped in the last fog, drenched by soft rain, a whitish sky hiding the sun.

He will hear the sounds of his father in the next room, and go and stand in the doorway, leaning against the frame.

'You can hardly complain about the weather and the landscape, dad. End of April and you'd think it was summer. At home I get up, I open the window, and every morning I see the footpath, two or three bicycles and some old woman with her shopping bag. You have the rocks, the sea, the islands . . .'

'Well, that's true,' Vittorio will reply with a half-smile. 'But isn't that exactly what's wrong? Small pleasures rather than big dreams. A beautiful view, sun and the best ricotta cheese in the world.'

'I was trying to look on the bright side.'

'The bright side? There is one, I'm aware of that. You can live well here, if you want to. But I don't. I want something else, can't you see that?'

Pierre will shake his head and turn away in silence, resolving not to put himself in a bad mood. There is no more impregnable fortress than pessimism whatever the cost.

Better to forget the whole thing and hurry down to the beach.

President Tito's private yacht crosses the waves at a steady rate. Cary, sitting at the prow, dangles a hand over the side and collects spray to wet his head, as empty of thoughts as the sky is empty of clouds.

The only annoyance: the three bodyguards, heedful of his every movement, always alert, always armed. Never a moment to relax.

Relax. Swim, read, sunbathe, stroll along the beach. The day's schedule is all there, a cure-all before the exhaustions of a new, long journey. Before going back to Palm Springs and then meeting up with Hitch and Grace Kelly on the Côte d'Azur. Better than staying at home, a wealthy pensioner, yoga, Ayurvedic massages and David Niven's wisecracks.

Until then, however, Cary has made up his mind not to think about it, and just wants to be left to his own devices.

He puts on his sunglasses, makes himself comfortable and opens the book at Chapter 23.

The lens of the spyglass frames the scene.

Zhulianov adjusts the focus and sees the yacht dropping anchor about a hundred metres from the beach. The dinghy lands in the water with three men on board. The bodyguards are in military uniform. Grant is wearing a blue polo-neck and a pair of swimming trunks the same colour. He has sunglasses on, and is holding something in his hand. Perhaps a book.

*

They are called the Elaphites, a group of about ten small islands between the eastern end of Mljet and the port of Dubrovnik. The name has something to do with deer, but it isn't clear whether it is down to the presence of those animals, all of which have now disappeared, or the appearance of the archipelago as a whole, which recalls, as a constellation might, the features of a deer.

Šipan, Lopud and Kolocep are the only inhabited islands. On Šipan, the largest one, there are two settlements, Šipanska Luka and Sudurad, on the other side.

Halfway between the two villages, hidden between rocks and gorse bushes, a shabby house looks down upon a stretch of uninhabited and inhospitable coast.

Perhaps that is why Vittorio Capponi, who has been living there for about two months, has never seen anyone drop anchor around here. At most a passing fishing boat, early in the morning, or at night off the coast, fishing with a lamp for squid. But a yacht of those dimensions, never. So big it can carry, hoisted by two pulleys at the stern, a four-seater motor-powered sloop.

Tourists? Hardly. Do you think anyone with a boat like that would come and swim there, at the most deserted point of the whole island? The kind of thing really posh people get up to is being seen all over the place, in the most fashionable places, on famous beaches, not halfway between Šipanska Luka and Sudurad, amidst the goats and the squid fishermen.

And yet. Vittorio narrows his eyes and puts a hand to his forehead to shield his eyes from the sun. And yet they are, Radko, look. They're lowering the sloop into the sea, heading for the beach.

Those aren't military uniforms, are they?

Bloody hell! They're coming to get me!

Pierre is enjoying the spring sunshine lying on the sand, bare to the waist and trousers rolled up to the knees. He is thinking about Angela, what she's likely to be doing at that moment, the things he will tell her when he gets back to Italy. Her perfume, her hair and endless details of her body suddenly come flooding into his mind. A kind of shudder runs through him, all the way from his feet to his shoulders. He thinks of the things he would like to tell his father, the knot he would like to loosen once and for all.

He decides to get up before he fries. Legs left liquid by the heat, steam in his brain.

He shakes off the sand and stumbles unsteadily towards the shoreline.

He rests his bottom in the clear water and is sorry he never learned to swim. Aunt Iolanda had tried to persuade him loads of times, but he was having none of it. He couldn't understand all that effort, just for the pleasure of crossing the river Santerno, from the little pond where he used to bathe in the summer. The water was cool even by the shore, and you had to sit down to get in up to your neck.

But the sea is something else. This one makes you want to swim, look at the beach from various different viewpoints, swim way out, towards the waves, towards the gulls.

When he hears the sound of the engine he gives a start. He creeps over to the rocks that separate him from the other beach, and peers over the edge. Three men are dragging a large boat ashore. The fourth is a loose-limbed man who looks around as though admiring the landscape, then sits down on the sand and opens a book.

A tourist would be fascinated by the rocky backdrop, covered with anemones and Neptune grass.

With a kick of his flippers he would follow a shoal of little scad on their sudden unanimous twists and turns.

Or he might plunge into the depths in search of a starfish, or to see the eye of a cuttlefish peeping out from the sand.

He would slip loose the knife tied to his thigh to pry limpets from the rocks.

A tourist would delight in the sight of the loggerhead turtles, rare in these waters.

But Ivo Radelek is not a tourist.

The only thing he's interested in looking at is right in front of him: the white hull of President Tito's private yacht. As it approaches he tries not to think of the months he spent in Goli Otok, the Cominform hell, where Tito locked him up so that he could forget all about him. Now he's going to make him pay for it, and he is going to have to be clear-headed and efficient.

Gripping the raised gangway, he hoists himself gently up on to the stern. He calmly takes aim, and only when he is certain of hitting his target does he blow into the blowpipe.

The third guard brings his hand to the back of his neck and barely has time to gurgle before the drug reaches his brain, leaving him lying sprawled on the deck.

The scuba-diver takes off his wetsuit, undresses the guard and puts on his uniform. Finally he takes a walkie-talkie out of the waterproof bag.

'The net has been cast. Repeat: the net has been cast. Proceed.'

'Let's go,' Zhulianov whispers to the other two.

The journey has been carefully planned. They can swoop on the beach unseen.

The two bodyguards are keeping their distance from Grant. In the shade of the sun, in their uniforms, just below the escarpment.

Three lizard men creep silently along, under the cover of the bushes. They freeze.

Twenty metres from their goal.

He walked along the waterline on the hard golden sand until he was out of sight of the inn. Then he threw off his pyjama-coat and took a short run and a quick flat dive into the small waves. The beach shelved quickly and he kept underwater as long as he could . . .

Cary hears a thump to his right and lowers the book. One of the guards is lying on the ground, and he doesn't appear to be sunbathing. The reflex action conditioned by thousands of clapperboards: an expression that filmgoers around the world have admired on countless occasions.

Fractions of a second. The other man throws himself down, shielding him with his body, but there is a dart for him, too. Cary finds himself crushed by the dead weight of the brute, and lets out a curse.

He manages to disentangle himself, and with a somersault worthy of Archie Leach he pulls himself up and begins to run towards the rocks.

He just has time to glance behind him: three men in black are coming after him.

There are four of them.

One at the front, one in the middle, the rest behind.

No uniforms now, but they sure as hell aren't tourists. They are running. Towards the barrier of rocks that separates the two inlets. The inlet they are anchored in from the one where Robespierre is standing.

Vittorio tenses his jaw. Drenched in sweat, apart from the hand clutching the Mauser and the finger pressed to the trigger.

He lowers his head, eye aligned with the barrel, and takes aim.

The loose-limbed man is first to spring from the rocks. He runs with great strides, like a sprinter. The other three struggle to keep up with him.

As they gradually approach, Pierre can see the man's expression. Tense, frightened. He doesn't look like an athlete in training. More like someone escaping. And his face is extremely familiar.

The shot has the effect of the starter pistol for the hundred-metre sprint.

He heads for the slope, leaving a cloud of sand behind him.

The second bullet takes the Slav just above the ankle. He goes down, like a slaughtered deer. The third shot whistles a few centimetres past the right ear of Zhulianov, who curses. He hadn't predicted this. He creeps over to the injured man and helps him to his feet, dragging him to shelter from the gunfire. He switches on his walkie-talkie and speaks quickly: 'Drop the lobster pot! I repeat: drop the lobster pot! Force 10 gale, come back immediately.'

He clambers over the still sleeping bodies of Grant's bodyguards, helping the Slav to his feet. They set off up the path among the rocks.

The opium of failure and the adrenalin of flight do battle within his nervous system.

Never underestimate the enemy.

There is a kind of cave at the edge of the beach, quite shallow, just a dent among the rocks. Pierre noticed it on the way down, and now he slips inside, head first.

The loose-limbed gentleman is right behind him. He slips in beside him and sits with his back to the wall, to regain his breath.

Pierre turns round, still electrified by his running.

They look at one another.

It doesn't occur to Pierre for so much as a moment that he might be seeing things. Too many times he has studied those features in photographs and on the big screen, centimetre by centimetre, trying to work out the secret of perfect style.

'Fuck me, it's Cary Grant!'

The emotion dulls his brain, he appeals to his English to help. His jaw refuses to close.

What should he say? What should he say!

'This is a film . . . isn't it?' he says in English. A Hollywood star on a forgotten beach in Dalmatia, being pursued by three sinister figures. What else could it be?

Grant peers over the rocks. 'I'm afraid not.'

It isn't! What the hell is it, then?

Another effort, not taking his eyes off him.

'What's . . . happening, Mr Grant?'

An expression halfway between worry and self-irony. 'Believe me, I haven't a clue!'

Glue! What on earth did *glue* have to do with it? Try again.

'You don't know . . . who are . . . these men?'

If only Fanti could see him, talking in English to Cary Grant!

'Absolutely not. And you? Where have you sprung from? Who are you?'

Understanding only half of the last question, Pierre rummages for something from Fanti's first lesson, and says, 'Nice to meet you. My name is Robespierre Capponi. I'm twenty-two and I'm from Bologna, Italy.'

Perplexed, the most stylish man in the world studies the hand that the boy is holding out. He shakes it quickly, and turns round again to glance towards the beach.

'Robespierre . . . We might as well call Napoleon and Lafayette to save our hide.'

'What?'

*

The voices emerge from the cave.

The gunfire did for three of them. The fourth must have captured Robespierre. He's interrogating him.

Vittorio creeps forward, careful not to make a noise. He skirts the wall that opens on to the cave, until he is a metre from the opening. He concentrates for a second, then jumps forward, Mauser levelled, ready to fire.

'*Stoj!*'

The shout resonates, and the echo mixes with Robespierre's voice. 'Don't shoot, dad, I'm with Cary Grant, don't shoot!'

When they reach the other beach, the bodyguards are still lying there.

Cary patiently listens to the questions of the Italian with the French name, a pleasant young man who has seen lots of his films and wants to learn to smile the way he does

His father, surly and shabby, insists on having a question translated, but the boy doesn't give him too much encouragement.

In any case, shabby or not, he was the one who fired, putting his pursuers to flight.

Cary is first to hold out his hand, as a gesture of gratitude. The boy asks him not to tell the bodyguards they are on the island.

'Cross my heart!' Cary replies, running a finger across his chest.

Behind him, a bodyguard struggles to wake up.

Heavy arms, misty vision. Captain Franko Spiliak tries to get to his feet, but his muscles aren't responding well. Three men, or perhaps only one multiplied by the narcotic hallucination.

In fact, when he manages to get back on his feet and his eyesight has returned to normal, he sees there is only one man there.

Cary Grant, safe and sound, sitting more or less in the same position as before, the same sunglasses, the same polo-neck and no book in his hand.

Seven hours later, even more confused, Pierre will go down to the beach to inspect it.

'Fine,' his father urges him. 'He didn't know who those people were. But have you asked him what *he* was doing around here?'

'Yes, dad, I told you. They want to make a film about Tito and

Cary Grant came to meet him. That's all, there's nothing strange going on.'

'So who were they? They turn up, they knock out the bodyguards, chase after the American and run off after three shots have been fired. All that, when he's just here for a film. No, Robespierre, something isn't right.'

'In any case, you've got nothing to worry about. They didn't come here for you, did they?'

'You never know. This is the kind of thing that attracts attention. Soldiers could turn up here tomorrow. You've got to think hard about what we'd have to do.'

A few feet away from the cave, the dog will bury his nose in the sand and start scratching.

'Radko, show me, what have you found?' Pierre will hold out his hand under the animal's muzzle.

A book. Nine bleeding hearts around the title, gold letters on brown cardboard. *Casino Royale*, by a certain Ian Fleming. In English.

He will turn it around devotedly in his hands. He will curse the swiftness of events and the Babel of languages that prevented him from prolonging the encounter.

Like winning the lottery and losing your ticket.

He will flick through the pages in the hope of finding some trace of the owner, a surrogate, however small, for an actual autograph.

But Cary Grant will not have written anything: not on the frontispiece, nor at the end, nor anywhere.

Chapter 53

'I've been thinking: on this forgotten island I've met my favourite actor and you've saved his life. But what do you think about it?'

'He might well be famous, but he didn't seem as bright as all that. You say women like him?'

'Are you joking? All the women in the world! And I didn't even ask for his autograph. No one's going to believe me!'

'You did well, Robespierre. He'd have told you to fuck off. In English, but he'd have told you to fuck off if you'd asked him for his autograph.'

They laughed, and the tension of their farewell eased.

Vittorio handed Pierre a leather bag.

After so many years without speaking the language, the days he had spent with his son had done wonders for his Italian.

'Thanks.'

Pierre closed the case. Dawn was just beginning to filter from behind the hill, and the stars were still visible in the sky.

'So is that all clear? You go to Dubrovnik on the coach. You go to the harbour, to Petar's taverna. There's a famous sign, everyone knows it, with a . . . what do you call it? A dove. A homing pigeon, you know?' Pierre nodded. 'Once there, you've got to ask for Dragan Petrovic, remember, Dragan is a tall guy, very strong, he has two fingers missing from his right hand. He lost them in the war when we were fighting together. Tell him I sent you, that you're my son, and that you've got to get back to Italy. Is that clear?'

'You're sure he won't give me away?'

Vittorio shook his head. 'I saved his life once, during the war. Listen: you can send me a little message through him.'

'How?'

'Dragan keeps homing pigeons.'

'He's a pigeon-fancier!'

Vittorio tried for a second to work out what he meant, and when he worked it out he nodded his head. 'He can give you a pigeon in a cage. You bring it to Italy and when you let it go it'll come back. Then Dragan tells me. That way I'll know you've managed to get home, and everything will be fine.'

The extraordinary coincidence made Pierre smile as he thought of Renato Fanti, perched on the roof of the building among his dovecotes.

He said, 'Perfect. But what are you going to do?'

Vittorio stroked the barrel of the Mauser that leaned against the door frame. 'What do you expect me to do? I'm going to leave too. After all that's happened, they will come to the island, and if they discover that I'm here, they'll find an excuse to send me to Goli Otok.'

'Come to Dubrovnik with me, then.'

'No. I'm going into the mountains.' He glanced towards the horizon, which was now tinged with pink. 'I know the mountains. I've fought there. I'll tell Dragan where I'm going. I trust him, so when your message arrives I'll know what's happened.'

'But you can't go on living like this. Always in hiding, always at the risk of being caught. You've got to do something, you've got to leave!'

'And where am I going to go? In Italy they'll put me in jail. And they don't want someone who's been friends with Tito. What am I going to do? Same as I'm doing here. I'm too old, Pierre, and defeat is like a weight you carry inside yourself, it drags you down.'

They said nothing for a while, each immersed in his own thoughts, searching for words.

Pierre understood that the defeat weighing on his father was not just the loss of the cause he believed in.

He had thought long and hard about it during those two weeks. Many times he had been on the point of talking to him about it, to loosen the knot he could feel deep in his stomach. But each time he was anxious. Anxious that he wouldn't be able to explain himself. Anxious that his father wouldn't want to talk about it. He realised that he couldn't leave like this, without saying anything. He hadn't set off on this journey just to know what had happened. Not just for the adventure.

He opened his mouth, still trying to find the right words, but it was Vittorio who spoke first, as though a kind of telepathy had formed between father and son.

'I haven't been a good father to you and your brother. A good father would stay with his children, even if he went to jail. I would have come back to Italy and put up with my trial. But what should I say, Robespierre? I did what I thought was the right thing to do. Helping these people to build socialism. That's what I fought for. And now I think it may not have been worth it. Now everything's crumbling. I'm like an exile. Milena has passed away and I'm alone like a dog, without children, without a companion, without a country and without socialism. And you know what I regret the most?' It was a sincere, stunned question. 'That I can't bring myself to be sorry. I can't think that it was a mistake. It was right to try, and if you want me to speak with all sincerity, I'd say it wasn't wrong, even now that Tito's turning into Stalin. Perhaps I'm wrong, Robespierre. I know it wasn't right for you and Nicola, I know you deserved a more normal father who would sacrifice himself for you. But here I had met Milena, I had fought shoulder to shoulder with her, we loved one another. Here there was a country to make, there was socialism, there was the revolution, you understand? A new society. And in Italy there was no such thing. If I had come back, I would have spent the rest of my life regretting that I hadn't done my part here. There you are, I've told you quite openly, and perhaps now you will hate me even more than Nicola does. But it's the truth, and now you're grown up you'll be able to understand. If I could go back, I would still make the same choice.'

Pierre saw himself again in Italo's cellar, at the age of thirteen, next to Nicola, a thin and bony 21-year-old. His father was a vague, dark outline and a deep voice. During the war years, he had been a fairy tale character for him, a presence that visited him at night, before he went to sleep, in Aunt Iolanda's stories and his own childhood fantasies. He imagined he was fighting against innumerable ruthless enemies, on the hills of a foreign land, like a warrior of old. His last tangible memory was the smell of his black leather jacket,

that night. The smell of tanning. 'Nicola, Robespierre, listen carefully. I can't stay with you. I've come back here under cover, you
understand? In hiding. Because if they discover that I've come back
to Italy they'll put me in jail. I have to go away again. But Aunt
Iolanda will look after you, she loves you as though you were her
own sons. I'll always write to you. And one day you will come to
live in Yugoslavia, in a better country, where the people are free and
happy. But you can't do that now, it's too dangerous. I've come back
to tell you this. Nicola, look after your brother, you understand?
You're the head of the family now.'

Pierre woke as though from a dream and clearly knew what it was
that he wanted to say, what for days he had carried within him
without getting to the bottom of it. He looked at Vittorio, sitting
on the camp bed, enveloped in the same darkness as before. But he
was no longer swathed in a mythical aura. He was just a man. And
he was his father.

'Nicola doesn't hate you, dad. It was disappointment that made
him like that. He admired you too much, and he felt betrayed. You
understand? He went into the mountains with the partisans because
you had taught him to be an anti-fascist. You were the one who
brought him up that way. He joined the brigade for you as well.
And he wanted you to see him, to admire him. And instead he took
that bullet in the leg, and when the war was over you decided to
stay here. He wanted to show you he was proud of what you had
done. You were our hero. You were the one who had never bowed
his head to the fascists. The one who had deserted so as not to kill
innocent people. The one who had gone to a foreign country to fight
the revolution that he hadn't been able to fight in Italy. But you were
also our father, Christ alive! And although you were fine as a hero,
as a father you had abandoned us. They were hard years, of course
they were. Aunt Iolanda bent over backwards to make the best of
things. It was a stroke of luck that the bar came up. It was the Party
that dragged us out of the shit, not you. You were far away. As far
away as Ulysses. You can't choose your parents. And you can't not
love them. Or hate them if they abandon you.'

Vittorio Capponi looked at his son. What he was looking for was
a lesson, a lesson in life from a man half his age, whom he had abandoned one day to follow his fighting nature. At that moment he

would have accepted anything at all, all the hatred in the world. He was ready, perhaps he had been for ten years.

Pierre screwed up his face, he made an effort, but understood that he would have to let the words flow.

'And yet parents, before they are parents, are individuals. That's what I think, I've taken a great deal of time to think about it. Perhaps I came here specifically to tell you that. For many years I wished I had a father like everyone else. A father who would have helped us, who would even have risked jail to take care of us. But the truth is that if you had made that choice, you wouldn't have been you. You would have given up what you considered the right thing to do. And that would have made you a failure. A failure as a person, I mean. By making the choice you made, you failed as a father, but you followed your ideas, your feelings. So you taught us that living means believing in justice and building your own destiny, not having it imposed upon you by other people. And for that reason, in spite of everything, you're a better person than many of the people I see in the bar, who have a house, a moped, *L'Unità* in their pocket, they have time to chat with their friends, and they don't want to make any choices any more. Perhaps their children are graduates and post-graduates now, perhaps they have good jobs, but they will never know what I know.'

Two tears hung from his eyelashes. They stayed there, poised, they didn't fall and they didn't dry up. His father remained motionless; perhaps he had the same lump in his throat.

Pierre went on: 'There, that's what I came to tell you. That what has happened cannot be erased, but it's too late to hate you and it's too late for you to go on feeling guilty. It doesn't do anyone any good.'

He gritted his teeth. Pierre hated sentimentality, he could only be sentimental with women, not among men, not between father and son.

He got to his feet, picked up his case and opened the front door. Radko slipped out, hungry for the morning air.

On the threshold the two men considered one another for a moment, embarrassed by the intimacy of their words.

'You've said some important things, Robespierre.'

'I've spoken the truth, dad.'

Vittiorio produced two envelopes from his shirt pocket and handed them to his son.

'One letter for Nicola and one for Iolanda. I find it very hard to write in Italian, but I think they'll manage to read it anyway. Talk to your brother and tell him I love him.'

Pierre nodded and didn't say anything else.

They shook hands like old friends.

'Good luck.'

'You too.'

Finally they hugged.

When he had reached the top of the hill overlooking the house, his father's whistle fetched back Radko, who had escorted him to that point.

Pierre turned around and saw him standing in the doorway, the old communist partisan exhausted by life. What he felt was not compassion. It would not have been fair; Vittorio had made his own choice and had not regretted it. He knew he had not said everything there was to be said, that he had held some things back, and for a moment his instinct told him to run back down there as well.

You've passed on your illness to me. I've made false papers to come here. Even I can't accept the destiny they want to impose on me. I've got a job, a talent for dancing, a lover and no prospects. I can go on being a barman, dancing myself breathless, meeting my girl-friend in secret, while she still wants to do that. Is that all? Is there nothing else? Is that supposed to be enough for me? No, dad, it's not enough, there's got to be something else, perhaps somewhere else, perhaps in another world, just as there was for you. Perhaps that's also why I've never managed to hate you. Because I'm like you too. I need more than the conversations in the bar.

He gripped the handle of the case, raised his arm in a farewell gesture and set off up the path.

Chapter 54

The old man's spit hit the eye of far-right MP Giorgio Almirante. A metre further on, meanwhile, a monstrous gash rent the face of his twin.

'That takes nerve,' Garibaldi cursed as he cleared his throat and prepared new ammunition. 'A fascist like that, coming here to speak to us, in Bologna, on the 1st of May. What does he think he's doing?'

'It's like this,' the other man agreed. 'It's all very well saying that we're against the atom bomb and all things like that, but if they give one to me, a nice bomb, and they tell me me to fire it on Washington, the Americans would be scared shitless, the wankers, and stop telling us what to do, you can be sure I'd press that button, I don't care about women and children, I'd press it and there's an end to it, because if you have to choose between two misfortunes you have to choose the less severe.'

'Let's just drop it, shall we, let's not say another word about it, we're late already.'

'Yeah, you're quite right, that's quite enough: last time the doctor told me terrible things about my liver, and I'm not to excite myself.'

'You never told me you had liver problems!' Garibaldi said in surprise. 'Do you want me to give you a little piece of Chinese mushroom?'

'Do I hell.' Bottone's face screwed up as though someone had held some shit under his nose. 'I don't even want to *see* that filth.'

'But it's good for you, you know? It won't make you sick or anything. You put it in your tea, and it turns into a broth, you drink three cups a day and you'll be right as rain.'

'I think it's all nonsense, that's what I think. One of those medicines that are good for everything and nothing.'

'But if the Chinese drink them, they must have a reason, don't you think?'

'Oh, the Chinese!' Bottone muttered after spitting at his umpteenth Almirante poster. 'They're strange people, the things that do them good don't do us good. And listen, if that muck there comes from China then *I born Vatican City, Shanghai Plovince, you not know that, honoulable Itarian comlade?*'

Bottone smiled stupidly, wagging his head from side to side, and Garibaldi told him to go fuck himself.

Noises were already coming from the intersection of Via Irnerio and Via Indipendenza, and the people were flowing through the gates in only one direction, towards Piazza dei Martiri, from where the procession would soon be setting off for the Margherita Gardens.

Above the heads of the crowd, the red banners of the Trade Union Headquarters, which was based not far away and organised the whole festival, with food stalls, merry-go-rounds in the gardens and a speech by comrade Montagnana in the afternoon.

Alongside the banners, which were gradually increasingly in number, some signs and placards were appearing.

'Garibaldi, you've still got your eyesight, can you read what it says up there?'

Garibaldi pulled the corners of his eyes with his fingers to help himself focus.

'Sadry, honoulable comlade, I Chinese, I no understand.'

Bottone advised him in no uncertain terms to engage in sexual congress with himself.

'It says: "No to Italy in the EDC", "EDC = SS", "Dollars and bombs: recipe for new Nazis."'

'Oh, fine,' Bottone said, rubbing his hands enthusiastically. 'Let's see if we can't get hold of everyone else, it looks like things are about to get going here.'

'What d'you mean, Bottone?'

'Don't you know? The police have forbidden any placards against the government, the atom bomb and so on. It's Labour Day, they say, so you can talk about work and don't fret over anything else. I'd say the fists'll start flying shortly.'

Bottone has seen a good few demonstrations. The first time was in 1911, a procession against Giolitti and the war in Libya. But he had felt a blow from a rifle butt only eight years after that, during the revolt against the rising cost of living, when the shops were looted. He had ended up in hospital with his head split open, and stayed there for almost a week, but the scar, under his hair, had never gone away.

The experience had left him with an ability to sense the moods of the crowd and the police, to work out when and where the sparks would fly. He grabbed Garibaldi by an arm and dragged him into the middle of the street, elbowing his way through to the other side of the square.

At the head of the procession, on Via dei Mille, were the union big-shots, some city councillors and even Senator Zanardi. The police would never charge at that point. They couldn't afford to do so over by Via Marconi either, because that was where Trade Union Headquarters was, and they risked getting a damned good hiding. For that reason, Bottone worked out that the attack would have to come from the station or somewhere behind it. But he ruled out the latter hypothesis, because there were very few controversial placards there, and the riot squad needed a pretext for sounding the charge.

In fact, at the designated crossroads, they found themselves facing the classic scene: rifles on one side, red banners on the other, and in the middle an invisible and magnetic trough, as there is when you try and bring together the same poles of a pair of magnets.

'This is your last warning. Hand in the forbidden placards or we will be obliged to break up the demonstration with the use of force.'

The reply was a unanimous shout, and hundreds of fists raised to the sky. 'One, two, three, four, Scelba you're a fucking whore!'

Then everyone launched into a rendition of the Internationale while Bottone and Garibaldi were sucked towards the front ranks.

It was then that something unexpected happened. The script had allowed for another minute or two of confrontation, then the marshal would give the order to charge and the first round would begin. Instead, at the first notes of the workers' anthem, a solitary individual, immediately identified by certain experts as Giuseppe Zanasi, a former amateur boxer, broke away from the cordon of comrades, took four steps forwards and went and took up position right in the middle of the magnetic field.

There was a moment's hesitation in the ranks of the riot squad, then one of them advanced towards Zanasi with his rifle raised, intimating that he should leave.

He didn't move a muscle, arms along his sides, eyes fixed on his shoes. The cop got even more aggressive and struck him on the shoulder to persuade him to shift. The former boxer's hand grabbed the barrel of the rifle and forced the cop to lower it. The two men stared at each other for a long time. Zanasi said something that many people later swore they had heard perfectly.

'He said, "Put this away, it's *nasty*," that's what he said.'

'No, no, I heard him very clearly, he said "So now what are you going to do? Shoot me?"'

'What are you on about? He said, "This would look better up your arse." And there's an end to it.'

Bottone and Garibaldi weren't near enough to have a version of their own. Neither did they hear the order to charge, but that was because, in the confusion of the moment, nobody had remembered to give it. Bottone didn't see the fist coming either. Garibaldi did: he was taller, and saw it very clearly. Zanasi barely looked up, as though his boxer's instinct suggested where he should strike. The cop went down like a tree. Then they were swept aside in the clash.

Zanasi was arrested along with another man who had just taken a few knocks, two riot police ended up in hospital, and five placards were confiscated.

Bottone was limping by the time he arrived at the gardens, from a kick in the shin that he claimed had been delivered by the marshal in person; Garibaldi's shirt was torn off in the scuffle, and Walterún, by way of consolation, offered him a glass at the wine stall. But there was nothing to be done, he would just have to live with it, and he was worried that his wife would chew his face off when he got home.

Chapter 55

At the end of the day he didn't mind the sea. Let's not get carried away, now, but he had developed a certain affection for it. Ok, the smell of the docks turned his stomach, he hated the salt on his skin, and the lounge bar millionaires with their passion for sailing; in spite of that, when he fantasised about the place where he would spend his last years, without even doing it on purpose he always found himself there, with his arse in the sun and the sea in front of him. It wasn't a conscious choice: his selection was guided by more important criteria.

First of all a place where Luciano wouldn't have any contacts. That ruled out a good proportion of the planet: at least all of the United States, a good chunk of Central America and the more civilised countries of the old continent.

Second, there couldn't be any fanatics around, it would be politically calm and the laws were very comprehensive, with citizens dedicated to alcohol, gambling and fornication. That completely ruled out Muslim countries, Soviet satellites and colonies in ferment.

Third, there would have to be at least one bar within a radius of five kilometres where the barman didn't serve bourbon instead of Scotch, and was capable of shaking up a decent Manhattan. Which ruled out Central Africa, India and possibly even Japan.

Fourth, the most you would need in the depths of winter was a woolly jumper. Out went Scandinavia, Canada and England.

Clearly, the sea wasn't on the list of basic requirements. And yet it came up time and again. Perhaps because Steve had learned his geography from cabin boys and bo'suns and couldn't think of a single town that didn't at least look out on an ocean.

Or perhaps because he had always lived in cities by the sea, even if, in New York, there are children in Queens who have never been to Coney Island or Orchard Beach, and don't even know that the ocean begins just beyond the Verrazzano Narrows Bridge. Because, in the end, Upper Bay is very like a lake, and you can be sure that the guy who drives the Staten Island ferry wouldn't be able to pilot a dinghy on the open sea.

So, to recapitulate: Montevideo? Full of Italians. And they have cold winters down there. The Bahamas? Too many goddamned Americans. Or how about Sydney? No, Steve, too many Italians in Sydney too; what about New Zealand? No, it would get cold down there too from time to time. Hong Kong? Singapore? Could they make a decent Manhattan in Singapore?

The sailor had told him to behave himself in there and make sure nobody saw him. It probably wasn't in the captain's interests to report him once they'd got there, but it wouldn't be a good idea to worry him, either. He wasn't a very understanding guy.

For the first two hours of the journey, Pierre remained true to the task. Crouching in his hole, with the little cage between his knees and the leather bag under his arm, he did everything he could think of to go to sleep, the only way he could give his stomach peace. But not even a fakir could have put him to sleep in those conditions. There was a terrible heat, the air was dense, a compress of salt and lubricants on the skin, the taste of rotten fish in his mouth and nose. Chin resting on his knees, Pierre kept his eyes on his travelling companion, concerned that it might drop dead at any moment.

He knew it would not survive for long.

He had to get out of there. Stick two fingers in his throat and that would be that. Otherwise, he risked throwing up in his hiding place, and drowning the pigeon. A terrible way to go.

The outline of the mountains dissolved on the horizon, there was nothing but water all around. Zollo headed towards the hold for his usual mid-crossing check. With a cargo like this, you could never be careful enough. He chucked his cigarette end over the parapet and started climbing down the stairs towards the lower deck.

When he had reached the bottom, just before he got to the hatch, a noise to his right attracted his attention. If it was something human, it was not unlike the final appeal that J. J. Clancy Frongillo had made to the world, before dying with his windpipe crushed by the thumbs of Steve Cement. Zollo leaned forward, over the base of a gigantic goods lift, and saw someone behind it, bent double, one hand on the wall and the other clutching his guts. Between his open legs, a pigeon stared at him from behind the bars of a cage.

'Who the hell are you?' Zollo asked the pigeon, when the retching noises stopped.

The guy just turned his head, didn't change his position. A boy. He mumbled something incomprehensible, then managed to articulate, in English: 'Wh-what?'

The trick of speaking English always worked with the police in Bologna. It gained you a couple of minutes, long enough to make up a story. Pierre undoubtedly needed it. The guy with the Sicilian accent standing in front of him was pretty big and, to judge by his clothes, he didn't come up with the last drop of rain.

'You're not in the crew, are you? Who are you?'

As with Cary Grant, Pierre managed to catch only the last part of the question. The guy spoke much better English than he did. That had never happened with the police in Bologna. Better get a move on.

'My name is Robespierre Capponi,' he said in Italian. 'I embarked at Dubrovnik.'

'You did? And how the fuck did you get on board?'

The sailor had told him clearly: if they discover you, don't give my name. They won't touch you, they don't want any problems with customs. I'd lose my job.

He had an answer ready. 'Last night, as they were loading the ship, I hid among the cases and climbed on board.'

'You've really fucked up. Why?'

'I was supposed to be coming back with a friend, but I had a mishap and had to leave early.'

'What kind of mishap?'

Pierre shook his head. 'If I told you, you wouldn't believe me.'

Zollo went over to the boy, wearing a face that would have put the wind up a wolf.

'Listen to me carefully, boy. I don't give a flying fuck about what happened to you. Now tell me the whole thing again, but cut the crap this time, ok?' It was one of the longest sentences he had ever spoken to a foreigner.

'Done,' Pierre replied, icebergs in his veins. 'I'll start at the beginning: I was on an island, to find my father, and we were minding our own business when someone tried to kidnap Cary Grant, who was on the island as well, I know it's incredible, but that's what happened, I swear, so then my father fired and the kidnappers escaped –'

'Horseshit!' Zollo interrupted. 'What does Cary Grant have to do with it? Yesterday evening the ferry set off for Bari. If you were in such a hurry, you could have taken that.'

'What? Where would I have got the money?'

'I see. The money's the problem.'

'Yes . . . that is no, in fact, I told you: this thing that happened . . .' Pierre didn't mention the actor's name again to avoid annoying the man. 'Hang on, look at this, I've got proof.' He rummaged in his bag and took out the copy of *Casino Royale*. 'You see this book? In English? You can't get it in Italy. He gave it to me in person, that is, he left it on the beach and I . . .'

Zollo stood there with Ian Fleming's book in his hand, and instinctively started flicking through it.

'Unfortunately,' Pierre went on, coming to stand beside him, 'there's nothing to show that it's really his. The underlinings in pencil are all mine, words I've got to check in the dictionary, you see?'

'Shut the fuck up!' Zollo exploded. 'Just pray that the cops don't come looking for you, or you've had it. But if they see you wandering about the ship, if you get into trouble, I'll chuck you overboard with an anchor around your feet.'

'Fine,' Pierre gulped. 'I won't give you any problems.'

Zollo stared at him for a long time, then turned on his heels and clambered over the goods loader, and when he turned around to ask what the hell that pigeon was all about, the boy and the cage had disappeared.

He went back up on the upper deck. He liked the cool evening air. The boy with the cage was just some poor bastard, probably crazy. What was all that crap about Cary Grant? You end up meeting the strangest people. Nothing to get worked up about, though. Not now that things were going his way. He'd creamed three kilos off the last cargo. Along with what he had already set aside, that meant a decent pension for Steve 'Son-of-a-Bitch' Cement. Once he was in Naples, he'd put the three kilos in safe keeping along with the rest, as he waited to arrange his appointment with Lyonnese Toni. He had to be careful. Luciano would send him to Marseilles to take care of the bulk of it. No nonsense. Steve 'Careful' Cement in action. Meeting the buyers for *his* drugs. The trip to France on Luciano's behalf was the best cover in the world. Loyal Steve sells the snake's heroin, and without anyone noticing, he sells his own as well. All nice and clean. All sorted. All he had to do was decide where he was going to disappear to.

Zollo saw the glowing cigarette-end roll overboard, perform a perfect parabola and extinguish itself among the waves. From his pocket he took the little flask and allowed himself a consoling swig.

Chapter 56

He turned up, jolted about in a nameless truck, after a journey that was anything but peaceful. Blows and shakes must have damaged him, but he couldn't expect the care he needed from yokels like these. The guy with the big hands and the beret over his eyes loaded him on to his shoulder with a jerk of his elbow. The door opened in front of them: they could barely get through it.

A fat, dark man with a toothpick sticking out of his mouth pointed to the niche in a chest of drawers, suitable at best for the basic model. Who the hell did these troglodytes think they were dealing with? A McGuffin Electric Deluxe isn't just an accessory, he's an essential part of the furniture of a modern house: a beauty, twenty-eight inches by twenty-four high, with a seventeen-inch rectangular tube, available in various colours to adapt to the shade of your furniture. Shovel-Hands, with Toothpick behind him, pushed with all his might, but there was nothing to be done, that much was clear, and fortunately he noticed, a stream of invective later, before scratching the wood-effect cover, ideally matched to a walnut buffet table, and entirely out of place on blue formica.

In the end, they laid him on two chairs placed side by side. Toothpick took three steps back and studied him with his head on one side, like Michelangelo contemplating one final touch to his statue of Moses, then walked over again to put in the plug and shouted a name, something like Concetta, two or three times, until a fat, aproned woman appeared and launched into an interminable series of condemnations of the size of the new arrival. *God*, what ignorance!

Toothpick stared obliquely at the floor, in a desperate attempt to restrain himself, a titanic effort that proved to be unsuccessful. 'Shut up,' he exploded a few minutes later. 'Bloody hell, woman, shut up!'

When silence had been accomplished, the man rubbed his hands a few times, as though to charge them with miracle-making power. He stepped forward ceremoniously, pointed a finger at the various switches and selected one. He returned to his wife, almost running, clutched his chin, tilted his head on one side and waited. McGuffin gave no sign of reacting. He repeated the manoeuvre from the beginning, including the rubbing of his hands. He chose the switch next to the previous one, but as the result of some kind of electrical confusion, it was his wife who sprang to life.

'That's some crock they've dumped on you,' croaked the shrew.

Toothpick didn't lose heart. He tried every solution, including slapping the poor McGuffin like a disobedient child. As her husband waved his fist at the screen, uttering menacing words, the woman approached the precious machine, convinced that she could make an essential contribution.

But sadly there was nothing to be done. He had been damaged, that much was plain. Rattled from side to side in a van, without even a blanket around him, along the twists and turns of a potholed road, what else did they expect? He was solid, but not indestructible. And repairs would cost a pretty penny.

The witch's nose brushed against the speaker grille. She had noticed something.

'There it is,' she said, beaming. 'That explains everything!'

'What's that?' asked Toothpick, stuck between the television and the wall.

'Look over here for a moment: you see this writing? It's American, you see?'

'Yeah, so? What difference does that make?'

'So? So it's obvious, isn't it? This machine can only pick up American programmes, and we don't have them yet. And don't you remember Maria, when she was sold that American fridge that didn't work with the electricity we have here? It's the same thing. We're in Italy, you need an Italian machine.'

Toothpick's perplexed eyes shuttled two or three times between his wife's face and McGuffin's lifeless screen. He read and reread the writing, took out the plug and put it back in again, clutched at various straws in response to her objections, tried out the remaining switches and finally had to yield to the idea that perhaps you should involve your fellow villagers when you're choosing your television, the same way as you do with wives and cattle.

She was a beautiful woman, Marisa. Wasted on a guy like that, who never spat out his toothpick even when kissing. She must have had a good reason for cuckolding her husband with such a squalid individual. Certainly, gifts like a McGuffin Electric Deluxe, with a commercial value of 250,000 lire, for those in the know, were sufficient reason in themselves. But if you looked carefully, there seemed to be something else as well.

Marisa bent to straighten the sofa, her generous cleavage mirrored in the screen. Then she turned around and did the same with her bottom. Her thighs might have been a little fat, but apart from that they were in no way inferior to the athletic physique of some American women. Hard to say what age she was, perhaps about thirty, and she'd clearly looked after herself.

When her husband came home, she ran to the door to greet him, deafening him with some nonsense about some new thing waiting for him in the sitting room.

'You know that raffle at the butcher's, the one with a television as a prize? You remember you bit my head off because you said that ten tickets was money thrown away? Well, come on, look what I've won, when you were going to spend a 160,000 on that trash we saw the other day!'

Her husband came into the sitting room and opened his eyes and mouth wide at the sight of the McGuffin. Seeing him like that, a complete jerk with a dazed expression, his narrow sloping shoulders in his grey jacket and a fake leather bag in his hand, it was not hard to find another reason for Marisa's adultery, given that Toothpick, coarse though he was, had at least a shred of manly fascination.

'Darling,' the milksop observed, straightening his glasses. 'I take back all I said about the wasted money. While you prepare the dinner, I shall try and make it work.'

The woman placed a traitorous kiss upon his wan cheek and disappeared. Milquetoast loosened his tie, slipped off his jacket, rolled up the sleeves and, feeling like a little Einstein, faced his battle with technology.

Ten minutes later, as the squid simmered in the white wine, Marisa heard the first slaps. By the time she added the peas, he was on to the bloody-hells. Giuliano was not a patient man: his nerves almost always ended up on edge, and afterwards he became intractable, rough and rude. That was certainly the underlying reason why his wife could not bear him and preferred that man Ciro, who at least kept his hands in the right place and, when he lost his temper, didn't shriek like a fairy.

As the tomato joined the other ingredients in the pot, Marisa heard him calling in an angry voice, 'Marisa, damn it to hell, you've been screwed yet again!'

The woman gave a start. Squid and everything spilled over the stove. How had he found out? Hadn't the sofa been tucked up nicely? Were there compromising traces? Could it be that the television also worked as a cine camera? Or perhaps Ciro had talked to the wrong people, people who worked in television?

'Marisa, never mind first prize!' the voice insisted, getting shriller and shriller. 'This fucker doesn't even work!'

'What did you say? It doesn't work?' the woman put a hand to her chest, closed her eyes and sighed deeply. Could be worse.

She stayed like that for a while, before attending quietly to the squid, trying to return it to the pot with a wooden spoon.

Vincenzo Donadio lowered the shutters of the workshop just after seven. He had wasted more than an hour trying to fix a broken telephone, and hadn't had time to look at that great pachyderm of a television. On the other hand, he couldn't claim to know a great deal about such machines. They were new, complicated, specially for people like himself who really specialised in motor scooters. But Vespas and Lambrettas had only come out recently, you didn't see very many of them around, and if a man wanted to work, he had to spread his area of expertise: radios, televisions, record players, pretty much everything as far as Vince was concerned.

He locked the big padlock in its iron ring and set off whistling 'Viale d'autunno'.

Less than six hours later, in the dark, deserted street, enlivened only by quarrelling cats, a furtive outline bent over that same padlock, armed with a bunch of fake keys. It tried out ten of them, with nerves of steel, until it found the right one. It lifted the shutter just enough to slip inside, as the headlights of a small truck appeared at the end of the street.

McGuffin was on the worktop. It was no coincidence that the break-in occurred that very evening. Its arrival had not gone unobserved.

After sliding a large consignment of small radios into the street, the man poked his head out from under the shutter, checked that everything was quiet, exchanged a couple of words with someone outside and very carefully raised the shutter until it was almost halfway up.

He wheeled the first Lambretta around the corner and helped his mate to load it on. He went back inside to grab a second scooter and loaded that one on too. If you had wrung out his sleeves, you could have filled a glass. When he held out his hands, they were damp with sweat. But there was no point being fussy: this providential intervention saved McGuffin from Donadio's quixotic attempts at repair, which would have compromised his delicate mechanisms for ever.

'Bloody hell, an American TV!' exclaimed the driver the moment he saw him. 'Maybe it can pick up American programmes, what do you think, Nené?'

'Don't talk bollocks, Peppino. Get the blanket, come on now!'

They wrapped it up well and wedged it between the Lambretta and a transistor radio to avoid any damage.

Finally he was being treated in an appropriate manner. Finally someone seemed to have grasped the great value of a McGuffin Electric Deluxe, even one that had been slightly damaged, with fake walnut finish and with a seventeen-inch screen.

The door closed. The truck screeched on the porphyry, terrifying the life out of two cats, then vanished with a murmur into the Naples night.

Chapter 57

General Serov laid the documents out on the desk, the sheets perfectly aligned. The 'Leach Grant' file now consisted of a considerable number of typed pages. Zhulianov's report was meticulous. Just like the internal communications of MI6 that had just come in from London a few moments before.

The British secret services had had their worst quarter of an hour since Hitler's bombers had flown over Westminster. The kidnap of Cary Grant had been a failure, but they had had their result. Tito had lost face with the British; the British had lost face with Grant and the Americans. Sources revealed that the actor's conclusive comment, once he had resumed contact with MI6, had been: 'Gentlemen, fuck off the lot of you.' The file also reported Dyle's embarrassed reply: 'I'm mortified. Is there anything we can do for you, Mr Grant?' and the retort: 'Certainly. Call me a taxi for the airport.'

The general chuckled to himself, imagining the scene.

MI6's film project ended up in the dustbin of history before it even saw the light of day.

He could be satisfied with that.

Perhaps they would go on the attack once again, but if Cary Grant's character profile was correct, he was willing to bet his colonel's stripes that the actor would never again be flattered by these bunglers.

It would be important to watch what Grant did next. He made a note on a piece of paper and turned his concentration back to the crucial questions of the day.

The world was facing new threats. The Soviet Union would have to assume its responsibilities. And he was there to do his part.

In Indochina the Vietnamese communists had the French colonialists on the ropes. General Giap put the final squeeze on the siege of Dien Bien Phu: the days of the Foreign Legion contingent, barricaded up on the high plain, were clearly numbered. The Americans were ready to supplant those shreds of fascist arrogance. They would never let Indochina turn red.

On the other hand the Chinese were ready to play the game to become the leading communist country in Asia. They had got used to it and won their stripes in Korea, and now they wanted to have their say.

The Chinese. You had to be careful with the Chinese; he had said as much to Khrushchev as well, when he had asked him his advice about the events of the day. There were so many of them, too many, with a leader no less charismatic than Stalin. But you never knew what they were thinking. When you thought about the Chinese you had to think in a completely different way. The General wasn't afraid of anything, not after everything he had seen in his life. The French were buffoons. They thought they still had an empire, but they borrowed money from the Americans to keep it on its feet. They reminded him of faded aristocrats in ragged trousers, braying things like, 'Don't you know who I am?' The British, good soldiers, certainly, but with all those stupid habits, like taking tea under bombing raids. Without the Americans and the Russians they would have been serving tea to Himmler, while that maniac Goebbels would have been raping their awful princess in the next room. How disgusting.

Then there were the Americans. The Normandy landings had been one of the most costly and absurd actions in history. All to get to Berlin before the Russians did. They had no idea of how to fight a war. Just fire-power. That was their only weapon, sounding the charge, trumpets blaring, atom bombs, helicopters, and now that new invention, napalm . . . If they went on like that they would end up like Custer, chopped to pieces by people with bows and arrows.

No, it was the Chinese that frightened him. Six hundred million people in the same line of fire. They had made it to the negotiating table in Geneva, to discuss the fate of Indochina. Khrushchev had called in old Molotov, dusted down his good suit and sent him to Switzerland to do his best. He wasn't sure that the experience of that crafty and decrepit revolutionary would be enough to resolve the situation in favour of the Soviet Union. Probably not.

Meanwhile the Americans were manoeuvring in the shadows. They had made contact with Bao Dai, the emperor of Vietnam, and filled his pockets with money to persuade him to go back to his own country and act as their puppet. Hundreds of thousands of dollars from American taxpayers being handed over to a decadent Indochinese aristocrat, who threw them away at the casino in Evian. Because it was there that he had decided to wait for the outcome of the Geneva Conference. And they bankrolled him and his court of dwarfs and belly-dancers, to use him as a joker and reinstate him in Vietnam. The Americans were the least parsimonious people the world had ever seen.

The general shuddered with rage. He started jotting down some notes on a piece of paper. He would have to activate the Swiss resident, and the French one: any scraps of phrases exchanged in the corridors of Geneva would have to be on his desk within the hour. No less important: keep as close an eye as possible on Bao Dai. If the Americans planned to put that feeble alcoholic back on the throne, he would have to be informed of it in good time.

Finally he got to his feet, cracked the joints of his neck and his shoulders, and walked the ten paces that separated him from the window. The curtains had gone. He looked outside and once again he had the sensation of being part of an enormous clockwork mechanism. Part of history.

Chapter 58

As the plane came down over Los Angeles, Cary felt that energy again. It had just been a shiver behind his ears, when, in his sitting room at home, they had suggested his mission to Yugoslavia. Then it had turned into emotion, concealed with aplomb, at the moment of his meeting with Tito. It had turned into fear on the island of Šipan, when they had shot at him and he had had to turn himself into a hundred-metre sprinter. And those two strange Italians who had helped him . . . He hadn't been able to work out what they were doing down there, but they had been nice, and equipped to deal with such a weird situation.

He looked out of the window to see the hills, but he couldn't get his bearings. They would be landing at the same military camp from which they had left. They hadn't added anything else, perhaps because no one knew (it was still a secret operation), and certainly anyone who did know was ashamed of what had happened. They hadn't come out of it looking all that great. And not just Her Majesty's Secret Service, but the Americans, who had supported the operation.

How had Bondurant coped in his place? When he finally got through to Betsy, on the private line put at his disposal by the military, she had given him nothing but the vaguest of hints. The business about the regimental tie was water under the bridge, he could almost laugh about it now. His good humour had really returned. His enthusiasm for things, which he thought he had lost, and which he had thought would never return, the enthusiasm that Betsy had tried without success to help him feel again as they travelled around the world, had grown back within him like a climbing plant. He couldn't say why, but as he headed for home he felt regenerated.

Once again he was a mature actor, nostalgic for himself, but even more nostalgic for other people, keen to be put to the test again, to demonstrate that the public, that boundless expanse of anonymous eyes, still wanted him.

Once again he was Archie Leach, a little boy receiving his first applause, and running to old Pender with a face that said, 'I did it, you see? And they're clapping for me!'

Archie needed that, it was his nature. Showing himself that he was still capable of getting excited, and of getting other people excited. Coming out of his shell and challenging the world to tell him to his face, if it was brave enough, that he no longer knew how to walk on his hands or throw skittles. He wanted to confront them with the grim countenance of a man who has conquered life at considerable expense, and doesn't want to let it go.

Cary would follow him. For him, too, it was a question of narcissism.

Clusters of houses at the edge of the city emerged between the gaps in the clouds. The young pilot assigned to them told them they would be landing in a few minutes.

Cary fastened his belt and relaxed into his seat. He could concentrate on the years that had passed, without rancour. Clearly, the age of Cary Grant was coming to an end. Marlon Brando and James Dean were conquering eyes and hearts. Handsome and introverted, problematic, a little boastful and a little insecure. Cary knew that the old-style fascination of his generation of actors would make way for the new army of male stars, with their pose of tender-hearted rebels. But that meant nothing. He was still there, his shoulders weighed down with experience and grooming. He would never wear a singlet or a leather jacket, he still had something to teach. Yes, they still needed him. They needed the reassuring smile of a man holding a door open for a woman to let her into the bedroom. They needed the ready quip and the double entendre. The secure, relaxed expression, for every man who wanted to see himself mirrored in Cary Grant, and imagine that his fascination was perhaps not something out of reach. That ideal friend and lover, whom anyone would have been happy to meet in a train, reading a good book and willing to chat amiably about any topic under the sun.

He nodded to himself. He still wanted female conquests. He

certainly wouldn't have said that to Betsy. But when he had phoned
Hitch to tell him he was there, and that he had been reassured by
the fact that Grace Kelly was going to be his screen partner, he had
realised that this was yet another challenge. Old Hitch knew how to
tease him; he was better at it than anyone else. They had understood
one another from the very first: Englishmen on American soil, in
love with Hollywood, but capable of changing it, attached to the
cinema, as one with the movies, and in some ways inseparable for
almost fifteen years.

Grace Kelly was the most beautiful woman of the moment. With
sex deep inside, not on the surface, as Hitch liked it. Sex had to be
part of the mystery, not spoken, implicit in a look, in the right line
in the script, in a detail. Sex was a subtle allusion somewhere between
romanticism and irony. Something made to measure for Cary Grant.

Working with Hitchcock again was what it would take for him
to start again. He was the only person capable of understanding his
passion for details, capable of talking for hours about the level of
liquid in a glass, and who could at the same time size him up with
a glance.

The pilot leaned back from behind the curtain, displaying his best
smile. 'Mr Kaplan, we're there. We're about to land.'

That ludicrous pseudonym again. As though the pilots hadn't
recognised him. Military protocol was truly idiotic.

He started thinking once again about the fifty years of his life,
and wondered how many active years he still had ahead of him. Five,
ten?

He smiled at his reflection in the window.

What did it matter? He would play the game until he was breathless. Without overdoing it, without claiming to be able to keep up
with the young guys, but also without being left in the shadows. He
would walk rather than run, he would stroll down the same street
with impeccable style, as he always did. People would have to wait
with bated breath for the day when he said 'enough'. He would leave
them yearning for more, and how!

The plane came down quickly and landed with a slight bump that
gave Cary a jolt to the stomach. Finally it stopped and its engines
came to a standstill.

When the door of the military aircraft opened up on the bright daylight, Cary narrowed his eyes and hunched his shoulders. Then a smile known to millions of people settled on his lips. He put on his sunglasses, picked up his bag and walked towards the light.

The words echoed in his heart: 'Hey, I'm back!'

Il Resto del Carlino, 19.4.1954

Easter Day in Rome
CONDEMNATION OF ATOMIC WEAPONS
IN PONTIFF'S MESSAGE

Il Resto del Carlino, 26.4.1954

COMMUNIST PRESSURE MOUNTS IN DIEN BIEN PHU
Giap's proclamation to the Viet Minh troops:
'The hour of victory has sounded'

ASIAN CONFERENCE OPENS TODAY IN GENEVA
Uncertain fate for Korea and Indochina

Il Resto del Carlino, 27.04.1954

THE FATE OF INDOCHINA DOMINATES
NEGOTIATIONS AT THE GENEVA CONFERENCE

Il Resto del Carlino, 28.04.1954

TITO'S INTRANSIGENCE OBSTRUCTS
A SOLUTION FOR TRIESTE

L'Unità, 29.4.1954

EXHUMATION OF WILMA MONTESI'S CORPSE

L'Unità, 3.5.1954

Asiatic Premiers call for peace in Indochina
RECOGNITION OF CHINA
AND ABOLITION OF ATOMIC WEAPONS

L'Unità, 5.5.1954

HO CHI MINH'S DELEGATES COME TO GENEVA
TO OPEN NEGOTIATIONS FOR PEACE IN VIETNAM

Il Resto del Carlino, 5.5.1954

DIEN BIEN PHU FALLS
AFTER TWENTY-HOUR BATTLE

PART TWO
McGuffin Electric

Chapter 1

Life's a pile of shit. So is death. Dying with your face in horseshit. I'm bricking it. What can I do what can I do what can I do? I start shouting, I'm bricking it, I implore St Anne who's abandoned me, all the Madonnas I caused to weep and now they're taking their revenge, I implore their forgiveness, yes, I'm pissing myself, forgive me forgive me forgive me Holy Mother and Steven Cement.

They're going to hurt me, *mamma mia* why? They're going to make me long for this shitty, icy cell. What can I do now that my luck's run out, what did I do?

He just slapped me once and now I can't hear out of my left ear, my eye hurts and my cheek stings like St Anthony's fire. He's tied me to this chair, he's walking back and forth, an animal, snorting like the nearby horses, Jesus, he's thinking about how to finish me off.

What lousy luck, what a bloody awful way to go! Salvatore Pagano known as Kociss, who hasn't said a word, I swear on my mother's life and all the saints, who knows what he's been told, some grass or other, not a word, what did I know, it was that pig of a police commissioner Cinquegrana dumped me in it, he was the one, cursed be his children to the seventh generation! Those questions about Don Luciano, Cement, everyone will have heard them, he dumped right on me, the disgusting swine. But I never said a word! Everyone knows that Kociss doesn't speak to guards or grasses or gravediggers.

I'd really like to tell Sister Titina, right now, because she always told me that I would live for a hundred years at least, because 'Christ doesn't want sad flesh', isn't that right, Sister Titina, so what do you say to this? Go and tell that to Steve Cement, or bring Jesus Christ down here, right now, Sister Titina, right now this minute.

So are you saying I'm crazy? That I was going around blabbing my mouth off about Don Luciano? Why are you doing this, I don't know a thing, my Lisetta, I didn't say anything, shame about that dress I bought you, what a catastrophe, and the pure silk trousers, you were happy, don't cry, never again will I smell your sweet fragrance that drives me out of my mind, Jesus, never again will I see Lisetta's curly head jiggling as she laughs, don't cry, that fawn's muzzle saying, 'Salvato', you're mad, you are!'

And what if he wasn't that resolute?

Why hasn't he killed me yet? Maybe some fuckhead, some absolute bastard gave them my name and told them I was in jail, but without saying 'that guy's been singing', no, just for the sake of saying some-thing, perhaps. Or maybe it's just that he hasn't made his mind up where to chuck the corpse, *mamma mia*, no!

No, no, we don't know for sure that he's going to kill you, take a good look at him, Salvato', he's as pissed off as a *holymotherofgod*, he's snorting like a steamboat, but he seems to be thinking about other things, other matters.

Think, go on, think, Salvato', quickly, think of something that will save your life, bawl your eyes out, fuck up his brain, anything at all, because otherwise you can forget all about Lisetta and this shitty life.

Steel myself. I've got to steel myself, and talk. Talk and say, 'Signor Cement it's all a terrible mistake. Salvatore Pagano known as Kociss is an admirer and Don Luciano's devoted servant and yours as well, and never, ever, ever could he say a bad thing about you . . .'

Yes, I need to steel myself, my throat's dry, my eye hurts, steel yourself, come on, *and* I stink.

'*A-hhm*, Mister Cement, *lissentumi –*'

'Shut up, shithead! Where is that fucking TV?'

The television?

'*Mistestiv*, don't worry, I'll get it straight away, sure, don' you worry, if that's all it is, I bring it back, no worry!'

The television.

But how on earth could it be his?

Chapter 2

The queue of people going into the dancehall started in the Piazza VIII Agosto. 'Seventh Heaven' was going to be packed to the rafters.

The musketeers weren't impressed, and stood on their pedals to get up the slope like Coppi on the last stretch of the Gavia, Brando at the head, Sticleina and Gigi sprinting along, and Pierre bringing up the rear on the racing bike borrowed by Bortolotti.

'What the fuck did they do to you in Yugoslavia, brainwash you? You're not like yourself!' Brando had observed a few days after his return.

As he pedalled, Pierre reflected that his friend was right. There was something strange: Bologna no longer seemed the same. But in the course of that week, what on earth could have happened? Nothing, the usual stuff: two punch-ups on 1 May, the thousand-mile driver who'd knocked over a kid in Via Murri, Bologna FC's victory . . . No, there was no getting round it, it was he who had changed. Wasn't Fanti always saying that seeing new places renews the eyes?

He thought once again of his dinner that day, at Aunt Iolanda's, with Nicola. After the roast meat, his brother had risen from the table, saying he was taking a stroll to help his digestion. The truth was that he didn't want to hear his brother's stories about his trip to Yugoslavia. He had told Aunt Iolanda everything, even about the strange absolution with which he had left his father. She was a fine woman, Iolanda, almost a mother to him. He had never realised how similar she was to her brother Vittorio, the same eyes, the same shape of chin. She was just a bit younger, but she had the wisdom of someone much older. Not the mean wisdom of the countryside, no, something like a kind of common sense acquired over the years, when you're someone who has seen war, the evil that men do, someone who has been in love but never married. When he looked back, to his childhood, Pierre saw her as a rock. The only person he would never leave, always able to cope with even the most critical situations.

Nicola, on the other hand, was critical all the time.

As they got back to Bologna, in the van, he had wanted to have his say.

'Benassi hasn't taken this business about Yugoslavia at all well.'

'What's Benassi got to do with it?'

'If Benassi gives me a message to pass on, the message comes from the Party. And they didn't much like you going there.'

'I went to find my dad. If he'd gone to Sweden, I'd have gone there too. Would Sweden have been better?'

'You're not nearly as smart as you think, you know. Everyone knows you've been acting pretty strangely.'

'There was no other way. And if they've got something to say to me, why don't they say it to my face, rather than getting Benassi to do it?'

'You're a real idiot. You should be grateful that they say something, that things don't turn nasty for you. If you went to the Section a bit more often and went dancing a bit less, the cogs in your brain would start turning better, and you might even even learn something. But oh no, young sir has to go and take private English lessons, from Professor Fanti.'

'You're right, I should have studied Russian, so that when the Red Army shows up I could work as an interpreter.'

'Oh, wind me up all you like, go on. But in the meantime, given how much of a prick you want to make of yourself, just be careful you don't go too far. And that guy Fanti isn't even a comrade. He must be a liberal, or something like that.'

'Could be. And I'm a communist. So? Tell Benassi to mind his own business, tell him I've never seen him getting whacked by the riot squad, and last time I took three blows to the head. At times like that, for some reason, I'm a great guy again.'

The conversation had been left hanging like that. Nicola had just shaken his head and gone on driving.

*

They chained their bikes to the streetlights, straightened their clothes and went in.

'They don't have places like this in Yugoslavia, eh, Pierre?'

'Dunno. I certainly didn't see them.'

'Go on, go on,' Gigi teased him as he handed in his coat. Then, in a low voice, 'Did you see the tits on that cloakroom girl?'

Pierre lagged behind to buy cigarettes from the cigarette girl, and Brando took advantage of the fact to stay on his own with him. 'Hear about Angela?'

'No, how could I have done?'

'Well, if nobody's told you, I will. While you were away her brother had a fit. He went clean right round the bend, punched out a nurse and I believe he hurt himself as well. Nasty business.'

Pierre wanted to leave immediately; what the hell was he doing there? He was going dancing, and maybe Angela needed to talk, to let her feelings out. Remorse gripped his heart, but Sticleina was already taking him by an arm and dragging him towards the tables.

They sat down with a carafe of wine, Pierre staring at his shoes, the others glancing around in search of *pasturage*.

Ferruccio had been ill. Shit. And what about Angela?

'Right, then! We didn't come here to say the rosary! Gigi and I are going to dance. What about you?'

Pierre waved distractedly and lit a cigarette.

The two of them slipped on to the dance floor, calling, 'Tossers!'

'You already know what I think about you and Angela,' Brando began. 'Christ almighty, find yourself a girlfriend, look how many girls there are!'

But Pierre's mind was elsewhere. His aunt's words were whirling around in his head: 'It's as though you were here just by chance. As though you were weighing yourself up.' He couldn't stop his thoughts racing, the music of the band slipped under them and carried them away.

'Don't turn round right now, *bello*, but the Redhead's looking at you.'

'Who?'

Brando shook his head. 'What do you mean who, Gilda the Redhead! Gilda Stanzani, don't you know her? She puts out, everyone knows that. She looks like Rita Hayworth, *and* her name's Gilda. A friend of mine had her in a car. At least that's what he says. Anyway, she isn't a virgin. She's looking at you, I promise she is. What more do you want?'

Pierre looked up.

In the middle of a cluster of girls, a striking young woman was smiling at him.

'Buxom,' Pierre commented without thinking.

'*Buxom?* What on earth sort of a thing is that to say? One fantastic pair of tits! Really fantastic!'

'She isn't looking at me.'

'Oh, no: it's the third time she's turned around! Go over there right now and ask her to dance.'

'Don't feel like it.'

Brando rubbed his eyes: 'Excuse me? Would you repeat that for me please? I've just heard the Filuzzi King saying he doesn't feel like dancing?' He kicked him under the table. 'You're going over there right now and if she says yes, I'm going for one of her friends. And if you don't . . .'

Pierre heaved a big sigh. He looked at his good suit, his gleaming shoes. He thought of his fine appearance, the fact that he was twenty-two. Redheads have hazel or green eyes. He bet on bright hazel. He stood up, got a slap of encouragement on the back from Brando and went on the attack, one hand in his pocket, his loose-limbed walk.

As he approached, he noticed something special about her. It wasn't her tits. It was the brazen way she stood there, watching him do his Cary Grant number. As though she were playing with him, after provoking him just so that she could enjoy the scene.

He had to make an effort to maintain his front.

He smiled. 'Good evening, may I ask you why you've been looking at me and laughing for the last half-hour?'

'Because you're gorgeous.'

She said it quite naturally, and Pierre frowned, as though he had been given a piece of bad news. He didn't know what to add; his instincts told him to go and sit down, perhaps after mumbling, 'Thanks for the information.'

He concentrated, called on St Cary for help and said, 'You too. Shall we dance?'

She nodded without saying another word, and they found

themselves on the dance floor, pressed against each other because of the crowd.

Light hazel. Pierre felt her breasts pressing against him, and struggled to coordinate his movements and keep his cool.

She was a good dancer. And if he was holding her too tightly, she wasn't complaining.

'You're Robespierre Capponi, aren't you?'

'Yes, and you're Gilda Stanzani.'

'They say you're the best dancer in Bologna.'

'That's what they say. And what about you, do you often go dancing?'

'Every now and again. You work at the Bar Aurora, in San Donato, isn't that right?'

'What are you, a secret agent, knowing all these things?'

She laughed, white teeth. Pierre felt a winge in his stomach.

'We haven't seen you dancing for a while.'

'I've been away, in Yugoslavia. Finding my father.'

They stopped to applaud the orchestra.

'I'm thirsty.'

'So am I, let's go to the bar.'

They managed to slip their way among the people crowding against the bar and ordered their drinks.

'So what's Yugoslavia like?'

'It's like Italy. They even speak Italian.'

'And why did you come back?'

Pierre gave an embarrassed smile. 'What would I have done there?'

Gilda the Redhead glanced around. 'You like it so much here?'

'Why, do you want to leave?'

'I should find a rich man to take me round the world. I'd like that. There are so many places to see. Instead I'm tearing tickets at the racecourse. And my wages aren't going to get me very far.'

Pierre thought about his own wallet, his debt with Fanti and the one he had with Ettore. His stomach lurched again. He said, 'You have to keep your feet on the ground.'

'While we're on the subject of feet, are you on foot yourself, or could you possibly give me a lift home? I live in Mazzini. Usually I come here with my flatmate, who's got a bike, but she's gone to see her family in Molinella.'

It wasn't hard to work out what was going to happen. It had never happened to Pierre so quickly. And not only that, but she lived on her own, with a friend . . . Brando was right, she really was 'easy'. She had fallen from the sky for him. All of a sudden he thought of Angela, Ferruccio who had gone round the bend, and who knows how she must be feeling. He couldn't take so much as a sip, he felt as though he was hunched inside his suit.

'I'm sorry. Really. But I'm walking too.'

Gilda's bitter smile spoke volumes. 'Some other time, then.'

'Yes, definitely.'

At that moment, Gigi appeared out of the crowd and grabbed Pierre by the jacket. 'Pierre, the bend-down-and-turn-around! Let's go!'

As he was being dragged towards the dance floor he heard Gilda calling to him.

'Pierre!' She was wearing a sly expression. 'Careful you don't keep your feet so firmly on the ground that you bash your face against it.'

Half dazed, he found himself dancing again, trying to follow the urgent rhythm of the band. He had to make an effort, he felt he was always late on the beat, but he tried to do his best. As the music swelled he was emboldened, let himself go, his feet moved very rapidly, yes, damn it, he was still the best! He let himself be swept away by the rhythm, more smoothly than ever, quick and coordinated, light as a feather, the people were clapping . . .

It happened in a fraction of a second. Someone must have spilled something on the dancefloor. His leading foot went off all by itself, he instinctively tried to jerk himself upright again, he went careering forwards and couldn't stop.

When he lifted his face from the floor he noticed a few drops of blood on the tiles. His nose hurt like hell.

Gigi and Sticleina helped him to his feet, the band had stopped playing. The accordionist leaned forwards from the stage, worried. 'Son, are you ok?'

'It's nothing, I just slipped,' said Pierre, dabbing at his nose.

He looked around, everyone was staring at him. That had never happened before. He could read a strange anxiety in their eyes. They felt disappointed and betrayed: the king had fallen from his throne, and he hadn't even been pushed.

'And give that floor a good clean,' snarled Gigi as he shoved Pierre towards the toilets.

He asked his friends to let him go in on his own and they, like faithful vassals, lowered their eyes modestly as they moved away. They went and stood in front of the door, like a picket.

He washed his face with the freezing water and stopped to look at himself in the mirror, his mouth and chin striped with blood.

What the hell was happening to him? Was it a punishment for leaving Angela on her own? For not taking Gilda home?

As he wiped his face with his handkerchief he murmured to himself, 'That would never have happened to Cary Grant.'

Then he became aware of a presence behind him, looked up at the mirror and saw him emerging from one of the cubicles. He was elegant, almost dapper, and wearing a good suit.

'It looks as though the king has lost his sheen.'

Ettore's voice was soft and insinuating.

He washed his hands, dried them carefully, straightened his narrow moustache and adjusted his collar.

'You came back sooner than expected. Problems?'

'I ran out of money. I came back on a ship.'

Ettore nodded.

'You and I had an agreement. I hope you haven't forgotten it.'

Pierre leaned on the basin.

'I know. Don't worry.'

'Fine. Then drop by the office one of these days and we'll talk about it.'

He was already halfway out the door when he turned round and added, 'Ah, Pierre, a word of advice: stay away from the Redhead, she's trouble. A good few guys have lost their heads over her. Mark my words.'

He went out, closing the door behind him.

Pierre stared at the floor and thought about how complicated life could get from one day to the next.

Chapter 3

Ettore didn't ride a bike. He preferred to walk. 'I cycled in my partisan days,' he said, 'and now I don't cycle any more.'

He lived near Porta San Felice and walked to the workshop. To go dancing or go and see a film, he put on a good suit with a well-pressed collar, the right tie and gleaming shoes. He preferred to walk under the arcades, to show off the crease in his trousers falling like a plumb-line.

And if you had a woman, why carry her on the bar of your bicycle that hurts her bum, rather than taking her by the arm? Strolling, as though there was nothing worth hurrying for, not even making love.

It was a reaction to the 'job' he did: always up and down, back and forth, never missing appointments, getting the goods there on time, putting his foot down, covering the greatest possible distance before he got tired.

In his free time, he wanted nothing to do with wheels and speed.

And anyway, he lived in the centre, on his own, and his bed was big enough for two. Bringing women home was easy.

That night, leaving 'Seventh Heaven', Ettore was alone and thoughtful.

He was thirty years old and he had a vague but well-founded reputation as a layabout. The Party and the National Partisans' Association had expelled him for 'moral turpitude' in 1949, but no one knew the real reason. People talked about drugs, prostitution and who knows what else.

It should be pointed out that these things were said in his absence, to avoid a good kicking.

*

Ettore Bergamini had been a partisan at Monte Sole, in the Apennines, with the 'Red Star' Brigade led by Mario Musolesi, the mythical *Lupo*, the 'Wolf'.

He had been involved in extremely violent and interminable gunfights.

He had used explosives, stretched ambush wires, executed enemies, fought shoulder to shoulder with Englishmen, Czechs, Russians and even one Indian. Sad. Not a redskin, an Indian from India, with a turban on his head.

He had seen Ettore Ventura, the 'Aeroplane', charging Germans riding on a white horse.

He had seen Fonso's mother turn up right in the middle of a battle, heedless of the bullets, an expedition of several kilometres, to bring her son a bowl of zabaglione.

'Poor thing, you've been fighting for hours, and you haven't had a bite to eat!'

Fonso had looked at her, shocked, unable to believe his eyes.

Then he had drunk the zabaglione, and said, 'Thanks, *mamma*. But now get yourself to safety!'

On 27 June, because of serious strategic and political differences with the Wolf, Sugano Melchiorri had formed a new battalion of forty-six partisans. One of them was Ettore.

After a thousand vicissitudes, 'Red Star' Sugano had gone down into the plain and joined the 7th partisan group, Anzola detachment. Those had been the last times Ettore had used a bicycle. There he had met Amleto Benini, 'Bianco' (because of his grey hair), who would later give him a job. *This* job.

In October '44 they had taken part in the battle of Porta Lame, three incredible days, the only open clash between Germans and partisans inside a European city.

On 21 April '45 Ettore had liberated Bologna, along with his other comrades.

Sure, but who had they liberated it from?

The fascists, the ones who'd been given amnesty.

The partisans, thrown out of the newly formed police corps and persecuted by the law courts.

Sugano, victim of a judicial set-up, forced to escape to Czechoslovakia, like many other comrades.

Ettore had also ended up the focus of a few inquiries. Minor stuff, accusations of extortion and looting. He had always been released, but he still had some charges pending.

And the *Carlino*? It had changed its name time and again, it was still churning out lines as when, on 11 October 1944, it had denied that the massacre of Marzabotto had ever taken place. Ettore had kept the cutting. He had reread it so many times that he knew some passages off by heart.

The usual uncontrolled rumours, the typical product of galloping fantasies in time of war, ensured until yesterday that in the course of a police operation against a band of outlaws, a good 150 people, including women, old men and children, were massacred by German troops mopping up in the town of Marzabotto . . . So we confront a new ploy by the usual reckless characters destined for ridicule because anyone who had bothered to question any honest inhabitant of Marzabotto, or even a survivor from that area, would have learned the true version of the facts.

Shitheads.

Pain, tears, fear, hatred. But also euphoria, the desire to see an end to the war and to fascism, the longing to create a new Italy. Life had a meaning in those days; it wasn't just a matter of running from hour to hour, dragging yourself from one day to the next.

Why deny it? Ettore knew: those months in the mountains had been the finest in his life. Afterwards, there had been nothing of *real* interest.

He didn't head for home. He turned into Via Lame, and arrived at the Porta. The sky was full of stars, hundreds of stars, maybe thousands.

He had done it a thousand times, and he did it again.

He remembered the battle, shot for shot.

There was fog, and someone shouted, 'Garibaldi's fighting!'

He had yelled with all his might, 'Red Star is winning!'

Chapter 4

*Report produced for the Italian authorities by Charles Siragusa,
District Supervisor, US Bureau of Narcotics, on 6 May 1954*

In my opinion Salvatore Lucania, alias Charles 'Lucky' Luciano, comes back under the jurisdiction of Chapter V of the control of Italian Public Security, relating to police internment, and could be destined for the penal colony of Ustica.

He would come under category 3 of article 181, relating to a person who pursues and intends to pursue criminal activities damaging to Italian national interests.

Since his expulsion from the United States to Italy, his activity has been such as to compel the forces of Italian Public Security and customs officials to investigate him thoroughly.

Lucania has maintained contact with the principal American criminals, through various avenues, and in particular through members of the underworld. Proof exists that Lucania has received considerable sums of money from these individuals, given to him personally by gangsters who had come from Italy with that specific intent.

He has already been incriminated in and fined for the illegal importation of American dollars and an American automobile. His name has been mentioned in various important inquiries conducted in Italy concerning the traffic of narcotics and the smuggling of large quantities of heroin into the United States. He has even been discussed by the United States Narcotics Commission.

Unfortunately the traffickers implicated in these investigations would never make declarations damaging to Lucania. This is understandable, given the terror that he provokes among the Italian underworld. Lucania has not been found guilty of the charges relative to the narcotics market; but that is not to say that he is not implicated in the trafficking. It is, furthermore, impossible to explain how he is able to enjoy such a luxurious lifestyle, without having any apparent source of income.

A person with his professional experience does not act in such a way as to have himself arrested by any police force for matters relating to drugs or anything of the kind. He is extremely skilful and surrounds himself only with loyal associates. This makes it difficult to investigate him in any depth.

The presence of Lucania is harmful to Italy's prestige. Even the communist press has made contemptuous comments about this. By sending him to prison, the Italian government could neutralise Lucania and his wicked international criminal activities. It would be preferable to imprison him for the maximum period contemplated, five years.

Miscellaneous

The secretary-general of Interpol in France has distributed to fifty member nations of Interpol a printed circular about Lucania, as a suspected drugs trafficker of international importance (see 'Allegation D'). Lucania has been interrogated by the Italian tax police on 5 May 1951 and 15 May 1951 for matters relating to the trial of Frank Callace and Joe Pici for narcotics trafficking.

He was also interrogated by the tax police for the illegal importation of a 1948 model Sedan Oldsmobile, which had been brought to him by a New York gangster, Pasquale Matranga, runner for a certain Willie Moretti, a known gangster from New Jersey, later murdered. Lucania told this to one of my informers. On 7 June 1951 the trial concerning this automobile was held in Naples, and the car was confiscated and he was fined 32,000 lire. He was subsequently interrogated by customs for the illegal importation of 57,000 US dollars. On 27 March 1952, with decree no. 4621 D.G.T. 28853/228/7212, the Naples court found him guilty and ordered him to pay a fine of 2,500,000 lire.

The Public Security officials maintain that Lucania's two 'lieutenants' are implicated in the homicide of Umberto Chiofano, a petty criminal said to have slapped Lucania in public, at Agnano racecourse, last January. They are:

Victor Trimane, forty-three, expelled from the USA in 1949 after being found guilty of manslaughter by battery and four years' imprisonment in Riker's Island, New York State.

Stefano Francis Zollo, alias 'Steve Concrete', alias 'Steve Cement', thirty-five, originally from New York, already close to the Anastasia criminal family. Has lived in Italy since 1951. There are no extradition procedures currently under way for him.

Numerous confidential sources have declared that Lucania has been rigging the results of horse races in Naples by paying sums of money. A jockey, Vittorio Rosa, double-crossed Lucania when a race was being run. Lucania had paid Rosa for a certain horse to win. Instead Rosa made the horse lose. Lucania is then said to have threatened to kill Rosa. Rosa escaped to Mexico. On his return he was interrogated by Lieutenant Oliva, on 20 September 1951.

Among the people mentioned by Rosa as involved in the confidence tricks is Gennaro Iovene, forty-one, racecourse veterinarian.

Although he is not officially its owner, Lucania possesses a building at no. 484 Via Tasso, Vomero, Naples. Lucania paid 100 million lire for the building. He occupies one of the two luxurious top-floor apartments. The registered title-holder is a certain Carlo Scarpaio, but he is not in fact the owner. Lucania has been living there since June 1952.

In March 1952 it was learned from a reliable source that Lucania had 100,000 US dollars in a suitcase at his home.

Lucania also possesses a property at no. 184 Via Aurelia, at Santa Marinella, 2,000 square metres in area. He also owns 10,000 square metres of land and a small villa near the railway track, to the south of Via Aurelia.

Lucania receives secret telephone calls from Italy and the United States on telephone number 20738, a line registered to Salvatore Scarpati, Via Grandi Grafici, Naples. It was the headquarters of a carpet company, now closed.

*

Lucania is also said to be implicated in the smuggling of cigarettes from Tangiers to Italy, or to have financed that activity. In April 1951, he was with Contessa Iolanda Adorni Campagnoli at the Hotel London, in Naples. The woman in question was an associate of known cigarette smuggler Sol Charles Mirenda, a United States citizen, and Alvey Sheldon, the British subject who owns (it is believed) the well-known smuggling ship *Sayon-Miami-Flo*.

It is claimed that Lucania is a habitual opium smoker, and that he uses a pipe.

Chapter 5

Bologna, 7 May

Dizzy Gillespie filled the room with blue flames, like the flames of a Bunsen burner, hanging in mid-air, then down, towards the floor, notes hanging from tiny parachutes. 'Good Bait', a searing melody, short solos alternating with reprises of the theme, and you can't help snapping your fingers.

Robespierre Capponi had finished telling his story, a little Dalmatian odyssey enriched with scenes worthy of Tom Mix or Roy Rogers and featuring an incongruous appearance by Cary Grant. Fanti was turning around in his hands a copy of a book in English, with a garish cover: *Casino Royale*. The first five pages full of underlined words, as though someone was deciphering a coded message.

'They're the words I had to look up in the dictionary. Can you see that I didn't make it all up; where would I find a book like that? You can't get it in Bologna, or in Yugoslavia.'

'I believe you, Pierre. It's all too confused and difficult for anyone to make up. The English lessons are starting to bear fruit, I can see that.'

In English: *'I guess they do.'*

Cary Grant in Yugoslavia for a film about Tito. Really curious. He would have to think about that.

'Show me this pigeon, Pierre.'

Young Capponi held up the cage he was holding between his legs. Inside was a creature with dark-grey plumage. A bit thin and slightly bald, but a good specimen nonetheless.

'Have you kept it in there ever since you got back?

'I was worried it would fly home without a message. And I don't want that to happen. I already know what to write to my father, but

I don't know how big the paper should be, or how to attach it to the pigeon's leg, I could tie it with wire and it would fall off. You're a pigeon-fancier, so –'

'Fine, I'll show you later. Sorry, I've got to change the record.'

Gillespie and his combo had finished their track, the needle clicked at the end of the groove. Fanti raised his arm, lifted the disc and put it back in its sleeve. The void was filled by a more recent piece, *23 Degrees North and 82 Degrees West*, by the Stan Kenton Orchestra. Latitude and longitude of Havana, capital of Cuba. It announced the exploration of the Caribbean and its exotic rhythms, midway between Spain and Africa. Twenty-three degrees north and 82 degrees west: according to Kenton, the coordinates of the future.

'*Professore*, I expected to find more people who spoke Italian.'

'I think that many of them, although they can speak the language, refuse to do so. After all, as far as the Slavs are concerned, it was the language of the invaders, they forced them to speak it during the racist "italianisation" programme: surnames were changed, schoolchildren were obliged to answer in Italian so as not to be beaten by the fascist teachers. I'm not surprised they want nothing to do with it. To understand how much they have suffered, you just have to look at the revenge they took in Istria, throwing people into holes in the ground.'

'Ah, the Italians they killed and threw into those deep holes in the limestone.'

Fanti didn't reply, and *watched* the music. In the bass, intricate horn riffs charging full tilt to the first break. It was like watching them diving into the sea from a cliff. Holding their breath. The trombone solo advanced like a flame along a fuse, to the explosion of the sax, like the space rockets you see in the newsreels. A new pause, a full horn section, furious phrasing to the final apotheosis, the whole orchestra as one, a colossal club whose blows *struck* the song as though it were a sacrificial animal being led to the sacrifice. The drum roll the body's last spasm before the death blow. The end.

'A frenzy! What do you think, Pierre?'

'Fantastic. It's like a mambo, but more complicated. And very hard to dance to.'

'To get back to those holes: they didn't have it in for the Italians as such, Pierre. Sure, many innocent people ended up in those holes, but many of them were fascists, collaborationists, informers, people who had enabled the Germans to capture and torture the partisans, carry out massacres, burn whole villages. After 8 September the whole region was effectively annexed to the Third Reich. They were no longer content with taking the *k*'s and the *j*'s out of people's Slavonic surnames, or rapping children over the knuckles. An indescribable repression was unleashed. No one who has collaborated in an act of slaughter can expect the victims' relations to show mercy when they manage to get their hands on you. Even around your way, in Imola, the people responsible for the Pozzo Becca massacre were lynched by the crowd.'

'Yes, I know. My brother was out in the streets that day.'

Fanti took a sip of Lung Ching Dragon's Well, a sweet liquorice aftertaste. For a while they talked about Tito, Djilas, Trieste, the Communist Party line on Yugoslavia, then Fanti looked at the pigeon and lost himself in fantasies about the journeys it had taken and those still to be travelled, accompanied by reminiscences of his life with his wife, the years spent in England. His mind landed across the Channel, while his eardrums languished in the Caribbean.

Pierre could not shake off his torpor, and went on drinking his tea, beating out Stan Kenton's rhythm on his left thigh until the music stopped.

Fanti came to, muttered a phrase of apology, got to his feet and changed the record. Bud Powell's elegant 'Sure Thing' accompanied him as he took off his dressing gown and put on his jacket.

'Come on, let's go up to the pigeon loft. I'll show you how the amazing pigeon post works.'

And so it was that Josip III, scion of a family of intrepid flyers, grandson of a heroic courier in the partisan war, set off on his return journey to Dubrovnik.

Chapter 6

Cary told her everything, including the bit about the swapped coats.
Retrospective worry for Betsy. Whole-grain rice and macrobiotic
food, welcome home. Darling, you risked being injured, you risked
death . . . But I'm alive, and I'm fine. If I'd known . . . What would
you have done? I wouldn't have advised you to . . . It's all over, Betsy,
and I'm fine. I called Hitch. I'm going to do the film. I feel strange,
darling . . . I know, I know, I would feel like that too if I knew what
sort of close shave you'd had . . . I don't know how. But if you'd
been involved in a railway accident, or, what do I know, a shipwreck
. . . Don't say it even as a joke. It's bad luck. To change the subject:
what did Mr Bondurant get up to while I was away? Betsy tells Cary
about the photograph sent to the newspapers. A blunder. Mr
Raymond thought it might reinforce the credibility . . . But the regimental tie? Mr Bondurant bought it, poor thing . . . He was so fond
of it. He felt dreadful when he found out you were cross about it.
I'll send him a telegram full of apologies and thanks. Will you really?
Of course? You know, he's a good person, he's simple and he's honest.
He'll have gone back to his own life now. He was Cary Grant, and
he can't tell anyone anything about it. But just think, he'll have material for his imitations, genuine material, not like those people who
imitate you and say 'Judy, Judy, Judy . . .' in that hateful tone. You've
never even said that line. Not in any film or any radio show.
    Let them do it. I'm Cary Grant, they aren't.

Dear Mr Bondurant,
    Please accept my apologies (I have been a little harsh on you).
I should like to thank you for your work. You have all my

gratitude and esteem, and I have no doubt that people higher up than I am will demonstrate their appreciation.

The two suits made to measure by Quintino have been left in my house. They are all yours, a gift from the Commonwealth. I shall have Mr Raymond send them to you.

Hoping to be able to meet you again,

au revoir.

Cary Grant

They are enjoying the sunset by the pool, Cary and his old friend.

James David Graham Niven. Nicely trimmed moustache, the aplomb of the declining empire, years spent in His Majesty's infantry. The epitome of the British actor. His success. His curse. Stereotyped roles. A charming, distinguished accent. He works by accepting the parts turned down by Cary because they were too damned *English*.

What has Cary got that David might envy? He's English, American and a citizen of the world. David can't do that: he appears and you hear bagpipes, echoes of novels by Kipling, the 'white man's burden', the changing of the guard at Buckingham Palace. Life and soul of the party. A wise and constantly surprising wit. Forever *the Englishman*.

What has David got that Cary envies: medals and honours. Everyone knows he fought. On his return to the States, Ike in person awarded him the Order of Merit, the highest honour for a citizen of a foreign country.

They offered me the part of Phileas Phogg in *Around the World in Eighty Days*. Another part as a perfect English gentleman. Did you accept? Of course I did. You accept too many parts. Listen to your critics. The kine are getting leaner, my friend. Soon I'll be reduced to working in television. Cary thinks about his own trip around the world, or nearly. So what have you been up to over the last two months? I saw you in a paper and you looked curious, something wasn't quite right. Cary invents a convenient version, I was busy, preparing to go back on to the screen, etcetera. I'm leaving for the Côte d'Azur. The plot of *To Catch a Thief*. Not a bad story. A bit light for Hitchcock. Sure. When we're on the subject of stories, I read a ludicrous and revolting book written by somebody called Fleming. The protagonist is an MI6 agent called James Bond. Brief summary. Incoherent, indeed. They'll never make a film out of that! Laughter.

It's reality that's incoherent, my friend. Joe McCarthy on TV every night, pointing the finger at this one and that one! I have a feeling he's overdoing it, he seems to be getting further and further up the ladder, someone's going to react. Someone *must* react. Have we reacted? We're just actors. You remember Frances Farmer? I don't just remember her: I read an article about her, not long ago. What? Moments of consternation. And what happened to her in the end? She went back to Seattle. She worked as an usher in a cinema, if I remember correctly. Strange, it was about her, but the only person who spoke was her mother. She's about to get married. It must be a plot. Her mother has a guilty conscience. We *all* have guilty consciences. You know what they've done? Yes, there are rumours going about. Electroshock, 'hydrotherapy' . . . They force you to sit in a vat of icy water. Naked. I heard that the nurses were prostituting her to soldiers on leave. Is that true? They say she's been lobotomised. She didn't seem lobotomised to me. Certainly, she looked like she'd been through it but . . . Years in a mental hospital. Like my mother. Sometimes this country frightens me: it creates beauty, it spreads ideals of freedom . . . and then it puts someone like McCarthy on the stage. Apparently Ike hates him. We have to put our hopes in him. I can tell you: I voted for him. What about you? I'm a British subject, you twit! Who's McCarthy got it in for now? The army. Incredible. Remember the story about the Adam Hat Company? He attacked Drew Pearson's radio programme, and hit hard at the sponsor, saying, 'Anyone who buys these hats is giving a contribution to the cause of communism.' The company withdrew its sponsorship. And what about the money he gets from private citizens? Some people send him five- or ten-dollar bills, but I've heard that others are sending five or ten *thousand* dollars. He's said to reply to everyone in person, so I sent him a five-dollar bill, giving my cleaning woman's name. He wrote back thanking me and asking for *more money* to help the 'hard and costly struggle against communism'. Where is that money going to end up? Reliable sources tell me he spends it at the racetrack. The bastard! The charlatan! And how do you think he dresses? Sloppily. He looks as though he's slept in those badly cut suits. He goes on TV with a gravy-stained tie, I've seen it with my own eyes.

Voices from inside the house, the maid, you're not allowed in here, how dare you? Fuck off, I'm a federal agent, I'm a fucking G-man! Where's the boss? You're drunk, you can't just . . . He turns up in the garden. The maid apologises: excuse me, sir, I tried to stop him, but . . . Cary and David get up from the sofa. Cary recognises him: Bill Brown. FBI agent. Plastered. Black suit, white socks, white shirt, black tie. No hat. You prick, they told me you were back in town. Weren't you going to kick me up the ass? How dare you say Mr Hoover's a faggot? Who's getting kicked in the ass now, eh? David, let me introduce agent Bill Brown, of the Federal Bureau of Investigation. I don't believe it: *this guy here?* Do you have a warrant, Brown? This is trespass. You commie-lover, you're not even American! Mr Brown, what you are doing violates all the Bureau's rules of conduct. I'm actually beginning to doubt that you *really* are a federal agent. I ask you to leave my property, or I swear that this time I will act without further warning. What the fuck do you . . . Cary's right fist smashes into Brown's jaw. Brown staggers, slips, falls into the pool. He is unconscious, and in danger of drowning. David jumps in. Ten minutes later the ambulance shows up. I am a witness to the fact that it was self-defence, my friend. No, David. I struck the first blow. What does it matter? You did well. That G-man has a glass jaw. Damnation, I nearly broke my hand, just before my return to the screen! Better stick it in the ice bucket. This is going to make Hoover furious. Can you imagine tomorrow's headlines! No, nothing's going to get out. Hoover will muzzle the reporters. In any case, you'd be better off heading for the Côte d'Azur. One day I'll write a book. I'll put all the strange Hollywood stories in it. Well, don't write about this. Fine, old man. The moon's out. Look at it, Cary, the moon's a balloon. This is just one big stage set. Tell that to Frances Farmer. A sigh from David. You're right. The moon *looks like* a balloon.

Cary thinks about something else, hand in the bucket, next to the bottle of champagne.

What do you think of Grace Kelly?

Chapter 7

Let's be clear about this: we in the Bar Aurora are not like those old women who are forever looking at other people's plates because they have only bones on their own. Sure, from now on we won't have to go on and on about the great fucks we've had. But even without that there's still stuff to talk about, you bet, because the times we live in are a disgrace because of the nuclear 'experiments', and Bologna FC are a disgrace because Coach Viani is too defensive even when the team plays scrubby teams like Legnano, and Italy is a disgrace because the priests are in charge.

Every now and again we've all got a friend with problems, and when that happens it's normal for him to talk about them, and it may lead to gossip, but usually you'll find some way to help him. So if this friend is the one who jollies up your evenings, and he's got a long face, everyone else ends up feeling the same, so his troubles become a shared affair, something you have to resolve together.

Maybe people who don't hang out in bars can't fully understand this, but there's nothing worse than when the manager has his bollocks in a twist. You can't joke about anything, no one gets a drink on credit, you have to avoid a whole series of topics, and even the espressos taste of chicory.

In short, for almost a month now Capponi has been like a trapped bluebottle, forever muttering, and since his brother got back it's been even worse, the two of them are barely talking to each other except to say 'pass me that'. The worst thing of all is that you can't talk about the problem as though it wasn't a problem, you have to keep your trap shut, and because you're in their bar everything gets complicated. The only way is to sit everyone down around the table, with

L'Unità in the middle, pretending to read it and comment on it, and every now and again Bottone reads out a headline and if Capponi comes over to our side of the bar Garibaldi starts talking about Indochina.

'Oh, listen to this: "The banner of Free Vietnam is flying over Dien Bien Phu. The latest attack lasted a few hours . . ."'

The Walterún periscope emerges over the sea of white and bald heads. No one in sight. La Gaggia fires first: 'As far as I'm concerned, it's Pierre's fault. He suddenly disappears, as though he was the only person in the world!'

'Well?' Bottone butts in immediately. 'Didn't your son do exactly the same thing? Had he gone to his mum and said, I'm going to shoot at the Nazis on the Cansiglio, she'd have tied him to the bed, isn't that right?'

'Excuse me,' Garibaldi interjects. 'What does it matter who's to blame? I'm fed up to the back teeth with both of them: why don't we ask them to tell us what's up, once and for all; they can fuck off if they want to, but at least they can stop this nonsense.'

'"Solemn obsequies at the coffins of the thirty-seven workers pulled from the Montecatini mines. Fifty thousand Italians at the funerals of the victims of Ribolla . . ."'

'Because in my opinion Pierre hasn't told us the whole story. Doesn't he think it's obvious that he's worried about things? If his father really was as well as he says, he wouldn't have that face on him.'

Bottone licks a finger and turns the page. 'Come on, come on, where does his father come into it? It's a fight between brother and brother, there's nothing any of us can do about it, it'll pass in due course.'

'You reckon? Then you don't know Nicola Capponi, "the Bear".'

'You're right! A leopard can't change his spots!'

Garibaldi raises his hand to tell us to stop, and Bottone lowers his head to read: '"Asti, 7 May. We regret to announce the death at around 4 p.m. today, in his home at 20 Via Cavour, in our city, of the very popular former cycling champion, Giovanni Gerbi, known to all fans of the sport as the Red Devil."'

'Really? How old was he?'

'No age at all. When would he have stopped racing? 1910, was it? I remember it clearly.'

'Listen to this, while we're on the subject of cycling: "Giro d'Italia, live television reports from the stages, in those towns that have a TV connection."'

The advertisement is met with more sighs and groans than the abuses of power in the Montecatini factories. The fact is that in the Bar Franco, next door, they've just bought a television, and until yesterday nobody cared much, but while television may be a miracle, there's never anything to watch on it, and anyway the people in the Bar Franco had looked like a bunch of wankers, throwing away a shedload of money to show that they're better than everyone else. Then Bortolotti, on the day of the Milan–San Remo cycling race, didn't show up here to listen to the radio, and the day after he came and told us that the sprint, there on the screen, is incredibly exciting. And he also pointed out that the World Cup starts in June, and they're showing the games on television, and Franco told him that in that month alone he expects to recoup what he paid for the set, by adding on ten lire for coffee and fifty for alcohol.

Nicola, behind the bar, muttered something and that was enough to make us understand that that he doesn't even want us to talk about this. Anyway, the way he is at the moment you could tell him the Red Army was entrenched in Budrio and he wouldn't bat an eyelid.

'Why don't we have a collection?' Walterún pipes up all of a sudden.

'A collection?'

'Yes, everyone gives a bit, because if we wait to win the lottery, we'll never see the damned thing. On the other hand, if we all put in a bit, we'll soon get the 150,000 together, or am I wrong?'

'Well, maybe,' Bottone comments under his breath. 'A fine communist strategy, Walterún; the problem is that we need money for the aerial and the subscription, and the whole thing'll come to 30,000.'

'You know what I say? Bollocks to a collection: true communism means squeezing the money out of the boss. Let Benassi pay for this television. Isn't he the one that cleans up, after all?'

'"Has the fourth H-bomb been exploded in Bikini?" Gaggia, this one'll interest you: "Piero Piccioni and Montagna shortly to be interrogated by Sepe. Today in Geneva, conference on Indochina."'

As soon as Capponi moves away, the group splits up. Some rage against private property, some want to organise a lottery, some announce that they're refusing to drink any more bitters until Benassi chickens out, and some suggest asking Gas if he's got his hands on any televisions.

'What?' Garibaldi explodes, 'No, no, no, no! If you want to let him swindle you, you can forget about any money from me.'

'Come on, Garibaldi, do you honestly think he's going to do us all over? Don't we know where he lives?'

'It's a matter of principle, I —'

Pierre brushes past Bottone's back holding a tray, face like grim death.

'Bloody hell, look at Pierre, what a mug!'

As Pierre heads for the other room, Bortolotti leaves his game of billiards and joins our table.

'Have you seen the state of Pierre? I heard that things didn't go as well as they usually do at the "Seventh Heaven".'

'Ah, that's it, you see in Yugoslavia he forgot how to do the twirl. But it's not serious, call him, go on, and we'll try and cheer him up.'

'Never mind, Walterún, I'm afraid today is St Grudge's Day, there's nothing we can do.'

'You're right, Bortolotti, at this point it's better to let the two of them stew in their own juice, and turn our attention to this business about the television, because the World Cup's getting closer, and Italy isn't going to be much cop, but they did beat the French 3–1, and Cappello's playing, one of ours, from Bologna FC, like back in Schiavio's days. In short, it's worth the trouble, just so that those two grumpy brothers can be dragged into a state approaching euphoria.'

Or at least let's hope so.

Chapter 8

'Oh, I did bust my balls, though. These people from Naples, from the Deep South, they're always yelling their heads off, why do they always have to shout so much? And the children? Let's not even talk about them, they're animals, *fuck 'em all, I'd shove their teeth down their throats, think about that,* their teeth down their throats! And the streets are in one hell of a state, full of holes . . . And I've got piles! One of them's the size of a doughnut, absolutely bloody enormous, you know the way I've always got cream with me? Look how greasy it is, and just smell the stink of it!'

'Palmo, if you stick your fingers under my nose while I'm driving one more time, I'm sending you back to your parents in Portomaggiore, and believe me, I'll kick you all the way there. If I find out that you touched that doughnut of yours before shoving your fingers under my nose, I'm going to pull the fucking thing off!'

'You'd almost be doing me a favour. At least I'd bleed to death and there's an end to it! Every month, up and down, up and down, and when we find a room then that's fine, but when you have to sleep in the truck, it really hurts the back! I'm thirty-three, and if I'm not careful I'll be ready for the scrapheap before I make it to thirty-four. But can't we tell Bianco to change our route? We've been going back and forth to Naples for months now, it's a long way, and there's always the risk that the cops or the customs will sniff out the fact that the boxes have double bottoms, that there's half a metre between the wall and the cabin. Why can't we go to France instead? I'd be more than happy to swap with Spanézz!'

'Palmo, I haven't got the papers you need to go abroad, I've got charges pending. That route would be even riskier. Spanézz doesn't have any charges pending.'

'How come? Doesn't he carry the same stuff as us, watches, cigarettes, lighters . . . ?'

'Palmo, you really don't understand a thing, do you? "Charges pending" is when you have a trial coming up but they haven't passed sentence. I've still got two or three little things that the judge isn't willing to forget about, and there's no way out, at least until Martelloni, my lawyer, resolves the situation.'

'And have I got any charges pending?'

'No, what have you got to do with anything? You've never even been a partisan! And don't worry about this smuggling until Bianco greases the right wheels.'

'Fine, and how come Spanézz doesn't have any problems? He was a partisan too, wasn't he?'

'What's with all the questions? When I drive you're always quiet as a mouse, nearly sends me to sleep, but today you're like a public prosecutor!'

'Come on, Ettore, I know you're tired of going to the South all the time. Why don't we ask Bianco to change our route, where's the problem?'

'The problem is that I have to take care of business in Naples, ok? The others are getting impatient, and the ones down there aren't *easy*; if they get impatient they're quite capable of getting the knives out, and bang, you're finished, kaput, pushing up the daisies! And Spanézz was in a socialist brigade, he might have fired the odd shot. I was with Comandante Lupo, in the real war, you see? If you want to go with Spanézz, just do it, what's holding you back?'

'Spanézz is a ball-breaker, he's a terrible fusspot, he corrects me the moment I open my mouth, he starts laughing even if I've said something serious, then he says, "You really are from Ferrara, aren't you!" One of these days I'm going to knock his brains out.'

'That's enough, now. Spanézz goes his way, we go ours.'

'You're right, fuck him! But how did we get on to Spanézz?'

'You were the one who brought it up, you were complaining that you didn't care much for southerners.'

'So do you like them?'

'There are some serious ones. The American, Trimane, he's serious.'

'He gives me the creeps. Yeah, he's serious all right, serious as death. And the other one, the one he mentions from time to time, as though to say, "If you don't fall into line I'm going to fetch him in"?'

'"Cement" they call him. I've never seen him. He may not even exist, he's like the bogeyman.'

'So tell me, what are we taking on today?'

'Pharmaceuticals, painkillers, I don't know how many boxes. Ten or twelve of Wilkinson razors. Lighters. French cigarettes. That guy from Frosinone says there's also one of those modern things, a television.'

'No idea what they are, they say it's like a cinema, but it's small and fits in your house. Any idea who you'll sell it to?'

'We aren't going to sell it, we're not even taking it to Bologna; we're dropping it off with someone near Rome, who'll pay us for our trouble.'

'Pay us: does that mean the money's ours, or do we have to give it to Bianco?'

'No, it's ours. Fifteen thousand, he's giving us. We'll go fifty–fifty, even if you have been getting right up my nose today.'

'It must be a stolen television.'

'Nothing to do with us.'

'Ok.'

'Ok.'

'So what are these charges pending?'

'Just you go and cream your doughnut.'

Chapter 9

Naples, 9 May

'Don Viciè, you've got to tell us everything, ok? This is an important matter, Don Vincenzo, some mistakes have been made that never
should have been made.'

Vincenzo Donadio, hands resting on the counter, listened intently
to Salvatore Pagano's doleful voice. What unsettled the twenty-stone,
five-foot-seven bulk of Don Vincenzo was the big man standing next
to the boy, silent, the knot of his tie protruding, hands folded in
front of his balls.

'Young man, have you any idea how many things shouldn't have
happened between the war and now? Too many to mention! And
you know why? Because here, in this accursed and forgotten land,
things that shouldn't happen are always happening, let's not even talk
about it! There's no point going down in the morning, opening up
the workshop, working your arse off, sweating your way through the
day, who gives a fuck, with all due respect, petty thieves are the only
ones who want to do anything, and they just want to go skirt-chasing,
again with all due respect.'

'Don Vincenzo, the television . . .'

'What did I just say? You have no idea how much trouble I'm in.
Trouble! And it wasn't just for me, that massive great thing that
weighs a ton, you have no idea; it was a present I was going to give
to a friend of my granddaughter's, you know, they say they're going
to be showing football matches on it, but the thing didn't work, and
I'd planned to take a look inside, open it up and see if there was any
chance of fixing it, and if there wasn't, then fine, I'd get my mate
on the case. So I'd put it on the counter, there, just at the side, it
weighed a ton, you've no idea!'

'Um . . . And did you fix it?' The mute had spoken.

A stupid question, Don Vincenzo thought, but the tone of voice and the physical appearance of the questioner demanded maximum respect.

'Certainly not, certainly not, sir. I had put it up there because it was Saturday evening, *positively* planning to sort it out on Sunday, the day of rest. And on Sunday morning they come and call me, Don Viciè, come quick, they've broken into your shop, they broke the lock, and I went running, if you can call it running what with these legs and all that they have to hold up, that much is obvious, but they'd got the television, the bastards! Perhaps I should have put a sign on it saying "out of order", who knows!'

'Don Viciè, have you no idea who it might have been? Maybe someone who doesn't like you, maybe some lowlife in financial difficulties; please try, Don Vincenzo, please!'

Salvatore Pagano pleaded. Salvatore Pagano begged.

Salvatore Pagano implored.

'Hmm, what should I say. Vincenzo Donadio has no enemies, big or small. If you give respect, you get respect back. Don't stir things up. Don't poke your nose in where it isn't wanted. Let these be the commandments of Vincenzo Donadio. Having said that, thieves and villains are as thick on the ground hereabouts as the locusts in the Bible! In this street alone there are four or five: Pinhead, the Korean, Peppino the Creep . . .'

Salvatore Pagano smiled hopefully.

Towards evening, Vincenzo Donadio, sitting at the table, wiped away the sweat with a big blue handkerchief folded in the palm of his hand. Every now and again he snorted, then took another sip of Gragnano. He couldn't help thinking that that double-breasted Minotaur whom the boy called Mistestiv was a real devil, but a lot of good that did him. And it showed that he was right. In less than half a day, however, all the villains on the street had come out like mushrooms, and the whole district had been turned upside down. It had been satisfying to see that ignorant wretch Peppino the Creep crying, asking forgiveness and swearing on the life of his mother who had thrown him out all that time ago. But there was no sign of the set. Peppino had pointed the finger at another villain who was a friend of his, Nené, and another one who didn't seem to have anything to do with it. Mistestiv the American had terrorised them, but nothing came out of it. Shitting themselves with fear, they had already flogged it at a filling station somewhere near San Giovanni a Teduccio. To Latina, Formia, Frosinone, possibly Rome or even further afield. The lorry drivers went to all those places, sometimes beyond. Nothing. Goodbye to the television. There was no point beating yourself up. Things happened as they had to and that was that. Because then, Don Vincenzo reflected, if they found it, what would happen? No, because he had bought it, second-hand . . . But hang on a minute. Another sip of wine. He thought he could still hear the voice of Mistestiv before he drove off in that luxury American car, saying to the boy, 'Get in, you piece of shit!'

He really should mind his own business.

Chapter 10

Was she sure? No, but it didn't matter. It was over between them. They had always known. Perhaps that was what had made it so beautiful. They had savoured every minute snatched from normal life, to be what they were supposed to be: the Filuzzi King and Signora Montroni. The princess and the dancer. Now the moment had come to admit it. To stop the race.

She saw Pierre waiting for her at the funicular railway stop.

Angela waited for everyone to get off. Then she stepped out.

Pierre understood immediately. From her face. From her posture. He didn't even try to hug her.

He said, 'They told me about your brother. I'm sorry.'

His voice was embarrassed.

She stood a little way apart and lowered her eyes. 'He's better now. How was Yugoslavia? Did you see your father?'

'Yes.'

They stood there in silence. They both knew, but couldn't bring themselves to speak.

Finally Pierre said in a thin voice, 'It's over, isn't it?'

Angela nodded, her face hard.

'You can't live on fairy tales, Pierre.'

'Not even if they make you happy?'

She tried to find the right words.

'We were happy, that's true. But there are other things in life.'

'Your husband, your brother. Is that what you mean? You've told me so often –'

'It's not just that.'

A leaf carried on the wind caught in her hair, and Pierre couldn't help taking it out. Her hair was soft.

'What is it, then?'

'You're twenty-two, and you don't like what you've got, it isn't enough. You went to Yugoslavia, you've had your adventure, you've seen your father again. That won't be enough either. You're like a child, Pierre. You've got to find the right way. I've already found mine.'

Pierre wanted to reply, but Angela went on. 'Maybe fate forced it on me, but you also have to know when to grit your teeth. I'm not a little girl any more, I'm almost thirty. I was poor, and now I want for nothing. My brother was finished, good as dead. Now he had people to look after him. Find your way, Pierre. I wish you all the luck in the world. Let's leave it there.'

He didn't know what to say. It had to happen sooner or later. His journey and her brother's relapse must have unleashed something within her. Perhaps he should have flown into a desperate rage, and instead he just managed to feel stunned, submerged by those words, by that calm. He would suffer like a dog, afterwards. He would beat his head against the wall. But not now, not here.

His vision clouded over. He felt her kiss on his cheek, and when he managed to focus his eyes again Angela was already moving away.

There, it was over. A clean blow. Like a swig of grappa on an empty stomach.

Bologna slumbered at the foot of the hills.

He tried to take a step forwards; where was he to go, he couldn't stand this place any more, this view, he would hate it for ever. He couldn't move. He sat down and put his head between his knees. His head filled only with a succession of curses.

Chapter 11

The television didn't work even if you slapped it, but now he didn't give a damn.

Now. At first he had been annoyed. He had immediately called Frosinone to tell them that either they were to give him back his money, all of it, or they were to find a way of fixing the television.

As predicted, they had let themselves 'off the hook. It wasn't the fault of the television, which was American and first-rate, checked by the only person in the whole of Naples who knew anything about it, and it was ok, as though it was fresh out of the factory.

Bollocks.

But wait a second, did he have an aerial? Did he have a subscription? Then of course he couldn't see anything. You couldn't pick up images just like that, and until half-past five in the afternoon there was nothing, there weren't even any programmes. Before saying that the TV didn't work, he would have to be sure, check that the aerial was properly connected, that the subscription was in order, that his district was covered by the signal and the broadcasts had already begun. Just wait for a month, and meanwhile the opportunity, that prodigious American-brand television, with a naturally luminous seventeen-inch screen, would have passed. He'd be better off keeping it, listen to the advice he was being given, and if at the end the set proved to be defective, they would give him back all his money with interest.

'Interest, yes, but sparing myself any further bother would be quite enough,' Carmine had thought.

As he hung up, the idea flashed through his mind.

Whether the television worked or not, it was no longer a problem.

*

He went to wait for her at the school gates. Cleaned and polished as though for an evening in a nightclub. Halfway through each cigarette his comb passed carefully over his temples, which gleamed with brilliantine. He would offer her a lift on his scooter and set the plan in motion.

He glanced around, to be sure that that poor character Nosé was nowhere around. He wasn't. He would think about him later on.

Giuseppe Orlandi, known as Nosé, was a piece of crap, a porter in an apartment block in Garbatella, always badly dressed, battered hat in the winter, patched cloth shoes in the summer. He didn't have a penny, he didn't wash much, and yet Marisa thought very highly of him because he was an 'existentialist', he spent hours at the little table in the Bar Le Rose pretending to meditate and read. In fact the level of the wine bottle went down before your eyes, while the book, always the same one, never seemed to come to an end. It was called *La Nosé* by Jonpolsart, as he put it, but the cover said *Nausea*, and that was probably what it provoked.

Marisa's parents were nice people, sure, her father never let the women in his life go short of anything, and her mother was a great housewife. They knew Carmine, and they were nice to him. But they also knew that stupid Nosé, and although they knew he was penniless, they let their daughter go out with him a lot, much more than with Carmine. Her mother thought he was a 'harmless' boy, while her father suspected he had tons of money stashed away somewhere. The fact was that going out with Carmine, getting on to his 1100, having your ticket to the ballroom bought for you, were proper things for a *signorina*, a gold-digging slut excited by the size of a man's wallet. Forbidden. And she would be thinking of wallets when it was time for marriage. Having an ice-cream with Nosé and his lousy friends, going to the Villa Borghese to look at the stars, going up to his place to give him back the latest book by the latest wanker, that was all fine, as long as she tidied up her lipstick before she came home and never tried to suggest that pauper as a future son-in-law. That guy Carmine, on the other hand, so fashionable . . .

Bollocks to marriage and the senator who wanted to close down the brothels.

The school caretaker opened the gate. Carmine threw his cigarette a long way off, straightened his tie, and repeated the deadly
words through half-closed lips.

Her parents gave their blessing.

Nosé was astonished by the invitation.

She happily accepted.

After dinner at Carmine's to watch *Just Say It, Please*. A few friends,
the right music, Nosé to pick up Marisa, Nosé to take her home.

Carmine's plan provided champagne and tobacco for the existentialist. Three or four glasses. Smaller doses for Marisa: he wanted her
to be responsive. The guests, all friends, ready to slope off at the
right moment or watch discreetly. That useless wanker out of action
within an hour. He tries to get the television working. A brilliant
phrase to test the lie of the land: 'Marisa, don't pull that face, didn't
I invite you to watch television? There it is, watch it for as long as
you like, you can't say I don't keep my word, heh, heh.' A sugges-
tive phrase in preparation for the attack: 'What rotten luck, I thought
things were going so well this afternoon. Ok, then, Marisa, let's not
get depressed about it; we don't want this horrible contraption to
ruin our evening.'

All calculated. Couldn't fail.

And, before bringing the set back to Frosinone, he would give it
to his sister to humiliate that starving husband of hers. And if the
tosser started causing problems, he really would put him to shame.
Have you got an aerial? Have you paid your subscription? Did you
switch it on after half-past five? Have you checked that there's a
signal? And you claim it's working? Only a Zulu would think you
just had to plug the thing in.

The jerk would be offended and give back the present. Then he
would take it back to Frosinone and get the money back. His sister
would realise for the umpteenth time what kind of a shithead she
had married.

And all without spending a lira.

Chapter 12

'Your friend Teresa didn't come today, either,' Ferruccio said reproachfully.

He was sitting on the bed, his back leaning against two cushions, and wearing the blue pyjamas she had given him for Christmas

Angela smoothed his ruffled hair. 'She may not be coming for a while.'

He frowned, and a barely perceptible tic ran across his neck.

'Have you had a row?'

'No, Fefe, don't worry, she's just been busy.'

'And what about you, what are you doing? You're on your own.'

'I came to see you.'

He shook his head hard. 'No, no, you're on your own.'

Angela smiled at him, stroking him again. Ferruccio had worked out that something had happened between her and Picrre, and he couldn't get used to the idea.'

'No, Fefe, I'm not on my own. I've got you and Odoacre. And you love me.'

Ferruccio sighed, looked around, then turned to stare at her.

'No, no.'

'No what? Don't you love me?'

'I do,' said her brother curtly.

'So does Odoacre. And he loves you too. When you were ill he came rushing back from Rome, because he was worried. He got a real scare, did you know that? He'll always be near us.'

Ferruccio clamped his jaw and clenched his fists around his sheet.
'Why didn't Teresa come?'

Odoacre said not to let Ferruccio brood on things too much, it made him ill, he became obsessive.

'Listen, how are things going with the new medication? You seem better to me.'

'It gives me bad breath.'

'And you've got to brush your teeth, how many times do I have to tell you you've got to brush your teeth, because dentists cost an arm and a leg.'

Ferruccio nodded, looking elsewhere.

'It scares me. The monsters come out of my mouth.'

Angela hugged him. 'What's that? You're always going on about monsters!'

At that moment there was a knock at the door and Marco, the nurse, came in with an affable smile on his round face.

'Here I am, hello, madam.'

'Hello, Marco.'

'It's time for his medicine.'

Ferruccio's mouth was fixed in a pout. Then he turned to the nurse and exploded, 'Why did you go away?'

Marco prepared the pills and poured water into the glass.

'I was on honeymoon, Fefe, I got married.'

'Really? And how's your wife?' asked Angela.

'We're both fine, thanks. We've set up home in Corticella. And your husband was kind enough to extend my leave by a week. Thank him again from me. Unfortunately it was only when I got back that I found out that Ferruccio had been ill. Come on, Fefe, swallow it down, all in one go.'

Ferruccio obeyed, then wiped his mouth with the sheet.

'It was better when you weren't there.'

Angela rebuked him: 'Fefe, what are you saying?'

Marco shook his head. 'It wasn't better. You went mad, do you remember?'

'I didn't have to brush my teeth. No medication, no plughole.'

'Stop talking nonsense,' said Angela, helping him into his jacket, 'and now that you're dressed, I'll take you for a walk.

*

Angela glanced nervously at the telephone.

Couldn't make up her mind. Just chewing her nails and two words. No medication.

A strange thing, the brain. First of all absolute zero, then obsession. Treacle smeared over every gesture. Hang up your hat, no medication. Put down your keys, no medication. Step into the corridor, no medication.

There are certain questions that Odoacre doesn't like. He's always saying: you're not a doctor. He says: certain things seem strange to lay people, but the doctor knows what he's doing. You have to let him get on with his work.

Suspicion of your doctor impedes the healing process. The gospel according to Odoacre Montroni.

There are certain questions he doesn't like: he forestalls them. He tells you everything. Never a gap, never a misunderstanding.

Trust. Odoacre in Rome. Marco on holiday. An oversight and Fefe goes out of his mind.

So now you pick up the phone and you call Marco.

You remember what Fefe said that morning, that when you weren't there he didn't take his new medication? Well look, I've talked to my husband. No way. Terrible idea. You've talked to the head of department: what else do you want?

A mistake? Impossible, he said. You would have been informed. If not straight away, then on my return.

There you are. Exactly. By the time you returned the damage was done and your locum didn't get round to telling you everything. Quite normal.

Jesus Christ, Montroni spoke in parables. When you spill salt on the tablecloth, just throw it over your shoulder and you avoid disaster. No damage, no harm done. Not in the clinic, though. If you hide the damage the harm gets worse. Contrary to professional ethics. My locum is an excellent doctor. He has my every confidence.

You don't even know the locum. Can you trust people through an intermediary?

Fine. Then Fefe must have made a mistake. What do you expect, he's 'handicapped'. He thinks monsters are coming out of the plughole, how do you expect him to remember what medications he has taken. You're right, Odoacre, how stupid I am, to pay any attention to that fool of a brother of mine.

The usual reply: no one said your brother was a fool. But he isn't a doctor either. Put facts and instincts together: the bad breath and the medicine. But there's nothing in his therapy to give him halitosis. Unless it was in combination with something else. What do I know: coffee. Marco is a really good person, but he always allows Fefe a drop of coffee and he shouldn't. So the correct sequence is: no Marco, no coffee, no bad breath. Fefe couldn't know that. He only looks at what pills they're giving him. He swallows them down and that's it. Believe me. That's exactly how it was. I'll check tomorrow.

Reassuring.

Convincing.

So why are you uneasy? Don't you trust Dr Montroni? Don't you trust your husband? Of course I do, of course he's right. But Fefe is my brother. When he's ill, they tell Odoacre. One week I take him to the sea, and Odoacre is responsible. He says something strange, and Odoacre explains it to me.

That's exactly how it was. I'll check tomorrow.

Angela takes her eyes off the receiver.

No medication.

Chapter 13

Bologna, 21 May

Waiting made him nervous.

Since he was a child. He never did anything without asking what came next.

You need patience in life, aunt Iolanda repeated. Learn to wait.

Patience or not, he had learned.

Ritual cigarette, dark corner of an internal courtyard, glance into the street through the open gate.

Perfect ceremonial. All that was missing was the watch. The gesture remained. Dart of the wrist, fingers on the sleeve, eyes low. Four thousand lire for a Lorenz. A gift, if you listened to Sticleina.

Wait.

Filuzzi sweat, spring heat and a lot of ground covered at a fast walking pace. No bicycle, that'd been sold too.

He stubbed out the cigarette-end in the dust, reached the gate, turned around. Clear night. Stars everywhere and the cries of cats in heat.

Almost running, from the Florida to the Bar Aurora. They had said two o'clock, on the dot. Half an hour had passed, and there was no one to be seen. The flame of the lighter lit the bunch of keys. He tried the lock for luck. The one time you let your attention lapse you'll get nicked. He had to pull it back a little but it opened.

Another glance into the street, another cigarette. The last one. His change that morning had been just enough to buy six.

Wait. He had been forced to learn.

He had done nothing else.

His father, the letters, Angela. And what about that Redhead? The

same. The revolution? Hey, my boy, you'll have to wait, this isn't the
time, it's going to end up as it did in Greece. He knew the lines by
heart. He had no idea about half of the lines they came out with,
no idea what had happened in Greece, but he knew it was something big, ask Benfenati, if you don't believe me.

When comrade Benfenati talked about fighting within institu-
tions, Garibaldi was the only one to have his say. As in 1921, when
the bosses said they wouldn't respond to provocation, they wouldn't
yield to violence, and meanwhile the fascist squads were out there
beating people up, and not just that, and in the end it had taken
twenty years to send them home. 'We were fighting within institu-
tions,' he replied, 'and meanwhile they were going their own way.'

The cat miaowed more loudly. The sound was melancholy, but it
still sounded as if it was enjoying itself. No doubt about that. No
alternative. Just the right instinct. Fanti said that man's intelligence
is in opposition to his instinct. But if no one convinces you, or you
don't see the whole picture, why pretend that waiting is a strategy.
Bollocks, it's just an excuse to stop looking. A clever boxer can think
himself a clever strategist, but he'll still end up on the floor. And
when you hear on the radio that Mitri is waiting for his adversary,
you imagine him not with his eyes lowered, thinking about sex, but
concentrating on the slightest distraction, ready to explode.

Glancing around for the umpteenth time, Pierre noticed the light
on the other side of the road. Bloody hell, the baker. A big problem.
The baker wasn't the kind of person to mind his own business, he
was always in his doorway, keeping an eye on everyone, always well-
informed, always asking questions of the people passing, pretending
to be cordial.

All of a sudden the cat fell silent.

The sounds of a car filled the silence.

Three headlamps. Pierre gripped the gate. The truck passed him
as it reversed into the courtyard. The baker's door was shut.

Palmo switched off the engine and jumped out.

'You're late,' said Pierre.

'You're here, that's the important thing,' Palmo replied calmly.
'Come on, hurry up.'

There were six boxes. Palmo picked up three. He nearly lost his
balance on the stairs, while Pierre lit the steps with the candle. He

had cleared a space behind the sacks of coal. No one would touch them until the following winter.

The boxes would arrive once a month. No more than five or six, twenty sticks each. Most of the load would be sold in a few days, they'd all been pre-ordered, but there was always something left over, and it wasn't wise to keep it in the shed. Some people used the trick of sending them around the place, by post, like parcels. But then you had to keep your eye on the address, and ten minutes after the package had arrived, you would turn up as a postal worker, apologising for the error and asking to have the box back. Too risky, they'd already got burned a few times using that method.

Palmo put down the second load, and wanted to check the hiding place. Ettore must have recommended it. The coal sacks seemed to convince him.

All was quiet in the bakery. Anyway, weren't the old ladies of the district forever complaining that the bread wasn't the same since Gino had stopped getting up in the night and passed the baton to his sons? Gualtiero and Lorenzo weren't a problem.

Pierre waved and went up stairs. He tried not to make a sound, as always, so as not to wake Nicola. The engine of the truck made more noise than his shoes.

'Who brought you home?' asked his brother, turning around under the covers.

'Eh? No one, who was supposed to?'

'Didn't you come back by car?'

'No.'

'I heard a car –'

'I came back on foot.'

'Oh come on, you'd never get here without a bike. But you did insist on selling it, and now you're cadging lifts off everyone with a car, and look where you've ended up.'

Pierre bit his tongue and didn't say a word. The phrase 'go fuck yourself' exploded in his brain. He folded up his clothes on the chair, grabbed a length of sheet and thought of Angela without too much conviction.

Chapter 14

The park was pullulating with grandmothers and nannies pushing tinies from nought to eight around in pushchairs and prams.

Ducks and swans carefully cleaned their feathers on the edge of the artificial lake.

The man opened the paper bag and threw a handful of maize over the fence.

A confused throng of webbed feet. Even a few abusive pigeons.

A few old men on their own, or perhaps with a dog, out to see a bit of the world and renew their interest in the meteorological conditions of the afternoon.

The man praised the patience of those animals. He too would buy a dog, one day, an animal that wanted him to watch it while it shat.

The man was tall, loose-limbed, with greyish-blond hair and blue eyes. The man was forty-five years old. He wore a beige raincoat. He was sitting on a wooden bench, legs apart.

Another handful of grain. A flurry of wings and beaks trying to get to the front.

The swans stretched their necks. The ducks pushed from underneath. The pigeons hopped about on the margins, looking for gaps.

The birds were fat and clumsy.

The duckling bobbed towards the shore. It was a yellow dot in the midst of the dank green of the lake. A grey shadow appeared beneath it and for a moment the chick disappeared under the water. Then it re-emerged, drenched and breathless.

'It won't make it.'

'I say it will. It's too big, it won't be able to swallow it.'

'On the contrary, those creatures are pretty impressive. I don't even know what they are.'

The little bird swam towards the middle of the lake, so frightened that it had lost its bearings. The shadow followed it and dragged it underneath again.

This time it stayed under for longer. It re-emerged once more

'It can't possibly make it.'

'Five hundred francs says it will.'

'Done. What time is it?'

'Quarter to five.'

'If it's still afloat by five to five you've won.'

'Fine, ten minutes, then.'

The duck went on swimming, but was starting to tire.

The fish dragged it under for a third time.

On the bridge the two spectators held their breath.

The duckling re-emerged.

The duckling was breathless now.

'It's had it.'

'It's too big a mouthful, it can't eat it.'

'Doesn't matter. It'll pull it under, drown it and eat it one piece at a time.'

'It isn't as simple as you think.'

'I know that, but the fish doesn't. It's just hungry. I'm betting on its ignorance. And it's enormous, didn't you see its shadow?'

'Water distorts proportions, it makes everything look bigger. And time is passing.'

'While we're on the subject, what time's the meeting?'

'Five.'

'Bench?'

'Bench.'

The duckling was running out of strength.

It was starting to get too tired to swim.

The fish pulled it under again, and this time it took a long time to come back up to the surface. It had taken on more water than the *Titanic*.

The duckling threw up, tried to quack, but no sound came out.

One leg was half eaten.

The duckling was starting to get too tired to live.

'One minute and you've lost.'

'Wait.'

A massive shadow, much bigger than the other one, emerged from the bottom of the lake like an ink stain. An impressive mouth gaped beneath the bird and swallowed it up with a sinister sucking sound.

'Won!'

'Far from it, my dear fellow.'

'Because?'

'Because you were betting on another fish.'

'But what the hell are you saying? You were betting on the duckling and the duckling is kaput, finished, sunk. Get out your money.'

'I bet on the duckling. You bet on the fish. You said that you were betting on its ignorance. Your fish lost, like my duckling. So it's a draw. No winners.'

'You're a con artist.'

'I had a good teacher. It's late! Let's get moving, or he'll be gone.'

The man saw two guys approaching.

He recognised them by their straw hats. Then he noticed their loud suits, the orchids in their buttonholes, their showy bow ties. Affected manners *à la Wilde*, tuppeny literary quotations. He had been told that was the style of the two Italo-Frenchmen.

They sat down beside him, on the bench, looking at the swans.

'Good evening. Did you choose your clothes to avoid being conspicuous?'

'On the contrary, Monsieur Verne, in order to be recognised.'

'You must be Monsieur Azzoni.'

'As I live and breathe.'

'And you will be Monsieur Mariani.'

'How did you guess? A fine name, Verne, did you choose it with reference to any particular work? *Twenty Thousand Leagues under the Sea? The First Men in the Moon*? Do you think we'll ever get to the moon? Who'll get there first, them or us? And what about the centre of the earth?'

'I want to talk about work, not literature, if you don't mind.'

'Certainly, that's what I'm doing, Monsieur Verne. Do you know *Waiting for Godot*, by that Irish genius Samuel Beckett? Jean and I saw it on the stage in Paris a year ago. A masterpiece!'

The man didn't take his eyes off the lake. 'I don't follow you, Monsieur Mariani.'

'Neither you nor anyone else, luckily. Ok, you see, despite our Italian origins, he and I are rather like those two characters, Vladimir and Estragon, who wait and wait for someone who never comes.'

'I was told about your eccentric ways, Monsieur Mariani.'

'And were you informed of the cost of our loans?' the other man replied.

'You make it sound like a sinister kind of prostitution, Monsieur Azzoni.'

'And isn't it?'

'They assured me that you weren't short of idealistic motives.'

'You see, Monsieur Verne, what my friend Lucien here was trying to say is that you have kept us waiting too long, and our hopes of a world of equals have, how would one put it, rather subsided. Hope is always the last to die, that is true, but in the meantime we also have to live. And it is better to live well. So, at the point at which we are now, it is easier to act for money than for passion. That provides better guarantees for you, too, among other things. A mercenary cannot be disappointed because he has no illusions. You will never be able to disappoint us, Stalin's already thought of that. What my friend and I do we will do for money alone. We thought it best to be clear about that.'

'Well said, Jean.'

'Thank you, Lucien.'

The man chuckled and threw another handful of grain to the ducks.

'You are right to clear the field of misunderstandings, Monsieur Azzoni. You will be paid on time.'

Mariani handed him a little piece of paper.

'This Geneva bank account, please.'

'Certainly. How do you plan to proceed?'

Mariani gestured elaborately to let his friend pick up the conversation.

'The Emperor is already ours. We chatted him up at the casino, and he was easier than a dockland whore, if you'll forgive the expression. The Emperor plays big-time. The Emperor loses big-time, very big. Given that the money isn't his. Fees from American taxpayers rolling on to the green table. He has a court of prostitutes that he puts on the CIA expense account under the heading 'Imperial Cinematographic Troupe'. Then, let me think: two dwarfs, a pack of dogs that piss and shit all over the place, four bodyguards who look like Sumo wrestlers, three cooks, a food taster, two drivers, a butler, a wardrobe assistant, a tailor . . . am I forgetting anyone, Lucien?'

'The masseuse and the masked man.'

'That's right. And now us too.'

The man brushed grains from his raincoat. 'And could you say he likes you?'

'Like us? He dotes on us. We are his favourite humorists. He won't leave us alone for a moment. He even maintains that Lucien brings him good luck at *chemin de fer*.'

'And Jean at roulette.'

'And what does the Emperor think about the Geneva conference?'

'The Emperor wakes up at two o'clock in the afternoon, eats his breakfast, has someone read him the newspaper headlines, has a bath, has sex between three and five, takes the dogs to piss, comes back at half-past six, has a game of chess with one of the whores, has dinner at half-past eight, shows up at the casino at ten on the dot and stays there until dawn. When would he have time to think about the conference?'

'Have you noticed anything strange happening around him? Have the Americans tried to get close to him?'

'Not for the time being. They just pour his money into a Berne bank account.'

'Any information could be very precious.'

Azzoni rubbed his thumb and index finger. 'You pay, we inform. The first piece of news is that the Emperor is about to leave Evian.'

The man gave an involuntary jerk of the head. 'He wasn't expected to leave town before the end of the conference.'

'We know. But Bao is dying to go and enrich the casinos of the Côte d'Azur. He leaves in a few days, and we're going with him.'

'How did you plan to stay in touch with me?'

Mariani butted in. 'What do you think of homing pigeons, Monsieur Verne? I've always been fascinated by the way they find their bearings. I've always wondered whether they can only find their way home, or whether they can go in the other direction as well.'

Azzoni silenced him with a gesture. 'We will communicate our movements by phone, with the code that you used to contact us. Although beforehand, we will check the payments into our current account, obviously.'

'Obviously,' repeated the man.

Mariani did a half-military salute, bringing his hand to his straw hat. 'Agents Vladimir and Estragon, ready and waiting.'

The man smiled, it would not be easy to write a report on these two.

General Serov would disapprove.

He got to his feet, brushed down his raincoat and rolled up his bag.

'It's a shame you no longer believe in history, gentlemen. Because you are fighting for the right side. If you were aware of it, you would do it better, and it would fill you with pride.'

Azzoni took his straw hat and put it over his heart. 'Did you hear that, Lucien, I want you to write this on my tombstone: "Here lies a fool who fought on the right side and never knew it".'

His friend did the same thing and, with a contrite air, almost weeping, said, 'Poor Jean, while waiting for Godot he made a pile of money and never knew why. He died sad and broken, without a cause to fight for. And nonetheless they will bury him in the Kremlin.'

The man didn't know whether to laugh or tell them to go to hell.

'Goodbye, gentlemen. Enjoy your day.'

The two men waved their hats in unison.

Mariani spoke in an affected voice. 'Pass on our greetings to the Central Committee, and tell all the comrades there's one author they really must read, his name is Karl Marx, remember that!'

The man did not turn around.

General Serov would disapprove.

Chapter 15

KGB archive, report no. 22227
Classified: level 1
Decryption code: 43
From: resident 04, 'Jules Verne', Geneva, Switzerland
Date: 22.5.54
Object: information recruitment

I communicate that information recruitment concerning Operation Indochina has taken place according to orders received.

There are two subjects at issue.

JEAN AZZONI, born in Lyons on 14.2.1920 to a French mother and Italian father, higher education, bachelor, declared profession: actor.

Of communist family, he has always declared himself to be such, but has never been a member of the French Communist Party or any other left-wing organisation. On more than one occasion he has shown his disapproval of the policies of the Soviet Union. Studied for three years at the Academy of Dramatic Art in Paris (1937–40). When the Nazi invasion took place he escaped to the south and lived by his wits, until he joined the partisan formations. Between 1942 and 1944 he was involved in several undercover spying operations on behalf of the Resistance. Has demonstrated the same qualities working as an actor in a popular Parisian theatre between 1947 and 1953. His flaunted opposition towards the French colonial occupation of Indochina is sincere and tested. He declares himself to be an admirer of Ho Chi Minh, and equates the Foreign Legion with Hitler's SS. In 1952 he was approached by French resident no. 03, and showed an interest in working for us. He skilfully exploited the infatuation of a young admirer employed by the French Ministry of the Interior to acquire information and pass it on to our resident in exchange for an agreed fee. He currently lives off smuggling and fraud at the expense of wealthy businessmen and Parisian entrepreneurs.

*

LUCIEN MARIANI, born in Nantes on 22.5.1921 to Italian parents, bachelor, declared profession: actor.

Of libertine tendencies, he professes himself to be a 'communist and libertarian'. He spent eighteen months in a reform school for theft (1937–38). In 1940 he joined the French army. When the Maginot Line was broken, he deserted and went into hiding. Under the Nazi occupation he survived for a few months by stealing from black-market traders. Subsequently he moved to the South and joined the Resistance, among the ranks of the 'maquis', where he met J.A. Together they carried out some sabotage operations against the German army, showing great inspiration and cunning. A reasonably good expert on explosives, known for his loose tongue and eccentric manners, between 1948 and 1952 he scraped a living by performing as a character actor in a Parisian bar of ill repute frequented by intellectuals and decadent artists. His irreverent imitation of Marshal de Gaulle was reported to the police. From 1952 he has been associated with J.A. in the same semi-illegal activities. L.M. also entertains a profound hatred for French policy in Indochina.

Recently the two subjects have been responsible for an act of sabotage against the Foreign Legion in Marseille, selling a consignment of tins of contaminated beans to a military transport ship leaving for Saigon. Dysentery decimated the crew, forcing the vessel to disembark many of the troops in Suez to allow them to recover in hospital.

There can be no doubt that these are two ambiguous figures, parasites without any ethical principles. Nonetheless, it should be stressed that for this very reason they are perfect for the task that they are to perform. This is proved by the extreme ease with which they managed to infiltrate the entourage of Emperor Bao Dai. Furthermore, the personal experience of the two subjects should guarantee their operational ability and allow us to keep the Emperor under constant and total observation, at least until the work at the conference is finished.

J.A. (in subsequent communications 'Vladimir') and L.M. (in subsequent communications 'Estragon') will follow Bao Dai's every move and report to the undersigned on a weekly basis. Payments will be made to an anonymous account in a Geneva bank (see Appendix 1).

Chapter 16

'Come on then, let's get going.' The spoon rings out against the bottle and Capponi's rough voice grates out its comments. Hungary 7, England 1, straight from the radio. Hard to think about anything else.

'I spoke to Benassi this morning, and this is his suggestion: he pays the subscription, we pay for the set and the aerial.' He quickly raises a hand and stifles everyone's protests. 'Silence! We're not in the marketplace! Listen: as comrade Bortolotti suggests, on important occasions the price of drinks will be upped. Benassi suggests that this money be used to cover the subscription, until each of us has paid his quota.'

Sunday. Extraordinary opening. Absent without justification: no one. No one can remember more than two such meetings at the Bar Aurora. The first one in 1945, to decide whether the bar was going to return to its glorious old name or find another, more modern one. And the second during the days of the attack on Togliatti, on a more delicate matter.

The café strike, proclaimed by Garibaldi and observed by more or less everyone, provided the first results. Plenary session of the regulars and first conciliatory offer from comrade Benassi.

But Melega refuses to be charmed. 'Sorry, Capponi, but can you run that past me again? We pay for the television out of our own pockets. When we come to see it, we pay a surtax on the coffee, and with that surtax, which is still our money, Benassi covers his costs? It sounds like a swindle to me, I can't speak for everyone else.'

About ten heads nod, convinced. 'Melega is right!'

'It's a swindle!'

'Who does this guy Benassi think he's trying to kid?'

Excited by this consensus, Melega spreads his legs in the pose of Pecos Bill. 'One of the two: either he pays, and then we hike the price to get his expenses back, or we pay, and the prices don't get hiked.'

Capponi strikes the bottle as though it were an anvil. Bottone's counter-suggestion is quick to come. 'I say: fine. We pay. But,' he counts on his fingers, 'no surtax for anyone who's contributed to the collection, and all the extra revenue to be placed in a communal kitty for at least three years, because if our income exceeds our out-goings, I don't know, either we lease out the table football or we buy a ticket for the stadium.'

Convinced looks are exchanged.

Someone insists on paying in instalments. 'Listen, lad, if you ask me for the 5,000 now, all at once, I'll have to sit this one out, because in August I'm going on holiday with my family, ten days in Torre Pedrera and that's 40,000 in a third-rate B&B. Can you tell me where I'm going to find the money for the collection? I've barely got two coins to rub together.'

'Come off it, Marmiroli,' someone else comments acidly, 'do you tighten your belt all year to go to the Riviera? Give your kids more to eat, they'll starve to death, they're like dry twigs already.'

Nicola has done enough shouting, and lets his brother reply: 'The instalment idea isn't too bad, but it might be better to accept Gas's suggestion: a single payment, and a saving of almost 80,000 lire on a luxury model.'

Gas's scalp, freshly shaven, is shinier than ever. But most eyes turn towards Garibaldi, who spreads his arms dolefully and takes a sip to control himself.

'Ok, ok, what are you all staring at?' Then, with a burst of pride, he jumps to his feet and points his finger at the bald man. 'But be careful, ok?'

He must be sure of himself, our entrepreneur. He doesn't say a word. He takes a long draw on his cigar and arrogantly blows away the smoke. He has accepted the challenge.

'Ok, then,' Pierre goes on. 'The approximate figure is 250,000. The collection will raise 200,000 at the most. We'll have to work out what comes out of the other initiatives. Not least because time's marching on, and the World Cup starts in mid-June. Bottone, what about your *tarocchino* tournament?'

'We'll win, easy. First prize: a nice Langhirano ham, we've already found a buyer for it, and it'll make us about seven or eight thousand lire. Let's hear what Benfenati has to tell us about the contribution from the Section.'

Silence falls, even with the bottle untapped. First, because what's at stake is a share in at least 20,000 lire; second, because everyone knows that the problem has been hotly debated, above all for ideological reasons, and we're all expecting a definitive political judgement; third, because Benfenati is one of those people who can wet the bed and say it was sweat, and people will discuss his intervention, turn it around however you like, in the days to come.

'It gave me a lot of pleasure to hear that Benassi in person is going to pay the subscription charge. We would have refused straight away.' The voice rises over the buzz of surprise. 'You know what we've discovered, with the other comrades, reading the text of the convention carefully? Listen to this . . .' He rummages in his shirt pocket and takes out a piece of paper: '"Clause 16: In case of financial or economic information of special importance, and information of general interest, the concessionary body will follow the instructions of the Chairman." Pretty, isn't it? Just so we know who we're dealing with.'

This surprise reading prompts comments. In the midst of 'what bollocks', 'did you hear that?', 'fascists!', Walterún's voice addresses his neighbour.

'Garibaldi, I don't get it: are they paying, or are they not?'

Benfenati, like a good primary school teacher, has radar in his ears and continues without missing a beat: 'Comrade Santagata rightly wonders whether we're paying. Let's get to the nub, then. Today we don't know much about television, but like any technical innovation, we know it will be useful if used judiciously, and damaging otherwise. Take the radio. Very useful, everyone agrees. But have you ever listened on a Tuesday evening? Have you heard that yankee fop who answers to the name of Mike Bongiorno? "How old are you? Are you married? What do you do for a living? Fine, Signor Grimaldi, tell us, for 450,000 lire, which liquid are they talking about in this advertisement?"'

'Hey, good idea!' Gaggia explodes. 'If he rang us up we'd have solved the problem.'

'Comrade, what are you on about! That's exactly what they're trying to tell you: that nothing involves any effort now, that life is one big joke, provided you know what's really important, like learning the words of 'Vola colomba' off by heart, devoting an in-depth study to the life of some princess or other, or taking an interest in the fantastic properties of Colgate toothpaste. If he phoned me up, I'd ask the questions, you bet: "Tell me, Signor Bongiorno, for 400,000 lire, how come my brother broke his back in the field and now he lives on a basic pension of 4,000 lire? In your opinion, how does he do it?' Those are the questions that need asking. However, to cut a long story short, specifically given the ambiguity of the new machine, we have not reached a common position, and we have decided to pay according to our consciences. Each man for himself, each one his own share.'

He sits down. He has finished. Ruling of Solomon? No one wants to be the first to comment.

'An angel has passed!' Garibaldi says sententiously as he usually does when a sudden silence falls. The tension eases, and everyone settles down, one after the other, smoke, chatter and the smell of feet.

'Ok, I'm off,' says Brando, 'I won't be in tomorrow, I've got things to do. I'll see you Tuesday.'

'As long as we're still alive,' Pierre shoots back with a laugh.

'Eh?'

'Haven't you heard? Some loud-mouthed fools are saying the world's going to come to an end on 24 May, at midnight. And so does Padre Pio, that priest who converted Macario. There's no doubt about it: the world is on the brink of destruction.'

'He'd be on the brink of destruction if I had anything to do with it. Take care of yourself.'

Chapter 17

Bologna, Villa Azzurra, 31 May

Tired and battered, the swing creaked beside the pond. A pint of oil would not have eased its arthritis. Hopeless there, in the bed of roses and petunias. Visiting relations often asked what the point of that old crock was, and someone had even put a hand on his wallet, just in case contributions were required. That wasn't the point.

While he's here, Signora, we can't take it away. We've tried, haven't we? Isn't that right, Fefe? You should have heard how he started shouting. Can you shout at night? Oh, you know it's not ok. Give me an example. What does Marco say to me if I start shouting at night? Eh, Fefe, how many times have I told you, if you need me, call me down.

He really loves that swing. He doesn't care if it's old and broken. It swingy-swings up and down and keeps you company. And the bench under the cypresses is ok too, but it doesn't say anything, complete silence, good for a nap. An afternoon nap does him the world of good, doesn't it? Say it, say it: Fefe is going to let you have a nap on the bench.

Do you want a cigarette? No, no, no cigarette, they're very bad for Davide, you mustn't give him any. Why on earth did I want to go out naked today? Tell me. Can you go out naked? Not at all. And there's pie later on. Mimma has made that lovely pie with carrots. Come on, put your trousers on or you won't have any.

But nothing's happened. What do you mean, naked?

He wanted to go out like that, you know? Then he wouldn't eat the carrot pie, then Giorgio went to the kitchen and scoffed the lot.

Can you eat a whole pie? No, Fefe, you can't eat it, and now Giorgio
won't have any coffee for a week.

When he saw all the pie was gone, he was in a bad state at first.
Then he went up to his room, took everything off and went outside.
With that great dangler of his, he nearly gave Signora Maffei a fit
of the vapours. I won't give you the whole scene. Did something
happen? No, nothing happened at all. Say it, say it. What will Marco
say if I do anything like that again? He'll get pissed off.

So pissed off!

'Fefe, what are you shouting?' Angela, behind him, silent on the grass
of the lawn. 'You don't have to use bad language.'

'No, no. Go away! Why have you come?'

'Well, that's a nice welcome. We're in a polite mood, I can see.'

She sat down on the swing in front of him, her arm outstretched,
stroking his head. He was sulking.

'Your friend doesn't come any more. I really liked her, but she
doesn't come any more.'

'Be patient, Fefe. She's very busy at the moment, but she really is
coming back.'

'If Giorgio hadn't eaten the pie, I could have gone out. What does
naked mean?'

Angela smiled, looking for the usual bar of chocolate in her
handbag.

'Hey, ok, you're just pretending. Marco told me all about it. You
did your act again.'

'Do I deserve some chocolate? There was no pie left and I went
out.'

'And did you have to go out naked?'

'But there was no pie left! It's your fault your friend doesn't come
any more. You have to stop coming. You've got your own business
to attend to, so much to do. Tell her to come.'

'"So much to do".' Angela knew that Fefe knew. She let her eyes
slide towards the top of the swing. Storm clouds were swirling in,
merging with one another.

'How are your teeth? You are brushing them, aren't you?'

'Marco says it's because of the coffee, that he can't give me any more. No, I'm going to pull out my teeth, so that Marco will start giving me coffee again. Like with the pie.'

'Come on, Fefe, don't even say that as a joke.'

'And then you won't have to come any more. You'll have to send your friend.'

Goodness, but Fefe was obsessed. 'Can we change the subject? Please?'

All of a sudden Fefe starts hitting himself on the head.

'No! You mustn't come ever again, never again!'

'Calm down, Fefe, that's enough.'

He wouldn't calm down. Angela tried to hold his arm. He broke away from her grip with a squeal of annoyance. He jumped to his feet, two steps back. Still thumping himself, he stared at his sister. 'We should throw that swing away. It's ugly, old, it swingy-swings all day. It's broken my balls. If there's some pie, you can't go out. But without any pie, do whatever the fuck you like! Say it!'

It wasn't a good sign when Fefe launched a verbal attack. You had to nip it in the bud, or he risked going incandescent.

'We don't use words like that.' Angela glared at him with serious reproach. Usually that was enough.

'Why not? Give me an example.'

'No examples. Those are horrible words and I'm getting angry.'

'Then get angry, so that you'll send your friend next time.'

'Exactly. If you go on behaving like this, Teresa will stay at home.'

'Then say goodbye from me. Hello, Teresa. Bye-bye, Angela. Bye-bye, old swing. Let's throw it away. It's broken and no one likes it. Bye-bye, Fefe.'

He resolutely turned his back and walked along the gravel path. Angela watched him go, then came after him, at a distance of a few metres. Once he had calmed down you had to leave him alone for a while.

Marco had said: unstable weather always makes him agitated.

Odoacre had said: it's the aftermath of his fit, it's perfectly normal.

Outside a summer storm was brewing, and Fefe hated them. The thunder reminded him of the bombs, the death of his mother, fear.

But Fefe's condition was not what it had been. He was more nervous, more obsessive, less tranquil.

That wasn't the only thing that worried her.

Fefe spoke a language of his own, but there was a meaning to his words that stayed in his head. Angela was used to scenting it out. Picking up references and hidden information. Even when there was no connection and the collage seemed to be casual. There was always a vague impression.

As Odoacre said: most of the time we are reflected in the incomprehensible. But beyond sophistry and personal empathy, Angela understood Fefe better than anyone else.

Their meeting that afternoon had worried her more than usual.

'Go away,' he often said to her. It meant: 'don't worry about me.'

It wasn't the first time she had seen him thump himself on the head like that. Odoacre called it 'self-harming'.

It wasn't new for him to want to go outside naked. He tried it every now and again, but bribery like the pie was usually enough to hold him back.

She'd seen it all before. So why couldn't she breathe? The phrase about the swing?

The first thunderclaps shook the windows.

Drops as big as marbles bounced off the windowsill. The dirty white of the sky pressed down on the roofs and hills. Angela ran to bring in the sheets on the line and put them in the basin. She put a hand to her heart, as though to stop it from leaping out. A flash of lightning.

Who knows, Fefe. From the first rumbles he got it into his head that he had to get outside, away, into the open. He was always worried that the ceiling might come crashing down on him. The storm itself didn't really worry him. In fact, he said he liked the rain, the smell of damp grass, the 'clean world' as he called it. They locked him up in his room, officially 'to ensure that he didn't fall ill'. In fact, during the warmest months there was no great risk of colds, and a drop of rain wouldn't have hurt him. Afterwards, though, he had to be undressed, dried, dressed again. Even Marco preferred to avoid the whole procedure with a turn of the key. Poor Fefe.

The image of her brother crouching under his bed with the pillow over his ears made Angela's state of mind even worse than it was already.

Water and hail hammered relentlessly on the glass in bursts. Five minutes like that and the rain would start coming in. On the other hand, even just leaning out to close the shutters would mean getting drenched from the shoulders up.

A fresh clap of thunder drowned the ringing of the phone. When Angela heard Odoacre's voice, nausea choked her. He was calling from the clinic.

Fefe. A terrible thing. A tragedy.

Chapter 18

Would have been a Thursday evening, that's right, first time I saw him, in the club, must have been a Thursday evening. I remember, because on Thursdays Frankie 'the Cockroach' Pistocchio brought in the new women to show themselves off and ask if there was a job for them. He lined them up, studied them, touched their asses and their tits. They didn't like that: Frankie was completely disgusting, he thought with his cock, and it was always hard, an animal, he was, and if he hadn't been a distant cousin of Joe Bananas, he'd never have set foot in the club, let alone worked there. *Scaravagghiu*, the 'cockroach', his mum called him, because when he was a very small boy whenever he played football he came home so absolutely filthy that he looked as though he was covered with shit and piss. As a little boy and, my God, as a grown-up too: an animal. But the fact that he thought with his cock could be useful sometimes, it was as though he had an antenna fixed to his head, he was like a radio that could pick up whether a girl was a slut or a plank in the sack. One glance and he knew if she was a good fuck or if she wasn't, if she'd let you in the back door, if she liked sucking dick or if she didn't. A genius, Frankie.

She was a beauty: dark-haired, tall, black eyes and lips you could have stared at for a quarter of an hour. Tits, ass, thighs, everything in the right place. I don't remember her clothes because I was looking through them, like Superman. I was behind the curtain, peering through the crack. She couldn't see me, but she was looking in my direction. She knew I was there, and she wasn't frightened. Frankie felt her tits with those hands that looked like shovels, and she smiled as though to challenge him. Frankie lifted up her skirt to see how she was built under there, and she gave a little laugh. Frankie was all sweaty and filthy, he really did look like a cockroach, and he asked her why the fuck she was laughing. Then he took one of her hands and put it on his dick. She kept it there, gave another little laugh that sounded like a mosquito flying like a bubble of blood after it's bitten you, and then she said out loud, 'Is that it?', looking towards my eye in the gap in the curtain, even though she couldn't see it.

Frankie went as if to strike her, but before he made that terrible mistake, breaking the face of the best whore he had ever got his hands on, I shouted, 'Stop!', then came out and turned towards the girl: 'Forgive me, miss, but I sometimes wonder what the hell's going on in the head of this employee of mine.' I waved away Frankie, who looked as though he was the one who'd been slapped, then said, 'Listen to me, miss, you'll be just perfect working for us. What's your name?'

She looked at my scar, and my right eye a bit lower than the other one, and then she did something no one ever did. Two things. First of all, she didn't give an immediate reply to my question. Then second, she asked me, 'What happened to your right cheek, sir?'

My right cheek. I did something I never did, and told her about the time I got attacked in 1929. Then I asked her her name again.

Her name was Mona, the daughter of an Irish father and a half-Italian mother, from the Abruzzi. I told her to come back the following evening, because Friday night is fucking night, it's pay-day and you take some of it home and the rest you spend on women and drink. That is, I didn't put it quite like that, I just told her to come back the following evening. But all of a sudden it occurred to me that Mona wasn't a piece of meat to be chucked in a brothel to work six nights a week. She was *poule de luxe* to tempt the big guys. And that was exactly what happened. She was a volcano who sent all the customers' spunk boiling.

The strange thing is that I dreamt about Mona last night. Fuck, I miss that girl. They were good times, we were doing well with the races, the gambling and particularly the whores. We were fucking twice a day, different women, because I might have had a droopy eye but my dick was good and stiff. Even today, even though I'm not as young as I was, I'm still a well-respected cocksman. I have one good fuck a day, and it doesn't just last three minutes.

Good times, yes, then that great bastard and cocksucker Procurator Dewey, Honest Tom, shows up, and what happens? The whores perjured themselves in court, saying I was the biggest exploiter in the Americas, that I had my fingers in all kinds of pies, may God strike them dead, and among the whores I see Mona, who I'd always had in the palm of my hand, and who I'd given a stack of money to, and I made sure the people she fucked weren't weirdos. But I'm not pissed off, you know, women are all whores in their minds, not just in their cunts.

The strange thing was that I dreamt about Mona last night. I can't believe you can end up in jail over a woman.

The really weird thing is that I didn't dream about the embarkation. In 1946 my lawyers are about to demonstrate that Honest Tom has corrupted, threatened and bribed the witnesses, when they free me on the spot and send me here to Italy, so as not to have me stuck in the middle of the whole mess. Honest Tom wants to stand for the presidency, it's in everybody's best interest for me to fuck off to the back of beyond. So it seems strange that the *capo di tutti capi* was released from prison all of a sudden; they put about the rumour that I have rendered service to the country, talking to the local boys to encourage the Allied landing in Sicily, so they pay me back with freedom and repatriation. Such bullshit that the American admirals still hate me for it.

Now this *paisà*, Siragusa, wants them to send me to jail, he's getting in a sweat about the car, and what the fuck does the car have to do with anything? Am I supposed to go about the place in a fucking *cinquecento* like a bum? The insults would be flying from both sides of the street! The cops are breathing down my neck, that great whore-fucker.

And that other one, that journalist who came last autumn, wants to write a book about me. Without my permission.

Freedom of the press is a fine thing, but it would still be better if we didn't have it.

Now Steve Cement is heading for Marseilles, so we're winding up that operation too and thinking about it a bit, because things could change. He's seemed a bit strange lately. I understand, he's homesick, our boy, he misses Manhattan and Brooklyn, and maybe he misses the shoemaking job he used to do on the wharf. Here all he gets to do is whack some lowlife over the head with a monkey wrench. Someone with his abilities has no way of distinguishing himself. A good fella, but strange, he barely ever speaks now, and they tell me he's always hanging out with that boy they call Kociss.

Then things are happening that I don't understand, but I'll get there, because I'm in hiding here, I live well, I'm retired, but I have my eyes and ears everywhere, even in my dick.

Chapter 19

Between Rome and Frosinone, 31 May

Too many damned mistakes. Steve 'Prick' Zollo.

You know how things are going to end up when all the bullshit begins.

Level crossing. Colleferro ten kilometres. Another country full of sheep and bumpkins like the one we've just left. Frosinone, a hole in the ocean. Another spin of the ball. Zero.

Two weeks following a trail leading to the asshole who got his hands on the TV, with a boss throbbing for business and brothels. The guys from Marseilles, that son of a bitch Siragusa, Sicily. Don Luciano, and he can be twitchy and unbearable. Another flame under my already scorched ass.

The end of the trail: Antonio Cammarota, a wine dealer, Frosinone. He was supposed to be the buyer, and he is, but the television isn't even there. He wasn't home. There wasn't anyone there, not even the television. At the wine warehouse I got the bad news from Cammarota's colleague, a guy called Paride. Antonio is out on a delivery and won't be back before nightfall. It's true that he has bought an important television, second-hand. He was supposed to be selling it to a guy in Rome, outside Rome, not far from Rome, he couldn't really remember.

The television didn't actually pass through Frosinone, because Antonio knows the guys who were transporting it on the truck, and they brought it all the way to Rome.

The lorry drivers might have been called Ernesto, or Ettore, he couldn't remember, and the other one was Palmiro, but Antonio had been closer to Ettore.

Nothing. Colleferro ten kilometres. Fucking level crossing.

'But I'm sure we'll find it, Stiv. A bloody great thing like that can't just vanish into thin air.'

'Shut up! Shut up, do you hear me? Are you going to go on like this the whole way? I'm thinking!'

It can't be true.

I'm going to France, Côte d'Azur.

Meeting the guys from Marseilles, for the organisation, for Don Luciano. Don Luciano thinks I'm hours ahead. Don Luciano is worried.

Meeting Lyonnese Toni. On behalf of Steve 'Jerk-off' Zollo, and his new colleague, Shithead, king of Agnano. My turn to buy him clothes. I couldn't leave him on the loose. He's fastened to me, tight.

This last spin of the ball is fucking your pension, Steve. Sorry, Toni, I've lost twelve kilos of pure heroin inside a television, but I'm going to get it back, you can be sure of that. I'm going to get a helping hand from Shithead, king of Agnano.

No.

I've got the sample. Three kilos straight away. The rest in a month, Toni. The rest when you want it, *oui, avec plaisir*. The rest in hell, Toni, I'm sorry. You bring the money, the stuff's there. In a month, *oui*. My pension. The stuff's there. No funeral. In hell, Toni.

Since he's been with the Italians, McGuffin hasn't known peace.

Shoved about to right and left by louts, thumped and cursed at, having things thrown at him, forced to reflect fights and ignominy, stolen, scratched, violated with a screwdriver, abandoned for hours, then the scorching darkness of the canvas-covered truck, bouncing around over asphalt chasms, gravel, scorched earth, the slabs and cobbles of ancient streets, up and down, all the time, making it long for its first journey, that boy's bike with the platform on the front, the sweltering oilskins and the stench of stables and leather.

Now he was on the move again, had been for at least an hour. He was certainly leaving Rome.

Cruel fate! Used to cheering up the public with reassuring images, mute witness to acts of squalor and violence. Nothing to fight back with. A void facing the void.

The pointless seventeen-inch screen still seemed to reflect those last scenes, performed shamelessly before its wide-open eye.

The man had lost patience. Quickly, though. Earlier than expected. Before trying him out. Before doing anything. He had come home, pointed his finger at McGuffin and exploded: 'What the fuck's that supposed to be?'

His wife hadn't been able to reply, silenced as she was by the second question. 'Who the fuck brought it?'

Ignoble fate! Used to warmer welcomes, joyful children with their hands outstretched, excited women, relations visiting to do homage to the new arrival, and what was happening now? Contempt, tools jabbing into intimate parts, punches, even spit.

'It's a present from Carmine,' the woman had said sententiously.

The man had turned grey with fury. 'A television? We haven't even got running water, and he gives you a television! Well done!'

Oh fantastic! And where's the harm, excuse me? If you haven't got running water in your house, do you have to spend your whole time dwelling on the shame of it? Sooner distract yourself than fret your life away. And what better way of doing that than amusing yourself with a fine McGuffin Electric Deluxe television, which, with its naturally luminous screen, doesn't even tire your eyes?

The car lurched to a stop. The vibrations of the engine shook McGuffin like an attack of delirium tremens.

'He wants me to torment myself, as always, to make me feel like a jerk, eh? May his parents roast in hell, he'd have been better off paying the rent on this hole rather than chucking his money away on a pile of useless crap.'

Certainly, the discussion hadn't got off to a terribly good start. Nonetheless, room for reasoning might yet be found. Old popular wisdom, very down to earth, something about not looking a gift horse in the mouth. But there must have been bad blood between the two of them. Something must have happened during an earlier episode: it would have been nice to have a quick résumé. But the timing of the squabble was all wrong.

The rattle of a train drowned out all other sounds. The car set off with a jerk.

'Whose parents? Tell me again, whose?'

'Don't provoke me, Giulia! We're taking this gadget back, and there's an end to it.'

'Whose parents are to rot in hell? Come on, let's hear it, whose parents?' A proud girl, no denying it. A bit short of content, but proud.

'Be careful, Giulia, I'm warning you. Don't make me say it again. Tell your brother to come and get it back, or I'll go down to Porta Portese and sell it.'

The apple caught him right in the eye, along with the stream of insults.

'Carmine's parents are mine, too!'

Things weren't looking good for McGuffin. Fat chance of pouring oil on troubled waters. On the other hand, always a bad idea to get between husband and wife, let alone if you're a seventeen-inch-screen television. The man had climbed over him as the woman hurled herself towards the door.

Too late.

No American television channel would have dreamt of showing, uncensored, what came next. Enough to say that in the end four hands grabbed McGuffin, lifting him up from a cemetery of broken plates and crockery that had flown round him like shells on a battlefield.

He had a black eye, she was black and blue all over.

Derisory payoff! They gave McGuffin back without even knowing that he didn't work.

Chapter 20

'Shit! You've coughed up a bit of lung!'

'What the fuck are you on about, Swede? *Cough! Cough!* Tell me right now if you're planning on talking bollocks for the whole journey, and I'll drop you off right here and you can get the bus back to Paris.'

'I'm not talking bollocks. It's there on the dashboard, it's a lump of something, don't you see it? There's a drop of blood on it, too.'

'That thing there? That's nothing, *cough!* It's catarrh with a bit of blood. Quick rub with a handkerchief, it's gone. You see?'

'Yes, but not with *your* handkerchief, look, it's covered with red stripes! Don't rub at it, you'll leave a stain! Do we want to end up on the Côte d'Azur like this?'

'What d'you mean, a stain, it's easy, look!'

'Not with your sleeve! Do you want to show up at the casino in Cannes with your clothes covered in blood? Do we want to be spotted straight away? They won't let us in like that!'

'Swede, you're worse than a finger up the arse. Calm down, *cough!*, we still have a few hours' driving ahead of us. For months now everybody's been going on at me for going to the South, the sea, the mountains, because it'll be good for my, *cough! cough! cough!*, it'll BE GOOD FOR MY FUCKING LUNGS and so on, but if I have to drag those lectures along with me on top of everything else, I'd as soon stay in Paris.'

'Toni, I'm worried: one, that you're going to die; two, that you're going to die *now*, because I've never seen this guy Zollo; three, that we're going to turn up looking like a dying man and his friend who's about to call for a priest. If the guys from Marseilles find out what's going on, they're going to clip you, and they're going to clip you hard. It'll be even worse with the Zips and that fucker who sells washing machines in Naples. We've had enough bother with the Sicilian darkies already, let's try not to be too conspicuous, ok? Style, that's what we need! Like Jean Gabin in *Touchez-pas au Grisbi.*'

'Would you shut up about that bloody film. How many times have you seen it now?'

'What's that got to do with anything? Did you understand what I said, or not?'

'Sure, do you want me to swear on God almighty and the whole gang?'

'Toni, you're in danger of losing it. Try and get yourself back in shape, everyone's been saying as much for months. You don't muck around with tuberculosis.'

'After this deal, let's do the thing with the jewels, then I'll get some rest.'

'Yeah, and you might even think about having the operation.'

'A lung operation? Your arse. I'm not having them sawing through my ribs and leaving me going around the place like a cripple for the rest of my days. That professor guy, Blafard, does "alternative" cures. I've booked myself in to see him.'

'Fingers crossed, then. You heard about the inside man, though?'

'Yeah, brilliant plan, couldn't fault it. But they're a bit too fond of the whores, it's risky, when you're preparing a coup, *cough! cough!*, whores talk and they make you talk, too.'

'Tell him to keep his dick in his trousers, then. We're already running too many risks. By the way, what's that guy Zollo like? Can we trust him? He's not about to rip us off?'

'No, I can tell if someone's ok, and he's one mastodon-sized son-of-a-bitch, in fact he's the mammoth of all sons of bitches, he's big and cold as a block of ice.'

'Did you know that mammoth means "son of the earth" in Mongolian?'

'Am I supposed to give a fuck?'

'I was just giving you some information.'

'Oh, thanks then! I don't know how I'd manage without you spouting non– *Cough! Cough! Cough! Cough!*'

'Go on then, try and tell me that isn't a shred of lung!'

Chapter 21

The boy had scented the air of home. Air of respect and danger. He
had stopped asking questions. He seemed to be concentrating, to be
at ease. He seemed to understand the incomprehensible words and
exclamations echoing from the street. He had worked out that he
mustn't breathe.

Zollo was finally able to allow himself a long, hot coffee. How
many hours had he driven without stopping? His feet were on fire,
his legs were made of marble.

Irrelevant details. For what he had to do. For the people he had
to meet. For where he was. The *taverne* was in the rue du Refuge.
The landlord said his name was Dédé. He had immediately held out
the pack of cigarettes with their meeting place written on it. The
district was Le Panier, the drainpipe of Guerini-town. The paradise
of *nabos, babis*, Corsicans, and other assorted scum from the rest of
the four continents lovingly thrown together by a single task: to
dominate the port and the trades of Marseilles. In the pay of Antoine
and Barthélemy Guerini, the lords and masters of the district, and
with the terrestrial blessing of Gaston Defferre, the socialist mayor
of the city. Tough customers. Big business all over the planet. Solid
political relations. Clear understandings and *carte blanche*. Manna
for Luciano. The spider span tirelessly. The web covered the whole
world. From Marseilles it ran straight for almost 20,000 kilometres,
all the way to Saigon, Laos, Thailand. Indochina: the route of opium,
powder, weapons. The French had been wallowing there for a century.
Now it was a complete shithole over there. Kill kill, slaughter
slaughter, fuck fuck. The ideal conditions to prosper in.

The Guerini brothers had very clear ideas.

The go-between over there was one Jean-Philippe Mesplède, an ex-Legionnaire who worked with the Americans as well. He seemed to have slaves, plantations and alliances with local tribes. Everything he needed for profitable activity and secure prospects. It was from there that the raw material set off, unlimited availability, or already treated or half-treated, but inferior in quantity and quality. That was the problem. The climate was too wet. Equipment and chemicals were too poor. Staff too under-motivated. Every now and again one of them would try and escape. He would have to be killed. Others died of hunger or exhaustion. They had to be replaced by relatives.

Luciano and the Guerini brothers were solving the problem. Efficient, up-to-date labs in Sicily and Marseilles. Excellent raw material. Reliable chemicals. Steel covers. White powder and top-quality brown could set off towards the East, back to the brothels at the front; to the West, to America.

The whores liked it.

The yellow men liked it.

The negroes liked it.

Even those depraved faggot communist artist musicians liked it.

People liked it, in short. They paid to have it. They paid well. They wanted it every day.

Zollo swallowed down the last sip of coffee and pulled a Gauloise from the pack that the landlord had given him. The boy pressed his face to the glass and looked at the street outside the bar. He was half smiling.

Zollo got to his feet. It was time. The Guerini brothers didn't like waiting. The day's timetable was as follows: visit to the brand-new laundry, pleasantries, as agreed.

Afterwards, whatever he wanted.

'Salvatore. I'm going to the Vieux Port. I'm going on my own. The people I have to see don't much care for new faces.'

'You've got important people to see, eh, Stiv?'

'Yes.'

'And are they friends of ours?'

'They're friends of Don Luciano.'

'*Mamma mia*, Stiv! I'd really like to come with you, but I understand. They don't like new faces.'

*

The shed was old, big and dilapidated. The revolting stench of fish rose even from his arsehole.

His chaperone was called Charles Zucca. He was wearing a blue suit over a big yellow tie and shiny black shoes. About thirty, an accountant and lawyer with the organisation, the son of Pascal Zucca, famous lawyer, a meritorious member of the French Resistance and a strategic adviser to the unscrupulous operations of mayor Defferre.

The preserving and canning of sardines.

Charles Zucca walked ahead of Zollo at a steady pace, silently, holding a handkerchief pressed to his mouth and nose. Towards the rear of the building, he reached a little door half hidden by piles of rotten wooden crates. It led on to a narrow metal spiral staircase. As they climbed down, the stench of fish gradually made way for another effluvium, no less intense, the product of a mixture of various chemical agents, sickly, thick, pungent.

Welcome to Guerini pharmaceuticals.

'We consider it very important that M'sieur Luciano be kept informed of the great leap in quality that the new equipment permits. In the Far East, M'sieur Zollo, things aren't going so well for our heroic armed forces. But there is always room for good business. You have to invest, modernise, be independent. We have first-rate chemicals. We produce heroin and base morphine of excellent quality. We can treat large quantities of it. Our supply bases are in Laos, near the Vietnamese border. The fields of Ba Na Key. It's a region of the limestone rock indispensable for poppy cultivation. Dozens and dozens of big plantations. We have others too, in Saravan, further south and further away from all the trouble. We transport the raw material on cargo ships bound for Europe. It takes up more space, obviously, than refined goods, perhaps it's also riskier, but the quality and the profits are multiplied more than tenfold.'

Zollo looked around: bags of lime, ovens, drums, filters, test-tubes. A layer of lime powder lay over everything. The stench of sediments and caustic agents. Tens, maybe hundreds, of jars, stacked and labelled: ammonia, chloroform, muratic acid, hydrochloric acid, sulphate salts. All used to refine the poppy sap to obtain base morphine. All used to refine the base morphine and obtain heroin.

Drug heaven. Zollo was filled with a sense of nausea.

Zollo said, 'Don Luciano will greatly appreciate the standard the organisation has reached. Same in Sicily. He too is always talking about independence and investment in modern equipment. The secret of business is success, he repeats often. He sends his respects and reassurances to the Guerini family, and asks whether the prohibition on your cities still holds.'

Zucca's reply came quickly. 'Absolutely. The Guerini family is absolutely firm on this point. We are very familiar with the effects and consequences of this stuff. Antoine and Mémé Guerini are forever saying that as long as they are here, Marseilles and the rest of France will not see the living dead wandering the streets. Business comes before everything else, but the powder mustn't soften the brains and muscles of our boys. I hope M'sieur Luciano understands this and doesn't take it amiss.'

'No problem. Don Luciano will understand. He can't bear the sight of drug addicts either, he just wanted to be sure that his French friends' rules remained the same. When's the next cargo?'

'Before the end of the summer.' Zucca cleared his throat. 'A big one. Two ships. One's going to pass by Palermo. All the details will be made clear in due course. The Guerini family likes it to be known that doing business with them is synonymous with absolute security and guaranteed profits. And while we're on the subject we want to confirm to M'sieur Luciano that half a million francs are bound for Geneva. By tomorrow at the latest, trusted hands will deposit them in the account indicated to us, with the thanks and best wishes of the Guerini brothers.'

'Don Luciano will be grateful to you in his turn.'

'M'sieur Zollo, I hope you will pass on my greetings to someone I consider to be one of the men of the highest quality and the keenest intelligence who live on this planet.'

'Don't worry, Mr Zucca. It will be done.'

Chapter 22

Bologna, 2 June

Black.
   Dark.
   A dark corner. To vanish into.
   Concentrate only on footsteps, one foot in front of another. No more than that.
   You can't survive grief. It's unfair. Stay and suffer.
   Stay.
   The whirlpool sucks up gestures, thoughts, breaths.
   Breathe. Almost impossible.
   Think. Think that Fefe isn't there any more. You *can't* believe it.
   Black. Dark. One foot in front of the other.
   The dog bites inside, the heart dies, one piece at a time. Then it lets you get your breath back, so that you can walk.
   Imagine the final moments. When he broke the window.
   Think of his terror of thunder, the chill that must have gripped him.
   Think of the moment *before*. Think of what he was thinking. *Before* the void, *before* the trench. Terror. You had to get out of there, Fefe, you had to escape, outside, where the ceiling couldn't fall on your head, as it did that day so many years ago, clinging to our mother's body under the rubble, hour after hour.
   The dog sinks its teeth in still deeper. You have to stop. Grope about. Wait till it passes, till it loosens its grip. Another shred.
   Black. Hell is a dark corner of the heart.
   There's nothing left. No point in anything.
   Your pockets are full of *his* things. Useless things. Knick-knacks.

Relics. You mustn't lose anything, not even the smallest piece of fabric, not even a handkerchief or a toothbrush. You've got to keep them all.

You've got to keep *him*. What he left you. What remains.

Dead. He's dead. He no longer exists.

Knees *want* to give. But you won't fall. No one must touch you. You don't want anyone. The hands that touch your body, that restore it to you and tell you you're alive. Remind you that you must eat, drink, wash. Again. Even now. Even tomorrow. No. You *can't* believe it. You can't live with a hole where your heart should be and a stomach smaller than a fist.

Black. Snuff out everything. Snuff out the day. Snuff out the church candles. Snuff out your eyes. Leave me with darkness.

I'm here and I'm walking. But I'm not me.

I'm not longer *alive*. I won't be.

Fefe, come on, get up. Don't just lie there. Get up, please. Get up and let's go away from here.

What to say? What to do? You can't hug her, you can't hold her. You can't do what would come spontaneously. You won't even be able to look at her, but who cares, you look anyway. Seek her eyes, black eyes that have burned their way inside you since the first time you saw them, and which have now disappeared behind dark glasses. Angela, I'm here, do you see me? It's me, Pierre. Angela, look at me. Let me hold you, let me cuddle you, caress you. Even if you no longer want me, even if it's over, a hug is a hug. And you can't deny someone a hug. You can't deny yourself that. Grant yourself one hug, please. Even if it's the last time, I'm still me, I'm Pierre. We loved each other, perhaps we still do.

But you aren't here, you're somewhere else, you're dead too.

I hate funerals. You shouldn't ever have to go to them. You shouldn't ever have to go into a burning room. See him there, behind a box. Is that the last image you want to keep within you? It's not fair. You shouldn't have come, Angela.

There he is, your husband, the great Odoacre Montroni. Incorruptible, upright. Condolences, processions of black outlines with bent shoulders. Suffering in silence, grave, composed suffering of a solid man. There's a queue to shake his hand, as though he was the one who had lost a brother, not you. You are a woman, you can suffer and abandon yourself to grief. You have to be left there, a hug from Teresa is enough, and you push her away without rancour, no one must touch you.

He has noticed that I'm looking at you, he's certainly noticed, but I don't care. Angela, I want you to turn around, read in my eyes, read the desire to be close to you.

He *sees* how I look at you.

He *feels* that I'm chafing.

He crucifies me with his eyes.

He is saying: don't come closer. Don't do it. You *can't* do it.

He hates me.

He has understood.

He knows.

'Signora . . . Signora Montroni . . .'

Angela barely turned her head. It was Marco, the nurse, Fefe's friend. Shattered, eyes red and face wrinkled, he looked as though he had aged ten years. He was holding something back, it was obvious, bent beneath a weight he had to shed, not knowing where it should go.

Angela said nothing.

'Signora, I've got to tell you . . .' Marco choked back air and sobs. 'Perhaps it's irrelevant, but I must tell you, I don't want to add to your grief, but if I keep it inside I won't be able to go on.'

She waited for him to summon the strength to speak. It didn't seem possible for her to be able to listen to someone, to absorb any information into her brain, except the absence of Fefe for the rest of her life. Marco looked down and spoke: 'A month ago a mistake was made, a terrible mistake. The new medication that Ferruccio was taking cannot be stopped all at once. The dosage has to be reduced gradually, to avoid any harm to the patient. That's why Ferruccio had that relapse and your husband had to come rushing back from Rome. It was a mistake.' He ran his hands over his face as though he felt guilty. 'I'm sorry, I wasn't there, I was on leave. If I'd been there, perhaps –' He couldn't finish his sentence, his sobs tore him apart.

Angela heard her own voice murmuring, 'Then it was true, Fefe was telling the truth. They suspended his medication.'

'Yes, Santo told me, he heard Dall'Oglio ordering the suspension. I don't know why, perhaps it's irrelevant, I mean, some time has passed, and the cure had been resumed. But I had to tell you, I couldn't . . .'

Angela touched his face. 'What can it matter now, Marco? It's not your fault. You loved him.'

She managed to hug him, as though he was the one in need of consolation.

She walked away, leaving him standing there, a wreck washed up among the tombstones.

As he left the Certosa cemetery, along Via Andrea Costa, Pierre couldn't get Montroni's expression out of his mind. It frightened him. It was ice, that was it, it reminded him of ice, a little cube of it sliding along your spine. No one had ever looked at him like that before. Shit! The fucker *knew*. He knew about him and Angela, he had read it in his eyes. But how the hell had he managed to find out? And yet he was sure of it, he would have put his hand in the fire. It wasn't the expression of someone wondering *why* he was looking at his wife. It was the expression of someone who *knew*, and knew why.

Montroni could go fuck himself. His brother-in-law was dead and the fucker was worried about being cuckolded!

Poor Fefe. And poor Angela. The world was collapsing on top of her. A brother who had killed himself and a husband who might have discovered her betrayal. She was in the shit. She was finished. And there was nothing he could do about it.

He clenched his fists on the handlebars, anger and tension swelled his muscles, he regained control, a car sounded its horn, *drunkard*!

He pedalled harder, head down, like Coppi, he wanted to tire himself out, get home exhausted and throw himself on the bed and go to sleep. To sleep, that was the only thing. To be unconscious. Not to think. That was all he wanted. His problems were laughable in comparison with Angela's. But he was going off the rails as well. On the home straight, he instinctively tried the brakes. As though he had to slow down on the brink of the abyss.

Chapter 23

Cannes, 2 June

The Municipal Casino was a blaze of artificial lights.

Cary was wearing a blue tuxedo. Blacker than black. The effect of the artificial light. The first person to have noticed it had been the most stylish man in the world (along with Cary and Fred Astaire), a man whose subject Cary had once been.

The Duke of Windsor. The former sovereign of the British Empire, under the name of Edward VIII. Someone who had *really* retired.

Cary, on the other hand, had not succeeded in abdicating. He didn't *really* want to. Now he knew. He smiled.

Relaxed. As always, when he worked with Alfred Hitchcock.

Hitch.

During the shoots for *Suspicion* and *Notorious*, Cary turned up whistling on set.

His understanding with Hitch was perfect. Telepathic. It would be this time, too.

He was back.

Once Cary, reading an interview with Hitch, had burst out laughing at the sentence, 'Do you think I would have chosen to look like this? I would have preferred to have played a leading man in life. I would have been Cary Grant.'

No, Hitch. Right now you'd be Archibald Alexander Leach. Cary Grant isn't born. Cary Grant *becomes* himself. Cary Grant is a gift to the world. *I'm back.*

Hitch was by his side. That famous profile, the prominent paunch, the bald head. A face abrim with sarcasm, every cubic centimetre of the body intent on digesting its dinner. Hitch was a slow, anthropomorphic stomach. The sarcasm was hydrochloric acid, the imagination a play of enzymes, Hitch *digested* the life forms around him, the proteins and vitamins that made up the *corpus* of his works.

Then there was Grace. A dark-blue evening dress, blacker than black.

Cary had met her a few days previously. He had admired her at a distance, now he was admiring her from close up. Concentrated, but without forfeiting lightness. Provocative without being aggressive. Beautiful and blonde without being showy. Beautiful and blonde.

A sensation of *déjà vu*. Just for a moment.

He couldn't wait to start filming.

Three backs turned towards the casino bar, three smiles, six eyes, human diversity beginning to swarm.

Nine p.m. Hands at ninety degrees.

Bowing at the same angle, the liveried porters greeted the entrance of the imperial court.

At the front, six girls of about twenty, décolletées and slits up their skirts that seemed to meet in the middle, catwalk strolls despite the needle-thin stilts beneath their heels. Dozens of male eyes swept through the hall to settle on the prettiest. Not Mr Hitchcock's, which were held by summer fruits and crème chantilly. Nor Mr Grant's, or perhaps surreptitiously so as not to offend Grace Kelly.

The same number of ladies, although these ones were striking because of their jewellery alone, followed the trailblazers with less boldness in their gate.

Immediately behind them, five elegant young men, pinstripes, hats and cigars, walked five different pedigree breeds on leads. A champagne-coloured Afghan hound, a Dalmatian, a charcoal-black Great Dane the size of a calf, a Dobermann called Anubi and a restless Labrador.

The rules of the casino forbade the presence of dogs. And the moment they had crossed the threshold another group in turn took charge of them, some servants paid specifically to dedicate themselves to their piss. It would have been wiser and more economical to let them run about the park *du Château de Torenc*, but the emperor did not hold this opinion.

Once the cynophile squad had passed, four bodyguards standing side by side barely got through the door. Masked by their backs, three eccentric men stepped forward, deep in conversation. The ones with the blue tights and the orchids in their buttonholes were the emperor's special advisers. In their midst, Bao Dai distributed waves, smiles and 100-franc notes. His Korean jacket gave him the air of a serious statesman, like Nehru, but juxtaposed with the purple *cache-col* that burgeoned forth from beneath the top buttons it looked more like the latest discovery of a Parisian *flâneur*.

Apart from the dogs, apart from the trio, the series was then repeated symmetrically: imposing gorillas, elegant young men, ladies in jewels, half-naked models. The moment the door of the casino swallowed up the last marble posterior, twenty different car doors, all belonging to the emperor's collection, slammed in unison and the drivers switched on the engines.

Spoken phrases, quiet gossip, inexpressible thoughts and eloquent expressions seethed around the courtyard like oil in a pan. Every evening, Emperor Bao Dai tried to catch one phrase from the crowd, helped by his special advisers Azzoni and Mariani. He was delighted by all this attention, but he took even greater pleasure in replying to spiteful comments.

A man of about forty, still slobbering over a girl's tanned legs, spoke just a little too loudly as he turned to his friend. 'Pretty girls, Henri, but all of them whores.'

Mariani jabbed his elbow into the emperor's ribs. Almost everyone had heard the appraisal. The news reached the others a second later.

Bao Dai stopped, spread his arms, and aimed the long slits of his eyes at the man who had spoken. Bao Dai tilted his head to one side and raised his chin. Bao Dai said, 'You are mistaken, Monsieur.' A nod caressed the ladies in his entourage. 'These women you see, my friend, are not whores.' His hand struck his chest. 'I am the whore.'

Cary smiled. Good timing. Good joke. Someone clapped.

The procession reached the *chemin de fer* table. Bao Dai took his place. The lips of Azzoni and Mariani met the emperor's ears. Behind him, the wall of heads, necks and pectorals belonging to the body-guards went up. Bao Dai scribbled out a cheque and held it out to the attendant. A wheelbarrow of *fiches* was about to be heaped out on to the green table.

*

'Have you heard, Stiv? Fifteen!'

Words uttered by Salvatore Pagano at the exact moment when, because of his fabulous but, oh dear, pointed and recalcitrant footwear, he stumbled over a strip of carpet and performed a pratfall, like a personal visiting card in the casino hall.

It certainly wasn't a problem of *clothing* as such. Kociss was dazzling: twenty years old, olive complexion, gleaming Saracen eyes over the regulation tuxedo hired by Zollo with all the necessary frills. If Lisetta had seen him, this Lebanese prince, she would have jumped on him in a second. Steve hadn't neglected the details. To the hiring of the smoking-jacket he had added the purchase of some decent clothes and a massive helping of instructions consisting of brief, fragmented phrases, and most particularly instructions to be quiet, be quiet, be quiet.

No, the problem was one of *bearing*, of posture, a long habit of uncontrolled gestures. Like saddling a wild horse. A lot of trouble for little satisfaction.

The Laurel and Hardy sketch drew everyone's attention. Zollo, unsure whether he should kill him there and then, or calmly later on, opted for the third solution, which also seemed to him to be most risky.

To flash a bosom buddy smile and dash over to the dickhead lying in the middle of the entrance hall, which was lit up like Times Square on New Year's Eve, help him to his feet, brush him down, still smiling, slap him on the back, 'Sal, what are you doing? You haven't even had a drink yet and you're on the floor already? Let's go to the bar, come on!' crushing his left arm in his vice-like grip.

'Salvatore. That's enough crap from you.'

'Sorry Stiv, sorry, but I feel like I'm wearing flippers . . .'

'*Shut up!* Enough crap, I said, *capisci*?'

'Yes, Stiv,' Kociss mumbled as he rubbed his arm.

'I've got work to do. Important people to see. I told you. No nonsense. Stay around here. In the bar. Lose some tokens in the fruit machines. Don't go to the tables. Do you hear me? No tables. Don't make me regret that I took you here. I'll be an hour at the most. Wait for me here.'

'Yes, Stiv, don't worry.'

'Salvatore. No crap from you.'

*

So it was that Salvatore Pagano, known as Kociss, feeling as though he'd just stuck his arm into a termite's nest, found himself alone in this incredible place.

Amazing women. Ludicrous clothes. Lights that made the *Piedigrotta* festival in Naples look like a joke. That one there, was she made of gold? He couldn't believe it. And let's not even mention the ones he had seen earlier on. It was their fault he had stumbled. Christ, what women! Then a crowd of weird-looking blokes, with an endless zoo of dogs, fifteen, he had asked, with that Chinaman in the middle waving all round him like the Pope, but surrounded by those amazing women who would have given the Pope a headache.

Filled to the brim with visions, lights and colours, Kociss took a few minutes to wander through the first wide hall, the area in the middle occupied by four large roulette tables, to the north and south the blackjack tables, and along the walls a long line of chromed, glittering slot machines.

That rapture of the senses, almost as though he had left his body, was interrupted near a roulette table, less crowded than the others.

He was holding Steve's chips. No tables. The fruit machines.

But that at least was where the people were. Some incredible-looking girls. There was really no comparison with the fruit machines.

What did the boss say when he set the ball rolling? *Rien ne va plus?*

Forget the fruit machines.

A chip. The Chinese guy's dogs. Fifteen.

Obviously Kociss couldn't suppress a cry of joy and surprise when the croupier, in that language that he couldn't understand but grasped intuitively, announced that the ball had stopped in hole number 15, black, odd.

The same croupier, the boss, deposited a substantial hoard of *fiches* right beside his winning chip on the 15 square.

They were his, he could take them, he *had* to take them. But wouldn't it be boorish to take them all, in the middle of all those rich guys who were perfectly happy to throw their money away, they had so much of it? Kociss made a big gesture: he left slightly less than half as a tip, to hell with the expense, if Kociss can win anyone can, who gives a damn? But that fool of a boss left them there, without touching them, on the 15, and rolled the ball again.

Fifteen.

'Pas mal, le garçon!'

'Oh la la!'

At that point there was a bit of a hubbub, he distinctly heard someone saying 'beginner's luck', because without a doubt the boy had done well. Two wins in a row. On the same number. Multiplying his stake tenfold at the second attempt.

Kociss turned purple when he saw the boss depositing, right in front of him, a real mountain of chips, while everyone slapped him on the back and smiled at him.

But how much were those chips worth? They belonged to him. A long way from the fruit machines, Stiv!

While two guys helped him to put all his coloured pennies from heaven into cloth bags, the vision arrived.

'Lucky Italian boy,' she said with an accent from who knows where. She was extremely beautiful. Her skin seemed to be made of gold. She had red hair like Lisetta. She smiled and touched his left arm, which didn't have pins and needles in it any more.

He followed her without a moment's hesitation.

There were two of them.

Zollo sat down at the table and stared into Toni's face.

'I thought you were going to be on your own.'

The Lyonnese calmly stubbed out his cigarette in the ashtray, then pointed towards the friend sitting beside him.

'Jo, this is Stefano Zollo, known as "Steve Cement". Zollo, this is Jo, known as "the Swede", *mon associé*. Jo and I are too old to remember when we first met.'

Jo gave a nod of the head that Zollo did not return. Lyonnese Toni was even more skeletal than the last time he had seen him, in Marseilles, a pile of bones wrapped in a thin membrane of skin. He was very striking, and there was something horrific about his face, something very similar to death.

His friend was a well-built, fair-haired man, who wore his suit with a certain class and had a youthful air, even though he must have been over forty.

A screen separated the reserved table from the rest of the hall. No one could hear what they had to say to one another.

'Everything ok?' asked Toni, lighting another cigarette.

Zollo had already prepared his role.

'Certainly. You've just got to tell me when and where I have to meet the buyers.'

'*Garçon, s'il vous plaît*,' said Toni, catching the waiter's eye. 'What are you drinking?'

'Jack Daniel's. On the rocks, please.'

Toni spoke to the waiter, who disappeared behind the bar.

'Tomorrow. On the beach,' said Toni. 'There's a little bistro, it's called *Le Grisbi*. You'll have no trouble finding it, everyone knows it.'

The other man said something in French. Toni smiled, and Zollo waited for him to translate.

'Jo asks if you've seen the Jean Gabin film, *Touchez-pas au Grisbi*.'

'I only know American films.'

'Shame. This is the capital of the cinema. Even Hitchcock is making a film in Cannes.'

Zollo didn't move a muscle, he wasn't there to chat.

Toni understood and reached his conclusion. 'The meeting is scheduled for eleven in the morning, when there are more people around.'

The fair-haired man spoke again.

'Jo's asking if you've got a swimming costume. You might stand out if you were wearing evening dress.'

Zollo glanced blankly at the fair-haired man.

Then he said, 'Tell him I haven't got a costume. I'll come dressed as the Emperor of Japan.'

Toni translated and Jo laughed heartily.

'You've got the sample, I imagine,' said Toni.

'The first three kilos.'

'It isn't that I don't trust you, *mon ami*, but I'm the go-between in this deal, and I'd like to check the quality of the goods. Can you see that?'

The waiter interrupted their conversation by placing the glasses on the table.

Zollo picked up Toni's glass, slipped something underneath it and pushed it in front of him.

Toni picked up the envelope, tested it with his finger, and passed it to his associate, who did the same thing.

'*Ça va.* If they're happy, they'll pay for the three kilos. They'll settle up for the rest.'

'I need some sort of assurance as well.'

Toni understood. '*Pas d'problèmes, Zollò.* You can come unarmed. We're all businessmen, and Cannes is *trop belle* for bad blood.'

'How many will there be?'

'Just one. Monsieur Alain.'

'How will I recognise him?'

'He's a fat guy in a white suit. We'll be sitting at a table nearby.'

'So how are we going to do this?'

'Tell me if you're happy: the two of you talk on your own, when you've finished you get up and walk back to the coast road, you take a right and after a hundred metres you go into the restaurant *La Provençale*. I recommend the duck, it's the house speciality. I'll join you there, and you tell me how it went.'

Zollo nodded. He downed his whiskey in one and got to his feet.

'Who's the boy?' asked Toni.

'Which one?'

'The one you came in with.'

'Oh, that's nobody.'

Toni looked at him and nodded.

Zollo waved them both goodbye and went back into the hall.

'Justine, my vision of loveliness! I had no idea that the many gifts that nature has so graciously blessed you with included such acute perspicacity! If only I could recognise a *parvenu* in a crowd with such unfailing success! And Italian at that, and with a considerable consignment of *fiches*, too! I bow to anyone who can uncover hidden talents. Introduce me right now this instant!'

Jean Azzoni had wasted no time. In a few minutes, despite his initial reluctance, he had first borne down upon, then overwhelmed, then taken in and bent to his purposes a Salvatore Pagano still confused, shaken, stirred by his great win and by the celestial exhalations of the siren with the golden skin. On the other side of the green table, Lucien Mariani had winked, as he began to envelop Bao Dai in a fog of bullshit.

Azzoni had had it easy, not least because of his origins and his perfect knowledge of Italian, but there could be no doubt that his ability to identify the leading players for his explosive theatrical *pièces* touched on the sublime.

The boy could make this A Night to Remember. As long as the masters of ceremonies, Azzoni & Mariani, acted as they were expected to.

It would not be a problem. That was why they were there. And to earn the precious Soviet caviar to spread on their croutons.

He immediately introduced the boy to the rules of *chemin de fer*: you play one against one, you are given two cards, you can ask for a third, the aim of the game is to make eight or nine, the highest points, or at least better than your adversary; when you win you don't just get your stake, you get the bank as well, you need cool nerves, luck, memory and instinct.

'It's like "seven and a half", I know how to play this one!' Kociss observed, full of bravado.

Jean Azzoni had no objections to the one mandatory clause that Salvatore imposed on their new fellowship: that Justine, that goddess, should stick with him like a cup and a saucer, otherwise that was that, he wouldn't even think about it.

'When Justine identifies her prey, she certainly doesn't let go of it,' whispered Jean 'the Wink' Azzoni.

He swapped his roulette winnings for the equivalent of the much costlier *fiches* of the *chemin de fer* table, considerably reducing their volume. The right moment came to enter the game. A slack period at the table, a less coveted bank. Bao Dai swathed in Marianiesque anecdotes, sudden quotations, feints to the lower abdomen and scraps of melody sung in in fake English.

The boy didn't disappoint. Eight first go. Victory, and the bank paid out.

The boy emanated confidence.

Azzoni was the shadow behind him, dispensing advice. Justine, the fairy who turned the frog into a prince. Mariani, the python paralysing his prey.

By the fourth win in a row, the kitty was starting to get interesting. For Azzoni, that was the point when the show really began.

Lucien Mariani concluded a rambling speech about the hidden meaning of Italian gestures designed to ward off evil, with particular reference to touching one's balls. He allowed Bao Dai to enjoy the

final game in complete tranquillity. The boy was winning hands
down. He crossed his fingers. He had Justine lay hands upon him.
He flourished his horns. He protected his scrotum from the darts of
the evil eye.

An imperial hand tapped delicately on the green table: Bao Dai
was rising to the challenge.

The much discussed, whorish, hated, bankrolled, hoodwinked
Asian nabob against the little Italian boy with the bewildering luck.

All eyes quickly converged on the table and the game. Bow down
before the talent and wise direction of Jean Azzoni and Lucien
Mariani.

'But you know the Chinaman, don't you?'

Four winning rounds later, two eights and two nines, everyone had
worked out that the imperial hand belonged to the boy.

By the ninth win, there was enough money on the Municipal's
table to solve the problems not only of Kociss, but of the whole
district of Sanità.

Bao Dai, obviously, didn't bat an eyelid. He called, 'Banco'.

Mariani was delighted. Azzoni smiled. Justine stroked the back of
Kociss's neck; he was in a trance.

All around, a real crowd of people was desperate not to miss the
most exciting clash of the past few months.

The croupier took two cards from the *sabot*. He handed them to
the emperor.

Bao Dai studied them, a slight flicker of his right eyelid, and after
a few seconds he spread the two cards face down on the table. Card.

The croupier gave him a nine of spades. It was Pagano's turn. He
studied and revealed the two cards. A king of diamonds and a three
of hearts. Azzoni murmured behind him. 'Difficult hand. We're going
to have to call for a card.'

'We haven't needed one before now,' came the reply, and before
Jean Azzoni could do anything, Kociss's voice was heard to utter a
single, mad word of only four letters: 'Pass.'

The silence all around turned into a murmur of surprise and disapproval. Bao Dai's eyelid trembled again, as he turned over the two
cards that were still covered. Queen of clubs and two of spades. With
the nine already gone, the emperor had one point.

Pagano's three was more than enough.

'Bank wins.' The croupier couldn't hold back a smile of wonder, or perhaps of sincere appreciation.

Pagano shouted.

The public applauded.

Justine touched Kociss's bottom, then the bottom of an incredulous, stunned, ecstatic Jean Azzoni.

Lucien Mariani burst into a sustained paean he had stored up for several days.

'As Napoleon said,' he began, 'only great men commit great mistakes. I should add: it is by their errors that you shall know them. Nowadays, too many things can be bought. A plebeian can be accompanied by an imperial procession, as long as he has the money to pay for it. A yokel can buy an imperial palace. Even the throne and the title of emperor are the object of a trade that is far from noble. So how are we to distinguish the true emperor? What is it that money cannot buy, and no instructor can ever teach? Not the imperial gait, nor imperial speech, however difficult it may be. Not court ceremonial. No. Nor the soul: as Faust teaches us, it can be acquired by the most skilful businessman.' He paused and shook his head. He looked around and allowed his eye to rest on Bao Dai. 'It is the way of losing, I tell you. It does not depend solely upon the individual's possessions, but also on the serenity with which he can renounce them, even if he is down to his last few pennies, precisely because the rich man without money is just a poor man, but the emperor without money is still the emperor. Yes, gentlemen: I assert that Waterloo consecrated Napoleon more than any victories whose dates and locations I cannot, I confess, even recall. As to you, your majesty, today you have demonstrated that your way of losing is, without any doubt, truly imperial.'

Cary, Hitch and Grace *saw* the murmurs and laughter rising like a tidal wave, crossing the hall, sweeping away all whispered conversation, forcing heads to turn and finally crashing against the walls of the casino. Everyone, absolutely everyone, was watching the *chemin* tables.

'It's the emperor! Sitting with him is a real-ly fun-ny Italian boy,' said a balding man, accentuating those two words in a ludicrous falsetto, and accompanying the whole phrase with the gestures of an orchestral conductor.

'Bao Dai?' asked Cary.

'Yes,' replied Hitch.

'Let's see this emperor at work!' said Grace with a smile, moving towards the table that was the source of all the hubbub.

Cary looked at his enchanting leading lady, her way of walking, her head floating elegantly on a splendid neck . . . and yet again there was that feeling of *déjà vu*, like a sudden flush. He put one foot in front of the other, followed her, meanwhile wondering what on earth . . .

'More than an emperor, he's an interesting character,' muttered Hitch. 'And his companions, you must have noticed them. They're as bizarre as he is, and even showier.'

'The two popinjays? Of course, old man,' Cary replied. 'And yet they do have a certain sarcastic, coherent style.'

The Italian boy, on the other hand, seemed to have *someone else's* style. Someone (his girlfriend? his parents?) had dressed him and smartened him up, his clothes looked like a prosthesis, worn more with enthusiasm than confidence. He snorted, he rejoiced, uttered strange incantations, ran his handkerchief over his forehead, had the comments of the bystanders translated by one of Bao Dai's two companions, whom he called 'Signor Azzoni'.

Azzoni snorted, rejoiced, uttered strange incantations and ran his handkerchief over his forehead.

The emperor snorted, uttered exotic incantations, ran his hand-kerchief over his forehead and had the boy's comments translated by the second companion, whom he called 'Monsieur Mariani'.

Mariani snorted, laughed at Azzoni's incantations and ran his hand-kerchief over his forehead.

The boy won and laughed, narrowing his eyes. The emperor lost and distributed polite smiles.

The whores blew kisses to all and sundry.

Each time he won, the boy got up and hugged the whores, who adored him. Azzoni dragged him back to the table.

Salvatore Pagano alias Kociss alias 'Totore 'a Maronna' alias 'Shithead' leaned towards Jean Azzoni and asked, 'But isn't that man over there an American actor? Isn't it Gary Cooper?'

'No, *paesano* . . . Gary Cooper's taller, I can assure you of that. It's Cary Grant, and before we speak his name we should all wash our mouths out with soap.'

'And who's the blonde? Marilyn Monroe?'

'No, my ignorant and wretched friend: her name is Grace Kelly. Everyone's talking about her.'

'And the fat guy? Is he Winston Churchill?'

For two seconds Azzoni didn't speak.

'Yes, that's exactly who it is.'

'The Italian guy's luck is incredible. How long is he going to go on winning for?' Cary asked Hitch.

'All evening, I expect.'

'But it isn't possible –'

'Shall we bet that he isn't going to lose a hand before the emperor withdraws?'

'Oh, come off it.'

'No, I mean it. If I win, I'll suggest giving him a part in the film, and in one scene you'll wear a hat. Are you on?'

'I'm on. A part in which scene?'

'The flower market.'

'Brilliant. And the hat?'

'John Robie when he's in hiding, sitting on the wharf. Pretending to be a fisherman.'

'Good idea. But you'd better resign yourself, you're not going to win, it's a matter of probability. And God doesn't want to see me in a hat, he knows they don't suit me!'

Half an hour later Azzoni and Mariani were almost drunk and increasingly dishevelled. They egged on the players as though they were at a bullfight, they yelled comments in an incomprehensible argot and provoked the mirth of the onlookers.

Azzoni slapped his protégé hard on the back.

Mariani consoled the emperor, telling him that it wasn't his money anyway.

The emperor laughed and said, *J'en ai rien à foutre! J'en ai rien à foutre!*'

Cary and Grace laughed. Hitch digested the scene.

Cary leaned towards Hitch and asked, 'What is the emperor saying?'

'His adviser is pointing out that it isn't his money, I don't know what he's referring to. The emperor agrees, and is repeating: I don't give a fuck.'

'Mind your language, old man! What would Her Majesty say?'

'But can he say something like that?' asked Grace, slightly too loudly.

'He's the fucking emperor, madam, and he may say whatever the fuck he pleases, if you'll excuse my saying so!' called Mariani in plebeian but passable English, his eyes reduced to tiny slits by an irrepressible smile.

Grace blushed and smiled. Azzoni and the Italian boy applauded her.

Cary burst out laughing and encouraged them by raising his glass in a toast.

The boy returned the gesture and called, 'I washing my mouth with the soap, Mister Grent!'

'What on earth is he talking about?' Cary asked Hitch.

'I haven't the faintest idea.'

Zollo came back into the hall and distinctly heard the word 'Fuck'.

In a place like this? Was that possible? Then applause and unbridled laughter. And Pagano's voice. You're not going to tell me that that great shithead . . .

'Stiiiiiv!' he heard someone shouting. It came from the *chemin* tables. He felt his blood boiling and heard a whistling in his ears, like a pressure cooker.

Don't go to the tables. Do you hear me? No tables. Don't make me regret that I took you here. I'll be an hour at the most.

'Stiiiiiv!' Come and see how much money I've won!' and more applause.

He took a few steps towards the *chemin de fer* tables.

Cary Grant. Really him.

And Alfred Hitchcock.

And the blonde from *Rear Window*.

Sitting down, surrounded by his court of whores and lackeys, that fucking oriental midget.

And standing up, fists raised above his head in a gesture of jubilation, Shithead. In front of him a mountain of *fiches*.

'Look at this, Stiv! I've won a pile of money! The Chinaman has given up, and Winston Churchill wants me in his film!'

Winston Churchill? *What the fuck?*

'What do you make of the Italian, Jo?'

'I don't know. He's got balls, I'll say that. We'll see.'

'What are you thinking about'

'I'm feeling a little sad, Toni. It happens to me when I see fireworks. Look how magnificent they are, over the sea.'

'I like them too, *cough! Cough! Cough!* Up they fly, no one can stop them, then they explode and fill the sky with colour, and everyone looks at them. A beautiful way to go: flying and colouring the sky. You know what, Jo?'

'What?'

'I don't want to die of tuberculosis.'

'What are you on about? You just need a bit of rest.'

'Rest? Rest your arse. But do you think I can be fooled like that? I've hardly got any lungs left, my mouth is always full of blood. The illness is consuming me, and I don't want to die like this. I want to die in action.'

'In action?'

'Yes, Christ alive, in action. Against the *flics*, against the darkies, against the Marseillais or the Italians, against whoever, what does it matter? But I want to die like a fucking firework, pal. I didn't choose this way of life to go out like a light, I didn't spend years in prison to die like a wanker.'

'You want to die like Jean Fraiger? Attack a police station, throw yourself against a wall of cops, all by yourself?'

'Christ, Jean Fraiger! *Cough! Cough!* That was one hell of a robber with guts. Haven't heard that story in a long time. When would it have been, '49?'

'That's right, he burst into a police station all by himself and opened fire on the cops, shouting "Shoot at my cock!" And they did, they shot at his cock two or three times.'

'Why the hell did he do that?'

'It's a long and complicated story, something to do with a woman.

I was told the story in the minutest detail, but I've forgotten it. In short, Toni, do you want to be shot in the cock like Fraiger?'

'Hmm, not in the cock, no! But I do want to die like a firework.

That sense of *déjà vu* . . . That thought that you hadn't quite grasped. Frances. Frances Stevens. The character played by Grace. A blonde called Frances. Frances Farmer. The ghost that torments you and Archie. Your friend Clifford. Joe McCarthy. The Cold War. A mission. Your mother. Your mother in the mental hospital. Frances Farmer in the mental hospital. Bristol. Passing through Bristol. Straight to Yugoslavia. Tito. The island. The shooting match. *The world has gone mad today*. Don't ask yourself too many questions, Cary. Don't ask too many questions, Archie. Don't brood. You're back, Cary. Sleep will cover everything, and tomorrow there's the film. You'll walk on to the set with a whistle. This Frances isn't that Frances. This Cary isn't that Cary. This world is changing, but it wants to take you with it. The explosions of the latest pyrotechnic display, remote, faint. Sleep will cover everything. You're back.

Chapter 24

He was woken at dawn, a good idea before a long journey. The sun was yawning in the east. He turned his head and let the light glide over him.

A sandy wind had swept the clouds away. It smelled of burnt grass and clay. A thousand other smells filled his nostrils, but some of them, pollen and fruit, were not new to him. The same ones blown round by the sun at home in the early morning.

Gulliver knew it was time to go. The sky was serene.

He sniffed the air once more and felt he was up to it.

When Garibaldi gave him the first big shake, he barely noticed it. It was only with the second that he lifted his head and looked vacantly at him.

'Hey, son, wossup? Your mutt popped its clogs?'

'What?'

'I said, what's wrong? Has your pet dog passed away?'

Pierre gave a vague wave of the hand that could have meant anything.

Garibaldi sat down slowly, carefully set down his glass of wine and pushed it towards him.

'A face like that can mean only one thing: women.'

Pierre gave him a forced smile, the best he could do.

'Are you going to give me some old and sage advice?'

Garibaldi stretched out his arms. 'Please! I wouldn't even consider it. Even at my age I haven't worked women out, let alone give you advice on the subject.'

'Nice consolation that is.'

'But it must mean something, don't you think?'

Pierre rested his head on his hand again. 'What would that be?'

Garibaldi lowered his voice and bent over the table as though to confess a secret. 'That we aren't as intelligent as we like to think.'

This time Pierre really did smile.

'How do you get a woman out of your head, Garibaldi?'

The old man took a deep breath and nodded seriously.

'Sure you want to know?'

'If you know, tell me.'

The old man tried to find the right words: 'Time. Time's a great healer. At your age you don't think it's possible, because you think you're going to have to do everything at a great rush, all at once, or else it'll all slip out of your hands. Then, one piece at a time, you begin to understand. That time is the solution to everything. And there's so much time, son, it doesn't seem like that to you at the moment, but when you reach my age and you look back, you'll become aware of how much time has passed and everything that's happened to you and then you work it out all by yourself. That time is the only capital we have.'

Pierre frowned, and straightened his head slightly. 'I feel rotten right now, what do I know about what's going to happen to me tomorrow?'

'Oh, I know you feel rotten. And I know that you've got to keep going, because they haven't got round to inventing a medicine for the thing that ails you. But let me give you one piece of advice: don't let your worries get the better of you.'

'Worries?' said Pierre.

The old man nodded. 'Yes. There are two things in the world that have no solution: death and sex. You're only lucky if they don't come at the same time. When you're dead, women stop complicating your life. So you've got to learn to let time take its course. If you get worried, if you try and find a solution to everything, because you're feeling too awful, you'll get even more bogged down, and there's an end to it.'

'I'm going round the bend, Garibaldi. I'm afraid of losing everything, I'm afraid of getting everything wrong, I can't think straight,' said Pierre hoarsely.

Garibaldi sat back in his chair. 'Don't do anything. You know what

Mao Tse-Tung says? There are times when the revolutionary has to sit on the riverbank and wait for the enemy's corpse to drift by.'

'Well, if Chairman Mao says it . . .'

'And he's not the kind of guy to fool around: first of all he's a communist, and he's also Chinese. And the Chinese are the wisest people in the world, everyone knows that.'

Pierre managed another laugh. He was depressed and confused, but of one thing he was certain. He would not let himself go, he would not stop looking after his appearance, he would not get drunk. If meeting Cary Grant had meant anything at all, it was that. He imagined Cary putting a hand on his shoulders and saying, 'Don't give up, Robespierre. The important thing isn't winning or losing, but staying impeccable. And that's the hardest thing of all, because in order to live we sometimes have to get our hands dirty.'

Pierre gritted his teeth, straightened the lapel of his jacket and uncricked his neck. Too difficult?

'Style is showing yourself that you're still up to the job.'

He smiled crookedly, the bitterest smile he had ever seen in the mirror.

After ten hours of travelling, Gulliver was exhausted. Never in his life had he felt so tired. A strong head wind had caused him difficulties for a long time. It might well have been the hardest thing he had ever tried to do.

But now he was starting to recognise places, he couldn't give up. He had already been to these parts in preparation. He clearly remembered the shape of the river, the geometry of the cypresses, the crumbling building at the top of the hill. Each metre he took gave him a sharp pain in the back, but he had done it. He was going home.

He saw the white tower in the middle of the bright grey of the meadow.

He saw the bridges stretched out along the river.

He saw the roofs and the chimneys of the houses. He knew every tile in the place.

He saw Tommaso waving his arms about, the banner in his hand. He folded his wings with one last effort and floated down over the dovecote.

He was welcomed with a mixture of joy and astonishment, an exchange of smiles and slaps on the back.

'You see who's back? There's no one like Gulliver!'

'Sasha will set off tomorrow, eh?'

'A shame he's the last one. It'll be a while before we do another swap with Dubrovnik.'

Tommaso took the dice-box from the pigeon's leg and read out the message to everyone:

Dear friends,

   We hope that Gulliver comes home safe and sound. Our Pale arrived without any difficulties. It is the first time that one of our birds has flown more than 700 kilometres. We are very happy. Along with this please find a message that you must pass on to ROBESPIERRE CAPPONI, Bar Aurora, San Donato, Bologna. Tell this person that he can reply with Sasha. So don't let him leave. Wait till the end of the month.

   See you soon.

   Stane and all your friends in the 'Brez Meja' Circle, Dubrovnik.

Chapter 25

On the winding road between Cannes and Nice, Zollo ran through the previous forty-eight hours in his mind.

He felt as though he was on the dodgems at a funfair, forced to drive while at the same time throwing hoops over the heads of ducklings.

Hard to understand the turn that things were taking. Just two days previously they had driven all the way up to Marseilles, for Luciano. Then the harder part: the meeting with Lyonnese Toni at the Cannes Casino. Negotiating the sale of *his* share of the drugs. Stefano Zollo's drugs, travelling around Italy in a television set. A reckless bluff. Going for broke.

Good thinking on Shithead's part, doing that number with the Chinaman. He had won a great pile of money, now safely inside the spare wheel. That fuckhead Pagano. All eyes on them: even those of Cary Grant, Alfred Hitchcock and that amazing woman Grace Kelly. So much for not getting noticed. Fuck, he hadn't seen many blondes like that. Eyes that flashed through you. If he ever managed to get the heroin back, he would pick one like that. He wouldn't leave her short of anything, he would spoil her with the best things available. He would carry her on his fingertips and make love to her until she was out of her mind. No more orders or bullshit to cart about in the truck, no more crap, just good restaurants and sun on her skin. Steve Cement's pension. A new man, a new life, even a new face if necessary. You can do anything at all if you've got the money. He *had* to find that television.

He rounded the bend, two wheels on the gravel, steered in and stayed on the road. He was in a hurry. Shithead had to be picked up as soon as possible, before he fucked anything else up.

He had been happy enough about the offer to shoot that scene just because that morning he was to meet Monsieur Alain and he wanted him out from under his feet.

The buyer for *his* drugs was an important fat guy. A sweaty whale in a white suit. 'Moby Dick' they called him, according to Toni. Affected manners, like a rich fag. Genuine interest. He had tried it. He had nodded. *C'est bon*, we'll do it. Zollo had said, 'A month.'

Not any more. He had to get that TV back. He had to work for Luciano. A month and he would be reunited with the whole of his share.

He had held out a sweaty hand. He had gone to the restaurant. He had met Toni and agreed the commission.

Then off to Nice, to pick up the silver screen's bright new star.

'Can you please explain to the boy that he's not really supposed to hit him?'

The assistant director finished dabbing the actor's nose and sent him off to the make-up girl to hide the bruise.

'The boy says it was self-defence,' said the interpreter.

'Defence? He butted him on the nose! Try and get it into his head that the scene's supposed to be realistic, not real!'

'I told him, boss, but the boy says he was was being suffocated, and he had to hit him to break free.'

The assistant director wiped the sweat from under his hat and glanced towards Hitchcock, who was sitting placidly behind the camera, looking amused.

What was so funny?

He went over to him. 'Mr Hitchcock, that Italian is a savage, he's almost knocked out one of our actors.'

'Fine, fine. The scene was perfect.'

'What? You don't want to do another take?'

'Sure, it's always good to have a few, but as far as I was concerned it was excellent. The boy is agile! Did you see that jump? Extraordinary!'

'But . . .'

Hitchcock waved the assistant-director away. He nodded to the leading man, whose hair was being retouched.

Grant rose to his feet and went over to him.

'So what do you think, are we doing it again?'

'Why not? It's the funniest scene in the film.'

Hitchcock turned to the assistant director. 'More flowers, I want more flowers, they've got to be drowning in flowers, ok? And tell the old woman to put some energy into those fists of hers. She's furious, they've just knocked over her stall.'

Grant glanced at him. 'I hope you're not planning on hiding a baseball bat in that bunch of flowers, old man? If I end up with a fractured skull who's going to finish the film for you?'

'Stop complaining. People will split their sides laughing, you'll see. That's all that matters with a scene like this: from Laurel and Hardy to Charlie Chaplin, from Buster Keaton to Douglas Fairbanks. But above all there's the original Cary Grant, the acrobat, his clownish mind. It's your *rentrée*, we'll show everyone we're still a duo to be reckoned with.'

'My tears are falling, old man,' Grant observed with an ironic smile.

'Back to work, before the light fades! And tell the boy to go easy.'

The scene was feverish, a brawl in the middle of the flowers, with Cary Grant's head peeping out, wearing a striped shirt and a red scarf around his neck.

An old woman started yelling something at him in French, and beating him with a bunch of flowers.

Zollo turned up just in time to see Salvatore Pagano, known as Kociss, along with two other guys, leaping into the fray.

Pagano tore mercilessly into his adversary.

'Stop! Perfect. That's enough, could someone tell the Italian to stop. Oi, you, stop! The scene is over! Will you let go? Jesus Christ, call the interpreter!'

The actor broke away from Kociss's grip, and made off, coughing.

Zollo approached the set manager: 'Can I take him away?'

'You *must* take him away, my friend. He's almost ruined one of my actors. Have you any idea of the insurance premiums?'

Zollo didn't stay to listen, but went over to Pagano and put an arm around his shoulder.

'Let's go.'

'Stiv! You should have seen me, Stiv! That animal was trying to choke me, so I nutted him one.'

'Sure, sure, get your stuff and be quick about it.'

'I've got to pick up my pay. That guy almost strangles me and I
don't even get paid for it? Wait –'

Zollo was starting to get impatient. He had a drive to Naples
ahead of him. How many kilometres would he be travelling during
those two days? Shit, once he had that money in his pocket, the first
thing he would do would be to tear up his licence. He never wanted
to see another steering wheel as long as he lived.

He lit a cigarette and watched Grant going through the script.

That was class. You only had to look at the crease in his trousers,
even when they were crumpled. And he wasn't wearing a belt, they
stayed up all by themselves. Everything seemed to be completely
effortless for him. He had read something in the barber's, in a magazine, about the film Hitchcock was making. The story of a retired
thief forced to come out of retirement because someone is trying to
frame him using the same modus operandi. A fine metaphor for
Cary Grant's return to the big screen.

He went over to him.

'May I just say how much I admire your work, Mr Grant?'

Cary looked up from the sheet and shook Zollo's hand.

'Ah, you will be the companion of that nice Italian boy. You were
at the casino the other evening.'

'Stefano Zollo, pleasure to meet you. And to see that you've decided
not to give up.'

'Excuse me?'

'To see you back in action again. There were rumours that you'd
quit the cinema.'

A smile spread across Grant's face. 'I did actually think about it.'

'I'm glad you had second thoughts. Hollywood wouldn't be the
same without you, believe me. You set a high standard.'

'Well, thanks, it's good to hear such things.'

'I had to tell you. Don't you worry about those two-bit toughs
who make the girls swoon. Even sitting on their fathers' shoulders,
Dean and Brando couldn't kiss your ass, with all due respect.'

Grant blushed and laughed heartily.

'A nice image, Mr Zollo. I couldn't have put it better myself. But
I mustn't speak ill of my colleagues.'

'Sure, you've got too much style even for that. But we both know that Dean is an addict. And Brando's a lard-bucket. By the time he's your age he'll be well over twenty stone.'

Grant laughed again.

'You really are an incredible chap, my friend.'

'Can I ask you a question?'

'Fire away.'

'Have you ever been to Yugoslavia?'

The actor gave a start, coughed and glanced at him strangely.

'Yugoslavia? No, I'd have to say that I haven't. Why?'

'I knew it. I met someone who insisted he'd met you on an island off the Yugoslavian coast. He even tried to convince me you'd given him a book. He must have been a lunatic.'

Grant held his embarrassment in check. 'Or a fantasist having some kind of joke. Are you leaving?'

'Yes, we're going back to Italy. I won't disturb you any further, Mr Grant. It was a pleasure to meet you. Remember what I told you: don't give up.'

They shook hands.

Grant watched Zollo walk away and join the boy, who was talking to the set manager, in improvised English, about his day's wages, then take his arm and drag him away.

Hitch's voice pulled him from his reflections on the absurd coincidences of life.

'Cary, are you ready? We're waiting for you!'

L'Unità, 2.6.1954

TODAY IN GENEVA THE FIRST ATTEMPTS
TO BRING ABOUT A TRUCE IN INDOCHINA

Il Resto del Carlino, 4.6.1954

Farmers' strike in Cavarzerano
POLICEMEN INJURED BY DEMONSTRATORS
Roadblocks, poisoned wells and barns ablaze

Il Resto del Carlino, 6.6.1954

Union agitation more severe
AGENTS OF ORDER INJURED BY STRIKERS IN FERRARA REGION
Attempted intimidation
to prevent the influx of non-unionised workers into factories
Denunciations and arrests

L'Unità, 9.6.1954

The three points of the wretched deal struck
to the detriment of the populations of Istria
THE ANGLO-AMERICANS ANNOUNCE
THEIR PLAN FOR THE PARTITION OF THE
FREE TERRITORY OF TRIESTE

Declaring that the Geneva discussions have already lasted too long
THE AMERICAN SECRETARY OF STATE THREATENS WAR IN ASIA
AND WANTS TO 'FINISH OFF' GUATEMALA
American marines off Central America
ready to disembark in Honduras to quell the strike
under way for thirty days against the United Fruit Company
and to hit out at Guatemala

L'Unità, 16.6.1954

LIGHTNING OVER GUATEMALA
How a large US company can
influence the fate of a small country

Chapter 26

The frescoes on the ceiling were frightening. Fat, unrealistic cherubs. Their smiles seemed to mask an infinite cruelty.

Impossible to turn on to her side. Or to close her eyes. Fefe's face re-emerged from the deep darkness. Every inch of her body in contact with the bed, as though hanging in the room. Her body, still young, and already exhausted, her childless body.

No more tears. Dried up.

Odoacre was a stranger who drifted from the hospital to the study at the end of the corridor almost without a word. She couldn't work out whether it was out of respect for her grief or fear that he could not share it in the same way.

You can't share grief with anyone. Grief is *yours*. You can be jealous of your own grief. You can transform it, turn it into a tool.

Fefe had understood. He knew that she and Pierre had left one another.

Fefe felt guilty.

Fefe felt that he was *the cause*.

Something had been unleashed in him. It had said: erase yourself and she will be *free*.

The guilt had been building up for years, it had grown inside him like a cancer. Guilt had turned to fear. Fear of thunder, fear of unhappiness.

Fefe couldn't bear it.

Fefe had *decided* to do it.

She drove the thought from her head.

*

Sante's expression was a mixture of pain and unease. The unease that comes from finding yourself in the presence of a grief so great it is beyond your comprehension. The fear of the unknown, don't tempt providence, embarrassment at the feeling of 'rather you than me' instinctively shared by the spectators of a tragedy.

He had kept his eyes lowered, as though ashamed at that involuntary thought.

'Excuse me, Madam, I was just behind that door. Dr Dall'Oglio had a word with the man in charge and said that Fefe's medication was suspended for ten days. That was when your husband was away in Rome.'

Dall'Oglio had managed to look her in the eyes from behind his thick glasses. He was a doctor, he was used to suffering. He knew how to confront other people's grief without embarrassment. He had received her as you receive a refugee, with all the understanding that he could muster, and the air of someone explaining the obvious to victims of their own ignorance.

'I never ordered the nurse to suspend the medication from one day to the next, but to reduce the dosage gradually. You see, Signora Montroni, the medication that poor Ferruccio was taking is very strong, it's habit-forming. You have to scale it down every now and again, or else the organism is affected by it and there can be very disagreeable side-effects, such as loss of memory, labyrinthitis. Your brother risked being poisoned. I prescribed gradual reduction of the doses.'

Dall'Oglio had nodded. 'I am sure that your husband was informed about this. We agreed the scaling-down of the medication together.'

Dall'Oglio had sighed. 'You may put your mind at rest, madam. Your brother's action had nothing to do with the reduction of his medication.'

In the taxi that brought her home she had wanted to cry. But her tears had dried up. She was empty. Empty of everything.

The cherubs on the ceiling didn't give a damn about her grief. They mocked her clumsy attempts to find another explanation. Seeking a secondary motive for Fefe's suicide was just a way of

justifying herself. To banish the idea that he had done it on her
account. Because he felt superfluous, to free her of the burden that
kept her from living, from choosing.

She couldn't shake off *that* guilt. She *didn't want to*. Her obsession was the only thing she could cling to if she were to keep her
mind clear. *Her* madness in exchange for Fefe's. Anyone could see
that. The sister of a madman, mad with grief.

Marco had told her he couldn't play around with the dosages
because it was a strong medication.

You can't live with suspicion. The final attempt to give a meaning
to what had happened.

The telephone rang.

She didn't move. The piercing noise repeated obsessively until she
managed to get to her feet, like an automaton.

The wardrobe.

The door.

The corridor.

The telephone.

'Hello.'

A hoarse voice: 'Angela, it's Pierre.'

'Hi.'

'I know Odoacre's at work. I've got to talk to you. I need to see
you, even if it's just for five minutes, please.'

'No. I don't feel up to it, I'm sorry. I can't see anyone.

'Angela, I . . .' She heard him cursing under his breath. 'I have a
million things to tell you.'

'I wouldn't listen to them, Pierre. I can't do it.'

'You're right, the truth is that I'd like to hold you and –'

'And what, Pierre? Console me?'

She was aware of the embarrassed silence at the other end of the
line.

'I'm going to have to say goodbye now, Pierre. Maybe we'll be
able to see each other at some point in the future.'

'Wait. There's something you must know.' His breath was almost
violent now. 'I know your husband knows about us. At Fefe's funeral
he looked at me in a particular way, Angela, I can feel it, I know.
He's worked everything out, it was written on his face, as though on
a white sheet of paper.'

She brought the receiver crashing down.

The telephone started ringing again.

Angela clenched her fists, her nails sticking into her flesh.

Chapter 27

Naples, 5 June
Record of the interrogation of Stefano Zollo, American citizen, born
in New York on 20 April 1919, resident in Naples, at 250 Corso
Vittorio Emanuele, carried out by Police Inspector Pasquale
Cinquegrana, on 5 June, and transcribed by officer Francesco
Gennaro. The subject has not requested the presence of an official
from the American Consulate

'Mr Zollo, you are also known by the nickname of "Steve Cement",
is that not so?'

'At your service.'

'And what is the origin of that alias?'

'Inspector, with all due respect, that is none of your business.'

'Is it true that you are the driver of Salvatore Lucania, better known
as Charles "Lucky" Luciano?'

'Yes.'

'What does your job as a driver involve?'

'I drive the car. I take Mr Luciano around the place.'

'And you are at his disposal every day?'

'Apart from Wednesday, which is my day off.'

'Could you define Mr Luciano's work for me?'

'He sells domestic appliances.'

'Do you know Mr Victor Trimane?'

'Yes, he's a friend of mine, an American.'

'Mr Zollo, where were you on 3 January this year?'

'At the racetrack.'

'A good memory. How do you remember so clearly?'

'It was the Grand Prix.'

'And you were there in the company of Mr Luciano?'

'Exactly.'

'Some witnesses maintain they saw a boy of medium height, well
dressed, hat, scarf and coat, approaching Luciano and giving him a
slap. Did you witness that scene?'

'I was there, yes.'

'And you didn't intervene?'

'To do what?'

'To prevent Luciano from being attacked.'

'It happened too quick.'

'And do you have any idea why that man might have struck Luciano?'

'No.'

'Let me tell you. It was a challenge. It appears that he had had a bet with a friend to see who would be brave enough to slap "Don Luciano" in public. You have no idea of the name of this hothead?'

'No.'

'Then let me tell you. Umberto Chiofano. A month later he was found with a fractured skull, dumped outside the hospital. It would seem he was thrown out of a convertible car. Now he's in the cemetery. Where were you on 30 January?'

'I can't remember.'

'Weren't you near the Marcianise farm, between Naples and Caserta?'

'No.'

'Mr Zollo, would it be true to say that you see all the people Luciano meets at the racecourse?'

'I don't pay attention to them all.'

'Some months ago, did Luciano receive a visit from some American friends, from New York?'

'Yes. He took them on a trip to Pompeii.'

'Were you driving that day?'

'Yes.'

'What did Luciano talk about to those Americans?'

'This and that.'

'Could you be more precise?'

'About women. About Italy and America. Loads of things.'

'You can't remember anything else?'

'I don't listen to other people's conversations.'

'Mr Zollo, did you take a trip to Sicily last April?'

'Yes.'

'For work or pleasure?'

'Pleasure.'

'Meaning?'

'I went to see my mother's family. She's originally from Prizzi, in the province of Palermo.'

'And did you spend the whole of your stay in Prizzi?'

'No. I'd never been to Sicily before. I travelled about.'

'And you didn't meet anyone else apart from your mother's relations?'

'No.'

'Have you left the mainland on any other occasions since your return from Sicily?'

'No.'

'Mr Zollo, have you ever visited the Dalmatian coast?'

'Excuse me?'

'Dalmatian, Dalmatia, Mr Zollo, the Yugoslavian coast.'

'I've never been to Yugoslavia.'

'And Marseilles? Have you ever been to Marseilles?'

'I haven't been there either.'

'Mr Zollo, do you read the newspapers? Do you know who Charles Siragusa is?'

'An Italian-American policeman who wants to make publicity for himself. He says Luciano is a drugs-trafficker.'

'He also says that someone is getting his hands dirty on Luciano's behalf. And that if we found that man, we might get back to the head of the organisation. Which is to say Luciano himself.'

'There are also people who believe in flying saucers.'

'You know that some people maintain that in 1943 Luciano contacted the Mafia to facilitate the Allied landing in Sicily?'

'Back in the States everyone knows that that story was invented by a state prosecutor in New York for political reasons.'

'Could you be more precise?'

'Sorry, I don't really know the story.'

'But you seem very sure that we can rule out Luciano's involvement in any kind of illegal business.'

'Luciano good, Luciano bad. Luciano servant of America, Luciano gangster. It's all politics. People believe what they want to believe. Interpol says drugs? People believe it. That's all I have to say.'

'It's an interesting observation. I'll refer it to Siragusa, when I send him a copy of the record of this interrogation.'

'If you've finished asking questions, I'd like to go.'

'I'm sorry, Mr Zollo, but I'm afraid we're going to have to keep you here for a while.'

'Let's not be silly, inspector. I'm in a hurry.'

'I'm not being silly: I have some eyewitness accounts from people who have heard one Victor Trimane asserting that "if anyone else was planning to slap Don Luciano, that little job I did with my goombah Steve Cement will make them think again". You should understand that before we release you we need to check these accusations very carefully.'

'You can't do that, I'm an American citizen, you can't hold me without a precise accusation.'

'You are suspected of murder, Mr Zollo, and you are working for someone under serious suspicion. I imagine that the American Consulate will be happy to make an exception for a case such as yours.'

Chapter 28

In her absent moments, Angela thought of nothing else.

Now that Fefe wasn't there any more, she seemed to have more absent moments than ever before. Angela couldn't work out whether it was a kind of woodworm that had hollowed out the hole, chewing away the tender wood of her days, or whether it had already been a hollow trunk, crushed by too large a weight.

She had expected Odoacre to mention her meeting with Dall'Oglio. He would certainly have been informed about it. She expected a sermon on the subject of trust. But there was nothing. She had expected illuminating phrases about the doctor–patient relationship. Not a word.

She didn't expect to bring up the subject herself.

I saw Dall'Oglio the other evenng. You're right to trust him, you know him, but I wanted to look him in the eyes, I wanted to hear him say: I did not suspend Ferruccio's treatment. I didn't say anything to you because I knew you wouldn't agree, but I needed to, Odoacre, I had to talk to him or else go mad. He told me that the medication was just scaled down because of dependency, because of labyrinthitis, I don't know, he told me you were informed of this. And what about me? Why did I know nothing about it? You've always told me everything about Fefe, even sometimes how often he took a bath. Why didn't you tell me this? Is it true that you knew?

He had finished dressing the salad. Calmly. A drizzle of oil, pinch of salt, knife-point of mustard. You did well to speak to him. I certainly wouldn't have stopped you, if that makes you feel any better. Did it make you feel any better? And yet what Dall'Oglio told you is true. We agreed that we would gradually reduce the doses. That is the usual practice with this medication. You start with quite a high dose, then you come down until you find the right quantity, which takes effect without damaging the organism. I thought I'd explained that to you when we started the treatment. That was why I never mentioned it again afterwards. It was nothing new, it wasn't a novelty, it wasn't even anything strange. You just do it, that's all. It's standard procedure.

Standard procedure. What about Sante? Sante was standing behind the door and heard everything. Could he have been mistaken? Could it have been an error? Fefe had said no medication. Was that a mistake as well, the delirium of a poor madman?

Angela piled up the dishes in the sink. The water was hot and foamy.

Why was Odoacre so calm? Why did he rule out any error on the part of Dall'Oglio or a nurse? To avoid making her anxious? Is that a doctor's standard procedure with the relatives of a dead patient?

Her fingers ran along the edge of the plate. The soap cancelled the friction. Water softened the fall. Unharmed. Not a day passed without Angela damaging something. Broken ornaments, needles in fingers, washing that came out blue or pink, cuts to the hands, burnt handkerchiefs. She picked up a cup and started rinsing it.

Dr Montroni had the advantage over Odoacre.

He left the kitchen and went into his study. Angela felt a little shudder run across her shoulder-blades. For some days she had been rummaging among his papers and opening boxes, even locked ones, with the help of a hairpin. She looked behind pictures, in card indexes, she flicked through books, moved them around. She turned off the water, holding a pan between her hands, and listened. *Ding*. The tiny ring of a bell. Odoacre on the telephone, the one in his study.

She had learned to recognise that sound. Walk down the corridor in silence, barefoot. Press her ear to the dark wooden door. Hold her breath and breathe in silence. Stay motionless.

'How many boxes did you say? No, look, we're not expecting any more, tell the police. What? Yes, yes, I know the longer we wait . . . sure, the accusation is getting more serious, the fact is that I can't wait any longer. Listen: have you thought about the brother? Yes, absolutely, he mustn't be involved, he's a good comrade, all the blame has to fall on that criminal. Yes, I know, and he'll shoulder all the blame, but the police won't believe him, basically the one responsible for the bar is the elder brother. And I'd recommend that the owner stay out of it too, he's another comrade. Taking photographs? How long do you reckon it'll . . . No. No. Too long. Let's just do it like that. Tomorrow morning you go to the police . . . try and find someone who's seen him, someone who lives near the bar, or we can drag up that business about Yugoslavia, we'll find a way . . . Fine, ok. Speak to you tomorrow.'

Still stooping, Angela tiptoed to the bathroom. She turned the key and sat on the rim of the tub. She had to repeat what she had heard. She had to get a better grasp, dissect every word. She had to remember everything.

The police.

The brother and the owner had to be left out of it. The criminal was to get the blame.

The manager of the bar is the elder brother.

And then, yes, the boxes. Boxes of what?

And Yugoslavia. Let's drag up the business about Yugoslavia.

Or someone who lives near the bar.

A light flashed on in her brain: Pierre was in danger.

His phone call, the litany of the past few days: 'I think your husband knows about us. He's worked it all out, it was written on his face . . .'

Chapter 29

'The Reds' bar was top of the list. Early in the morning, before it filled up.

The robbery at the butcher's had messed up the whole day. Two hours in pursuit, then the truck had taken a bad bend somewhere over by Castel Guelfo. Quarters of beef scattered all over the tarmac, and dead chickens lying in the grass. The thief's face had gone through the windscreen. Dead as a doornail.

Clearing the meat off the carriageway, sending out a report, waiting for the tools to show up, passing everything on to the traffic police. A pack of dogs was feasting on a carcase. Greedy flies were dealing with the rest. A pack of humans was collecting chickens as though they were potatoes.

Shortly after eleven, back to Bologna.

'Do you know where we'd find this Bar Aurora?' asked Sacchetti.

'Yes, turn right here, it's quicker.'

Tagliavini sniffed his fingers. They smelled of blood. Twenty years in the police, the war, and he still couldn't bear to smell it on him.

'So, Sacchetti,' he asked in a fatherly voice. 'Death always leaves its mark on you, doesn't it? Horrible business.'

Sacchetti nodded.

'Yeah. Back in the war I suppose we got used to it, but it's different now, wouldn't you say? Just think that within a few years you will have young colleagues who have never seen a corpse. No bombs, executions, mines, assassination attempts. I guess it'll be even worse for them.'

Sacchetti wasn't the type to say much. To tell the truth he hardly said anything at all. That's ideal when you have to get things off your chest after a chase. Tagliavini didn't want to appear tense. He particularly wanted to be sure that the boy was calm. You never knew with Reds.

'It's this one, isn't it?' asked Sacchetti.

'Yes, stop here.'

It didn't look too busy. The chairs on the pavement were empty. Tagliavini peered inside. Old men playing cards, a bloke at the bar. Hardly enough to put up any resistance. They crossed the street. A moment before he touched the door, wrinkled faces looked up from their game, a cup of coffee hovered in mid-air, hands polishing glasses suddenly froze.

Pure Wild West. The bounty-hunter who has travelled from far away to gather information in the saloon. The music stops, and the clocks.

'Are you Nicola Capponi?' the policeman asked into total silence.

'What do you want?'

Tagliavini chose a casual tone. 'We've got to take a look at your cellar, Mr Capponi.'

The man studied them, one at a time. He ran his tongue over his lips. Tagliavini thought he could read his mind. He was weighing up the forces involved. He was assessing strategies.

About ten men in their sixties left their tables to lean on the bar. No one pretended to be doing anything else. No one pretended not to listen. They stared at the policemen's uniforms, ears pricked.

The manager's voice was a dusty old record. 'I'm very busy today. Drop by again tomorrow, ok?'

Sacchetti gave a start. 'Oi, you're not to –' A hand gripped his shoulder: shut up.

'We need to act now, Mr Capponi, but if you cooperate it will only take half an hour.' Inflexible and conciliatory in a single sentence. A masterpiece.

A young man appeared from the back of the bar. Glanced at the little crowd. Turned to the other man. 'What's up, Nicola?'

Tagliavini seized the opportunity. 'We suspect that the cellar of this bar is being used as a warehouse for illegal goods. We have to proceed to a check.' His tone had now switched to bureaucratic. The regulars started whispering for the first time. The young man intervened confidently.

'Proceed away, then. We have nothing to hide, isn't that right, Nicola?'

A sideways glance was the only reply.

'Ok, then.' Tagliavini grinned. They didn't seem to be about to do anything stupid. 'The sooner you come with me the sooner we'll get it over with.'

As Nicola Capponi came out from behind the bar, one of the pensioners slipped through the door, with two others hot on his heels.

Tagliavini was clutching a paper towel. He wiped the sweat from his forehead, then rubbed it against his fingers. The smell of raw steak was giving him an appetite.

La Gaggia was hammering a heel on to a shoe. Bottone came in, completely out of breath. Garibaldi and Walterún right behind him.

He could tell by their faces that they weren't there for a game of cards.

'Capponi's in trouble.'

'Two cops at the Bar Aurora.'

'They want to search the cellar.'

It took a moment for him to get the situation into focus. The cellar of the Bar Aurora. The niche behind the cupboard where they kept the dishes. The box hidden there after July 1948.

'Are you sure?' he asked, stroking his sideburns.

'We were standing right beside him, and we heard him very clearly.'

'They've invented some kind of check on illegal goods.'

'Absolute balls. It's obvious what they're after.'

La Gaggia put down the shoe and his tools. A nail dangled from his lip. Could someone have talked? Didn't only five or six people know about the niche behind the cupboard?

'How did Capponi take it?'

'Pissed off, as usual. But he's going to take them down there.'

'In my opinion he shouldn't have given up,' said Garibaldi. 'He should just have called a few people in.'

'He did the right thing,' said La Gaggia approvingly. 'I'd stay calm: there's the cupboard, it's very heavy, you'd have to take everything out to move it, and then there's the plywood board nailed to the wall, and the old radio on top of that. We did everything properly, so either they know where to look already, which seems unlikely to me, or they're not going to find anything at all.'

'I'd call Benfenati,' suggested Walterún.

'Benfenati? What's Benfenati got to do with it?'

'Well, doesn't the Party always give a hand in these situations? If it wasn't for Benfenati, we'd be bringing Anselmo Lunardi oranges in chokey.'

'Yes, but he killed three or four of them, that's a bit different. Listen to me: we call Benfenati only if disaster strikes. Otherwise it's better if he doesn't know anything and we move the lot tomorrow.'

'In the meantime, aren't we going to take a look?' asked Bottone.

'Let's go.'

They went outside, leaving the stench of leather and rubber behind them. La Gaggia lowered the shutter. The bar was empty. Voices were being raised in the courtyard at the back. Opinions and observations rose above clothes lines laden with sheets, climbed buildings and balconies, echoed in the street, flew up and down the cellar stairs, from one doorway to the other on the legs of the little boys, rained down on cauliflowers and melons in the local market.

Anyone who had turned up just then would have known that Capponi had been arrested, that they had searched very hard, that much was clear; they had hidden something sinister among the junk just to frame him up, to throw mud at a true comrade, a hero of the 36th and Monte Battaglia, no, wait, maybe it was Ca' di Malanca. And maybe Purocielo. It was a provocation. An insult, that was what it was. Typical Scelba. You couldn't stand and watch.

The four *tarocchino* players pushed their elderly way down the stairs. A tiny amount of light filtered through the slits near the ceiling, supplemented by a few candles.

To anyone who knew him well, Nicola seemed rather tense. The usual hard expression, but the muscles in his jaw were contracted, fingers drumming on a thigh.

Pierre looked calmer. He was strolling about the room like a dancer. He moved tarpaulins, opened boxes, shone a light on hidden corners.

'Do you want to look in here, officer? Look, there we are, nothing but cobwebs, you see?'

La Gaggia remembered.

Pierre didn't know anything.

La Gaggia understood.

That was what Capponi was worried about. Not the hiding place, which was as safe as houses. If the cops hadn't found it straight away, it meant they had no idea where to look. Unless Pierre, with those itchy feet of his, those polite manners of a son of a bitch, went and caused trouble for everyone. You had to admit that he was good at it: serene, impeccable, more than willing to cooperate. The best trick of all. Without a doubt he was enjoying it. And most of those present were enjoying it as well, smug murmurs accompanied each affected nicety, each 'After you, officer', 'Can I help in any way?', 'And what about this box, we don't want to forget it, do we?' and 'Let's do this properly, now that you've gone to all this trouble, let's turn everything upside down, to eliminate any last doubts.'

Nicola was firing glances at him. Pierre wasn't fazed: partly the gloom and partly the excitement. And if he had noticed . . .

La Gaggia looked at the others.

Garibaldi was drenched in sweat, despite the cool of the cellar. Bottone had come up almost at a run. Walterún repeated obsessively that they should call Benfenati.

They understood too.

The older officer raised his candle and leaned over a pile of tables and chairs. He moved a few of them, stood upright again, and seemed to be satisfied.

Pierre threw open the crockery cupboard. Pierre pointed at the boxes on the shelves. Pierre said, 'That's the crockery: glasses, cups, saucers, plates. Two services used in turn. Shall we see if there's anything sinister in there?'

Bottone pushed his way on to the stairs to get back in position. La Gaggia looked as though he was paralysed. Garibaldi was thinking about their treasure: two Bren guns, two machine-guns with perforated barrels, ten magazines, eight hand grenades. Walterún wondered if it wouldn't be a good idea to warn Benfenati.

'Come on,' Pierre insisted. 'What are you looking for? Cocaine? Opium?'

The younger officer turned purple in the face. 'Spare your breath until we call you to the station,' he hissed.

The onlookers protested. The people in the front row informed the people behind, they told the ones on the stairs, then anyone passing through the courtyard, the little boys of the district and finally the greengrocers. Villain! Provocateur! Criminal! They haven't found anything and they're trying to provoke us into a fight!

Capponi, to the general surprise, sided with the policeman. 'He's right. Could we have a bit of quiet, please?'

Pierre had no time to disagree. The older officer held out a hand to say goodbye. 'Very well. Everything seems to be in order. We'll leave you to it.'

The crowd parted like a little Red Sea. Not quite enough to allow the guardians of the law to leave the scene quickly and comfortably. Little pushes, nudges, tripping feet and muttered insults.

Garibaldi gripped Walterún's shoulder with a spasm: the danger had passed. Capponi looked at Pierre with ice in his eyes and the promise of yet more fury to come. Bottone and La Gaggia headed for the stairs, just behind the policemen.

'Smell this, Gaggia,' whispered Bottone, tapping his nose. 'They really do smell of corpses, don't they?'

Chapter 30

Confidential document written by Charles Siragusa, District Supervisor, US Bureau of Narcotics, dated 13 June 1954. For the attention of Inspector Pasquale Cinquegrana with reference to the arrest and interrogation of Stefano Zollo

Dear Inspector,

The American Consulate has sent me the enclosed document in which it informs me, concerning the situation of Stefano Zollo, that the authorities of the United States can wait no longer and if, by the 16th inst., investigations into the Chiofano murder supply no fresh evidence, they will find themselves obliged to intervene to free him, as requested on several occasions by Mr Schifanoia, Zollo's lawyer, since allegations made against his client have proved to be unfounded.

Nonetheless, new evidence against Zollo would enable us to keep him in extended custody, and I consider this essential for the current phase of Operation Luciano.

On this subject, I have carefully examined the declarations made by our informer, Gennaro Abbatemaggio, eighty-five, concerning the so-called 'Montesi case', with particular reference to the visits to Naples of the suspect Ugo Montagna and links with the Neapolitan underworld and drugs trafficking.

Of the names mentioned by Abbatemaggio, none has direct links to Luciano.

This matter has struck me as a little strange, and for that reason, just yesterday, I obtained, on police authority, permission to interrogate Abbatemaggio.

It immediately struck me as apparent that the 'gap' in the previous declaration was due solely to reticence, and in particular to the fear that the figure of Luciano inspires in all and sundry.

Reassured about the protection that he will be guaranteed,

even more than he was at the time of the Cuocolo trial, and about the advantages of his cooperation, Abbatemaggio has supplied valuable information about the connections that Luciano's lieutenants maintain in the capital, and in particular with 'marquis' Montagna (see Appendix No. 2).

Abbatemaggio has declared himself willing to make an official declaration on this subject.

I therefore maintain that, by tomorrow, we should proceed to the interrogation ot Abbatemaggio, in order to be able to make fresh accusations to Stefano Zollo by the 16th inst., and interrogate him on this matter.

Yours sincerely,
Charles Siragusa

Chapter 31

He had missed the tram after fifty metres of useless sweat.

He decided to walk to the next stop. The meeting with Ettore was arranged for seven. He had time.

Ettore. How would he pay his debt?

Montroni had put the police on to him. Angela had warned him. Palmo had taken the boxes back just in time.

Montroni wanted to fit him up. Angela had said: he knows about Yugoslavia, too. Nicola had stopped talking to him: the spectacle in the cellar had left him furious.

Montroni knew.

Just to make the situation even worse, that morning, a letter from Pisa. Sent by the pigeon-fancying group 'Wings of Tyrrhenia'. Inside, two lines of explanation and a message from Vittorio Capponi.

His father. Hidden in an abandoned sheep pen in the mountains on the border with Albania. His father, man of few words. I've finished with Yugoslavia. Find out about conditions for a return to Italy. Hug. Vittorio.

Pierre checked the time on the wrist of a passer-by. Sultry, oppressive heat. The sun shining over Via Emilia, about to pass through Porta San Felice.

He had to pay his debt to Ettore.

He had to think of his father's return.

He had to pay Angela back for saving his arse.

He owed too much to too many people.

Angela had raised a suspicion. I think Fefe's death had something to do with his medication. They were supposed to scale it down and instead they stopped it completely. I asked Odoacre: he says it isn't true, but he didn't convince me, I think he's afraid. Afraid to admit that Fefe might have died because of that. Afraid I will hate him for the rest of my life. Afraid I will start seeing you again.

The pneumatic drill crushed his eardrums. Work on the new hospital was continuing. A deafening noise: the tram had passed him before he even knew it was there. He gave up running.

Who could help his father? Usually, the Party took care of such. But Vittorio Capponi had stayed with Tito when Moscow and the other comrades had abandoned him. And now that there was a rapprochement between Tito and the Soviet Union, he was with Djilas. So the only person he could ask for help was his son Pierre, who didn't have a lira, who had a debt to pay and didn't know how to do it, who had been abandoned by his girlfriend, who was in the sights of her husband, a big shot in the Bologna Federation. And what was he going to come back and do here, in Italy? Fifty years behind him, twice a widower, a whiff of jail, jobless, marked out as a 'Tito fascist'. A fine prospect.

Pierre crossed the tramlines and took the path through the middle of the stubble. The shed was covered by trees. He glimpsed the truck. They were unloading.

He passed by an improvised pile of bricks and tyres. He smoothed his hair and appeared in the dusty yard. Ettore emerged from behind the tank and nodded to him to come in. An oven, 400 square metres.

He stroked his moustache and skipped the niceties. 'So, tell me about this cellar.'

'Nothing to tell, Ettore, they're on to us.'

'I know that. How come?'

He spread his arms. 'No idea. Somebody grassed us up?'

'Someone who saw you unloading.'

'Probably.'

'I don't think we've got too much to worry about. No one has shown up here.'

Pierre lit a cigarette and put down the pack. 'I don't think it's any big deal. I think it's limited to the Bar Aurora.'

'That's what I think too,' Ettore smiled. 'And I don't think you're telling me everything.'

'What?'

'You know very well what.'

Pierre raised his hands over his head, palms facing the front. 'Ok, ok: the baker on the other side of the street. There's a girl involved, a long time ago. I thought he'd got over it, but it seems he's still got it in for me.'

From the silence that followed, Pierre deduced that the ball was in his court again. 'So Ettore, what do we do now?'

'What do we do about what?'

'I'm in the shit, look: I don't know where I'm going to get hold of all that money.'

'Ever thought of taking up robbery?'

'I don't think I'd be capable of it, but soon I'll have no other option.'

'There's one other alternative. We're getting a lot of requests in at the moment. Three or four journeys for a converted agricultural petrol company, and the usual trafficking. The petrol guys are about to pull out, but if we had one more mule, we'd be able to accept. What d'you think?'

Smuggling, that's all I need. So, better accept: better than this . . . He replied that he would think about it. Then he added, 'Isn't four journeys rather a lot? It only took me one to get to Yugoslavia.'

Ettore smiled.

Pierre shook his hand.

Chapter 32

Record of the interrogation of Stefano Zollo, carried out by Police Inspector Pasquale Cinquegrana on 15 June, recorded by officer Francesco Di Gennaro for the exclusive use of Charles Siragusa, US Bureau of Narcotics

'Mr Zollo, tell us the truth –'

'One moment, Inspector, you're starting your questions all over again! My lawyer, Mr Schifanoia, told me that accusations of the murder of somebody or other are without foundation, and that there are new, more serious allegations against me. Will you tell me what's going on?'

'All in good time, Mr Zollo. First answer the questions, then you will be informed. May I continue?'

'I'm only going to answer in the presence of my lawyer.'

'Mr Zollo, were you in Rome this year?'

'I told you I didn't intend –'

'Have you ever met, in Naples or elsewhere, Signor Ugo Montagna?'

'Inspector, what the fuck –'

'Mr Zollo, in your capacity as driver for Mr Luciano, does your work involve drug-dealing?'

'Listen, Inspector –'

'No, you listen, Mr Zollo. Your situation is far from brilliant, if I were you I would do my best to cooperate: the accusations of the Chiofano homicide have not been collaborated, it is true, but I am pretty much convinced that you killed the poor man, and if that is the case I promise I will do everything possible to make sure you end up in jail. Furthermore, you are accused of having supplied phoney marquis Ugo Montagna with a large quantity of heroin between February and April 1953. Now, we are well aware that the brains behind this drugs trafficking is your employer, Mr Luciano. You may be sure that we will catch him sooner or later. At the moment, however, we do not have sufficient proof, and we would be very grateful to any reasonable person who, with a view to extricating himself from an unpleasant nuisance, would clarify our ideas about a number of situations.'

'I don't know what you're talking about. Just find that person and leave me in peace.'

'I don't understand what your problem is, Mr Zollo. The ship is sinking: jump into the lifeboat while you still have time, leave the admiral to his fate. After all, you're just an ordinary seaman.'

'Your grandfather's the ordinary seaman. I've already told you that I will only answer questions tomorrow, in the presence of my lawyer. I'm only interested in knowing what I'm being accused of. Selling heroin to this man Montagna? Prepare to release me, Inspector.'

Chapter 33

When he saw her his heart leapt into his mouth.

She was waiting for him on the other side of the street. Black skirt, white blouse and dark glasses.

She looked fantastic. Pierre closed the padlock of the bar shutter and walked towards her.

'Angela . . .'

'Hi.'

She was running a serious risk in coming here. He didn't know what to say to her. A simple 'How are you?' would have sounded stupid and provocative. How was he to behave?

Fortunately she was the one who spoke.

'I need to ask you a favour. I don't know who else I can turn to.'

'Sure,' Pierre muttered, 'shall we go and sit down somewhere?'

He jumped into the dark, landing on wet grass. The sprinklers had just been switched off. The lawn at the Villa Azzurra was always well tended, in the English fashion: so green it looked fake.

Pierre crept over to the wall, staying out of range of the lamps.

The two nightwatchmen were always in their little cage by the entrance. They had an abundance of flasks of coffee, sandwiches and magazines. Every two hours they took a walk through the wards to check that all the lunatics were sound asleep.

There was no other way of getting in. After Ferruccio's suicide, Montrone had had all the windows barred, and now the lunatics were effectively in a cage. In fact the bars had been there before, but only on certain wards, those for the more seriously ill patients. Fefè's jump had changed everything. Pierre looked at the building submerged in shadow and shivered. It could have been a jail, or an army barracks.

He crept along the wall to the door and peered round the corner.

One of the nurses was sitting with his head on his folded arms, and Pierre thought he could hear a faint snoring.

The other man was flicking through a newspaper.

Pierre got down on all fours and crept towards the reception desk.

He breathed quietly and moved slowly. A crack in his joints would give him away.

The offices were at the end of the corridor, around the corner. At least six or seven metres to cross without being seen.

Pierre thought about the time when, as a boy, he had hidden from Aunt Iolanda when she wanted to bathe him in the tub. They looked for him everywhere. He had become convinced that if he didn't look at them, no one would see him. He had lain down in a corner, among the chicken hutches, and lowered his head. Then, motionless, he had waited. An ostrich strategy.

He stretched himself out on the floor and started to creep forwards gently, one centimetre at a time. If his movements were imperceptible, perhaps he wouldn't distract the watchman's attention from his paper. If the nurse's eyes remained fixed on the page, he wouldn't notice the long mass sliding along the floor.

He continued like that, nose on the linoleum, like an earthworm.

He bent his body to round the corner, without speeding up, twisting himself around and pulling his legs behind him at the last minute.

He had made it.

Incredulous, he got to his feet and walked to the office door.

Lifting it slightly to keep the hinges from squeaking, he opened it just enough to slip inside, and closed it behind him.

He took out his torch and started rummaging through the card index.

Malavas . . . Malossi . . . Mambrini . . . Manaresi.

Manaresi Ferruccio.

The shaft of light lit up the hospital file. A long list of medications, times and doses, with the doctors' signatures beside them.

In his head, Angela's voice suggested what he should be looking for: 'Check the time when Odoacre went to Rome. Check whether, before he left, he suspended Fefe's medication, and when they started giving it to him again.'

Pierre gave a start.

The dates matched.

So did Dr Montroni's signature.

Pierre understood.

Pierre felt his flesh creeping under his clothes.

Pierre felt sorry for Angela.

The day before he left for Rome, Montroni had suspended Ferruccio's treatment.

Fefe's 'relapse'.

Montroni leaves the conference and comes back to look after the family.

The sainted Montroni solves everything.

The forceful husband saves his wife's little brother.

His faithless wife who is cuckolding him with a *filuzzi* dancer.

His wife feels guilty and understands that she can't live without Odoacre the Magnificent.

Another shiver. Cold sweat. Drips on his nose.

Fefe had worked it out.

Montroni's dirty game. Fefe *couldn't* tell anyone about it. Fefe was *mad*. Fefe wasn't credible. Fefe was locked up. Angela was locked up too. Fefe was the weapon in the cuckolded husband's hand.

Fefe couldn't accept it. He loved his sister. He didn't want to be the cause of her unhappiness.

Bloody hell!

Pierre staggered, suppressed a coughing fit.

He felt nausea rising from his stomach.

He felt disgust in his throat, he felt dizzy.

Fefe hadn't wanted to *accept it*.

Fefe hadn't yielded.

Fefe had *decided* to take revenge on his brother-in-law.

In the only way possible.

By taking his weapon out of his hands.

Chapter 34

She's asleep.

She says she's very tired, that she was *working* until late.

Hell, what's a bloke to do?

You go and pick her up in a custom-built car that looks like a speedboat. The car that belongs to Stiv, that big guy, lent specially for the occasion. That is, not actually for Lisetta, in fact if he finds out I've taken anyone with me, he's quite capable of shooting me. In my pocket I've still got the piece of paper he gave me along with the keys, poor Stiv, so I'm sure I won't forget anything.

Salvatore, I want no crap from you. These are the keys of my car. It's in the courtyard of my building, in Corso Vittorio Emanuele. Take it. You'll go to Frosinone, straight there, find Cammarota, ask for the television and come back straight away. Go on your own. Don't talk to anyone. Not a word. I'll go out in a few days. If you scratch the car, you can forget your winnings. So no crap, ok?

When she's asleep, Lisetta is really beautiful. *Mamma mia*, I'll have to think straight, because I really don't want to hurt Lisetta.

But the car made no impression on her, except for the first five minutes.

'Totore! And where are we going in this lovely car?'

'We're going for a drive, I told you.'

'A drive? Dressed like that?'

Nothing. She hadn't even been impressed by the linen jacket, damn it. If it had been the monkey suit I was wearing at the casino, which even that goddess with the golden skin noticed, then she'd have been all over me, I wouldn't have had time to open my mouth. But Stiv had just hired that one, you could hardly say it was his fault, must have cost a packet, and as a reward he got this one for me, luxury goods, so you might say I bought it myself with those famous winnings of mine. Not a bit of it: Lisetta just had a good laugh because I was taking her to Frosinone in my best bib and tucker.

'And what are we going to do in Frosinone? What's nice there?'

'I don't know. Let's go and find out.'

'Sorry, Totore, why don't we stop by the sea? It's boiling!'

'Lisetta, I've got some things to sort out in Frosinone, ok? Afterwards we can go wherever you like.

The car drives like a dream, you've cleaned it and polished it and you're dressed better than you were dressed on your first communion. But she, Lisetta, is thinking about the heat. She's thinking about the sea. She's thinking that Frosinone is too far away.

So start with the story of those incredible days spent with big-guy Steve; just being around him meant more things happened than you'd expect in a lifetime. Tons of money, you couldn't even say how much, this game, *chemin*, where you've always got to put down nine, and that Chinaman who lost and lost without so much as a murmur, you'd never heard that Chinamen were so rich, he must have been the King of Siam at the very least.

'You won a heap of money and you didn't even bring me back a present?'

'What? No, Lisetta, what are you saying, it's just that you see I can't use that money yet. It's mine, of course it is, but you know what happens, word gets round, Salvatore's got a bag of cash, and all of a sudden some no-mark decides to come and rob him, or worse, cut Pagano's throat, or even kidnap someone he's fond of, you get me, you know how these things are, and I'm an orphan, I've got no one, but just imagine we'd been seen together a few times, and someone thought you were my girlfriend, the very idea that they might hurt you . . .

You arrive in Formia, you take the inland road, you take off your jacket and tie, open the buttons of your shirt, which just makes the heat even worse. Lisetta's in a sulk, you've just left the coast and the

sea's behind you now. You play your last card, the cinema, the scene
of the fight in the flowers, with that famous American actor, a big
movie that's going to be shown all around Italy, all around the world,
and then who knows how many other directors will notice this tough
young lad, that athletic jump, those oh-so realistic punches. That's
how it starts, becoming a great actor, opportunities like that open
the gates of Cinecittà, yes sir, Salvatore Pagano, the guy in the fight
among the flowers, that's me, an unforgettable, historic scene.

This time she looks at you differently. You seem to have struck
home.

'And what's the title of this famous film of yours?'

'Ah, Lisetta, you know I have no memory for names, and anyway
it was a complicated, American name, and here in Italy they're bound
to call it something else anyway, but I've written it down on a little
piece of paper, the title and the name of the star, the greatest of them
all, and before you say his name you have to wash your mouth out
with soap, and he was there next to me, close as you are, you know?
And the director, you won't believe this, Winston Churchill, of all
people . . .'

'Churchill? Totore, what the . . . ? And I was starting to believe
you there!'

Lisetta had started sulking again. Hell, maybe you'd got everything
wrong. Maybe you should have gone to Frosinone on your own,
then dropped by to pick her up and take her to the sea, and then
it might have worked, even if the car, beautiful, gleaming, luxurious,
wasn't really yours, your clothes weren't right for an outing to the
country, Stiv had the casino money and you couldn't even remember
the title of the film and it wasn't going to come out until next year.
What can you do?

Yes, without a doubt it would have been better that way.

When you got to Frosinone Lisetta had put her foot down and
said she didn't want to stay in the car, not even for half an hour,
and there was nothing to see in this yokelish countryside and if you
didn't bring her back straight away then you were a yokel too.

Fortunately, you found Cammarota immediately, and without
making too much of a fuss about things he told you everything about
the television: the man from Bologna took it, a certain Ettore, the

same one who took it to Rome, someone who had a rig and carried goods between Naples and the north. Yes, it could have been the 2nd or the 3rd of June. He was happy to take it, he said, because he had a taker for it, either in Bologna or in Milan.

Well done, Camarota. Well done, Kociss. Ettore from Bologna. Stiv'll be happy.

'What's this about the television?'

'What? The television? Pff, I know about as much as you do, it's something that interests my friend Stiv, who's very busy now, so he asked me to do him the favour of taking care of it, because he knows he can trust me.'

'And do you think it's normal to send a friend to Frosinone to ask for a television?'

'What do I know? He asked me a favour, and I'm doing it, I'm not going to ask him this and that, wouldn't be a favour then, would it?'

'Salvato', you're an idiot!'

Past Cerpano, a kilometre before San Giovanni Incarico, you see this lake, the trees, the shade. You turn on the indicator, turn down the avenue and pull up right on the shore. It's almost seven, it's not so hot, there's going to be a spectacular sunset between the water and the clouds.

You turn off the engine. Lisetta yawns. You take off your shoes and dip your feet in the water. Lisetta yawns. You wet your forehead, and remember the name of that lorry driver, Ettore the Bolognese, mustn't forget that. Lisetta yawns. She's tired. She worked till late. She goes to sleep.

She's asleep.

She's missing the spectacular sunset. She turns on to her side, revealing her legs, an earthquake of flesh. She's not wearing a bra. It would drive you mad.

You'd never hurt Lisetta, never. But a kiss, yes, a quick one, just to calm you down, not to do anything worse. A kiss, a little one like this, nothing important. Lisetta, you're driving me out of my mind.

There. A kiss.

'Salvatore, what do you think you're doing?'

Chapter 35

Sudden silence. Almost magical.

Heartbeats and breaths float between smoke and ceiling.

Lips form circles, utter heavy sighs. Oooh. Here it is, look, what a beautiful thing!

Nothing about Rocky Marciano against Ezzard Charles. Those blacks, even the old ones, are always animals.

Nothing about Guatemala, agrarian reform, the USA's ignoble attack to defend the interests of the United Fruit Company.

Nothing about Ethel Rosenberg, just a year ago. A whole year? Christ, how time flies . . .

Nothing about cycling is dead as a sport, someone should get involved, they should get rid of the cycling aces, the 'Bernina strike', they're taking too much money, Coppi has gone soft in the head, the *Carlino* says he has a lover, *L'Unità* says he hasn't, it must be a clerical attack on a left-wing sportsman, but he isn't the man any more, Bartali is forty and puts more grit into it, even without drugs.

Even Benfenati has stopped talking.

Carried in like an ancient pharaoh by the Capponi brothers, the set enters the throne room.

The Bar Aurora has never been so full. Everyone's there. The ones who hadn't shown their faces for months. The ones whose wives always keep them at home. The ones who aren't Bologna FC fans. The ones who have debts and, yes, they'll pay them tomorrow. The ones who think, in the age of motorised transport, that sitting in front of a piece of furniture is a complete waste of time. You'd think that Anselmo Lunardi, known as Baldo, incognito from Prague, was there, and even the Old Man, God rest his soul, straight from the

Certosa cemetery, so that he can say to his wife, when he's lying beside her again, 'Argia, you've no idea what you're missing.'

As they hoist it on to the tabletop, everyone wants to help, touch, join in. 'I was there!' they will tell their grandchildren.

Heave!

A little more to the right, that's it, lean it over a bit more, that's the way, all those dials. Christ it's heavy! Christ it's big! Christ!

Sure it's all new, but perhaps it should be said that all these people aren't just here to see a television, not least because, more or less, we know what it's like. And many of us, last week, were in Bar Franco enjoying Coppi's arrival in Bolzano, the only stage that he has really put his back into just to show everyone that when he wants to be he's still the Champion of Champions. But what do you expect, cycling isn't all that interesting, you see the finishing line, you see the people, you see Coppi pulling out, but you don't know how it was, in the mountains, or rather you do know, but you know it from the radio, and that isn't the same thing. Seeing a football match is another matter, especially if Italy are playing the game of their lives in the World Cup. With Belgium you win or you go home. And then you've got to hope that England will knock out the Swiss, weekend dilettantes; if you believed what Czeizler said they're almost as strong as the Hungarians. On Thursday some of us didn't even go to Franco's bar, because we didn't see much point in paying a surtax on coffee to see Italy–Switzerland. But we lost. And the ref disallowed Lorenzi's goal for an offside that never happened, but in the end all that matters is the result: 2–1 and thank you very much.

'And where does this plug go? What is it, the aerial?'

More than anything else, though, what we're excited about is that we bought the television by ourselves, for our bar. An American television, a luxury item. And from now on we won't be forced to emigrate, to go somewhere else, where the bitters are more expensive, the coffee isn't the one we're used to, and even the people's accents sound different. You feel you're on loan, it's no good. To cut a long story short, it's an event within an event, the Italy game and the television in the Bar Aurora, in between the article in *L'Unità* on the death of Stalin and Capponi's medal.

'Is there a piece of cardboard somewhere? Let's put it underneath so it's level.'

Meanwhile Benfenati launches off on a lecture about football. He hasn't said a word for ten minutes, it's a shame to waste valuable propaganda time. 'These footballers are paid too much.'

La Gaggia tries to grab our attention with the Montesi case. Alida Valli's embroiled in it now, because of a phone call to Piero Piccioni.

'I've had enough of this!' observes Bottone without letting La Gaggia finish. 'I don't understand a word of it! It's all far too complicated. If they find out anything that makes any more sense, come and tell me, ok?' He raises his voice. 'Now, let's see if we can get this contraption up and running, come on, the game begins in ten minutes.'

The seats are already reserved. Old guys at the front, younger ones behind them, a few standing up. Pierre starts fiddling with the dials.

We've got *less* than ten minutes. Direct link from Lugano. Italy–Belgium, commentary by Niccolò Carosio. World Cup.

'Give the Filuzzi King a hand, there, he doesn't look so good at fiddling with buttons.'

'He's handy, that one, he's practical, leave him alone.'

At Lugano stadium, Italy comes on to the field with Ghezzi Magnini Giacomazzi, Neri Tognon Nesti, Lorenzi Pandolfini Galli, Cappello – The guy from Bologna? Hey, fantastic! – and Frignani.

Nicola comes over. Pierre spreads his arms and shakes his head.

'Couldn't you have set it up earlier on?' asks Bottone.

'I said so, didn't I? Don't say I didn't,' almost in a whisper, like a prayer, the comment brushes Garibaldi's lips.

Five minutes. A glance at *Sport Illustrato* to bring down the tension. *Nesti, pugnacious and resolute, has given his all on the field, shone with his staying power and effective . . .*

'Oi! I'm off, I'm going to Franco's to see the first half, then I'll be back.'

'I'm coming with you, off we go, then, let's see if there are any seats left.'

'What did I tell you? Not to trust that bald guy?' Garibaldi's tone is getting heavy.

. . . He has often thrown himself into the attack and has made many passes to the forwards, skilfully demonstrating his . . .

'So?'

'I want my 5,000 lire back, what is this nonsense?'

'Don't say a word!' Garibaldi is getting agitated. 'It's all the fault of that good-for-nothing.' He points at Gas, beside the door. 'He's the one who swindled us.'

Four o'clock precisely. Now. It's starting now.

'How's it my fault? What did I know? Why are you getting on my case?'

Melega grabs the entrepreneur by the knot of his tie and pins him to the wall.

Garibaldi brings his face right up to Gas's face, or rather to his chin, and starts bellowing. 'And it's always the same story! Nothing but swindling, you'd cheat your friends, even your own mother! Criminal! Bum!'

The Bar Aurora empties. Some leave contemptuously, some quietly, some running, some shaking their heads. Only a few of us are left, unsure which is worth more: Italy–Belgium, or seeing Gas getting beaten up.

Capponi pushes his way through the chairs, followed by his brother. Furious expressions.

'You shouldn't have done that, Gas. Did you see how many people there were? Who's going to talk to Benassi now? You?'

'Talk?' Bortolotti intervenes. 'No talking! If I were you, Capponi, I'd get a refund. And this guy here will have to find another television as soon as possible.'

'Another one?' Gas protests. 'And where am I going to find one at that price? It was a special offer, an extraordinary price.'

'You'll find one, off you go,' Melega's finger stops just short of his eye. 'Otherwise we'll come and get you.'

And a moment after our cowboy's threat, the voice of the radio commentator imposes a truce.

Chapter 36

'*I regret to be a bad student.*' Pierre remarked after his umpteenth mistake.

Fanti smiled, sipped his tea and corrected error umpteen plus one: 'Wouldn't it be better to say, *I regret that I'm a bad student?*'

Pierre hid his face in his hands. 'It's all of a piece, *professore*. I can't even manage to say how bad a student I am.'

'Right. And I'd be a lousy teacher if I couldn't tell that it isn't your day.'

'Unfortunately it isn't just a matter of days, *professore* . . .'

With his usual *savoir faire*, Fanti avoided direct questions. He did nothing more than pour the tea, sniff it, sip it with a vacant expression. He could put you at your ease with the most simple and ordinary gestures, never overdoing it. If you wanted to speak, he was ready to listen to you. If you wanted a piece of advice, he was ready to give it. Provided that the silence was tamed by the fakirs of jazz, and he didn't have to clean the pigeon-loft and tend to the birds.

The oolong tea, with its hazelnut aftertaste, satisfied the palate. The swing orchestra satisfied the ears. Pierre's thoughts were drying up. His father, Ettore, Montroni, Angela. He hadn't talked to anyone, not even the musketeers, who had now stopped taking him along to the dancehall. It was as though no one could understand so intricate a situation; he could at best have enjoyed a bit of bar room chat, and thanks very much. No one could help him. He didn't like going around the place telling everyone his business. Angela said it was nothing but pride. Pierre called it dignity. Ok fine, a bit of pride, but not only that. It was just that nine times out of ten you knew in advance how people were going to react: someone would feel sorry for you, and you regretted not keeping your mouth shut; someone else would suggest distractions, women, wine, a night on the town, without understanding that when you're ready for those things it means either you've recovered or you're in the final stages, and it's the in between that makes you feel bad; yet another would start telling you his own problems, and you weren't in the frame of mind to listen; the worst of all told you it was nothing, or treated you like a fool if you didn't think their advice was utterly fantastic.

Having said that, sometimes pouring your heart out was a good idea, if you had the right person to do it with. The hard thing was knowing where to start.

'My father wants to come back to Italy,' he said finally, turning back to his cup. 'And he asked me to look into the question, but it doesn't strike me as such a good idea. What can I do for him? I've been through the mill myself over the last couple of months. If I could, I'd love a change of air as well.'

He stopped for a moment and glanced at the flowers on the terrace. It gave him a new starting point.

He started with Angela. He explained about Fefe and Montroni, leaving out hardly anything, as though looking into a mirror. As though Fanti had melted away among the notes of Woody Herman and the vapour from the teapot.

'And it isn't over yet, the best is still to come: to pay the people who took me to Yugoslavia, I let them use the cellar of the bar as a storeroom for some American cigarettes. Contraband, in short. Angela's husband found out, because he was keeping an eye on me and he wanted the police to get me. Except she heard him talking on the phone and came and told me. I barely had time to sort things out. Then Angela asked me a big favour, and at that point there was no way I could say no. She wanted me to creep into Montroni's clinic, to see if there was a file there with his signature where it said that Ferruccio had to stop taking that medication of his. I did it, and the signature was there. Now she's going to have a furious row with her husband, and he in turn will be furious with me, out of jealousy, and apparently he knows about Yugoslavia as well, and who knows what else he'll be able to get out of it, he's a big cheese in the Party, and even if he talks balls people believe him.'

In spite of everything, Fanti's face showed a certain amazement.

Partly because of the things he had heard and partly because he wasn't sure he had grasped all the plot lines. He sat there with his chin in his hand, almost motionless, until he was sure that Pierre had nothing else to add.

'So your father decided to come back at the worst possible moment.'

'I'd say so. And yet he's had plenty time to make his mind up.'

'Yeah, but things were different in those days.'

'For me too, I assure you. And my father isn't stupid: if all of a sudden he asks me to think about him coming back, it means he's in a very bad way. He knows as well as anyone that there's not much I can do for him.'

'A moment ago you said you'd be happy to have a change of air.'

As usual, Fanti avoided direct questions, or rather he threw back at you what you had already said, he made you explain it and analyse it more deeply.

'Yes, sir, if I could, I would go away, out of Italy. Didn't you say that journeys mean change? When you're in a tight spot you always regret your inability to fly.'

'Why, can't you?'

'And how am I going to go about it? You've travelled all over the place, to you it seems like the most natural thing in the world for someone simply to pull up roots and leave. But I have a thousand problems: I don't know where to go, I have no money to get there, and the only passport I have is fake. And on top of that I've got a father to help, he hasn't got a penny either, he's got a sentence to serve in Italy and Tito's political police are hot on his heels. What else do you want?'

'I'd say that a change of surroundings might be the solution for both of you.'

Pierre gave a resigned nod. That solution had already flashed through his mind, but in the end it seemed to create more problems than it solved. He could ask Ettore to give him a full-time job for just long enough to pay for two people to leave the country under cover. But what would happen then? To what lengths would Montroni go to bring more serious accusations down on his head? What would he live on once he was abroad?

The explosion of the trombones covered Fanti's words.

'What did you say, *professore?*'

'I said: if it's of any use to you, my wife's relations live in England. They're nice people, they'd be happy to help you out for the first few months.' He smiled. 'It might help your accent, don't you think?'

'Hmm, I don't know . . .'

'Think about it. I really mean it. They're well off, they have a big house, and they're used to having guests.'

'Really? Thanks, *professore*. Really, thanks. I'll give it some thought.'

Pierre wanted to add something more sensible, but it wasn't easy. No words could pay for hours and hours of free lessons, litres of tea to clear the mind, kilos of raisin biscuits, piles of books recommended and lent, Stan Kenton and Dizzy Gillespie, the journey of the first pigeon to Yugoslavia, 30,000 lire never paid back, long political discussions, advice given with no pressure, the right phrases to speak to Cary Grant.

And now England. His wife's relations. Hospitality.

Not the solution to all his problems, but enough to open the door a crack.

Chapter 37

Confidential report for the Italian authorities by Charles Siragusa,
District Supervisor, US Bureau of Narcotics, 24.6.54. Addendum

In addition to what has already been quoted in the previous report, I am happy to receive the news of the withdrawal and revocation of Lucania's Italian passport, No. 3243602, issued in Naples on 10 October 1950.

As we await the sentence of five years' imprisonment, which strikes me as extremely urgent, I suggest that further limitations be imposed on Lucania's freedom of movement, forcing him:
- to appear at the police station at regular intervals to confirm his address;
- to return to his apartment by 11 p.m. and not to leave it before 7 a.m.;
- not to visit public places of entertainment for several evenings in a row, so that Lucania cannot choose such places as a logistical base for his trafficking.

I should also point out that Stefano Zollo, who has also been mentioned, was arrested and interrogated by the police authorities on 6 June, in relation to the murder of Umberto Chiofano. Before that date, for several weeks, no trace of him had been found in his usual haunts. It is suspected that he may have been 'on a mission' outside the city on behalf of Lucania.

Stefano Zollo remains in the custody of the police authorities. His period of custody has been extended because of the emergence of fresh allegations against him, this time linked to the revelations of Gennaro Abbatemaggio concerning links between Ugo Montagna and the Neapolitan underworld.

Chapter 38

'Steve, Steve, Steve. Come in, my friend, sit down on the sofa, let's have a drink. How patient we have to be, Steve! You must forgive me, I hope you will. It's just because of your friendship for me, your sincere dedication, that a free American citizen can be treated like this on Allied soil by poor, miserable cops who know nothing and talk and go on talking and some politician or other comes and sucks their cock. How have they been treating you, Steve, in this stuffy cesspit, Poggio Reale? Anyone been taking liberties?'

'Don Luciano, no one's taken any liberties except to send you greetings and thanks, don't worry about that, it's just been a stay at the expense of this shitty Italian state.'

'The Italian state! Well done, Steve, a great subject. What is the Italian state? Where is it? Ehhh . . . You've said it yourself: the Italian state is shitty. But lots of people don't know how to answer the question. Look here, come on, Steve, take a look. Look in front of you. Naples, the bay, Vesuvius, the port . . . You see the port? You know the port very well, don't you Steve? They're almost as familiar as the old docks back home by now, aren't they, Steve?'

'With all due respect, Don Luciano, compared to the docks of New York, the port of Naples is a bathtub.'

'Of course it is! Of course, Steve Cement's bathtub. But let me tell you something. You know who's in charge of this city? Who's the boss, the mayor, the *sindaco*, the Fiorello LaGuardia of Naples? His name is Achille Lauro, the viceroy, and you know what he does? He builds boats, he's a shipowner, and he owns newspapers, the football team and the votes of the people. But his trade, his fortune, is the sea, ships, ports. And you know where he builds his ships, where he has his boatyards, this king of Naples? In Genoa, in La Spezia. Doesn't that seem strange to you? It's like if you were made mayor of New York and went and opened a nightclub with whores in Chicago, don't you think? But you'd worked all that out already, eh, Steve? The port of Naples is a bathtub, and you know who's taking a bath? The 6th US Fleet, and us, modestly speaking. We're a bit cramped, but if you don't tread on each other's toes you can get by, wouldn't you say, Steve? There's no room for commerce, for passenger ships, for dry docks, for expansion work. The bathtub was useful to us, and it still is. This man Lauro was like that with Mussolini, and then when we showed up, the liberators, he was arrested, just for a few days, to understand the situation, reach an agreement with him and his people, and Don Achille proved to be an intelligent man, a sound skipper. The dockyards and the ships ended up in Genoa, Don Achille keeps the people far away from the communists, and we and the 6th Fleet will give him a bath every day to keep him smelling sweet. So tell me one thing, Steve: can you see the Italian state from here?'

'I understand, Don Salvatore.'

'Hey, Steve, two words are too much for you, you understand everything. Steve Cement, a sure thing: strong as an ox and far from stupid, more trustworthy than anyone and silent as the grave. But have you got the balls of an ox as well? Sorry, Steve, I can't contain myself, but let me finish my speech and pour yourself another drink now that our period of abstinence is over! Maybe the boys in Palermo, the guys down the sulphur mines in Alcamo, maybe they know what the Italian state is? Or all the gentlemen and the poor fools who want to bring Sicily into the federation of the United States. What is the Italian state? Can you eat it? In Milan and Palermo, in Turin and Reggio Calabria they don't even speak the same language, they don't even understand each other, haven't you noticed that? What the Italian state does, says and thinks is decided in Washington DC. And since Washington is full of cock-sucking son-of-a-bitch politicians and judges spouting endless bullshit and acting like the flag-bearers of justice, "even fleas are starting to cough now", as they say in Naples, and they're trying to break people's balls. Now they're claiming we gave drugs to those perverts in Rome for their parties, their orgies, maybe they can't get it up without a bit of help. Because the politicians and other big shots were there, the kind of people who beat up girls and leave them dead on the beach. They're saying this guy Montagna came to Naples to get some drugs, from me! It's all made up, it's all lies, children's fairy tales to put in the papers. But you know who's spinning this bullshit, Steve? An American cocksucker like me and you! That loser creep Charlie Siragusa, who's trying to get his career back on course by instructing the cops down here. Ever seen the Italian cops, Steve? Fat, lazy, sweaty cowards. Charlie Cocksucker is fighting a losing battle. But even in successful battles soldiers on the winning side sometimes get killed. This guy Siragusa is scum, Steve. Scum. He's busting our balls, ok, but in the end he's a has-been. The only people they can get on side are losers, stoolies, but they've got to choose them well, not like that old nut Abbatemaggio. Eighty years old and forty of those he's been a rat. He knows nothing! Don't you worry, Steve, they'll come and beg our forgiveness, cap in hand, because they owe us everything, we're too important, we're making them *modern*, ain't that right, Chip? Have a biscuit, good little doggie. All kinds of decent, wealthy God-fearing people come and will continue to come to my shop asking for washing machines or the latest American TV, eh, Steve? Because they're all after it now, they all want it, this new miracle of progress. A gadget that'll allow them to forget their debts, infidelity, their problems and the fact that they don't matter a damn, do you agree, Steve? But now everyone's slobbering to have a television set, and the people who can't afford one are just going to accumulate more debts. They're so worried about the communists, but let me tell you that communism, Steve, is never going to take in Italy, it ain't going to happen, not just because we're here to stop it, but because the Italians are too lazy, they're too happy having the future sold to them to organise the present, to earn their daily bread and knock up every woman they touch. No, Steve, no communism here. Too much bother.'

'No communism, Don Salvatore.'

'There's one thing that interests me, Steve, that boy who's always with you, can he be trusted? You've got some kind of business going together, his mother pulls your dick every day, tell me.'

'Don Luciano, the boy takes bets at the racetrack. He's a *bravo guaglione*, as they say here, a sound lad. He's smart, too. But he's inexperienced. He got pinched at the start of the year, something about a theft, and while he was in there the bastard inspector who's on my back asked him a few questions about your business and mine. When he got out, he was scared, he came to see me, he came to tell me everything, that he wasn't a rat. So I thought it was better to take him around with me for a while, so that no one could ask him any more questions or make strange suggestions to him. So, Don Salvatore, the boy is my responsibility, don't you worry about him.'

'All right, Steve, you see, as long as you're not doing anything stupid, you're in quite enough bother already, aren't you? One last thing, by the way, Steve: at the end of the month I'm going away for a few days, to Meta di Sorrento, to the house of the *Cavaliere del Lavoro*, to get a bit of fresh air and sip on some of those wonderful lemon granitas they have down there. One week, ten days at the most. I'd like you to stay in town until I get back: come and check on the house, go and see the boys in the port, do a couple of collections, have Vic help you.'

'Please, Don Luciano, I'm feeling a bit tired. I was going to ask you for a few days off.'

'But of course, Steve! Why not? Do I not know that even Steve Cement is made of flesh and blood? It's the first time I've heard you say anything of the kind, do you know that? Although it had occurred to me. When I get back, you take a month off and go wherever you like, have some fun, screw a few whores. I know it's been tough on you staying here, that you're not showing it out of respect, that you miss New York like you'd miss oxygen. I've already talked to Albert Anastasia. He said you can go back to them at the end of the year. I can just imagine his face! Who wouldn't want to have Cement taking care of his affairs?'

'Don Luciano, thanks. It's an honour for me to be able to work for you. Even if I never see New York again.'

'No, Steve, you deserve every appreciation, the very idea that you mightn't always be with me fills me with gloom.'

Chapter 39

Genoa, 27 June

'Are you sure we're going in the right direction?'

'Of course. I've been here before.'

The labyrinth of alleyways and sheds ran monotonously past the window.

'Where does the harbour end?'

'It doesn't. That's why it's a good place for smuggling. When are the cops ever going to find the goods in this lot?'

They parked the truck. Ettore and Pierre got out near the imposing sides of the ships flying flags from half the countries in the world.

Pierre strolled along behind his mate, looking up. The cranes worked in a steady rhythm, the stevedores threw hundredweight sacks at one another as though they were footballs. Ettore gave him a nudge and tensed his biceps, laughing behind his moustache.

'What did you say our ship was called?'

'*Querida*. It comes from Venezuela.'

'What's the Venezuelan flag like?'

'How the fuck should I know?'

'Is this guy Paolino to be trusted?'

'With your eyes closed. He was a partisan, one of the really hard ones. During the war the SS tortured him, they knocked out all his teeth and he never squeaked.'

The black letters stood out against the side of the vessel, *Querida*, and underneath, in smaller letters, *Caracas*.

'There it is.'

Ettore walked towards a group of dockers, swapped a few words with them, and they pointed him towards the gangway.

It was filled by an enormous man. He was wearing a striped shirt with short sleeves and a sailor's cap. His arms were blue with tattoos: mermaids and dragons chased each other along his muscles. A half-lit stub hung from his lips, like an inseparable part of his sunburnt face. Impossible to work out how old he was.

His mouth twisted into what must have been a smile: the Nazis hadn't left much in there.

'Hi, Ettore. It's been a while . . .'

'It must be two years.'

'Who's the boy?'

'One of mine.'

Paolino pointed towards one of the warehouses. 'We've just unloaded the barrels.'

'Fine,' said Ettore, lighting a cigarette. 'Tell me, how's Venezuela?'

'Hot.'

When they had finished loading the drums of naphtha on to the lorry, Paolino offered them a drink.

'Do you travel much?' asked Pierre when he had taken a sip of his wine.

'All the time.'

'It must be interesting going round the world.'

The man looked at him as you might look at a turd on a footpath. 'The ports are all the same. Same whores. Same prison faces.' He sealed his sentence with a blackish gob of spittle on the floor of the bar.

No one present was shocked.

Pierre hunched his shoulders, but didn't stop asking questions.

'What if someone wanted to get a job on one of these ships?'

The sailor smiled. 'To go where?'

'Away. I don't care where.'

His smile broadened. 'Every now and again someone shows up who's in trouble with the police. But they have to be comrades, and they have to be able to pay. There are contacts. I know a load of people in South America.'

'When do you leave?' asked Ettore, trying to cut the discussion short.

'Ok, we're going down to Naples, on the way back we're stopping in Civitavecchia and Livorno. Then we come back up. In two weeks we're setting off for South America again. And we'll stay there for a bit.'

'The petrol's selling well. I can do you a deal on some if you like.'

'I'll bear it in mind.'

'We should get going now. We have to be in Bologna this evening. See you, Paolino.'

'See you, old man, see you soon.'

'So, cat got your tongue?' Ettore asked as they left the city.

'What . . . ?'

'Are you thinking about sex, or are you going to sleep? Eyes on the road!'

The vastness of the port opened up below them. From that distance the ships looked like toys, but Pierre thought he could still remember all their names.

Albatros, Marseilles. *Father's Blessing*, Monrovia. *Saint George*, Plymouth. *Catarina*, Buenos Aires. *El Loro*, La Habana. *Querida*, Caracas.

'I need money, Ettore. I mean, apart from the money I owe you.'

His friend gave him a strange glance. 'To go to South America?'

'If a big job comes up, keep me in mind. I'm not worried about the risk.'

Ettore grinned. 'There'll be a good opportunity, even for you.'

The arch of the Gulf of Genoa stretched towards the sea. The ships were arrows pointing in a thousand directions.

Chapter 40

Hollywood, California, 28 June

If I should suddenly start to sing
or stand on my head or anything
don't think that I've lost my senses
it's just that my happiness finally commences.

George and Ira Gershwin. 'Things are Looking Up'. A good
omen. Grace's voice from her dressing room. Hitch smiled.

'How come no one ever talks about Louis XV?'
    'And why should they talk about him, excuse me?'
    'I mean: people are always referring to Louis XIV, that is, the Sun
King, or Louis XVI, the one the revolutionaries sent to the guillotine, but no one ever says anything about the one in the middle.
There's no "*style Louis XV*" that I'm aware of. Am I right?'
    'About what?'
    'About the "*style Louis XV*". Have you ever heard anyone talk
about it?'
    'To tell you the truth, no.'
    'Or maybe they skipped a number?'
    'Who?'
    'The Louis.'
    'Why would they have wanted to do that?'
    'Umm . . . Because fifteen is an unlucky number in France?'
    'I really don't know.'
    'I've got it! Maybe the heir of Louis XIV wasn't called Louis! It's
like popes!'
    'In what sense?'

'In the sense that the new pope isn't obliged to use the same name as his predecessor. Perhaps between the two "Louis" there was, I don't know, a Jean.'

'I fear you've got me there, my darling.'

'Although I could be wrong. Louis XVI wouldn't have been called that if there hadn't been a number XV.'

'What on earth are we talking about?'

'When we have a child, you won't want to call him "Cary", will you?'

'Does this seem like the right moment to . . .'

'Ok, ok, calm down. Listen, I'm going to my Zazen session, I'll see you later.'

In Hollywood, in the Paramount studios, Cary and Betsy were watching the preparations for the magnificent, glittering final scene of *To Catch a Thief*: the masked ball, the night of confusion. Hitch strutted about among admiring female visitors and gigantic wigs, whalebone corsets and parrot cages on sticks, exotic masks, drapery and brocades . . . Betsy had asked whether the style of the costumes was Louis XIV or Louis XVI. Cary couldn't tell, but it all struck him as very baroque, and therefore, in his opinion, more XIV than XVI. Cary was thinking about something else. He was thinking about the dreams he'd been having over the past two weeks. He was thinking about Senator McCarthy who, after accusing the Pentagon of being a hotbed of communism, had realised he was going too far. Political observers said that his career as a witch-hunter wouldn't last beyond Christmas. Even the FBI seemed to be taken by surprise, lost for words and bereft of strategies: whatever you might say about Hoover, the army was the army. The end of a nightmare, in every sense.

Frances Farmer had come to see him. She was wearing Grace's clothes and saying the things that Elsie had said. She called him 'Archie'. She talked to him about McCarthy.

Today I don't even know where I am, Archie. Somewhere in America. When people see me they nudge their friend and say, 'Once she was a communist, now look what she's reduced to!' Today the friend could reply, 'You see communists everywhere.' It isn't revenge, no one will ever avenge me. It's a paradox. The knights enter Toledo and sweep away the Inquisition, but it's too late for me: there is no longer any space between one wall and the other. The witch-hunter will lend his name to this era. On the other hand, memory of me will slide into oblivion, so much so that no medium will be able to reclaim my spirit. Not even you will be able to.

I have come to you like this many times, Archie. I have not gone to Clifford. I have not gone to people much guiltier than you. I have not gone to anyone else. I came to you because you needed me. Just like that. Fate is a skilful and ironic scriptwriter, Archie. I, the falling star, left your life just as your mother was returning to you, a comet heralding a rebirth. For one woman everyone thought was dead, coming back from the hell of the asylums, another fell into it, and now they think she's alive.

In this world there is not an Orpheus for every Eurydice. But you are Orpheus, you are the Acrobat whose leaps enchant the wild beasts, and stop rivers and winds. You are the man who revealed the mysterious rites to the plebeians, and that is why the demons hate you, and the Maenads want to tear you to pieces. You have passed through Hell in search of my ghost, in search of yourself and your double, your double and your mother. You have done your duty in fighting the Dauber, you have run across deserts, over hills lit by the pyres of the witch-hunters, pursued by dogs, you have escaped ambushes to meet the Man of the East, and you are not even out of breath.

You are the ass that Apuleius wrote about, Archie. You are the palingenesis. You don't have to feel guilty, not for me or for yourself or for Cary. Each man has a different task to accomplish. There are ways and ways of saving witches. 'Things are Looking Up'. Let's raise a toast to the end of the Inquisitor.

> Bitter was my cup
> but no more will I be the mourner
> for I've certainly turned the corner.
> Oh things are looking up
> since love looked up at me.

Grace came out of the dressing room, ready to play the role of 'Frances' for the last time, happy and unaware of what was happening, imagined deaths and rebirths, metempsychoses and descents into hell.

She couldn't get the song out of her head, or off her lips.

Chapter 41

Bologna, 29 June

Italy eliminated.

Four goals in the play-off against Switzerland. Everyone home.

Gas had been mistaken. Apart from the World Cup, there wasn't much on television throughout the summer. They could talk about it again, more calmly, in the autumn. Or not. Melega and Bortolotti had paid him a visit. He was to find a new television, and be quick about it. They wanted to see *Anche oggi è domenica*.

A wretched programme. The listeners send in letters. They express wishes. Twelve of them are selected. Their wishes are granted.

An old man in his nineties had been in Rome as a boy. He had thrown a coin into the basin of the Trevi Fountain. According to legend, that gesture guarantees a return visit, but the old man had never been back. Can you resist the double temptation of saving an ancient legend and fulfilling the dream of a dying man? No. *Anche oggi è domenica* makes his wish reality. The old man smiles in front of the fountain. People are moved.

An Italian immigrant in the mines of Belgium is married by proxy to a Calabrian girl. He has never seen her. He hasn't the money to pay for the journey. Who will make their meeting possible? Exactly.

A girl from Florence got a bike as a present from her dad. The same day someone stole it. Now her dad can't afford another one. Don't worry, little one: *anche oggi è domenica*. An identical bicycle is delivered to the girl beneath the smug eye of the television cameras.

Gas had had a clever plan: why don't you lot write in? We've collected all our savings to buy a TV, but a thunderbolt struck the aerial and destroyed it. Now our children are crying because they can't see your programme. Help us.

Gas had dodged a slap. 'You write in.'

'If you make things up they can tell,' Bortolotti insisted. 'And then they'll report you.'

Gas had promised. He had gone to work. He had found someone he could palm off the television to in return for a Phonola. Not as expensive, but still a luxury item.

It was five by the kitchen clock. He would have to get a move on. He slipped his fingers into the side indentations of the great beast and struggled to lift it from the table. His sciatica was acting up.

He headed for the door.

The cat slipped between his legs in pursuit of its ball.

He lost his balance. He fell to the ground. He propped himself up on the elbow that had hit the floor.

He raised his eyes and immediately closed them again. He couldn't look.

Bloody hell!

The screen was shattered. The fascia on the back had come away. The cat was hunting around inside for its sodding ball.

He kicked it away. He knelt down behind the set to see if the fascia could be put back. A minor problem, given the state of the screen.

For a moment he didn't understand.

What the hell were those little white bricks inside the television? A moment later, he half understood.

That was why the bloody thing didn't work. That was the swindle. They'd taken out the mechanism and filled it up so that no one could tell the difference. Ingenious.

His third thought took him three-quarters of the way to complete comprehension.

Strange little bricks. Couldn't they have used rocks?

He stretched out a hand. He weighed one of the packages in his hand. Unrolled the cellophane.

White powder.

Well fuck me with a ragman's trumpet!

He had got there.

He went to run his hands through his hair, but just ended up stroking his bald pate. He had never even *seen* this stuff. What sort of stuff was it, in fact? Cocaine, heroin, morphine? Who the hell had put it inside the television? The package seemed to glow.

He tried to calm down. Fine, old man, here you are with – how much? Ten kilos? Twenty kilos? Of what? Heroin? Cocaine? It looks as though, potentially, you're rather a wealthy man.

Potentially: you don't know anyone who could tell you what it is. No one who could buy it. No one.

He tried to calm down. In the meantime you're going to have to hide it. Then phone Fattori and tell him you won't be selling the television. Then find a new screen and put in some real bricks and sell it again. But in the meantime you're going to have to sell that stuff.

Potentially, you're very rich.

Chapter 42

Naples, 30 June, 1 p.m., during the partial eclipse of the sun

Three men who were lost in the forest were captured by cannibals. The cannibal king told the prisoners that they could live if they passed a trial. The first step of the trial was to go to the forest and get ten pieces of the same kind of fruit. So all three men went separate ways to gather fruits.

The first one came back and said to the king, 'I brought ten apples.' The king then explained the trial to him. 'You have to shove the fruits up your arse without any expression on your face or you'll be eaten.'

The first apple went in . . . but on the second one he winced in pain, so he was killed.

The second one arrived and showed the king ten berries. When the king explained the trial to him he thought to himself that this should be easy. 1 . . . 2 . . . 3 . . . 4 . . . 5 . . . 6 . . . 7 . . . 8 . . . and on the ninth berry he burst out laughing and was killed.

The first guy and the second guy met in heaven. The first one asked, 'Why did you laugh, you almost got away with it?' The second one replied, 'I couldn't help it, I saw the third guy coming with pineapples.'

The boy had told the story on their long journey back from France. He had never stopped talking. Shithead. Nonsense, all of it, that was all he needed. Salvatore.

What was he to do? Shake him off, get rid of him?
No.
Are you getting old, Steve?
The boy knew almost everything. Too much, without a doubt.

He had a knack of getting himself into trouble, but energy, vitality, burst from every inch of his skin.

His instinct told him: the boy isn't the problem. You've got other problems.

'Because everyone's after it, everyone wants it, this new miracle of progress, isn't that right, Steve?'

Shit. Did the old man know everything? Was he delivering those long speeches just to give his fucking mouth some exercise?

Pay attention, Steve. The ball is spinning.

Rien ne va plus.

The number played, always the same one. Fifteen. The kilos stolen from Luciano. The pension. Three of them already at their destination, then another twelve inside the McGuffin. In Bologna. Fuck.

'Stiiiiiv! You have no idea, you can't even imagine what Lisetta and I have done. With the help of your car, obviously. Try and guess, Stiv, go on, try. No? Fine, then I'll tell you: we've found it. It's in Bologna.'

Yes, ok, Bologna. He could be right. But who had it? And after all this time was the powder still inside?

Almost impossible.

The meeting on the other side of the border was imminent. Skullface Toni was itching to collect his last cut. Monsieur Alain had the stinking breath of his Parisian friends on him: pimps, toffs and doped-up musicians.

'I've spoken to Albert Anastasia: you're going back with them at the end of the year. To New York. The thought that you might not always be with me already fills me with gloom.'

Luciano. The biggest son-of-a-bitch on the planet. Dull-eyed, gazing into the distance. Behind corners, behind walls. At racetracks, in televisions. That was why he was still alive. And still the boss.

What possibilities did he have? Pointless question, now. He'd have to get moving. *Rien ne va plus.* Try. The life-and-death triple jump of Cement Zollo.

Bologna.

The lorry driver.

Over the border. Alain the fat guy. With or without the powder: different plans, same result.

Paris. Airport.

Where to? Was there some asshole in the universe that Luciano's dick couldn't penetrate?

'While we were shooting the film, Stiv, there were these two guys, they were Italian as well, talking about a rich man from far away, someone like the emperor of China, and he'd bought this huge diamond, a thing this big that cost God knows how many millions. They said it was called *Durban*. The diamond. And that it came from Cape Town, which is in South Africa. And that in South Africa, in that place, it's full, can you imagine, Stiv, full of diamonds like that. So much so that I found myself thinking: why don't we go there, Stiv, why don't we go and take a look? We could buy the diamonds and then come here and sell them, eh, Stiv? To all those rich guys drowning in money who like that kind of thing. Sure, first we'd have to go and talk to the city boss. Otherwise he'd get pissed off, wouldn't he, Stiv?'

Durban.

Cape Town.

South Africa.

Why not?

Far away. Hot. Sea. Business.

Improvise, it might be the solution.

Cape Town. Why not?

The boy had balls. He had demonstrated as much. He pointed the way.

He would come after him. He couldn't stay in Naples. Then he would decide.

The ball is in motion, Steve.

A shadow has fallen across the sun.

You can't be Cement all your life.

Chapter 43

The Certosa cemetery was half deserted. It wasn't visiting day for the dead. In the summer, people want to think about life, so almost everyone was out on the street or in the hills looking at the eclipse.

Cemeteries didn't make him feel sad. Whenever he went there he always found himself reading the names on tombstones, with dates, photographs, Latin phrases, wondering what kind of life was hidden behind each of the tombs. He imagined lives consumed in a flash or worn away over a long period of time, to the very last drop. He thought of the friends and relatives that those people had left behind.

He was early, and he whiled away his time doing the same thing. He wandered about in the middle, flowers in his hand. When he felt his heart pounding he knew she was there. He looked up and saw her.

He didn't walk towards her, but took the path and walked to the grave, stopping and waiting for her there.

Angela had brought flowers as well. White ones.

Pierre reflected that she had more class than many daughters of the bourgeoisie. Perhaps it was something innate. Either that or it was simply taste, attention to detail, a graceful way of being in the world.

Fefe's photograph showed him smiling.

He had to tell her. He had so many things to tell her and he didn't know where to start.

She looked at him. Her features were more relaxed, and she had a strange gleam in her eyes.

Pierre was almost frightened.

She put the flowers in the vase.

'I wanted to tell you that I've decided to go away.'

The sentence struck him like a fist to the sternum.

He could only murmur, 'Where to?'

'I don't know yet. I've got a bit of money put aside. But I can't stay here any longer.'

He had to ask her, now or never.

'Come away with me. I want to leave too. I can't put up with all this any more.'

Angela gave him a hint of a smile, the first in weeks.

'No, Pierre. I'm going away on my own.'

The words stuck in his throat.

Pierre became aware of a profound sorrow within himself, something that would mark him forever, a barrier of hate and pain erected against the world.

She glanced towards the grave.

'It's the only way of giving any meaning to what happened. Because Fefe didn't die for nothing. He wanted me to be free.'

'He wanted you to be happy, Angela.'

'When he worked out that I couldn't be happy, he decided to free me. He gave us a lesson, Pierre, he gave it to everyone. He was too weak to rebel. And now I'm too sad. Throughout the whole of my life I've never been able to choose. Someone, something has always made my choices for me. Necessity, misfortune. Now I'm on my own. I want to start over from the beginning, in a different place. All I have here is horrible memories.'

Pierre felt like bursting into tears, but he contained himself.

'Am I a horrible memory, too?'

That half-smile again. 'No. But you too must make your decisions on your own. You can't stay in suspense for ever. What you have isn't enough for you, and I can't give you what you want.'

'I want you.'

'That's not true. Neither of us knows what we want. We just know that we have no future here. That's why we've got to go, each our own way.'

Angela seemed gigantic, as though he had always underestimated her, as though the person he had loved was now someone else, a thousand times harder and stronger than he. Pain had seared, turned her into iron.

She brushed his cheek with her hand.

'I love you, Pierre. But you can't share my pain. No one can.'

Once again, Pierre heard the thud of that door closing, leaving him in the dark.

He could think of no brilliant words to say. He couldn't find the right facial expression. He stood there, motionless, as she said goodbye to him.

'Can I at least ask you for one last kiss?'

She shook her head. 'No. Better not.'

'You can't deny someone a hug.'

She looked at him as you might look at a child. Her eyes lingered briefly on his tight sweater, his clinging trousers.

'You look like a boxer who's about to thump someone.'

She said it tenderly. She loved him. Really.

'Goodbye, Pierre.'

She walked along the path.

Pierre swallowed back the lump in his throat. Was this how it all ended? Was this how he would let her go?

No tears. No breaking voice. Master of the situation.

He gritted his teeth, caught up with her, and put a piece of paper in her hand.

Angela stared at it, perplexed.

'It's the address of an English family. Fanti gave it to me, and I trust him: he's a good person. Fanti will write to them, they'll help you. Go to them, Angela.'

For a moment he saw that light gleaming in her eyes, the same one that had made him fall in love with her.

He understood that she would have been enough for him. For the whole of his life, if it came to that.

Chapter 44

Ten hours' driving, three coffees, two simpamine tablets . . .

At dawn somewhere near Siena. Florence, another tablet. Bologna.

Park the car. Give the consignment to Shithead. Split up.

Morning spent on recces.

The bars, the main squares, the taxi ranks. Taxi drivers know every-thing about everyone. They drive, they listen, they see. Taxi drivers are involved in the black market. Retail deliveries and contacts.

The eight o'clock sun warms up the square. A pigeon feasts on a crust of bread. Small crowds gather beneath a kind of castle.

They are farmers. They are peasants. They are discussing the purchase of cows, hundredweights of beetroot, potatoes and calves. Where the fuck have you fetched up? In the Middle Ages?

You throw a few questions around. A certain Ettore, a certain truck. You get blank looks in return. The identikit spreads like an echo. Someone who carries freight between Naples and here. You get indecipherable comments and shakes of the head. Last shot: that lout in the foreground has the most incredible handlebar moustache anyone's ever seen!

You make for a bar on the other side of the street.

He runs towards you, hugging himself and shouting. Your eye freezes and you press your index finger between nose and chin. When the fuck is he ever going to learn to shut up?

He gets within reach. You grab his shoulder and drag him to the wall.

'What the fuck are you shouting about?'

He speaks under his breath, *now*. You can barely make out what he says.

'I've found it, Stiv, are you happy now? It's in a shed just behind the new hospital, right over there.'

The new hospital is a vast and dusty building site. The man stops the bulldozer and points beyond the fences to the area where the sheds are.

Storehouses for bricks, railway sidings, scrap heaps. You pull on the handbrake, you get out and ask. You go in and out, at a lick.

Your head is crushed with sleep. The simpamine returns it to sender. Bullseye at the fourth attempt. A mean-looking bastard.

'Ettore's not here, he's gone on a delivery.'

'Doesn't matter: you might be able to help me. I'm looking for a television. Signore Camarota, from Frosinone, told me you should –'

The bastard interrupted. 'A television? Yes, yes, wait, I think I remember. A nice big television?'

'A nice big one, yes, that's right.'

'Then that's the one. We delivered it to a bar in San Donato.'

Bar Aurora.

We're there. You push open the door, a glance around. The old men look up from their cards. No televisions, but there's another room at the back and the click of a game of billiards. Hope yet.

'Can I help you?'

'I'd just like some information: I'm looking for a television, big, American-made, I was told you had one.'

'We had one.'

Shit! Take the magnet off the zero. Toni, get the gun ready: time to get paid even without the stuff.

'You had it. Then what?'

One of the old men turns on his chair. 'Then it was rubbish, we couldn't get it to work. So we told the man who sold it to us to get us a new one, and there's been no sign of the layabout for a good ten days now.'

'You mean Ettore?'

'God no. Gas, they call him, or Castelvetri. Gaggia, you've got a good memory, what's his first name?'

'Adelmo.'

'Adelmo Castelvetri? Do you know where he lives? I can give him a good price for that television.'

'I think he lives in Via Mondo, is that right, Gaggia?'

The fiftieth cigarette since the start of the journey finds its way to your mouth without your noticing.

The old man's voice: 'When you find him, I don't suppose you could give him a couple of slaps from us?'

The front door is open.

'We got there, eh, Stiv? Are you happy?'

You no longer have the strength to get pissed off.

'Check the doorbells, hurry up.'

First floor: Galassi . . . Mazzanti . . . Zaccheroni . . . Second floor: Alvis . . . Monari . . .

Castelvetri.

'Who is it?'

'Package from the Bar Aurora.'

He opens the door. Gleaming bald head. Reflex action: foot against the door.

'We heard you wanted to sell a television.'

'A television?' The man blanches from his chin to the back of his neck. 'You were misinformed, I haven't got a television. Goodbye.'

He pushes the door but can't get it closed. A blow of the forearm opens it wide again.

Just as you reach for your belt, the boy's voice: 'Stiv, look, the television!'

It's on the floor, under the clothes horse. A cobweb of cracks runs across its screen. It has been eviscerated.

You are blind. Brain OUT OF SERVICE. All you can see is a patch of light. You yell like a wounded grizzly. Your fist gets him right on the back of the neck. He crumples to the ground. You turn him over with a kick, land heavy blows to his chest. The sound of breaking ribs.

'Where is it? Tell me where it is!'

You slap him. Back and forth. He licks away a tooth and tries to speak.

'Wh-wh-what?'

Your hand under his jaw, as though he was a bottle of champagne waiting to be uncorked. A toast to Steve Cement.

'The stuff that was in the television, *asshole*. Get it out. Right away. Salvatore, turn over this place like a cart of shit.'

Interstellar panic. 'It was empty, I swear.'

'Like fuck it was, you dickhead. You were too quick there, in the doorway.'

'I swear.'

Careful. If you let yourself go now, you'll kill him. No pointless wandering. Control. Steve Cement's style.

You rummage in a pocket. You flick out the blade. You wave it under his nose.

'Where?'

The vomit momentarily prevents him from speaking. He must have shat himself as well.

'On the bed, in-inside the pillow. Don't kill me, please don't.'

You run into the bedroom. You rip the guts out of the pillow.

Rien ne va plus.

Fifteen.

Chapter 45

On the corner of rue des Abbesses, a coughing fit took his breath away. He leaned one hand on the wall and the other against his chest, bent double by his retching. When the crisis had passed, he rested his forehead against a poster for the Quatorze Juillet, and stayed like that to get his breath back. A man asked him if he needed help. He was more or less the same age as himself. He could have been mistaken for a sick eighty-year-old.

He started walking again. The sultry weather of the past few days had put ten years on him. Tuberculosis did the rest. Two or three times a day he had near-fatal attacks. Then he looked around and decided, no, this wasn't a suitable place to kick the bucket. Public toilets, stairs of the metro, an anonymous footpath scattered with shit. He was starting to think he wouldn't manage to leave this world in his own way. Perhaps that was why he'd decided to take a break? If the jewellery job worked out, he would be gone. Destination: Martinique. The last journey of the old Indian warrior choosing a beautiful mountain on which to pass away in peace.

No, that was bullshit. Stuff for savages, far too spiritual. The Toni of former times would have laughed at the very idea. Dying at peace with the world! Far better to spit your last fragment of lung in its face. The ideas of today's Toni were more confused.

The moment he entered the bar, the sweaty pig gave him a nod from behind the bar.

'What's up, Joël?'

'Someone called Zollo rang. He says it's urgent. He left this number.'

Toni picked up the piece of paper, asked for a Pernod and walked to the phone.

Behind him, the usual doomsayers called him a 'ghost', 'unrecognisable', 'nothing but skin and bones'.

He asked for a line. He talked to a stranger. He waited.

'Toni?'

'Finally. I was beginning to worry.'

'Where and when.'

'Sospel, just beyond the border, in the car park of the old *relais*. Tomorrow, about three in the morning.'

'Fine. Within twenty-four hours you'll have the rest of your percentage.'

'You're a gentleman, Zollo. It's been a pleasure doing business with you.'

'The pleasure is mine. And make sure you enjoy your holidays, now.'

Chapter 46

Naples, 2 July

So Steve Cement isn't in Naples any more, no one's seen hide or hair of him. Trimane says he left with a boy from Agnano. At first I was furious, I was, then I calmed down because Salvatore Lucania knows the guy, and he understands him, and he knows it wasn't his fault, this fucking country turned his stomach like nigger wine from Harlem, and I understand Steve, because my stomach's like that as well. But Salvatore Lucania must be able to trust him, he must know that a dog doesn't start pissing indoors, he's got to know that a dog doesn't have fleas or mange.

That fucker Siragusa wanted to fuck me good and proper, and Steve Cement might just be the Vaseline; the cops drew lots, some kind of stunt to see if Steve Cement would sing, like that fucking jockey did, or that wretched Camorra man back when dinosaurs walked the earth. So did they think this was a festival, that the best singer wins a prize? And did they all think that Salvatore Lucania is a fucking faggot, that he likes to take dick up the ass?

But Steve's a good guy, when all's said and done. He won't sing.

But now the dog has mange.

Chapter 47

'Fuck it'

Zollo shut the bonnet with a terrifying thud.

Pagano curled up in the seat. Dish of the day: sour grapes.

Zollo sat back down in the driver's seat and lit a cigarette. He was tired, he hadn't slept for two days, he felt as if he had a brick where his brain should be.

'The carburettor's fucked,' he said, puffing away the smoke.

Pagano suggested, 'Let's look for a mechanic.'

'This is an American car, Shithead, you won't be able to get the right parts.'

Zollo was furious, he was tired, drained, but he *had* to think. That night they were waiting for him on the other side of the border. If he didn't show up the whole deal would go up in smoke, end of story, he would have to set off with the packages in his bag and try and find a buyer somewhere or other. Too risky. By now, Luciano must have noticed he had fled. His time was running out, there was no leeway any more, he had to get out *now*. Things have a time limit. To go beyond it is to risk exposing yourself. He had been exposed for too long. Luck had been on his side, it had helped him find the heroin. He couldn't ask any more than that. Now what he needed was an idea and one final burst. With the little breath he still had.

Think, Steve, think. You'll have the rest of your life to think as much as you want. Now you've got to finish the game . . .

He sprang open a false bottom under the seat and took out his Smith and Wesson.

Pagano was terrified: 'Oi, Stiv, I'm your friend!'

Zollo gave him a sideways glance, stuck the revolver in his belt and buttoned his jacket. Then he stuck the reserve magazine in his pocket.

He got out of the car, opened the boot, took the bag and slipped it inside.

He took out the spare wheel and leaned it against the back seat. He used his flick-knife to pierce the tube and transferred the piles of banknotes into the bag. Before he closed it he put a few in his pocket.

'Get out.'

Pagano didn't have to be told twice. He stood hesitantly by the car.

He saw Zollo taking the car registration documents and emptying the vehicle of all the rubbish he had placed in it: file cards, waste paper, street maps, postcards.

He tore it all up and let the wind carry off the scraps.

The file cards and the licence plate went down a manhole.

One last glance; nothing left.

'Let's go.'

Zollo walked along the pavement.

Pagano stayed where he was, scratching his head.

'What's going on, Stiv? Where are we heading?'

Zollo stopped.

He had that look on his face that frightened the life out of you.

'We're going back to France.'

'But how? On the train?'

Steve Cement waved the banknotes around.

'With these. Be sure and stay behind me, because if you do anything dumb, I'll shoot.'

He was serious. Extremely serious.

Pagano hurried to join him.

The warehouse was enveloped in summer haze. Ettore, sitting on the rocking chair, let the two men approach him. You could tell in an instant that they were foreigners.

When they opened their mouths there was no doubt about it.

'You're the one who brought the American television from Frosinone to here, isn't that right?'

The answer was implied. Ettore didn't waste his breath.

In many years of trafficking and smuggling he had learned to size people up at a glance. The guy standing in front of him fell under the category of people like himself. He could smell them a mile off. The ones who are neither bosses nor workers.

'And you must be the one who was looking for it.'

Zollo nodded.

'I have to get to France by three tonight. Without crossing at a border post.'

Ettore stroked his moustache.

He wasn't a cop. He could smell them a mile off too. He was a hunted dog like so many others. And usually people in a hurry are willing to pay well.

'Big place, France.'

'I just need to get across the border.'

'Menton?'

'Sospel.'

'Are the police after you, or is it some people you've swindled?'

Zollo ignored the question, took a couple of wads of notes from his pocket and threw them in Ettore's lap.

'There'll be the same amount again once we get there.'

Ettore counted the money. 'French francs. Clean?'

'Won in the casino.'

'That'll do fine for the journey. Are you carrying any other goods? I've got to know what sort of risks I'm taking.'

Zollo hesitated.

'The risks are high. That's why I'm paying decent money. If you don't feel like doing it, I'll go elsewhere.'

Ettore looked at the bag that Zollo was clutching.

'Is that all the luggage here?'

'Yes. There are two of us. There's the boy as well.'

Pagano waved in greeting, but his gesture looked thoroughly ridiculous.

Ettore weighed up the pros and cons. It was a hefty amount of money. A round journey. He knew the smugglers' route, he'd taken it on other occasions.

And getting to Sospel was easier than getting to Menton.

He wouldn't mention it to Bianco. The owner didn't approve of night transports. That cut out the other guys in the company. It wasn't wise to take the journey alone, without anyone watching out for your back. That guy with all the money looked as though he was in difficulties. Serious difficulties. Better to take the due precautions.

He got up and walked to the telephone.

'Are you ready, Robespierre? We need you tonight . . . Come to the warehouse straight away, we're going in an hour . . . I don't give a fuck about the bar, didn't you say you needed some cash? Well, there's a fair bit involved, enough to settle your debts and a bit more. We'll be back tomorrow . . . Ok, get a move on.'

Ettore came out of the cage that served as an office and planted himself in front of Zollo, who had lit his umpteenth cigarette in the meantime.

'Sorted. We're off in an hour.'

He went out to the back and opened the padlock of an iron box.

He took out a Thompson and two Lugers, wrapping them in a blanket.

Before closing the box he hesitated for a moment, and then picked up a couple of hand grenades.

Life had taught him to heed his forebodings.

Chapter 48

The tram was half empty. Pierre went and sat down at the back and slid open the window.

A fair amount of cash, Ettore had said. How much?

A risky journey. Where to? What for?

Pierre had skipped the questions to hurry to the meeting, but before jumping into the truck he would want some answers.

Risk meant: red-hot goods or a high likelihood of a check of some kind, customs perhaps. A fair amount of money meant enough to pay off his debt with a good bit left over. A hundred thousand? That was three times his monthly wage.

Pointless hypotheses. Better to wait.

Once it was empty, his brain found itself occupied by a new tenant.

Had Angela already spoken to Montroni? What had they said? Pierre imagined her cold, determined, as he had seen her after Fefe's death. What would she have told him about the hospital file? Would Montroni suspect him? Would he take his revenge? Without a doubt, Angela's departure was a kick in the pants for his uncertainties. The enemy wouldn't leave him alone. The enemy was very powerful. The trip to Genoa had come at exactly the right time. Ettore's money even more so.

The first right things at the right time that had happened to him since the start of the year. It could be a good sign. A reversal of a trend. Better not to have any illusions.

Angela. It's strange to think about a person so close to you whom you might never see again. You feel a void opening up, but not in the future, which is almost always a void. It's the past that seems to deepen, to pass once and for all, to become a photograph.

Even before he met her at the Certosa, Pierre knew that Angela wanted to leave. He had given her Fanti's contact in England.

He had done it because she needed it more than he did. Strong as she was, she was still a woman on her own, an adulteress, without a job, with nowhere to go.

But he had done it for himself as well. To allow a thread, however slender, to bind him to her, the only one that she wouldn't sever in an instant. If she decided to go to London, he would know where to find her. Fanti would pass on news from him. He could write to her.

A sudden jolt stopped his thoughts mid-flow. He had to get out.

He found Ettore, who was carrying two petrol cans to the lorry.

'Here I am.'

'Perfect. Help me fill her up, and we'll set off.'

'Where are we going?'

'France. Just over the border.'

Good guess.

'And how much are we being paid?'

'I haven't done the sums yet. For you it'll be around about 80,000.'

'Fine. You want me to help you load?'

'No, don't worry, no point.'

'No point? So what are we carrying?'

Ettore pointed towards a big guy who was walking towards them. 'Him.'

Pierre took a closer look. There was something familiar about the man.

Where had he seen him before?

. . . the cretin with the pigeon!

Zollo came and stood in front of Pierre's disbelieving eyes.

An image of the boy bent double to vomit, on the ship going back to Yugoslavia, flashed through the American's mind. Between his legs, the cage with the bird in it. The funnel inside his brain was suddenly blocked with thoughts.

Zollo didn't like coincidences.

He didn't try to guess. He didn't *want* to.

He raised an eyebrow slightly. He took a step forward.

He said, 'Cary Grant has never been to Yugoslavia in his life.
You've never spoken to him. He told me himself. You're a klutz.'

He walked towards the lorry.

Ettore finished checking the tyres. 'We're going on a long journey,
it's better if we swap names.'

The American nodded. 'Zollo.'

'Bergamini.'

They shook hands.

'Is he coming with us?' asked Zollo, pointing to Pierre.

'Yes. He's my helper.'

'Can he be trusted?'

Ettore pointed towards the warehouse, where Pagano was trying
to catch the air pump that he had inadvertently switched on, as it
fought like a snake.

'Can yours?' Ettore shot back.

No one spoke.

The two passengers climbed in behind, in the body of the truck,
where rudimentary seats had been installed, with sacks and blankets.

Ettore sat down at the wheel, Pierre beside him.

When the the lorry nosed on to the drive, Pierre felt a shiver
running across his shoulder-blades. He couldn't have said why, but
his instinct was to turn around and look at the warehouse.

'So do you know that guy there?' asked Ettore.

'I saw him on the ship coming back from Yugoslavia. He was
giving orders.'

'And what was he transporting?'

'I don't know. I didn't see any passengers on board.'

'What's Cary Grant got to do with it?'

'No, Ettore, it's far too long a story, and I'm starting to think I
dreamt it.'

Every time he climbed into the lorry next to Ettore, Pierre saw once
more, as from the top of a tower, the twisted paths that had brought
him here, further and further away from 'normal' life, from what
decent people consider *legal*. A clandestine expatriate, without
papers, on a smuggler's boat, then the bar cellar turned into a storehouse for American cigarettes, then Genoa, the theft from the archive

of the Villa Azzurra and now this new trip that even Ettore called 'risky'. And along with all that, as constant as arthritis, the empty wallet. The James Bond of the poor.

'I'd like to ask you a question: how did you end up doing this job?' asked Pierre, as the lorry jolted its way down from the Pontelungo, in the far west of the city.

'It was the middle way between bank robbery and working in a factory,' Ettore replied, speaking to the windscreen.

He was silent as far as Borgo Panigale, where he cadged a cigarette and picked up his thread. 'In fact, I've tried to do another job, but it didn't do it for me. I'd learned to drive a lorry in the military, and after the war I started doing this. It'd all be fine if the boss didn't pay so badly, so to make an extra bob or two I reached an arrangement with the companies and used the lorry for my own trafficking. One day the boss catches me at it and fires me. So I decide: *that's enough*. I had a bit of money put aside, borrowed some more, and bought myself a little rig.'

'And you worked on your own?'

'Yes, specially for cooperatives. That was the problem. In '48 I was thrown out of the Party and the co-ops turned their back on me. Then Bianco showed up, an old comrade from the brigade. He said, if you want I can fix you up with a job.'

'And how did they get involved in smuggling?'

Ettore smiled. 'I asked the same question. Bianco said to me, "Ettore, listen to me: Italy is a boot, we've tried to polish it, but the place for a boot is always in the mud. For the first little while, at least, things were clear: everyone knew that if you didn't have a Party card you couldn't work, and you took a few kicks for your pains as well. Now, because we're a democracy, things have got even dirtier. The law isn't equal for everyone. If you've got friends, if you do people favours around the place, then you do your trafficking, you get rich and no one is going to say a word to you. Otherwise, forget it. You can't do this, you can't do that either. And meanwhile the real criminals are making millions. So I tell you," he said, "that *my* war, now that no one's allowed to kill anyone any more, involves fucking over those criminals, their friends and the people who defend them, and making money right under their noses."'

'He wasn't completely wrong,' Pierre remarked, amused.

'Well, he certainly convinced me.'

Pierre would have liked to know something about Ettore's expulsion from the Party, but he thought he had asked enough questions. They still had a long journey ahead of them. He could save some for later.

'Stiv, what am I doing exactly?'

Pagano's voice reached him from another dimension, above the noise of the engine.

It wasn't a comfortable journey, the body of the truck was dirty and the sacks they were sitting on were hard.

'Did you hear me, Stiv? Now I . . .' he underlined the concept by pointing his index finger to his chest, '. . . *what the fuck am I doing?*'

The boy wore a strange expression, he looked as though he had resigned himself to a gloomy idea.

'Stiv, I think you want to kill me the way you would kill a mangy dog. And of course you wouldn't tell me, you're waiting for me to go to sleep or turn away from you, like, "Shithead, pass me that blanket," and I turn away and *pffft* with your gun that doesn't make a noise. Then you throw me into a ditch the moment the lorry slows down.'

Zollo said nothing, and lit a cigarette without looking at him.

'Ok, Stiv, listen, I want to tell you that I understand. That is, it's not so much that I like the idea of dying, it really makes me sick and I'm dying with fear, but I know you can't just let me loose, because I've worked out how things stand. You can't go back. You've put Don Luciano in this position' – Pagano crossed himself as though he had mentioned the devil – 'and he kills people for a slap, let alone for drugs. He'll flay us both alive and polish his shoes with our skins. And you can't trust me, because I'm an irresponsible wretch.' He hunched his shoulders, lowering his head. 'You know, Stiv, I enjoyed looking for that television. We went all over, we saw a load of places, we drove the car at speed, I drove it when you were in jail, too, we went abroad, to the casino, I won all that money from the Chinaman and then made a film, an American film, and when they see it in the local cinema they'll have to shut their traps and lower their heads when Kociss turns up on the screen.' He smiled. 'In short, it seems to me that even if I lived to be ninety, there wouldn't be a place for Salvatore Pagano any more. That's all I wanted to say to you, and I'm saying it because I've done a lot of thinking on the subject. Because if you do decide to shoot me, I won't hold it against you. It was me who sold you the TV, it was me who got you into this trouble.'

He fell silent, as though waiting for a reply.

Then, in a low voice: 'So, Stiv, what are you doing? Are you going to kill me?'

'Listen to me carefully,' said Zollo, rubbing his temples, 'I don't want to hear another peep out of you, ok? I have to think. If you go on talking I won't be able to. When we've crossed the border it'll be your turn again, and you can fuck off wherever you feel like it. As long as it's far away from me, ok?'

Pagano rolled his eyes as a bend threw him backwards. 'Thanks, Stiv, I knew you were a friend. I never really believed that you wanted to kill me, I was just talking for the sake of it, because after all, you know, hypothetically speaking, I mean, just hypothetically speaking if you *had* wanted to kill me, I would have understood, I'm not saying that I would have forgiven you, but –'

Zollo took out his Smith and Wesson and held it under Pagano's nose. 'If you don't shut up, I might just change my mind.'

Pagano apologised, folded his arms and kept his mouth shut.

Zollo felt his stomach burning: coffee, simpamine and cigarettes was not the breakfast of champions.

Think, Steve, think.

The boy wasn't a problem. He'd just have to keep him out from under his feet for long enough to do the deal. Then he would let him have his money and goodbye.

The problem was a different one. Toni had vouched for them all, and you could trust Toni. But you never knew what was round the corner. Right now, Luciano must have been chewing the carpet. He couldn't take that leap into the dark alone, he needed a cover. Someone to watch his back for long enough to get the money and run. Sospel was a one-horse town, he would have to reach a city, with a railway station or a coach station, and get to Paris from there. And from Paris to South Africa.

What was it that old Sam Giampa had said to him as he broke

the scabs' arms down at the docks? 'Professionalism, Steve, is giving the maximum even in the worst conditions.'

What he needed was a means of transport and a determined accomplice. He glanced towards the cabin: maybe fate had put the right person in his hands.

The last race, Steve, the home straight. The final details of an improvised plan coming miraculously to a good conclusion.

A few hours and it would all be over. Steve Cement would vanish for ever.

Grit your teeth, Steve, nearly there.

He knocked three times on the wall at the end and felt the vehicle slowing down.

Zollo nodded to Pierre to get into the body of the truck. The boy got out. He couldn't contain himself.

'Sir . . . I wanted to say . . . You don't have to believe me, but I really did meet Cary Grant. In Yugoslavia.'

Zollo looked him up and down. 'When this business is over, you can tell me what you were doing on the ship with that pigeon.'

He went and sat next to Ettore.

When the lorry set off again, they sat there in silence, one concentrating on the road, the other on the night around them.

Zollo couldn't find his bearings: he didn't know these roads. They seemed to run right through a great big void. Ettore drove in the summer darkness as though he had radar in his brain. But there was nothing out there, some fields, perhaps, houses. Very seldom they saw the headlights of a car. Otherwise, they could have been the last four men on earth.

'So?' Ettore asked, lighting a cigarette.

Zollo did the same, he had stopped counting them.

'I've got a problem.'

Ettore nodded. 'I know. You're on your own.'

Zollo became aware of something like a pin-prick at the base of his skull, the light that came on when his forebodings about someone were revealed to be accurate.

He made an offer. 'If you'll cover my back there's a pile of money in it for you as well.'

'What are we going to do?'

'An exchange.'

'Of what?'

He would have to tell him: a person who's risking his life wants to know what he's doing it for.

'Drugs for money.'

Ettore didn't flinch, eyes fixed straight on the road.

'How much?'

'Enough to change my job and move to a place in the sun.'

Silence again.

'Who's waiting for you?'

'The buyers. They shouldn't do anything silly. But you never know. There could be someone else on my trail.'

Ettore nodded, he had worked out from the urgency of the operation that the American friend had fucked someone over. Someone who was going to be seriously pissed off.

'The drugs aren't yours, are they?'

Zollo didn't reply, there was no need.

'How can we trust each other?' asked Ettore.

Once again, Zollo studied the void on the other side of the window, the void that was the Po valley. Few subjects for conversation presented themselves.

'How many people have you killed?' he asked all of a sudden.

'I don't know. In war, you don't count them.'

'Then we're equal. And we'll play as equals.'

Ettore thought that was a good reply. They both knew that their scruples had been left behind the moment the lorry set off. They knew they were dangerous guys. Their only guarantee: determination.

'Fine.'

Zollo opened the case and took out some more wads of francs.

'Here's a bit more cash.'

Ettore barely glanced at them. 'Put it back. We'll count it at the end.'

Once again Zollo felt that pin-prick at the base of his cranium.

He pointed back at the body of the vehicle. 'What about the boys?'

Ettore nodded. 'They'll stay in the lorry. They'll have their share. But if I'm going to keep you covered I want a free rein. I have a couple of old Lugers that'll fit the bill.

*

The lorry set off again with a sudden jerk. Pierre's eyes weren't yet accustomed to the dark. He lost his balance and fell into the arms of the Neapolitan.

A voice asked, 'What are you doing, you feeling me up?'

Pierre turned on to his side, smiled and held out a hand in the dark. 'My name's Robespierre Capponi, forgive me.'

'I'm Salvatore Pagano, known as Kociss, like the footballer and like Cochise, the Indian chief. Can you tell me yours again, I didn't get it?'

'Robespierre. It's a French name. Robespierre was a French revolutionary. But everyone calls me Pierre.'

Once again, Kociss didn't understand. Robberswhat? But the nickname was fine: Peer. Christ, what if he was a poof? You know the way French names . . . Close to his home there was a famous one, who taught the trade to drag queens, and everyone called him 'Sgiacc', meaning Jacques, although his name was Antonio. But with all the names there are already, why would you have to go to France for one? But maybe he wasn't a poof. Maybe he was just French.

'Were you born in France?'

'No. Near Bologna. I've never been to France.'

'Really? You've *never* been to France? Hey, it's a shame we have so little time, Peer. Because France is a great country. There are women there you wouldn't believe. I'm speaking from personal experience: I was in France a month ago, to make a film.'

'A film?' Who knew what he meant by 'film'?

'It seems strange, doesn't it? Now, because we're in the dark, but if you looked at me more carefully in the light, you'd recognise me. I'm sure you've seen me, I've got the kind of face that people remember. That's why the directors are always calling me up.'

'And what film did you make, in France?' There was a hint of sarcasm in the question.

Kociss gripped his quiff in one hand. 'Damn, look, I can never remember the title, it's an American title and I can't keep it in my head. But I can tell you the name of one of the actors, the best of the lot, before you say his name you have to wash your mouth out with soap, wait, wait, Gary Grent?'

'*Cary* Grant,' Pierre corrected him, certain that the Neapolitan was pulling his leg. He must have made an arrangement with that

other man. Mr Rock-Hard, who had asked Grant *in person* whether
he had ever been to Yugoslavia. No doubt on the next stretch of the
journey Ettore would tell him that Cary Grant was acting as an intermediary between the Red Star and Allied Command. That was what
annoyed him the most. To have met *a myth* and not to be able to
tell anyone. Like the story about the shipwrecked man and Marilyn
Monroe on the desert island. She fell hopelessly in love. On the fifth
day of unbridled sex he says to her, Marilyn, if you really love me,
dress as a man and let's meet on the other side of the island. She
thinks it's going to be some kind of erotic game. But the moment
they meet, he giggles, jabs an elbow into her ribs and says, 'Oh,
Gianni, you'll never guess what's happened to me! Incredible: for the
past four days I've been fucking Marilyn Monroe!'

'You don't believe me, do you?' Kociss's voice was disconsolate.
'Yeah, I know: you meet someone in the back of a lorry and he tells
you he's made a film with Cary Grant and Winston Churchill. Who
are you trying to kid? I understand you, but when the film comes
out, take a good look at the scene with the fight in the middle of
all the flowers. The guy in the maroon shirt.'

'I do believe you,' Pierre interrupted him. 'I believe you because
I've met Cary Grant as well, and when I tried to tell people, they
all laughed in my face.'

There was a moment of silence.

'Hey, you've made a film with Cary Grant too!'

'No, I met him in Yugoslavia. Some people were shooting at him,
and my father and I saved his life.'

'Oh, I see.'

Was he winding him up, or what? Was it a way of saying he didn't
believe a word? Or when someone says one thing, and the other
person has to come out with something even bigger? Like the bloke
with three balls on the tram who goes over to someone and says,
'You know that you and I have five balls between us?' And the other
man says, 'Oh, you poor thing, have you only got the one?'

Kociss locked his fingers behind his head and lay back on the
sacks.

Pierre did more or less the same thing, rocked about by the potholes
and the engine. A moment before falling asleep, he managed to catch
the beginning of a long monologue.

'Here, mate, I really did meet Cary Grant! And I wasn't giving you a load of bollocks about that film, either, I exaggerated the bit about being an actor, because at the end of the day I'm still at the beginning of my career, it was pure chance, I did make an appearance, but everyone told me I was really good, and they even paid me, and I'm sure that some Italian director . . . Oi, Peer, are you listening to me?'

In the war you didn't count them.

In fact some people did count them, and cut notches in the barrel of their gun.

In clashes in the middle of the woods it was hard to tell who was killing who.

And it had been hard at Porta Lame, as well. There was fog. There were smoke bombs. Ettore was sure he had killed at least fifteen, firing his Thompson gun and throwing two hand grenades.

There had been loads of them, in Bologna. More than a hundred partisans, between their base in the ruins of the main hospital and the one in the building in Via del Macello. At dawn on 7 November the Germans had encircled the block and captured some guards. The battle had begun at seven. The Germans, flanked by the Black Brigade, had had rifles, machine-guns, light guns and two cannon. They were shooting from the roofs of the nearby buildings as well. On the other side, nothing but automatic weapons, rifles and hand grenades. After five or six hours of fighting, with the block practically razed to the ground, the partisans had managed to move and take up position in another building.

The Krauts had brought in an armoured car, they had brought it into the courtyard and were shouting 'Giff up! Giff up!' A Houdini-style escape route had been found (that's Houdini the conjuror, not Houdini the greengrocer in the Cirenaica district): a wall was knocked down, and they had escaped along the canal, leaving smoke bombs to cover their retreat and splitting up into little groups. They had actually managed to evacuate the wounded. Late in the afternoon reinforcements had arrived. The partisan detachment from Medicina. Germans and fascists, taken by surprise, had made off, leaving behind 260 dead, a few injured and vehicles loaded with ammunition.

The partisans had got away with twelve fatalities.

He had never done a job like that before. But the game was worth the candle. There was the money. And there was the shiver along the spine. For too many years he hadn't risked his skin. His life had gone flat. No great joy, no great grief, no great rage. Many women, but no major relationship. One-night stands. Hours and hours spent with Palmo, who was a moron.

If I'd died at Porta Lame, or up in the mountains, my face would be up on the memorial in the Piazza del Nettuno. With my friends, for ever. With the fallen of the Valanga group, with Dubat, who killed himself in a cave rather than allow himself to be captured by the Germans, with Carioca, Ettore Bruni, Edoardo, Ribino, Aldo, Ferro, Silenzio, Renato. With Stelio, who had been tortured for thirty-six hours in Via Siepelunga, like Irma Bandiera, like Sante Vincenzi the night before the Liberation. Stelio disfigured, tortured, hanged in Via Venezian. 'Justice is done' was the headline in *Il Carlino*.

But if I die tonight, what will people remember of me? That I was a smuggler, a criminal. They've thrown me out of everything, I have no right to be remembered as a partisan.

Who knows what *Il Carlino* will write about me if I die tonight.

I should have died at Porta Lame. And instead here I am, protecting someone transporting drugs. A scary guy. I wonder if he's a friend of that famous 'Steve Cement', the one whose name is used to frighten children?

I would guess that in those little circles, no one is a friend of anyone.

Chapter 49

Time 2.40 a.m. Sospel. A hamlet. Pungent air. Around it, woods and mountains.

Ahead, the plain. The headlights reveal a sign: '*Relais l'Étape, 500 m*'. The white road climbs among the chestnut trees.

Zollo gestures to Ettore. *We're there.*

The lorry draws up to the crossroads. Ettore picks up his arsenal and jumps out. Thompson gun, hand grenades and a flare pistol. As in Porta Lame.

He runs through their roles again. 'The young guys keep an eye on the lorry. I go and take up my post. You show up at three on the dot.'

Zollo nodded. *Rien ne va plus.* He raps his knuckles on the back of the lorry. 'Ok, come out for a moment.'

They appear after a few minutes. They have the creased faces of people who have just woken up. They need to be reactivated. Two simpamine tablets for his migraine and two to fight their sleep. Ettore prefers to use dialectics.

'Lads, listen to me. If we get it right, in less than an hour we'll be walking happily away from here. To get things right you have to be alert. Each of you will have a gun, and eight shots. Only use them if you have to. Your task is to protect the lorry. If the lorry is damaged, we won't get away. Is that clear?'

Zollo looked at the ex-fighter. *We know what to do.*

Pierre turned the gun around between his hands as though it was a Martian's dick. Ettore gave him some hints about how to use it, then slipped into the wood.

The hamlet seemed to be enclosed in a silent glass bowl. A gigantic hand might suddenly have turned it upside down and unleashed a storm of fake snow. Pierre leaned his back against the lorry. Fake papers, an undercover expatriate, a storehouse of illegal goods, smuggling. Whether he ended up using it or not, that gun was the cherry on the cake.

The American gestured to him to get up, all three of them into the cabin. Pierre gripped the wheel and put the lorry in gear.

Kociss seemed to be hypnotised. Eyes wide open, staring. From the movements of his lips you would have said that he was praying.

Mr Rock-Hard said nothing. Every now and again he rolled his neck around and rearranged the gun in his trouser pocket.

It's all going to go smoothly, Steve, come on.

Precautions aren't the same as paranoia. The era of cock-ups is past. The age of the diamond is beginning.

Toni has given us a guarantee. Moby Dick is a decent son-of-a-bitch.

The breakdown of the car forewarned of the final cock-up. Turning up alone for the meeting, with twelve kilos of heroin and the king of Agnano keeping him covered. Script courtesy of Steve 'Dickhead' Zollo.

The *Relais l'Étape* hadn't served *soupe de pistou* for at least ten years. The sign that extolled its high quality and moderate prices was peeling. The lorry turned around the building. Zollo peered through the glass: not a table, not a chair. Empty.

The car park was badly lit. Old banners hung from a string. A flash of headlights greeted the arrival of the lorry.

'Stop here.'

Pierre parked on the right, by a low wall.

Zollo picked up the bag and jumped down. The gun barrel froze him, from groin to shoulders. Contrary to his usual form, he wore his shirt out of his trousers like a Hawaiian twat. Just to cover the weapon.

He took two steps forward into the dust, slipped his hand under his shirt and rested the bag between his legs.

Come on. Don't make me nervous. Be on your best behaviour.

Moby Dick was wearing his white suit, as he always did. The two bodyguards were dressed in black from head to toe. They looked like the keys of a piano.

Zollo stepped forward. Moby Dick was clutching a holdall.

The shots came from the roof of the restaurant.

The great white whale and the two sharks fell almost in an instant. Zollo didn't throw himself to the ground in time. The bullet struck his right arm. He felt the bone crack. He went down. He crept through the dust as another two shots shattered the earth. He reached the Frenchmen's car. Slipped inside. His arm was saying goodbye to him. He slipped the bag under his belly and gripped the gun with his left hand.

They're shooting from up above. From the roof.

Like the Germans and the Black Brigades.

Like at Porta Lame.

Open up a gap. Evacuate the wounded. To do that: kill the snipers. To kill the snipers: see them. To see them: light them up. The flare-gun. Gift from the cross-border guys, for use in emergencies. Use it. *Stoompf! Fiiiiiiiiiiii . . .*

The firework comes down and lights up two startled faces: Germans posted on the sloping roof, tiles fall, a helmet, one of the two is tied to the chimney pot with an improvised sling. The other gets to his feet, stumbles and slips sideways, shouts, dazzled, raises his arms to cover his face. The other tries to climb back up towards the chimney-pot, skids, more tiles fall. You shoulder the Thompson gun and fire. Got him. He tumbles clumsily, the shots deflect his fall. *Crash*. The sound of bones splintering. You shoot again. Got him. A head exploding. Corpse hanging from the rope. Throw yourself to the ground.

More gunfire, from beyond the low wall at the edge of the car park. Right at the back, invisible except in the flashes of machine-gun fire. Black Brigades. Three, maybe four. The torturers of Irma Bandiera, Stenio Polischi and many other patriots. Traitors and murderers, they must die.

The wounded comrade is alive, he's returning fire. But now it's me they're after. Holes in one of the lorry doors. It's going to take pluck. It's going to take courage.

We were criticised for always going on the attack. Lupo was made that way, he took risks, he raised the level of the challenge to the Germans, he made incursions that struck other people as foolhardy.

I must take risks too, or we'll never get out of this. Defend my comrades. Avenge the fallen. Myself. Give a meaning to all this.

If necessary, die.

Stiv is still alive. I saw him firing.

What'll I do now, Christ I'm scared!

They're all firing.

Is this a film too?

They're slogging their guts out. These are Don Luciano's goons. Christ alive, Stiv, shoot, shoot!

Now they're firing at the Bolognese guy. He's raising hell like no one else.

I can't believe what I'm seeing.

What the fuck am I supposed to do with this gun? Do I shoot? I can't see a fucking thing from here. Nothing but big black bogeymen.

Get it to Stiv? How?

Bastards, villains, murderers, Stiv, let's get out of here!

I start to crawl.

The Bolognese is a raging demon. Kill them. Kill them all.

Pierre had stretched out on the seats, and every now and again he peered out over the dashboard.

You can't be a match for *any* situation.

The windscreen had exploded. A splinter had grazed his leg.

They were firing at him again, and he had no idea who the fuck they were.

He couldn't breathe properly. He swallowed irregular mouthfuls of air. Acid throat. A chasm in his stomach. Guts under pressure. He felt he was sweating shit.

He raised his head.

He peered through the shattered glass.

He saw Ettore come out into the open.

He saw Ettore running like mad.

He heard the shots.

He felt fear twisting his guts.

'Red Star to viiiictoreeeeeee!'

Major Mario, look at me now. Fuck, if you were here to see me!

The shout and the running take them more by surprise than the rocket. They wonder what the fuck I'm doing. A few seconds. The two seconds I need.

Pullthepinfromthegrenadeonetwothrowandhurlmyselftothe-ground-BOOOOM!

Fragments of brick, blood, a pair of glasses falls on my hand.

Now they're firing from somewhere else, to the right. I roll forwards. The Black Brigade comes out into the open, bang! He's down. The injured comrade shot him, or maybe one of the boys.

Excited whispers, footsteps running in the dark. I must act first. Red Star to victory. I pull out the pin, rise on to my knees, onetwothrow-BOOOM! I hear them screaming . . .

Ettore was hit in the back by a hail of gunfire. Zollo saw him falling heavily and crouched there waiting for the bastards to come into the open.

Ettore had one set of balls, thought Zollo. He had had fist-fights, he'd killed people, but he'd never fought a war. The influence of the Anastasia family had kept him out of that. Ettore, on the other hand, had been there, he'd told him. One hell of a guy. He'd never seen a guy like him among the wiseguys.

He had saved his life, with the bright idea of the rocket.

He had to kill the bastards.

Not just to save his skin.

Pierre raised his head after the two explosions. His ears weren't working. The muscles in his back were so tense they hurt. He noticed that his fists were clenched, his teeth gritted.

He looked at the car park in front of him. Ettore was no longer there.

He lowered his head, took a breath, and looked again.

Ettore was on the ground. Motionless. The dust all around was clogged with blood.

Pierre's skin crawled. He succumbed to a fit of the shakes, unable to contain them. His teeth chattered like castanets.

He saw two men coming out of a shattered glass door behind Ettore.

One of them stretched out his arm and shot him in the head. The other one walked cautiously towards the Frenchmen's car.

Pierre gripped the gun. He crouched down, took a breath and tried to aim.

He was trembling. He was terrified. He had never fired a gun in his life.

He wouldn't be able to hit his target even at a third of the distance.

Not with a pistol.

He put down the Luger, slipped into the driver's seat and turned on the engine.

He lowered himself to one side, his cheek against the steering wheel, and put his foot down.

The lorry jerked forwards in a cloud of dust. Skidded to the right. Skidded to the left.

Pierre felt the impact against the mudguard, a dark mass was thrown beyond the front of the lorry. Pierre heard at least four shots being fired. He ran on and stopped beside the Frenchmen's car.

Pagano heard the lorry setting off.

He took advantage of the dust and the confusion and made his mind up.

In his hand, the pistol was no use to anybody.

In Stiv's, that was a different matter. Stiv might have run out of bullets. He hadn't heard him shoot for a while.

Maybe he was dead. No, he didn't even want to think about that.

He knocked over a drum, jumped out and ran, his back almost parallel to the ground.

He lost his balance. Rolled the last five metres.

Stiv wasn't dead. Not bloody likely. He was Cement.

'Here you are, Stiv.'

The boy. The Luger.

You grip the pistol.

A moment later the fucker stops shooting. The last one.

The lorry pulls up beside you. The other boy offers you his hand.

'Come on, get in, we're going!'

Zollo said nothing. Zollo just waited. Zollo listened to the silence.

Was that really the last of the fuckers?

'Help me get in, Salvatore.'

Zollo clutched the door. 'Go and get the Frenchman's holdall, now. Quickly.'

The boy ran off. The other man helped Zollo into the lorry.

'Turn round and drive slowly towards the exit.'

In the wing mirror Zollo checked the recovery of the booty.

Pagano picked up the holdall. Ran back to the lorry. Threw it in, into the back of the lorry.

Zollo opened the door and held out a hand.

Pagano took it.

Two shots. The boy relaxed his grip and rolled to the ground.

Zollo nearly pulled off the handbrake handle. The lorry skidded.

Zollo got out. He went over to the boy's body. The bullets had perforated his lungs.

He leaned over him.

'Stiv . . .' Blood rose into his throat, he tried to spit it out with a gurgle, his hand gripping the collar of Zollo's jacket. 'Stiv . . . Were you taking me with you?'

Zollo clutched that hand until he felt the grip relaxing, and Pagano's eyes turned to glass.

Pierre's voice reached him from the lorry. 'Is he dead?'

'Yes.'

Pierre released the handbrake and put the engine in gear.

'Let's get away! Come on, let's get away! They'll kill us, too!'

Zollo stared at the boy's corpse. He looked up, slowly. He saw the shadow waiting for him.

The last one. Vic Trimane.

A test of trust for him, too. 'Whack Steve Cement, Vic. Clip your buddy'.

You don't escape Lucky Luciano. You don't get out of the coils of the snake.

Again he heard Pierre, calling, 'Jump in! We're going!'

Zollo got up and started walking calmly, one step after the other, towards the advancing shadow. There was no hurry now.

He saw Vic lift his gun.

Zollo took aim and emptied the magazine without stopping.

The third shot hit its target: he saw Vic's brain spatter through the air. See you, goombah.

He fell to his knees.

The blood drenched his shirt. How many had he got? Two, three? Vic was a good marksman. He found himself staring at the last stars as they went out, up at the top of the sky.

Pierre had crouched down on the seat again. He stuck his head out through the door.

Mr Rock-Hard was on the ground, motionless, crucified.

The Neapolitan was on the ground, on his back in a pool of blood.

Ettore was on the ground, his head mashed in the dust.

Other bodies lay on the ground. Dead.

He was alive.

He set off down the road at a lick.

No pension, Steve. No diamonds. No South Africa. Shame, you nearly made it. Sorry, seriously, after coming so far. No point trying to lift your head, it's like you're made of wood. The bullet must have hit your spinal column. Your leg, one hand, the muscles of your face. Cement.

Stefano Zollo's triple death leap stopped after two somersaults. It was a good jump.

You can't be Cement your whole life.

Last spin of the wheel. Last look at the woman you would have loved.

What's she like, Steve? Gorgeous, of course. Really, she doesn't know what she's missed.

What a grand finale. You thinking about it, Steve? Cape Town, sun, green fields, and a manhattan always right in front of you. Do they know how to make manhattans in Cape Town? You've had a go, goombah. Don't be too hard on yourself, what happened happened.

There, the ball's at rest.

Fifteen, odd, black.

Chapter 50

She folded up the blouse and put it on top of the others. The taxi would be there any moment.

She counted the money she had changed, closed the bag and pulled the strap tighter than necessary.

She looked at herself in the mirror, smoothed her hair and put the finishing touches to her make-up.

The doorbell rang.

She had taken everything.

She dragged the cases to the door.

'I'll be down in a moment,' she whispered into the entryphone.

The corridor looked longer than usual. At the end, behind his study door, was Odoacre.

Angela didn't go into the room. She felt she couldn't get any closer, that she had to keep her distance. She felt the certainty of what she had to do.

She looked him in the eyes as she delivered her final words: 'You're an absolute shit. We both know why. Goodbye.'

She had nothing else to say to him. There was no need. She stayed on the threshold just long enough to fix that expression in her mind. Then she closed the door.

The corridor had shortened again.

Chapter 51

Shitshitshitshit . . . Pierre, suitcase in hand, jumped ditches stumbled over stones, splashed the hem of his trousers, stopped every now and again to throw up, then come on! come on! come on! get away from the slaughterhouse, *but who the fuck were those guys, where the fuck am I? where the fuck did they come from?* Malevolent spirits from the scrubland, Ettore and the other guy had returned their fire, Ettore had thrown the bombs, like when he was in the partisans, Ettore had died in combat, he had saved his, Pierre's, arse, and now here he was with a case bursting with *money, spondulicks, argent, dinero,* he had seen it, piles and piles of it, dollars and francs. And bags of white powder. Drugs. Without a doubt. *Too dangerous, shit!* He had thrown the drugs away, he had found a hole in the ground, under a half-uprooted tree, and stuffed it in underneath, covering it up again as best he could. He had to slip away as quick as he could, cross the border again, there might be more of those demons around the place, who could tell. Who were Kociss and Mr Rock-Hard? Why had he been on the same ship coming back from Yugoslavia? What did Cary Grant have to do with it? Who the fuck were those people who had tried to kidnap him on the little island? Was there a connection? He couldn't understand any of it. *That's the second shooting you've been involved in in less than three months. Both times partisans saved your arse. But you've got the money, Pierre. If you make it out of this forest alive and you manage to take a train or a coach, get back to Genoa, then stay in hiding for a while and take a ship to . . . To where? Ask Paolino, the longshoreman. And what will Paolino say when he sees me turning up without Ettore? I've got to tell him that . . . No, fuck, I won't tell him anything! Just that I want to leave as soon as possible. And the lorry?* He had driven the lorry two or three hundred metres back and left it in the depths of the forest. *Do I have to tell Palmo that I've left the truck there? What am I talking about, have I vomited up my brain as well? Christ alive, the French cops will find the lorry after they've found all the bodies and scoured the area. And I'll never see Palmo again. I'll never go back to Bologna. Nicola . . . never see him again . . . The bar . . . The musketeers . . . Professor Fanti . . . Aunt Iolanda . . . Angela. I'll never see her again. My father.*

I'll never see anyone again.

I'm a man on the run.

But I've got the money, and a ship to catch.

I'll take whatever ship Paolino can find me a place on, then contact my dad and tell him to come as well.

A man on the run.

Pierre stopped to throw up. He swore he would never vomit again as long as he lived.

He couldn't see a fucking thing. When was the sun going to come out?

Ten-hour train journey.

Genoa.

Paolino asked no questions. He put me up in the house of a friend of his and Ettore's. Maybe he guessed something was up, maybe he knows.

The radio delivered the first confused news of a bloodbath just across the border.

There's a ship bound for Mexico, it sails the day after tomorrow.

Money opens all doors, portholes, valves. Money can buy you the nutshell on which to plant a paper sail, a toothpick as a mast, go on, towards the Southern Cross.

Mexico. Veracruz.

On a crumpled scrap of paper I have the address of a comrade who's in Mexico City. He fought in the Spanish Civil War. Who knows, he might even know someone in the bar.

You see, Angela, you see that I'm managing to leave as well?

You're going to the cold, I'm going to the heat.

You're going north, I'm going south.

You're going across the Channel, I'm going through the Pillars of Hercules.

It's always been like that, basically. You go one way, I go the other. Sorry.

I've got the money.

A sea and an ocean away, Mexico.

What do I know about Mexico? Nothing.

And furthermore I don't even know where this money comes from. I don't know a thing.

But I'm alive.

'Hello?'

'Hello, Nicola, it's me, Pierre. Listen, I can't tell you where I am, but –'

'Are the cops after you?'

'What?'

'There's an article in *Il Carlino*, Pierre. Front page.'

'Shit.'

'Some people have been killed, near the French border. Ten or fifteen dead. One of them was a Bolognese smuggler, Ettore Bergamini, "ex-partisan turned criminal", it says in the paper. He was expelled from the Party and the Partisans' Association, years ago. I remember that guy.'

'Nicola –'

'They found his truck nearby. There were Mafiosi involved as well. There are photographs. One of them dropped by the bar a few days ago, he asked me for the television.'

'Nicola, listen –'

'No, you listen to me, Pierre, do you think I came up with the last drop of rain? Did you think I wasn't aware of what you were up to? I don't know what kind of a mess you've got yourself mixed up in, and I don't want to know. But if you're in the shit it's your fault and yours alone, and don't think I'm going to sort things out for you this time.'

'Nicola, for Christ's sake let me get a word in! I'm leaving Italy, for ever! It's all sorted. I can't stay here, it's dangerous, I've got to go away, I'm leaving tonight.

'Well done, good timing.'

'What?'

'Dad's just turned up.'

Chapter 52

When he saw it emerging on to the wharf, he immediately recognised the van of the Bar Aurora. It proceeded slowly; he had given precise directions, but in the labyrinth of the port it wasn't easy to get your bearings. It was dark; the only light came from the big, tall streetlamps that cast their light on the sheds, goods ready for loading and motionless crains.

Paolino spoke in a low voice. 'Is that them?'

'Yes,' replied Pierre, coming out of the corner and waving towards the van.

The engine was switched off and the passengers got out.

He saw them approaching. The Capponi family, reunited like this. Clandestine, and about to part again. He would never have imagined it.

Two men walking slightly apart, unable to escape the distance that time had imposed, the embarrassment and the difficulty of the situation.

Here we are, thought Pierre, the last survivors of the past half-century. The Capponi family. Partisans, revolutionaries, fighters, certainly that, defeated, perhaps disappointed, smugglers definitely, dissidents, stubborn. Vittorio, the hero, Nicola, the hard one, and Robespierre, the dancer. *Here we are, perhaps for the last time, to say goodbye and all the other things we have kept inside for all these years.* Was he ready? Yes, he had had time to prepare. And there was nothing left to lose now, he had to walk towards his fate with his head held high, whatever it might be. *A leap in the dark, that was what you wanted, Pierre, wasn't it? You wanted something different, you wanted to go away, what you had was not enough.*

He hugged his father.

'When did you arrive?'

'Two days ago.'

'How?'

'On foot. I still know the paths through the Carso. I couldn't stay hiding out in the mountains, Robespierre. I had to see you again.'

'Did you go and see Aunt Iolanda?'

'I gave her a shock: she thought I was a ghost. We talked all night. She gave me a pullover and a scarf for you.' Vittorio patted the travelling bag slung over his neck.

'Did you tell her we're going away?'

Vittorio nodded. 'She says that you and I are the kind of Capponi who can't stay in one place, the ones with the itch, the wretches. But she loves you from the depths of her heart.'

Pierre reflected that he would have given an arm and a leg to hug Iolanda and say goodbye to her as he should have done. But time was short. He would write to her, yes, once they had reached their destination.

His eyes met Nicola's, and he was surprised not to read the usual anger in them. In those dark eyes there was something not unlike resignation.

'Thanks for coming with dad.'

A mangy dog passed through the beam from a streetlight, a solitary shadow in the deserted wharf. Paolino pointed behind the cases and whistled. 'It's time. They're lowering the gangway. You'll have to board.'

A little mobile gangway was coming down from the side of the moored ship. There was no time left.

Pierre felt that the tangle of thoughts he had in his head would have to be loosened.

'Nicola, I've got a ton of money. It's dirty money, but I didn't kill anyone to get it. I found it in my hand, like that, whether you believe me or not. You can come with us. What are you going to do here?'

His brother looked at him and shook his head. His eyes were as hard as his voice.

'No, Pierre. It doesn't work like that. There are people who go and there are people who stay. I'm one of the ones who stay.'

Nicola looked at them both, then turned to Vittorio. 'You can't always leave. Not everyone can leave. Someone's got to stay behind. You went to Yugoslavia, you chose to make the revolution there, where the communists had won. I stayed here, even after '48, when times got hard, when we had to roll up our sleeves and defend democracy one inch at a time, in the factories, in the streets. Our resistance didn't stop when we came down from the mountains, it's continuing even now. And if we weren't there, if we had all gone as you did, who knows what this country would be like now. No, someone must stay in his place.' He spoke fluently, he spoke more than he had ever spoken before. 'I'm not angry with you any more. I'm not angry with my father who left us alone, or with my no-good brother who has given me nothing but anxiety. The fact is that your place is not here.' His lips narrowed and he added, 'I'm not forgiving anyone, but I don't feel angry. I'm happy that you're going away together, because you're the same breed. You're the kind people who leave.'

A long silence followed, interrupted by Paolino's irritable voice: 'Get a move on, you buggers! There isn't much time left, you've got to get on board!'

Pierre hugged his brother. 'I have one last favour to ask you.'

He put a string bag at Nicola's feet and added, 'This is for you. For the bar, if you prefer. I've got enough. Do what you want with it, burn it if you don't want to spend it, give it to the poor. But keep part of it for Angela Montroni. Don't ask me any questions, deliver it to Professor Fanti, he'll find a way of getting it to her.'

He waited for the reply. He had no idea how his brother would react.

Nicola looked down at the bag.

'Ok, then.'

'Thanks.'

The longshoreman gesticulated in the shadows. 'Come on! Get on board!'

Vittorio moved forwards and hugged his elder son. Pierre saw that his father's eyes were gleaming, but his expression was fiery.

'Nicola. Listen carefully: you're a better partisan than I am. Perhaps you're a better communist as well. And I'm proud to be your father. We'll see each other again. I'll come and find you, wherever we go.'

Then father and son walked quickly towards the gangway.

Nicola's voice reached them when they were already on the first steps.

'Hey, Pierre, you finally did it, eh?'

'Did what?' he asked, gripping the railing.

'Got yourself out of the shit and sorted everything out for everybody.'

Pierre thought he could glimpse a half-smile in the darkness of the wharf.

'You've been decent. A fool, but decent.'

Pierre returned his smile. He heaved himself towards the ship's rail, followed by his father.

L'Unità, 1.7.1954

From the Hiroshima bomb to the peaceful use of atomic energy
SOVIET NUCLEAR POWER
LAUNCHES A NEW PHASE IN HUMAN PROGRESS

WITH THE SIGNATURE OF THE SURRENDER
THE LAW OF THE TERROR OF UNITED FRUIT
RETURNS TO GUATEMALA

LARGE NUMBERS OF DRUG-TRAFFICKERS ARRESTED
IN ROME AND NAPLES

L'Unità, 4.7.1954

SERIOUS GAPS IN GOVERNMENT INQUIRY
INTO SCANDALS RELATED TO THE MONTESI CASE

L'Unità, 6.7.1954

SERIOUS TERRITORIAL LOSSES ANTICIPATED
BY THE PLAN FOR TRIESTE

TWO THOUSAND ARRESTS IN GUATEMALA
Repeal of the law for agrarian reform

Il Resto del Carlino, 11.7.1954

Days of waiting and trepidation
THE BANNERS OF TRIESTE READY
TO FLAP OVER THE BALCONIES OF THE HOUSES

THE DRUG ROUTE
A long and terrible route populated by dreams and drenched in
blood
with, in Italy alone, countless paths, highways
and even aeroplane runways.
A long and serious inquest into drug-trafficking,

also taking in the Montesi trial,
has been conducted by Lamberto Sorrentino,
who has, in the course of his laborious inquiry,
approached smugglers, dealers and idlers,
and even had a stay
in a clinic for addicts,
enabling him to give the reader of
Il Resto del Carlino
a version of this searing problem

Il Resto del Carlino, 1.8.1954

TRIESTE ACCORD
BETWEEN 9 AND 15 AUGUST

L'Unità, 2.8.1954

TITO MAKES NEW CLAIMS ON ZONE A

Il Resto del Carlino, 4.8.1954

ITALIAN TRICOLOUR HOISTED
OVER THE TERRIBLE SUMMIT OF K2

Il Resto del Carlino, 5.8.1954

SCELBA HAS REPORTED TO THE CHAMBER
THE DANGER OF A LEFT-WING DICTATORSHIP
'The threat hangs over the political life of the country'

Il Resto del Carlino, 6.8.1954

TRIESTE ACCORD TO BE ANNOUNCED
AFTER ASSUMPTION DAY

L'Unità, 19.8.1954

ATOMIC FALL-OUT OVER WASHINGTON
EIGHTY HOURS AFTER EXPLOSION IN NEVADA

L'Unità, 20.8.1954

SUDDEN DEATH OF CHRISTIAN DEMOCRAT LEADER DE GASPERI
A NATION MOURNS

L'Unità, 25.8.1954

'TOUCHEZ-PAS AU GRISBI' AT VENICE FESTIVAL
Latest Jean Gabin yields up its booty

Il Resto del Carlino, 26.8.1954

TRIESTE ACCORD MAY BE ANNOUNCED
IN MID-SEPTEMBER

L'Unità, 26.8.1954

'Witch-hunter' investigated on Monday
MCCARTHY BEFORE SENATE COMMISSION
FOR 'CONDUCT UNBECOMING'

Il Resto del Carlino, 31.8.1954

A MYSTERIOUS OBSTACLE
IN THE WAY OF SOLUTION FOR TRIESTE

L'Unità, 03.9.1954

THE UNITED STATES ALREADY HAS WEAPONS PREPARED
TO GIVE THE SOLDIERS OF THE NEW WEHRMACHT

L'Unità, 10.9.1954

The chain of silence must be broken and light shed on the Montesi affair
THE LEVEL OF PROTECTION ENJOYED BY THE LEADING PLAYERS CONFIRMS THE POLITICAL RESPONSIBILITY OF THE GOVERNMENT

Il Resto del Carlino, 20.9.1954

A speech by the Marshal at Celje
TITO EXTENDS HAND TO THE USSR
Prospect of 'normalisation' with the East

L'Unità, 22.9.1954

Justice on the way: two arrest warrants issued
PICCIONI AND MONTAGNA IN JAIL

Coda

Seventy-five parts potassium nitrate. Fifteen of charcoal with low levels of sucrose. Ten of pure sulphur, non-acidic; alternatively replaced or accompanied by starch, rubber, sucrose. The composition of the explosive powder.

Gunpowder.

The potassium nitrate releases oxygen and produces combustion.

It is almost certain that it was an eighth-century Chinese monk who gave birth to the age of bangs, with all its incalculable consequences. It was Roger Bacon, thirteenth-century philosopher, who passed on to us the formula as it is today, while Berthold Schwarz, a sixteenth-century German monk, was the first to use it to fire a projectile.

In any case, the art of fire is a very ancient one, much of it shadowy and unknown. In China, once again, there are records of pyrotechnic exercises from the second or third centuries AD. There are hardly any detailed publications on the subject: the essay by a sixteenth-century Italian, Vannoccio Biringuccio, *On Pyrotechnics*, in 1540, a treatise on technical chemistry. Then nothing until a dense manual from the late nineteenth century. After that, little more.

But mankind's fascination with the infinite variations in the art of fire remains immense, perhaps precisely because of the air of secrecy surrounding it. On the playful, popular level alone, no festival or fair, no mountain village or international metropolis, is complete without glittering luminous pyrotechnics, marvelled at by children, admired by adults.

Paris couldn't get out of it. Certainly not with a festival like the

14th of July on the horizon, even though French pride had been dealt a severe knock by events in Indochina, and the festivities were going to be in a minor key.

Fireworks are obtained by mixing metals with explosive powders. As they burn, carbonates and oxides of different metals produce the different tones and colours of each firework. There are rockets called 'chokes' or 'vortices' that rotate on their own axes and soar into the air leaving a luminous trail. The 'bombs' or 'aerial shells', on the other hand, need iron mortars fixed to the ground with wooden battens. Each one is a cartridge full of smaller fireworks which, once a certain altitude has been reached, explode in all directions. By modifying the arrangement of the charges within the main firework, different shapes and intensities may be achieved.

Toni knew these things because he had always admired fireworks displays. He had researched the subject, he knew a few things about it. He had often said it was how he would like to go. A nice multi-coloured bang lighting up the sky. Now they had 'Stars of the East', his favourites. Golden tears filling the sky. Toni watched the spectacle from inside his car, through the windscreen.

A rotten year for France, 1954. Who gives a toss? thought Toni.

He thought he'd fucked them good and proper. He'd fucked them twice over. The Marseillais. The bastards.

But he had been waiting for them. Dead-eye from Naples always settled his scores.

He had sent three of them to their creator. Toni thought of the other, less choreographic use of the black powder.

The blaze of the Stars of the East was at its peak, Toni could see it everywhere, increasingly blurred. The taste of blood filled his mouth.

Toni couldn't help noticing that it was not as he had imagined it would be. A nice polychrome explosion colouring the sky. It was different from the colourful geometric figures, the intestine bursting from his torn belly. And the gilded tears of the Stars of the East inundating the sky were different from the blood now flooding into the back space of the car and pouring copiously out of it, on to the pavement, tinting it a dark red. Fuck tuberculosis, he thought.

Toni thought about all these things. As he died.

McGuffin had shown cartoons of cats chasing mice.

The mouse called 'Jerry' lived behind the wainscoting of a spacious and well-furnished living room. Inside, a bed made from a matchbox, and various bits of furniture recycled from the rubbish. There was a housekeeper, but all you ever saw of her was her feet, and her fat calves.

She was trying to hit the cat with a broom. The cat had turned the living room into a complete mess. The cat's name was 'Tom'. He spent his days chasing 'Jerry'.

Mice and cats scampered around McGuffin, at the top of a mound of rubbish. Often a cat would doze off inside McGuffin. She didn't look like 'Tom'.

The mice had long fur and long tails, and they didn't look much like 'Jerry'.

At dawn, McGuffin's broken screen reflected the rising sun.

At sunset, the broken mirror in front of it reflected the red of the sinking sun.

At night, squeaking crickets, distant barking, insistent miaowing, the noise of shoes or bottles thrown at cats to shut them up.

A smashed chair. Radio dials. Irreparable gadgets.

McGuffin couldn't have known, but the smell was terrible.

McGuffin imagined it.

Never again would he capture electromagnetic waves to turn them into dreams or nightmares.

Never again would anyone stare at him with eyes as dead as the cigarette stubs that surrounded him now.

At least McGuffin had a purpose. The cat was pregnant. She would give birth before Christmas.

He had passed from home to home. Now he *was* a home. Someone really needed him, at last.

If he had had a mouth, a face, McGuffin would have smiled.

III

The moment of glory. The whole of Montreal seeing him evening after evening. Friends and relations, even the ones in the Ville de Québec.

Arsenic et vieilles dentelles. A rustproof *pochade*, the story of two adorable old ladies, a crazy nephew who thinks he is Teddy Roosevelt, a criminal on the run and a secret that must not be confessed. He played the role of Mortimer, the sane nephew, a newly-wed husband preparing to set off on his honeymoon.

Laughter, smiles, even requests for autographs. Jean-Jacques Bondurant ran, rolled his eyes, raised his eyebrow. Exaggeratedly, like Cary in the film version. He was perfect, the monozygotic twin of the most elegant man in the world. Apart from the fact that he delivered his lines in *québecois* French.

The audience adored him. Twenty performances at the Théâtre du Rideau Vert, and the bookings were still coming in.

Not bad for a benefit show, with most of the parts taken by amateurs.

He remembered the opening night. Charlotte in the front row, happy, proud of him.

In the photographs published in magazines, Charlotte and Jean-Jacques had eyes full of sapphires and emeralds. Cary Grant's double and his wife. They smiled towards the future. Alive. Strong.

The curtain was about to rise. The noise quickened his blood. His Quintino suit was a second skin.

He guarded a secret in his heart. Wherever he went, he took a note with him. The note consisted of a few lines and a two-word farewell. They bounced around his cranium, from one side to the other.

Au revoir.

The smile spread across Jean-Jacques' face until it filled his cheeks.

Merci beaucoup, monsieur Grant.

IV

Betsy had advised Cary to go and see Dr Clapas. All her friends had good things to say about him. The events of the past few months had banished depression, returning Cary Grant to the world that was clamouring for his return. Now they had to try to understand the reasons for his depression, to make sure that it didn't come back. Never again was the sun to darken, nor the hand that moved the razor to tremble.

Clapas was French. A pointed white beard, silver-rimmed glasses. He had moved to California with his wife in 1949, at the age of fifty.

If the truth be told, it appeared that he had *fled*, after a rather unpleasant experience culminating in a nervous collapse. A dangerous criminal had taken him hostage in his own home. The man was a patient and had turned up for his session, but the police, who had been on his trail for some time, had surrounded the building. Holding him at gunpoint, the criminal (a multiple robber and murderer with anarchist and subversive tendencies) had told Clapas of all the atrocities he had committed. Clapas's anamnesis had been so mercilessly accurate that the criminal had gone mad and, having managed to free himself, committed suicide in the most grotesque fashion: bursting into a police station, guns in hand, and opening fire on the officers. The press had reported his last words: 'Shoot at my genitals!' adding that some policemen had followed his advice. Dr Clapas had become frightened and, fearing an underworld vendetta, had fled the country.

In Hollywood he had modified his rigid Freudian approach so as to be more *à la page* and to attract showbiz people. Apart from concepts drawn from the oriental philosophies and religion, such as *karma, chakra* and *mantra*, he experimented with psychoactive drugs, which he believed induced local regression, as happens in dreams. In exceptional circumstances, he gave his patients a very new compound, lysergic acid diethylamide, better known as LSD, a substance capable of 'unlocking the casket of the id'.

Cary had told him about Archie Leach, about the invention of 'Cary Grant', about a father who had died a drunk and a loser, about a mother who had died and come back to life, about two failed marriages. Cary couldn't talk about Nazi spies, missions on behalf of MI6 or encounters with the socialist satraps of a far-off eastern country, but what he had talked about was more than enough. Clapas, sincerely struck, had decided to give him LSD, without telling him of its effects lest he provoke defence reactions.

'Same time tomorrow.'

Clapas hung on the actor's every word. Clapas sweated and clutched his linen trousers around his knees. Cary Grant was completely transformed, he spoke in a very heavy English accent, using idiomatic expressions from turn-of-the-century Bristol, and generally talked and talked and talked. Cary Grant was Archie Leach.

Cary watched his own past like a 35 mm film shown on TV, apart from the bright colours, crikey, bright as a fire in which your mother dies, a fire lit by your father. Widescreen, a more distant rectangle than usual, between two black strips. Events follow hot on one another's heels. Marriage to Barbara Hutton, friend to the friends of Mussolini, interminable parties and bombing raids on London (the latter probably the consequence of the former), Errol Flynn bombing London, Errol Flynn fucking a little girl up the arse in the cockpit of his Luftwaffe plane, MI6 catching him *in flagrante* and locking him up in a madhouse, every night Errol climbs over the wall dividing the male wing from the female one, managing to fuck Frances Farmer or Elsie Leach, here Cary bursts into tears, Clifford Odets's hand writes 'Here Cary bursts into tears' and brings the scene to an end, Senator McCarthy sends anyone who knows how to read and write to the pyre, the Gestapo tries to arrest Charlot, who defends himself and knocks them flying with his walking stick, MI6 free Elsie in exchange for his cooperation, Cary refuses and says, 'I'm not James Bond!' ('Who the hell is James Bond?' wonders Dr Clapas), then accepts because Elsie is stuffing him with hallucinogenic wheatgerm, so Cary has to go off on a long journey, he opens the clothes cupboard and inside is a naked Quebecois with a regimental tie around his neck, the Quebecois is Cary's double, and he is chatting with Josip Broz known as Tito ('Where the hell does Tito come into it? Clapas wonders), they go together to the Hotel Lux in Moscow, in the corridor papered with portraits of Stalin they are involved in a shooting match, policemen turn up in Louis XVI costumes, Robespierre shows up, grabs the wigs from their heads and tells them, 'Change, or I'll send you to the guillotine!' then introduces himself to Cary, who is now, who knows why?, wearing nothing but a pair of swimming trunks. The bathing attendant appears and says to him, *'Monsieur Bond, au téléphone!'* Cary repeats, 'I am not James Bond!' Sir Alfred Hitchcock says, 'Cut!' Guillotines are set in motion, heads fall into a single large basket. Cary rummages in the bucket and pulls out a head: it is Joe McCarthy's. Cary swims, Frances Farmer swimming beside him, then Frances Stevens (Clapas notes: 'Ask who that is').

Cary relaxes. Cary goes to sleep.

Cary hardly remembers anything. He wakes up. He feels good. Colours are vivid. His movements are fluid, his bones light.

'Very, veeeerrrry interesting, Monsieur Grant, but any anamnesis would be over-hasty. I shall administer LSD to you again. Are you available next Tuesday, at the same time?'

'LSD? Those drops were LSD? Why have you given me a hallucinogenic drug?'

'In a sense to return you to your childhood, Monsieur Grant, without the inhibitions of adulthood, beyond the reality principle.'

'I must have been coming out with some foolish things . . .'

'On the contrary, Monsieur Grant. Your visions have been highly instructive. I have a few questions to ask you, but let's not think about those now. We'll meet again on Tuesday.'

'I think the effect is persistent, it's as though everything were . . . underlined. As though every object were winking at me and saying, "I'm here, and I couldn't be anywhere else for any reason in the world" . . .'

'I shall make a record of your description of lysergic perception, *monsieur*. Is it pleasurable?'

'I would really say so, yes. It's as though everything has a complete shape, but not a fixed one.'

'It will last a few hours. In the meantime, try to see and hear as you have never seen or heard before.'

When he is on his own, Clapas writes:

First notes for anamnesis.

The subject has created an alter ego for himself, with a revealing name, the non-existent James Bond. 'Bond', a link, a connection. 'James Bond' is the super-ego, he is Hollywood, and by extension the American society in which the subject feels ill at ease. In fact, he defends himself a number of times against the accusation of being 'James Bond', that is, of having links with this society.

The reference to the alleged korephilic perversions and National Socialist sympathies of the actor Errol Flynn, who later couples with the subject's mother and a less famous actress, one Frances Farmer, is indicative of the same conflictual relationship.

The Quebecois double in the cupboard, surprised talking to the Yugoslav dictator Tito, represents precisely the fear of failure to conform (Quebec represents cultural anomaly, the stranger in the house), the fear of being accused of anti-Americanism and communist sympathies. The Quebecois double is naked, and hence in a state of innocence close to the truth, but at the same time he is wearing a tie, a sign of indecision between nature and civilisation. That might mean that the subject is effectively a crypto-communist, but that this causes him a sense of qualms and guilt. With regard to this, the parallel between Stalin, Robespierre and McCarthy, which is turned on its head by the execution of McCarthy *by Robespierre*, indicates an insoluble contradiction: the subject is well aware that democracy will prevail over totalitarianism, so he feels remorse for his communist sympathies, but also suspects that democracy, if it is to win, will have to sink to the level of the enemy, resorting to Terror. McCarthy has shown that this can happen. Given

this confused, if not undifferentiated reality, the subject feels
partially justified for his choice of communist. All the more so
in that there is no parental authority to reproach him or explain
to him that not everything is play and fiction, not everything
is a stage (see the reference to Clifford Odets) or a film set (see
the reference to Alfred Hitchcock). The constant tone is one of
rancour at a father who has not only killed the mother, the
object of the subject's Oedipal desire, but who has abandoned
his own role as a guide, leaving the subject in an eternal limbo
between childhood and adolescence. The situation is aggravated
by the schizoid doubling, even *tripling* of the subject's personality, divided between the child Archie Leach (who has emerged
as a result of locally induced regression, see the markedly English
manner of speech), the character Cary Grant and the mysterious 'James Bond'.

The tripled subject is constantly in search of three fathers
(perhaps the trio of Stalin–Robespierre–McCarthy?) and three
mothers. Could that be why he has had three wives? Or are
they Elsie, Frances Farmer and the unknown 'Frances Stevens'?
The last two swim beside him, a clear reference to the amni-
otic fluid of the maternal womb.

Clapas hadn't understood a thing.
However, Cary had discovered how to keep depression at bay.
See and listen. A few drops and every thread in the fabric of the
world appears before you.
The winter of his discontent made glorious summer by that lysergic
sun.

V

Dear Professor Fanti,

I am not good at writing like you, I have never written enough in my life and above all I started too late. But I will try.

I would like to tell you that I can't thank you enough for all the trouble you have taken. You write that you did it out of your friendship for Pierre, and I believe you, but that alone cannot justify everything. You are a good person, one of those you seldom meet in life.

The lodging that you have found me in the home of the family of your poor wife is very fine. I have a great deal of difficulty with the language, but have already managed to buy the book of translations you recommended, and am applying myself to it day and night. For the moment I only tend to the house, but Mrs Jean has said she wants to find me a job (or at least that is what I think she said). The money you sent me from Pierre, minus my first expenses, I have put in the bank until I decide what to do with it.

It seems incredible that my pain is fading. Perhaps I have merely managed to contain it, to lock it up at the bottom of my heart, where I can keep it along with my memories of Ferruccio. But perhaps this is only natural. Life goes on, and the things you have written to me about the loss of our dear ones are said by someone who has been through the same ordeal as myself. Thank you for that as well. They were beautiful words.

You tell me that you have received a letter from Pierre, from Mexico, and that he is well. I am happy. For now, please tell him my news yourself, tell him that I want for nothing and that I am well too. That I have kept his address and when I feel capable of doing so, I will write to him straight away. Mexico. How far away is Mexico? On the other side of the ocean.

You know, it's strange, but I don't miss Italy at all, the bad memories are still too recent. Apart from displacement, I am happy to be here, where I know no one and everything has to be started over again. I am the kind of person who is able to adapt. Just imagine, I have even started eating bacon and eggs for breakfast!

I don't know if this was the right decision. To tell you the truth I don't know anything at all. Perhaps I was only acting out of instinct, driven by the pain and the sense of betrayal. But it doesn't matter any more. I'm here, and I have to think about this new life.

I still can't find the words to thank you for everything, *professore*.

Write to me again and give me some news.

Affectionately,

Angela

VI

Renato Fanti stared at the card for a long time. A pre-Columbian pyramid standing out against a grassy plain.

On the back, a familiar handwriting.

Mexico City, 4 September 1954

Dear Professor,

There are teachings that we carry within ourselves, even on the other side of the world.

There are people you can't forget.

I think that the only way a pupil has to pay his debts is to confront life, bringing to fruition what he has learned.

I hope that I will succeed in demonstrating this. I hope that one day we will meet again, although I am not sure we will.

We will be the same, but we will be new.

Really, thanks for everything,

Robespierre

Fanti hid his emotion behind a half-smile. He chose the right record and put it on. He picked up his pipe and filled it with the tobacco he smoked on major occasions. As he took the first few puffs he watched the scented smoke rising in blue whirls, mixing with the notes of Stan Kenton, flying over the books, the English ornaments and the jazz records, *23 Degrees North and 82 Degrees West*. The coordinates of the future. Havana. The tropics.

He murmured, 'Good luck, Pierre. Good luck.'

VII

'You don't think Capponi's gone as well?'

On the lowered shutter, no sign, no 'Back soon', nothing, some people are driven to suppositions.

'Gone? Do you think he'd go away like that, without saying anything to us?'

'Why, what did his father do? He packed up everything, lock, stock and barrel, and went to South America.'

'What's that got to do with the price of fish, excuse me? Pierre had to get his father out of the country, he won all that money in Monte Carlo and he didn't think twice. And Capponi isn't a tramp like his brother.'

La Gaggia hears the voices slipping under the door and pokes out his head to see what's happening.

'Tell us, Gaggia, you don't know where on earth everyone's gone? Did the patron saint tell them to shut up shop?'

'St Petronius? Benassi has never closed for him. And remember that Capponi isn't from Bologna to boot, and I haven't seen him this morning, but even Garibaldi and Bottone don't know where everyone's got to.'

'I bet someone's died!'

'Hasn't Bottone been having troubles with his liver lately? I know he was persuaded to take "Chinese mushrooms".'

'That's enough bollocks about dead people and Chinese fungus, come on, let's be serious now, what could have happened? You don't think the cops came back?'

This allusion to the constabulary immediately prompts a change of subject. Because in early summer, in our place, but also in the streets, the shops and the other bars, any excuse is enough to talk about the Scelba government, whether it will survive, or whether it'll be packing its bags, whether it's going to be the turn of another Christian Democrat, or whether we'll be voting again, but in the spring, because there's no point even thinking about having elections in Italy between June and April. Someone's convinced that there is a reason, an anti-communist strategy put together by the CIA, but no one is able to explain it. Others merely say you can't have them in the summer because people want to think about enjoying themselves, and not in autumn and winter because people are too pissed off. With the bad weather, the cold, work, nobody's in the mood to think about politics, ending up in a rotten mood, digesting the usual pap, listening to the stuff the big shots come out with. But in spring, ah, that's something completely different, it's a bit warmer, the days are nicer, you start thinking about your holidays and work is less of a burden. And according to Bottone there's the question of luck: in 1948 the priests won because it was spring and now they're fixated on that date, no getting out of it, if you move it to some other time of year the harvest will be postponed.

La Gaggia has already forgotten all about work, all the urgent stuff, because it's soon going to start raining seriously and we all have to get our shoes on. And anyway, as we know, Scelba has two problems: first of all there's Trieste, because right now they're signing the treaty in London. They say it's going to be provisional, but they won't get us to swallow that: Tito has acted the lion and we Italians have been the lambs, because that was how it suited America. And the other issue is the one about Wilma Montesi, a terrible scandal, Minister Piccioni had to resign, his son went to jail along with that man Montagna, the police are passing the buck, the chief of police in Rome nearly ended up in the slammer as well. These days La Gaggia is the most sought-after expert in the whole bar, apart from Melega and Bortolotti, the match has only just begun, and on the Montesi issue our cobbler is the only one who knows everything inside out, because he has been following the story from the beginning, and he always told us that a few things would come out sooner or later.

'They don't know which way to turn, poor things! They dug up the girl's uncle less than a week ago: headline, Giuseppe Montesi accused of murder and now, pff, there's that bubble burst and they've got to blow another even bigger one.'

'Lucky the move on that poor uncle didn't work, eh, Gaggia? I've a feeling he was a comrade as well, that one.'

His voice becomes heated. 'It's because they've really cocked up, so they're trying to salvage anything they can. Because forgive me, let's say poor Wilma did get fucked by her uncle, or someone else, someone who wanted to fuck her, let's say it had nothing to do with Piccioni and Montagna. What difference does it make? Montagna's a criminal anyway, he had friends in high places, the various chiefs of police have bent over backwards to shelve the investigations . . . Piccioni, ok, he wouldn't come up smelling of roses, but Piccioni isn't the problem!'

At the end of the street, under the lime trees that were shedding their leaves, a bicycle appears.

'Walterún! Walterún!'

He stops. He looks annoyed.

'D'you know what's happened to Capponi?'

'Capponi? Isn't he in Imola? With Garibaldi, Bortolotti, Melega. There was the funeral of that really famous partisan, what was his name?'

'Bob! That's right! Luigi Tinti, known as Bob. Walterún, you must know him, he fought in Milan!'

In a flash, Bob ousts Scelba, Wilma Montesi, Trieste. The people who knew him well, like Capponi, are all in Imola, but even those who were too old, or too young, know at least an anecdote, and drag it out, asking whether he was really the protagonist or whether it might have been someone else. Almost all of them are stories that we have already told each other a day or two ago, when the terrible news arrived and Capponi wanted to send us all home, then he decided to stay, to drink to the Commander's health and remember his exploits. In the end we left after midnight, and the bar was fuller than it had been at six. Even the men from the Section arrived, and people we'd never seen here before, and for the first time since we'd known him Benfenati didn't say a word, he sat there in silence, listening to the stories, then he hugged Capponi and went home.

Today the speeches are more or less the same, but no one is

complaining, because it's better to repeat some things one extra time than to forget them.

But no sooner has Walterún said goodbye than Capponi and the rest of the gang turn up, Garibaldi, Melega, Bortolotti and Bottone.

Someone complains about the surprise closure, without even a note, a sign. Capponi replies that since Benassi sold him half of it, he too has the power to decide whether the bar should stay shut. And today, never mind the bar, he had to go to Imola so don't make a fuss.

'Garibaldi, you're good at this kind of thing, how many people would have been there?'

'At least 15,000.'

'And a few more. All the mayors of all the villages in the mountains were there, Bulow was there, and Teo and Piccolo carrying the coffin, there were partisan sections from the whole of Italy. Bergonzini was there, he gave the public oration along with the mayor, there were so many people there that they couldn't all get into the Piratello cemetery, there was a band, what did they play again?'

'The *Eroica*, by Beethoven.'

'That's the one. And they buried Bob with the other fallen of the 36th, in a part of the cemetery that also has Andrea Costa and all the best citizens of Imola.'

Bottone breaks away from the group and shakes his head. 'It's almost a good thing that he died so quickly.'

'What was that you said, Bottone?'

'Another ten years and who would have remembered Commander Bob?'

'You're wrong, Bottone,' Garibaldi corrects him. 'It's easier to be forgotten while you're alive, when you can still wind people up, than when you're dead, hoopla, you're a big hero again, time to get the banners out, sing a bit, and say that the spirit of the Resistance never dies. That's how it is, mark my words.'

Meanwhile Capponi is already inside and heating up the coffee machine, while Bortolotti hurls himself at the television and turns it on, he's wild about it now, and loads of us don't agree, we should all be able to make the decision, and only if there's something interesting on, not like that, not just for the sake of it. But what do you expect, it's a taste for novelty, and Bortolotti says there's no point having something if you don't use it. In fact, since they've had the table football he's almost stopped playing billiards, and he spends all his time fiddling with those little men. The coffee machine, the television, the table football, the gas stove and the new lights: all stuff bought with Pierre's money.

'But Brando, do we really know for certain that he won all that money at the casino?'

Brando doesn't reply, partly because he has to reply to Bortolotti's hand, but above all because he's been really down lately, poor guy. Pierre has left, Sticleina's got married, he's found a *real* job as a nurse in Piacenza and gone to live there, Gigi has found another girl who's a mambo fan and he doesn't much feel like dancing the *filuzzi* with his friend the barber.

Capponi walks over to the wall, to where his medal is framed, and beneath it he tacks up two photographs, neatly aligned, with drawing pins.

One is a picture of Commander Bob, in uniform, hair combed back, half his face in light and half in shade. It looks a bit like a holy image, but it's best not to point that out. The other is more blurred, two guys, isn't that one Pierre? Hey! That means the other one must be Vittorio. They are hugging and smiling, and above them is written, in marker pen: *Greetings from the New World to all our friends in the Bar Aurora.*

'Oh, Capponi, where on earth have they gone? To Venezuela?'

Then, in an undertone: 'And yet Melega says that Pierre was in no great rush to leave just because of his father. It seems there's something to do with Montroni's wife, who actually did leave more or less around that time.'

'Did she go to Venezuela as well?'

'Who knows?'

'It's all bollocks as far as I'm concerned. Do you really reckon Signora Montroni would cuckold her husband with a barman?'

'But she didn't *marry* the barman . . .'

'Ah, women, women . . .' says Stefanelli from the next room.

From the television, right next to the two photographs, comes the voice of the presenter, who is interviewing some characters who are passing through Rome.

'Why don't you switch that thing off?'

Garibaldi's request is the only sign of anyone paying attention to the television since Bortolotti switched it on. And you can bet that that will still be the case until closing time, because here in the Bar Aurora we haven't the slightest interest in some famous actor who happens to have arrived in Rome today, or some politician, and if it weren't for the football and the cycling we wouldn't have bought the television in the first place. We've got Bottone, with his atom bombs, and La Gaggia, who knows the Montesi case like the back of his hand. We have to work out whether Garibaldi is narrowing his eyes because he wants a certain card or because the smoke's annoying him. Benfenati takes care of any political doubts we might have, and any doubts about the pools, like the Carrarese–Parma game, are dealt with by Melega and Bortolotti. Everything else is just opinion: Montroni's wife, Pierre's money, how cold it's getting. And Gas, who knows where he ended up, because he still owes us the money for the old TV.

That's why that presenter is never going to be a great success in the Bar Aurora. And if it was up to us, we'd kick his arse all the way back to America.

The poet and architect Carlo Alberto Rizzi got up early and made himself a good breakfast. At his desk, he leafed through his notebook. That evening, at the club, he intended to declaim a poem about the 4th of November, about the commemoration of the martyrs, about the gold medal awarded to the city. He had jotted down some impressions, and was preparing to turn them into verse.

So clear a morning distance is erased.

An interesting note. He could exploit it to talk about the Italian people, distant yet close, on the opposite shore of the Adriatic. As though even the atmosphere had grown keener, on that 4th of November, to bring the irredentist lands closer to Trieste, cut off from the motherland by wicked and biased interests.

The merest breath of the bora *sets the banners flapping, on every balcony, on every building, specially two, huge, at the entrance to the square: the Tricolour and the Halberd of Trieste.*

Celebrations on land and sea, in the Piazza dell'Unità and on the ships moored opposite, in the San Giusto dock: the cruiser Duke of Abruzzi, *three white destroyers and an old-fashioned sailing ship, all shrouds and pennants, the training ship* Amerigo Vespucci *from the Naval Academy in Livorno.*

Soldiers and sailors standing in ranks. The crowd moving anxiously from one railway station to another. Waiting for President Einaudi and Scelba.

The wind and the banners gave the poet a shiver of inspiration. He picked up a white sheet of paper and smoothed it in front of him, as though to purify it with his hand. His biro scratched and nothing came out. He breathed on the tip and started again:

> The bora *stirred, and from the ship-filled sea*
> *Rose scents and memories that touched the heart.*
> *Trieste, our beloved city fair,*
> *Trieste – pride of all thy sons thou art!*

Fine, so that's the wind taken care of. And the banners? Mustn't forget them.

> *The buildings huddled on thy crowded flanks*
> *Bunting-clad and draped with banners bold*
> *Proudly salute the living and the dead;*
> *Thy blessings fall upon both young and old.*

He buttered a slice of bread, spread it with marmalade and after the first bite stared once again at the crumb-scattered notebook.

> *Twenty-one cannon shots raise flocks of doves on land and gulls on sea. The presidential procession arrives: ten cars, preceded by the horses of the curassiers.*
>
> *The President musters the soldiers. Women and children push their way to the front to touch, greet, stroke the uniforms. People in the trees on the lamp-posts: 'Italy! Italy!' At least 150,000 people.*
>
> *The authorities climb to the city hall and at 11.35 they appear on the balcony. The mayor reminds them of their sister people on the eastern coast of the Adriatic. Scelba explains why the government has signed an agreement that does not satisfy the expectations of the Italian people: Trieste had been waiting for too long, it had to resolve its situation at all costs. He reassures the Slovenes who have stayed on Italian territory of respect for pacts and the will to bury the past and ensure cooperation. If pacts are respected, minorities will become a reason for friendship between the two countries.*
>
> *'To facilitate useful exchange between the two countries', 'Italy and Yugoslavia must collaborate for the defence of peace and the prosperity of the two nations'.*

Rizzi remembers the whistles that had risen up from the square when the Prime Minister had uttered those phrases, too obliging to Tito and to a pact that flattered Yugoslavia just to keep it away from Moscow. The rights of the people were being trampled by the politicians: worse than in Korea and Vietnam, because at least there everyone spoke the same language, in the North and the South. Their regimes might have been different but their culture, their traditions, their spirit were not. If it had been up to the British, Trieste would have become another Berlin, divided into sectors, dismembered. And in Vietnam there had been talk of a referendum, of unification: why did no one think of asking the opinion of the people in Zone B? In the face of Wilson and the principle of self-determination.

But those gloomy thoughts, the image of Scelba's bald pate on the city hall balcony, were distracting him from his verses. So what was missing? The irredentist lands, close by in the distance. The hubbub and the sadness. His pen glided across the paper:

> Trieste! Italy! – yet our joy subsides;
> We think of others not so far away
> But cruelly severed from their fatherland
> Who should be celebrating here today.

Excellent. Nearly done. Just a few more lines in the notebook:

Einaudi pins the gold medal to the gigantic banner that Rome donated to the city. The loudspeakers articulate the reasons for the honour:

'Outstretched for centuries, pointing in Italy's name to ways of unifying peoples of different clans, proudly it participated with our country's finest in the independence and unity of the Fatherland, during the long vigil it confirmed with the sacrifice of the martyrs the will to be Italian. That will sealed with blood and with the heroism of the volunteers of the 1914–18 war. In particularly difficult conditions, under Nazi artillery fire, in the partisan war it demonstrated how great its yearning was for justice and for freedom, which it won by using its vital force to rout the oppressor. In recent dramatic events and in the humiliation of Italy, against the treaties seeking to part it from the

motherland, with tenacity and passion equal to its hope, it confirmed to the world its unshakeable right to be Italian. An example of inestimable patriotic faith, of constancy against all adversity, and heroism.'

The day had come to an end in San Giusto's. The Basilica was packed; so was the square, despite the *bora* that was just starting up. After the *Te Deum* of thanks, the bishop had recalled the dismembered diocese, the Istrian parishes transferred to the control of Lubljana and Parenzo. On the tower, the banner with the medal had greeted the crowd, along with the chimes of the big bell.

Rizzi thought about how chilly it had grown. He glanced out of the window: the wind wouldn't stop blowing, it was freezing. He would have to buy a new coat. A coat that was as warm as his old grey duffel-coat. The GMA agents had taken it from him without so much as a by-your-leave. An exchange of clothes, it seemed. In one of the cafés in the centre of the city. But then why hadn't they given it back to him? Given it back to him? They'd kicked his arse and sent him home.

His leg still hurt.

And his arse wasn't what it had been, either.

Moscow, the Lubyanka, 21 November

General Serov lays out the documentation on the desk, the pages perfectly aligned.

The latest information from Saigon, the capital of South Vietnam.

A report on Bao Dai, the pantomime 'emperor'. A moronic grin and a stolid expression on banknotes and stamps. He was outside history, if he had ever been in it.

Report on the new Prime Minister Ngo Dihn Dien, a pious man with an unhealthy attraction for crucifixes, in power in a Buddhist country. His brother: an opium addict with foolish pseudo-intellectual aspirations, and a passionate conspirator. His sister-in-law: a slut, consumed with hatred for the communists. A corrupt regime supported by America.

The latest information from Hanoi, the capital of North Vietnam. Russia's 'friends', with China up to its eyeballs in a quagmire of blood and shit.

An unstable equilibrium. 'Peace' wouldn't last long.

The latest information on Tito, on the Italians who were abandoning Istria and Dalmatia, on that scandal, the 'Montesi case'.

Information on Guatemala, once again the exclusive property of the United Fruit Company after the coup in which the CIA had toppled an 'inconvenient' government.

Latin America, the Americans' backyard, a thin stratum of land over seething magma. That was the new front, Serov would bet on it.

Dispatches from France and Switzerland.

Report on 'Vladimir' and 'Estragon'. Based in Paris, the Latin Quarter. They socialised with artists, pseudo-revolutionaries, compulsive liars, self-styled 'prophets' of even more self-styled movements. A

Romanian by the name of Isidore Isou. Utter nonsense. Azzoni and Mariani were wallowing in it all. There wasn't a single telephoto image that didn't show Mariani laughing, teeth on full view, cheekbones and eyebrows practically touching. Azzoni looked into the lens.

They would continue to use them. Clowns understand other clowns, and the world was now one great big circus parade.

Latest information on everybody and everything.

What a frenetic year. A year that had changed the face of the world.

The birth of the KGB. The Berlin Conference. The rearmament of Germany and its membership of NATO. The defeat of the French in Indochina and the division of Vietnam. Tito. The ruin of McCarthy. Tito and Cary Grant. Nuclear experiments in the deserts and the middle of the oceans. The end of the 'postwar period'.

The birth of monsters throughout the Soviet Union: two-headed lambs, calves without legs, a goat with only one eye. Inauspicious events loomed.

Just for a change.

General Serov rose to his feet, cracked the joints of his neck and shoulders, and walked the short distance that separated him from the window. He looked through the pane and once more, as he did every day, he felt part of a big clockwork machine.

Part of history.

X

'You really don't know the story of that bastard Rasputin? Ok, if you've never been to Moscow I can see you might not know it, *compadres*. You've got to know that when the conspirators went to get him, in the depths of the night, at his house, Rasputin, who was a pretty big bloke, tall and *fuerte*, managed to escape by throwing himself into the river from a window. But it was *invierno* and the water was freezing, so the fucker died of exposure after a few strokes. His corpse was recovered and carried to the shore, as stiff as a stock-fish. Everyone was amazed that his dick was *todavía* hard. The maid, who had served him for many years and who had also been his lover, had a real veneration for his cock. You know what Russian peasants are like, simple and superstitious. And she thought she could save the symbol of his manly vigour and his potency. So she cut off his knob. And apparently it was enormous, *más que treinta centimetros!* And she ran off with it. *De aquel* moment no one knows *lo que pasò*, what happened to the member. There are legends, certainly, strange stories, about the relic, but it seems that it passed from hand to hand, that it was sold for a fortune, that the White Russians were looking high and low for it, to turn it into a banner for the counter-revolution. And the Bolsheviks were after it as well, to burn it, and scatter the ashes to the *viento*. Moral of the story, now we know *donde está* Rasputin's cock. In the Museum of Natural History in Moscow. If you look in the case of the stuffed monk seal, down at the bottom, you'll see the seal pups, with their characteristic hood. Except that one of them isn't a seal pup.'

León Mantovani stared at the two people sitting at the other end of the table. They looked perplexed. But he was used to it, his stories often had that effect. They had shown up there looking for him. They had known that the bar was for sale, and they planned to take it over. Two Italians. A boy and a guy who might have been more or less the same age as himself. Father and son.

He had introduced himself. 'Leonardo Mantovani, pleased to meet you. *Pero* everyone here calls me León, have done since I got here, in '39, after the *derrota de España*.'

He had looked at them carefully. He guessed they might have an interesting story to tell. How many had he met in his life? Mexico was the *refugium peccatorum*, the new and ancient land where the persecuted and the rejected arrived in search of their fortunes. The land of the century's first revolution, the one led by Villa and Zapata, the one you couldn't work out whether it had been won or lost somewhere along the way, between the biggest capital in the world and the desert.

The older of the two had talked about another revolution. Yugoslavia, the Balkans. Another planet. The younger one had talked about a failed revolution. At home, in Italy.

León had talked about Rasputin's cock.

'You know, Stalin once told me that you should never say more than is strictly necessary. *Mejor*, as they say in the north American courts, anything you say can be used in evidence against you. *Pero* in these parts there's an unwritten rule: everyone who passes through here has a story to tell. Sometimes it's true, other times it's pure fantasy. Doesn't make much difference, if it's a good story. And since, from what people say, I'm the best storyteller around, every now and again someone tries to challenge me. But no one has managed to beat me yet!'

'You know Cary Grant, the American actor?' asked the younger man.

His father touched his shoulder. 'Leave it.'

'You really knew Stalin?'

'Angel, *esta cerveza está caliente*. The first time was in '22, when the Party sent me on a mission to Moscow, with a half-empty suitcase and a letter from Gramsci in my pocket. I've never been back to Italy since. On the other hand I've collected convictions all around the world. In Moscow I met Lenin, then Trotsky and Stalin, Bukharin and Molotov: cold, *compadres*, you can't even imagine how cold it is in Moscow in *invierno*. I never managed to shake off that cold, there was no wood for the stoves, there was no oil, *nada de nada*. The coldest revolution I can remember! And you couldn't complain, because what kept you warm was the revolutionary spark. *Spasibo* and off you go!'

'How long did you stay in Russia?' asked the boy.

'A few years. I did a relay to Paris. Back and forth. I brought Togliatti's orders to the exiled comrades in France. It was dangerous, specially after '33, when you had to travel through Poland and Czechoslovakia to get to Switzerland. Nazi spies everywhere, and in Paris you had infiltrators from the fascist secret police, *hijos de una gran puta madre*, who were after your blood. But I always managed to get round them, because I disguised myself, I did, always wearing different clothes, once even a false beard. I stiffed an agent in the bogs at the Gare du Nord. I shot him in the *frente*. And because he got me covered in blood, I left the station completely nude. I got pneumonia, but at least I sent that fucker to the grave!'

Laughter and swigs of beer.

From the adjacent room, where the old men were playing dominoes, the lawyer's exotic accent still rang out. A lot of high-flown words which must have sounded incomprehensible to the two Italians who had arrived only recently.

A distracted gesture in that direction: listen to the end of the story, *cabrones*.

'Then they transferred me to Paris once and for all, to organise *las Brigadas*, the International Brigades. With Longo, that's right. When I arrived in Spain, to defend the republic, there was such a mess I can't even tell you. We worked day and night, it was all meetings, consulting files, greasing rifles, organising the brigades. And what a confusion of tongues! Fuck, the English understood one thing, the Russians another, the Hungarians understood A, the Yugoslavs B, then the Americans, the Germans, we Italians, the Irish, *locos, loquisimos!, puta vida*, that's why we lost the war! No one understood anyone else!'

From the other room, the inexhaustible flood of words, slow, cadenced, stressed the lawyer's argument. Ah, but when you've got all those ideas in your head . . .

Father and son craned their necks to peer around the corner and see who that voice belonged to.

Get their attention back, straight away: 'Then, after the defeat, Mexico took us in. No one wanted us. We even built a monument *a los hermanos mexicanos*! If it wasn't for them . . . Ah, but I never went back to Russia, to freeze my arse off, no thank you very much. And so many things had changed. They'd got rid of everyone I had known in the twenties. *Traidores*, Stalin said. Fuck, you make the revolution, and they shoot you as an *enemigo* of the people. No thanks, give me Mexico any day. They asked me to help them kill Trotsky as well. I said no, you can do that without me, *el compañero* Mantovani is withdrawing from the fray. So they killed Trotsky with an ice-pick and I opened this *cantina*. Then one night they tried to snuff me as well. They waited for me in the street. There were three of them. Burying them in the field was a task and a half.'

The end.

The meeting in the next room, on the other hand, showed no signs of reaching a conclusion. León thought: if it goes as it usually does, this is going to be another late night.

So he made himself comfortable. Legs stretched out on the chair. 'Now I want to retire. The city does nothing for me now. I want to retire to the sea, where it's hot, and do nothing *todo el dia. Por eso* I'm selling the bar. And if you really are interested, I advise you to take advantage of the fact, because it's a good price.'

The two listeners re-emerged from the story rubbing their eyelids.

The father was the first to speak. 'Yes, it's a good price sure enough. But we also need advice.'

At that moment the river of words coming from the other room became more intense, almost a roar.

The boy couldn't help asking, 'Who is that man talking in there?'

'The lawyer. A great mind, and with two enormous great *cojones*. He's an exile too, like all the rest of us.'

'One hell of a harangue!' commented the boy. 'He's been at it for two hours now!'

'In his own country, that man there attacked an army barracks. A fine brain and balls *de hierro, entiendes*?, except when he starts talking . . .' A shrug of the shoulders. 'There are political refugees from all around the world here. If you stick around, you'll hear some good ones. Take the lawyer, for example: he's looking for decent people to train up some guerrillas. He wants to topple a dictator and free his island! Every now and again I tell him he's mad. Like *Don Quixote*, you know. Then it occurs to me that I've spent my whole life with mad people and I've never regretted it.'

A strange light gleams in the eyes in the older of his two listeners. 'Train up some guerrillas?'

Explain it to him: 'This is Latin America, *compadre*. You should never be surprised about anything. Think of the most ridiculous thing you can imagine, and it's perfectly normal here.'

At that moment the tall and corpulent figure of the lawyer approached the bar. Every now and again even his throat dried up.

'Abogado, qué tal? Deje que le presente a mis amigos.'

He wore an elegant black suit, his hair was short and curly, slicked back with brilliantine, a jovial, slightly chubby face, with a thin moustache. He couldn't have been more than thirty.

León Mantovani pointed to his guests: *'Le presento a dos compañeros italianos. Piense que el padre luchó junto al comandante Tito contra la dominación nazifascista. Estuvo en las montañas con la guerrilla . . .'*

The man shook hands with the old partisan.

'Muy honrado . . . abogado Castro Ruz.'

Then he did the same to the boy, and it was as though he had transmitted a strange sensation to him.

One that suggested that life, like history, would never be short of surprises.

End Titles

These are really the thoughts of all men in all ages and lands, they
    are not original with me,
If they are not yours as much as mine they are nothing, or next to
    nothing,
If they are not the riddle and the untying of the riddle they are
    nothing,
If they are not just as close as they are distant they are nothing.

This is the grass that grows wherever the land is and the water is,
This the common air that bathes the globe.

    Walt Whitman, 'Song of Myself', 17

On Cary Grant (1904–86)

Cary and Betsy separated in 1958 and divorced four years later. Cary
married twice more. He retired from the cinema in 1966, after about
seventy-two films. He became a director of the cosmetics multinational Fabergé. He died in 1986 and was cremated, and his ashes
were scattered to the wind.
    'I used LSD about a hundred times before it became illegal.' (C.G.)
    A subculture of Cary Grant fans lives and thrives on the web. The
most complete site is: www.carygrant.net
    You can also sign up to Warbrides, the email fan club:
www.carygrant.net/warbrides.html
    Among the many biographies and critical works, we would be
happy to recommend: McCann, G., *Cary Grant: A Class Apart*,
Columbia University Press, 1997.

Imagine that Cary amused himself by putting hidden references to his Yugoslavian adventure into his subsequent films. Have fun spotting them!

On Frances Farmer (1914–70)

Hollywood tried to salve its guilty conscience by dedicating a film to her. *Frances* (1982) is sustained by a mesmeric performance from Jessica Lange, and describes very effectively the progressive slide into misery and the descent to hell, even if it is strained in places. For example, there is no proof that Frances underwent a transorbital lobotomy. The film simply skips the last twenty years of her life and 'career': two marriages, odd jobs, moving from Seattle to San Francisco before finally settling in Indianapolis, where she fronted a television show, before dying of cancer, having written an autobiography, *Will There Really be a Morning?*, published posthumously in 1972.

Frances was buried in Oaklawn Garden Memorial Cemetery in Indianapolis, Indiana.

Nirvana dedicated a song to her, 'Frances Farmer Will Have Her Revenge on Seattle', on the album *In Utero*, 1993.

The daughter of Kurt Cobain and Courtney Love is called Frances.

Dedicated sites:

www.geocities.com/the mistyone/index2.html

www.people.virginia.edu/pm9k/libsci/FF/francesF.html

On Lucky Luciano (1897–1962).

In spite of the efforts of Charles Siragusa and his involvement in various investigations, Salvatore Lucania was *never* interned. He died of a heart attack at Naples airport on 26 January 1962. He is buried in St John's Cemetery, Queens, New York.

'Never have been a jerk and never will be a jerk.' (L.L.)

On Wilma Montesi (1932–53)

No concrete evidence has ever emerged that Wilma Montesi attended a party at the Capocotta estate, in Tor Vaianica. The geographical proximity of the estate and the stretch of beach on which her body was found was the only very feeble link with Montagna and his friend Piero Piccioni.

In fact, the sole foundation of the hypothetical accusation was based on Montagna's past as a fascist spy, confidence trickster and (especially) procurer, and on the fact that Piccioni was the son of the Foreign Minister, Attilio. The case was stuffed full of false testimonies and clockwork 'confessions'. Anna Maria Moneta Caglio launched the fashion for 'super-witnesses', who are, even today, indispensable figures in any judicial frame-up.

The case was exploited by the 'left-wing' of the Christian Democrats led by Amintore Fanfani (and keeping the Italian Communist Party and its press as 'useful idiots') to assume control of the party (recently bereft of its leader, Alcide De Gasperi), ousting the tendency of Piccioni, whose career was severely compromised by the scandal.

On 27 May 1957 the Venice court acquitted all the accused. The sentence described Anna Maria Caglio as an unreliable witness and a compulsive liar.

In the sixties and seventies, Piero Piccioni became one of the most important composers of Italian film soundtracks. In the nineties, to everyone's great surprise, he became one of the household names of so-called 'lounge music' and Exotica and the Sixties Revival subculture.

Update 2004: Piero Piccioni died on 23 July 2004 at the age of eighty-two.

The case has never been solved. Who killed Wilma Montesi?

On Joe McCarthy (1908–57)

In its session of 2 December 1954, the United States Senate officially condemned McCarthy's work, with a majority of seventy-seven to twenty-two. That put an end to his career as a witch-hunter. The senator succumbed to rancour and alcoholism. He died of hepatitis in 1957. He is buried in the Roman Catholic cemetery of Appleton, Wisconsin.
On certain inexplicable mediumistic phenomena

Steve Cement is clearly recognisable in the film *Lucky Luciano* by Francesco Rosi (Titanus, 1973, soundtrack by Piero Piccioni).

Salvatore Pagano, aka Kociss, appears in the film *To Catch a Thief* by Alfred Hitchcock (Paramount, 1955).

The film on the Fifth Offensive was made in 1973: *Sutjeska*, with Richard Burton (in the role of Tito), Irene Papas, Milena Dravic, Ljuba Tadic and Bata Zivojinovic. Colour, 87 minutes, the most expensive production by the Yugoslavian cinematic industry.

Thanks to:

Wu Ming 5 (Riccardo Pedrini), for his help, brainstorming sessions, and documentation on *filuzzi* and boxing.

Cinzia for the cover of the Italian edition.

Andrea Olivieri for his advice and translations into the Triestine dialect. Marco De Seriis for other linguistic advice.

Fabrizio Giuliani for information on the KGB. Giuliani has translated from the Russian the book by Yevgeny Primakov, *Storia del Kgb* (3 vols.), Hobby & Work, Milan 1999–2000.

Annamaria Cattaneo for the material on pigeons.

Istituto regionale 'Ferruccio Parri' per la storia del Movimento di liberazione, via Castiglione 25, Bologna.

Biblioteca comunale dell' Archiginnasio, piazza Galvani 1, Bologna.

The partisan fighters Mirco Zappi (36th Garibaldi Brigade) and Carlo Venturi 'Ming' ('Red Star' Brigade), for the material they supplied to us.

Vitaliano Ravagli, for the *epos* and his friendship.

Daniele Vitali, Luigi Lepri, Alberto Menarini and Gaetano Marchetti for their inestimable work in defence of the Bolognese dialect.

Roberto Santachiara, *hasta siempre comandante!*

54 contains explicit homages to the following ancestors and colleagues: Beppe Fenoglio (1922–63), Auguste Le Breton (1913–99), Léo Malet (1909–96), Walter Chiari (1924–91), Edwin Torres and Brian De Palma. We thank them too.

Thanks to everyone who has subscribed to Giap, our electronic newsletter. You can subscribe at our website:

www.wumingfoundation.com

We beg the forgiveness of the friends 'vampirised' in the novel: Stefano 'Zollo' Colombarini; Fabrizio Giuliani; Alberto Rizzi; Leo

Mantovani; Maurizio Melega; Giovanni Azzoni; Luca Mariani; Federico Martelloni.

In the name of Salvatore Pagano we thank: Lawyer Carlo Ercolino, for his patience; Salvatore Capozzoli and Davide Staiti for their company and moral support in Poggioreale prison.

Begun in May 1999, during the Nato bombings of Belgrade.

Delivered to the Italian publishers on 21 September 2001, awaiting the escalation.